Black Star

Books by Morton Cooper

MY LIFE WITH CHAPLIN (*with Lita Grey Chaplin*)
THE KING
BLACK STAR

Black Star

by Morton Cooper

published by
Bernard Geis Associates

*To Charlotte
as always
and, as always,
to Don Preston*

Corruptio optimi pessima
(The greatest evil is the good corrupted)

"You taught me language, and my profit on't
Is, I know how to curse. The red plague rid you
For learning me your language!"

CALIBAN

THE MORNING AFTER Jesse Nash was shot by an unknown assailant in New York, Phil Simms of Gundersen-Weber-Simms Associates read about it in the *Los Angeles Times* on an early flight to New York. He had never met Nash, and he had no wish to meet the man, but he was relieved to read that Nash was going to pull through.

The *Times* carried the story on its front page, which suggested to Simms that it was a big story indeed and would be covered as such around the country. Jesse Nash, thirty-three years old, Negro, had come a long way. Two years before, he had been a small-time comic, playing side-street clubs and nothing television shows. One year before, after a highly publicized altercation on a nightclub floor, he had burned his show business bridges and enlisted in FREE, one of the least moderate of the black protest movements. Today, he was FREE's chief spokesman and rallier, unofficially but for all practical purposes its head, and the country knew him because he was an artful, consummate agitator, a most angry and often irrational black man with a huge store of incontestable facts to support his anger. It was Jesse Nash, more than anyone else, who had kept the two-year-old killing of a Harlem boy by a yet-unpunished white policeman before the public's attention, continually hammering at it as though it were the single greatest violation of civil rights in history (and, in a somewhat far-fetched sense, it was, Simms thought, for all the ingredients in the case added up to something intrinsically evil in society), determined that no one be let off the hook—the cop, the New York Police Department, the Mayor, the District Attorney, the city, the state, America, society.

According to the *Times* story, Nash had been speaking last night, December 18, to an overflow Harlem crowd, demanding anew that the cop (whose name, almost too good to be true, was White, and who was still on the force) be brought up on civilian trial for murder. He reminded the crowd anew that an ofay grand jury had refused to indict despite a ton of evidence, that an ofay police departmental hearing had simply gone through phony motions of concern in its desire to protect its own, that more and more signs pointed to the likelihood that Willie Mae Hamilton wouldn't see a red cent from the city in her suit to recover damages for her son's death. Nash had reached a fury-whipping crescendo, and then a gun was fired somewhere in the crowd of Negroes and counter-picketing whites, and Nash clutched his side and fell. As of this morning's sketchy account, no one had yet been apprehended because, in the confusion, no one was certain where the shot had come from.

Sighing, Phil Simms sipped his second cup of black coffee in the hope that it would cure or at least narcotize his mild hangover. His wife Ruth, who could sleep anywhere, was asleep beside him. He gazed through his window at the billowy clouds below and wondered, as he had wondered numberless times before on planes and in bed, why GWS—Gundersen-Weber-Simms Associates, the most successful television packager and independent producer in the business—was wasting itself on crap. This Jesse Nash thing, for instance, and all the principals and principles directly and indirectly involved—this was pure drama. Dealing with it squarely, or issues like it, could be damned rewarding, personally and, hell, socially. Jesse Nash was what was happening on this day, in this year, in this decade in the United States of America. And until Charlie Gundersen died five years ago, Charlie and Phil Simms and Warren Weber had been responsible for the meatiest and most meaningful shows to hit the home screen—and earned profits in the bargain.

This season, Phil Simms and Warren Weber were responsible for the six most profitable series on national television. They were "Meet Ginger," Spy for Sale," "The Curly Custer Show," "Reckless Rangers," "Our Loving Husband," and "Champ the Chimp." Five years had zoomarred by, but there was no conceivable doubt that Charlie Gundersen was still, even at this moment, rolling furiously in his grave.

Who's that there in the woodpile?

Nobody here but us Mephistopheleses, boss.

Philip Leo Simms, forty-five years old, balding, bespeckled, invariably rumpled looking in spite of the precise Savile Row suits his wife ordered for him and made him wear, finished his coffee, set the *Times* aside, and made a promise to himself, the promise he always made on planes and in bed. He would talk seriously to Warren about their climbing off the crap treadmill and really get back to the business of why GWS had been formed: to raise the level of communication, not push it to its nadir. They had discussed this periodically, of course, and agreed that a return to responsibility was long overdue, but there was always next week, next month, next season, time enough to indulge in self-respect, because the profits to be realized from a series that clicked were such a bitch to resist.

And they had come a long way in this business of producing entertainments. Twenty-one million dollars—twenty-*one*, with six voluptuous zeroes—were tied up in GWS shows this season alone. He and Warren paid themselves $180,000 a year each, plus expenses. Each, this fiscal year, would net an estimated $1,255,000 beyond that salary because Philip Leo Simms, Phil Shimolovich the immigrant tailor's son from near Prospect Park in Brooklyn, had sold a major share of the firm to Pageant Pictures on a sumptuous capital gains deal. GWS was already in the artists' agency business, part time for now, dabbling in motion pictures, investing in plays and real estate, studying the record business and the radio station business, looking ahead, always looking ahead.

There had been misses, minor and momentous failures. But success had been, and was, a glittering reality, not a dream you had in that cramped closet of a bedroom you shared with three brothers in the railroad flat near Prospect Park, where the cabbage smell was constant, and where you were supposed to get accustomed to the subway trains booming past your window and your ear.

And now he and Ruth were flying back home after four days of studying the ledgers in the Los Angeles offices of GWS, of wrangling with the West Coast agency boys, of giving time-consuming dinner parties for directors, writers, and actors whom Warren had been brusque with or indifferent to the last time Warren had been in Los Angeles. Phil Simms had a mild hangover now because he had stayed up past midnight at a Beverly Hills mink ranch, cajoling superstar Tom Jordan into deigning to sign aboard to superstar for the third consecutive season of "Posse." He loathed wooing a lettucehead in the pursuit of a new unnecessary buck, and he had sworn he would never do it again. Yet he had done it, because Warren was tied up in the East and because Norfolk Tobacco had indicated it wouldn't renew if it couldn't have Tom Jordan, a semiliterate, semi-queer ex-rodeo rider whose acting talents were not visible to the naked eye. He had gone. He hadn't fought very hard.

This time, though, it would be different. He would get after Warren, if Warren would settle in one spot for five minutes, and he would nag at him until they both had restoreth their souls. And Santa is coming to town and there are fairies in the bottom of my garden, Simms told himself sourly. I'll talk, and Warren will listen, and nod, and that will be the end of it. And why won't I holler? Because even though I'm an equal partner and the organization needs me, if Warren died today so would the company. I'm a hell of an organization man and no one can touch me when it comes to the dollars and cents end of running a business. But I'm in no position to kid myself. Warren Weber is a bloody genius at creating a project and getting it to work, and a bloody genius at conning everybody—including himself, and me. If he says no dice, then it's no dice. On my own, I couldn't make an interesting film at a gang bang.

End of Indian wrestling with Mephistopheles, dat cute ole debbil. For the time being.

Ruth Simms came awake, about halfway through the flight, as Simms, hangover mercifully gone, was deep in a lapful of paper work. He smiled, and so did she. Ruth, good wife and good friend, never a beauty but a down-to-earth, *haimisheh* girl he wouldn't trade for a minute for all the available shimmering gash in L.A., had been his steadying rock during the four days and nights in the lush lunatic asylum that was Hollywood. Warren thrived in such an atmosphere. Simms would have gone berserk if Ruth hadn't been around, always, to remind him that the Tom Jordans of the world were nothing more than rodeo riders.

"I was dreaming Tom Jordan was trying to seduce me," she said.

"Did he succeed?"

"No. Oh, we necked a little, but at the moment of truth I told him I wouldn't go any farther because I'm happily married."

"What did he say?"

"He said I have a darn heck of a nerve, talking so vulgar."

Simms laughed and squeezed his wife's knee. "It'll be good to get back home."

"Phil? . . ."

"Yeah?"

"I'm so glad we're going home. I don't like me, or even you very much, when we're in California. We're not ourselves there, we start putting on airs. I feel so much safer when we're in New York."

The temperature at Kennedy was a numbing eight degrees above zero. George, the chauffeur, met them, drove Ruth to their childless and comparatively modest apartment on Beekman, then drove Simms to the main office of GWS, which occupied two floors of a large building on 60th Street and employed fifty-one people on its New York staff alone. In his own office, half the size and a third as splendid as Warren's across the hall because that was the way he wished it, Simms and his secretary Louise quickly went over what had happened of importance in his absence, even though they had talked at length twice or oftener each day by telephone. Work had piled up but, amazingly, there were no calamities. He asked if Mr. Weber was in, and she answered that she hadn't seen him but she would check. He flipped the intercom. Jeanne, Warren's secretary, reported that he was having lunch with McCann-Erickson at Four Seasons, and was planning to go from there to a "Curly Custer" run-through, but hoped to be back by five at the latest. She paused, then said uncomfortably, "Can you squeeze a minute in for me? There's something I want to talk with you about."

"Will it wait, say, an hour?"

"Sure."

"I'll get to you," Simms said, and spent the hour at his desk, returning urgent phone calls that weren't urgent at all, reading the important wires, letters, and messages and replying to those that didn't deserve to wait. He buzzed Jeanne. "Ready," he said.

Jeanne Prescott came in, with that no-nonsense walk, a tall, thin but not skinny Negress (no, wait, he corrected himself; there's no such word—why do I keep using it?), groomed as always to a faultless turn, a first-rate secretary who earned a horse-choking salary because she was smarter than a whip, because she could juggle fifty calamities at once and never let a ball drop, because her brilliant one-track mind played only one song—Warrenweberwarrenweberwarrenweber—and because her calming humor stayed intact on GWS's most calamitous days. She was in her early thirties, unmarried as far as Simms knew, nice to look at. Maybe Warren was banging her, which would have momentarily disappointed the essentially prim Phil Simms but wouldn't have surprised him: Warren was banging every female on both coasts and all continents.

"Pleasant trip?" asked Jeanne.

"Don't be sarcastic," he said, pouring the Sanka that Louise always had prepared. "My incipient duodenal doesn't appreciate it. What's up?"

She sat across from him and lit a cigarette. "I'm worried about Warren."

"Again?" Along with her other gifts, Jeanne was a mother hen who had the sense and subtlety to cluck-cluck without hovering. She would complain that Warren didn't sleep enough, eat enough, or vacation enough, but she kept the nagging light and easy. Simms gave her his full attention now.

"No, really worried. He's always driven himself, but I've never seen him the way he's been over the past month—the past week, especially. Have you noticed anything different about him?"

"I've been in Lotusland for four endless days, remember?"

"He's munching Dexies like peanuts, Phil."

Simms held his cup in midair and frowned. "Are you sure?"

"Positive. And his hands shake—those beautiful, strong hands—and he looks on the brink of exhaustion, and his temper's shorter than ever, and he looks just awful. And there's a capper—he's drinking with a vengeance. Never drunk—I mean, no reeling or that stuff —but he's got that bottle hit hard."

She was making it up, she was an hysteric, she was talking about three other guys. "All this Jekyll-Hyde in the four days I've been away?"

"Yes." She nodded. "It's all surfaced in these four days, anyway. What's been bothering him more than usual, do you know?"

"No. Do you? He's just my partner and my friend. How would I know anything?"

"Will you find out, without saying I snitched on him?"

He listened to more from Jeanne, who was not an hysteric but a sober and knowledgeable and sensitive woman, and his own amorphous concerns about the changes in his friend knit together into something quite specific, but he could not let Jeanne know the depth of his concern. He told her he would follow it up, and she left.

He phoned Warren's wife, Karen, on impulse, not taking the time to debate whether or not he was out of line. If Warren was drowning, the first order of business was to find a life preserver.

The housekeeper said that Mrs. Weber wasn't expected home till nine or later.

Simms worked. Five o'clock came, then five-thirty, then Jeanne buzzed to say that she had to leave for an appointment, then six o'clock arrived, and there was neither Warren nor word from Warren. He had been at the "Curly Custer" run-through for a while, Simms learned in a discreet phone call, and gone from there either to the Polliard taping or to keep an executive date—but with whom? what executive?—at NBC. Simms made more calls and couldn't track him down.

At seven o'clock, tired and hungry, Simms rose from his desk to go home because there was no legitimate reason to stay, because Warren, who was going to have slain all the dragons that dwelled on Madison Avenue, who was going to have squeezed and twisted the corporate balls of television until it yelled uncle, who suffered a nervous tic that could be defined as moral rationalization yet who was a good man, was more than a good man: he was a big boy, and you could worry but you couldn't mother him.

What does it all add up to? Phil Simms asked the east wall, which contained an Emmy, the only significant award GWS had received in too many years. And they'd got that for "Land Bright," a big gaudy special extolling democracy in song, a "Jimmy Crack Corn" here and a sprinkle of spirituals there. If I'm getting more dissatisfied with playing financial traffic cop, and if Warren, the world's smartest man, is having trouble keeping his marbles, what in hell does it all add up to?

He instructed the night man to have Warren call him at home when, or if, Warren came back.

On the car radio, riding home, he heard for the first time two of the day's news developments. Jesse Nash was at Knickerbocker Hospital, under police guard. The bullet had been successfully removed from Nash's left side, and he was truculently telling police and reporters that the only person who would have shot him was a white member of the Police Department, carrying out assassination orders. Police Commissioner Gaines called the charge preposterous and libelous, and added that personal contempt for Nash's vilification would in no way deter his men from promptly bringing about the assailant's apprehension. No one yet knew who the assailant was, though there were leads, Gaines claimed, and an early breaking of the case was expected.

The other news item, and a surprise, was officially unrelated to the shooting, but the timing strained coincidence. Police Officer Stuart Curtiss White, a football kicked for the past two years by a tangle of civil rights factions, keep-the-peace factions, and blatantly bigoted factions, would retire from the New York police force soon after January 1, a few weeks away, because of the flare-up of an old foot injury received two years before while breaking up a street-corner fight. There was no question in Simms's mind that the city was finally knuckling under to Nash's incessant agitations, nor was there any question in his mind that there would be repercussions, stormy ones from all sides.

It was the kind of story Charlie Gundersen would have dropped everything to cover. And, once upon a time, Warren would have joined in, too, with a ravenous appetite.

Phil and Ruth Simms spent the evening at home, but Warren did not call. Simms decided against phoning Karen Weber again. Shortly before midnight, preparing for bed, he decided to stop worrying—for the night, at any rate. Warren was a tough bird—a bit more erratic and unpredictable than usual, but tough. He'd be fine. Men like Warren always came out fine.

Shortly before midnight on that evening of December 19, Warren Weber collapsed in the East 76th Street apartment of a call girl who called herself Gloria Barclay. He had been working steadily for the past forty hours, personally supervising all the current and prospective Gundersen-Weber-Simms projects that were based in

New York, and he should have known better, for he was an intelligent man. But he ignored all the perfectly obvious warnings from his body, and so he collapsed.

He still might not have, had he gone straight home at ten o'clock when they'd finished the "Meet Ginger" run-through in the drafty midtown rehearsal hall, the barnlike room with the hardwood floor where weddings and Bar Mitzvahs were catered by day. Karen would have Benedicted some eggs, warmed some milk, readied the sauna, and done her best to help him unwind if he'd given her the chance. But he had been too keyed up to go straight home just yet. He supposed he should phone Phil, who had flown back from the Coast today, but he would do that later, as he would phone Jeanne later to explain why he hadn't returned to the office or even called in—he had lost all track of time, there weren't enough hours in the day to supervise all the out-of-office work let alone the office work —and to find out what messages there were. Rudi, his chauffeur, drove him to Danny's Hideaway for a nightcap, and on the way he recalled that he hadn't bothered to eat all day because he had sped from one meeting to another, one show to another, and because the Dexedrines had completely submerged his appetite.

Building himself a vodka and drop of tonic at the car's rear-seat bar, he realized he was alone for the first time in—how long? A hell of a day, he thought—and a foolish one, some voice in his head added. Chasing around this freezing town as if the sheriff's dogs were in hot pursuit was foolish because a good half of it was unnecessary. The increase of the Dexies was foolish because he had yet to meet anyone who had ever used them liberally and had the last word over them. The increase of drinking was more foolish; it was absolutely mystifying, for he had always drunk but never as much, as often, as dutifully as he had begun to drink in— when? . . . in the last couple of months.

Most mystifying, most upsetting when he was alone enough to let it upset him, was this unthinkable misplacement of his clean sense of order, his organization of time. The artful budgeting of time was a skill he had mastered long ago and kept, until . . . well, until when? Recently, right? There was no logical excuse for forgetting to call the office, to reach out for continuity.

A vacation, he promised himself, scalding his throat with the vodka. I'll take Karen, and maybe the kids, and we'll go away. Where? Anywhere. When? When Birnam wood to Dunsinane doth come, for Christ's sake. I'm booked solid, Jack. If I walked away from the company for half a day, the whole house would fall down and go boom.

He was trembling with nervous exhaustion when the car pulled up to the restaurant, but entering, walking tall with the assured steps of a perpetual winner, he was the robust, handsome, forty-four-year-old shaker and mover whose profession was the control of other men's destinies, and he was immediately bouyed by the reception he got. He returned the lavish greetings of the maître d' lavishly, hugged the smiling hatcheck girl as he gave her his camel's hair coat, and waved cheerfully to clusters of faces that beckoned or called to him to join them as he made his way to the rear table that was always reserved for him.

He held court over a promptly served drink, enjoying all the attention, even the clamorous toadying that normally made him impatient and curt. The job hunters, the transparent liars, stopped by. ("MCA's got three pilots they're begging me to consider, Warren. Any one of the three, I can have my choice. But you know I'd tell them to get lost if you came up with a property—in a hurry, that is." "That's sweet of you, Andy. We'll see what we have lined up and get in touch.") Andy Best, a character actor at Metro when the living was easy, hadn't had a good job in years and never would have again because age had hit and the confidence was gone.

The friends who didn't need anything stopped by. ("They tell me you're being snotty with Caleb again, Warren." "Nothing serious, Paul. Hello, Lorna—you're looking lovely. Caleb and I are sweethearts to the end.") Weber and Caleb Atwood, the charming swine in charge of all television activity at Vanguard, despised each other but did a great deal of business together because each needed what the other had to offer. A week before, at El Morocco,

Weber had bumped into Bart Snyder, the columnist, and had invented an accident for Atwood: "Caleb took a morning walk and was hit by a speedboat." Snyder had printed it. Phil Simms had given Weber hell, and so had some other friends, but Weber had thought the line amusing and, as he predicted, he and Atwood wrapped up an important deal two days after the item appeared.

The men with the envies stopped by. ("Tell the truth now, Warren—how did you snag Virginia Barrett? We've been trying to sign her all year." "Finesse, Manny. Finesse, kindliness, and tact —and we offered her the kind of money a ragpicker like you wouldn't have the wit or the balls to cough up. How's your wife, Manny? Karen saw her at Bergdorf's and said she looks terrific.") Virginia Barrett, the musical comedy star who was television's last major holdout, would make her debut in February in a special devised and sold by GWS. The Mannys *had* offered her more money than had GWS. But evidently the Mannys hadn't been as good to her in bed as Warren Weber had been.

The friends and the toads and the pretty women and their jealous escorts continued their pilgrimages to Weber as the fresh drink and small steak were served, and he liked it all. But then there was a gradual stirring in the room, an eddying away from his table, a buzz and turning of heads. He looked to where the heads were turning and saw the arrival of Caleb Atwood and a chesty blonde satellite.

A Presence had distinctly come, a Presence that sent ripples of whispering across the room and drew all eyes. Atwood was forty years old, lean and dark and coldly handsome, and he entered a room as if he had come to buy or sell each person in it. He, and the chesty blonde were seated three tables away, and, as the two men nodded to each other and smiled civilly, Weber felt the drinks go sour in his mouth.

He asked Emile for a table phone, to call Karen and tell her he was on his way home, but he remembered the whore on East 76th just before the phone was brought, and he called her instead. Yes, Gloria Barclay said, she would be waiting. Weber signed his check, assured the maître d' that the steak was probably superb as usual but he wasn't as hungry as he'd thought, and made a point of pausing at Atwood's table on his way out, because the room was watching.

The men shook hands and Atwood introduced the satellite as Miss Thornwood, who had just come from London after a successful run with the Old Vic. She reddened. Weber vaguely recalled her—oh, yes, she was an English hooker someone had supplied him with for an hour in Vegas a few years ago—but he played it straight. "I'm delighted, Miss Thornwood. Caleb, are you showing Miss Thornwood the sights here in the colonies?"

"In my small way. We wouldn't want to keep you from your appointment, Warren."

"That's all right. Let's have lunch soon, Caleb."

"Sure thing, Warren."

He left Danny's Hideaway, amazed that there still were times when Atwood could deplete him by dismissing him. He wanted to be home and asleep, yet he had Rudi drive him to the whore's place because it was necessary to keep on the move. That made no sense at all, he knew. But neither had anything else over the past days and nights.

Gloria, a statuesque redhead whose otherwise flawless alabaster skin was marred by permanent razor blade scars on her left wrist, whose sole yet sufficient virtue was that she could practice her craft with a minimum of words, had a generous J&B on the rocks prepared for Weber when he arrived. She mentioned that he looked tired, and she sounded as though she cared.

"Only old crocks get tired. I'm Joe College," sighed Weber.

The stiff drink didn't relax him, which was bad, nor did the pungency of Gloria's perfume, which was very good. A sign she had once stolen from Palisades Park was framed on the pale blue wall over her bed, and it read *Games Played Here for Amusement Only*. Weber sat on the bed in his lemon-colored shorts and his chest felt heavy as he watched her brush the long red hair that fell almost to her hips, watched her slowly remove every garment except the spike-heel shoes, watched her full breasts and firm buttocks as she walked to the record player and switched on some early Dick Rodgers. All of it was skillful teasing on her part, leisurely peep-show stuff calculated to stir him before they touched. Weber extended his arms, ready for her, striving to ignore the gathering pricks of pain at his temples, the sudden, absurd lack of feeling in his fingertips and toes, the growing tightness in his chest that, he suspected, had nothing to do with passion.

Gloria came to him, feigning lust splendidly, and gasped with nicely corny pleasure at his erection, as though this were the first rather than fifth time she had seen it over the past several months. For a moment, or more, as the preliminaries began, as she touched him and kissed him, the flood of tactile sensations blottered up the tensions of the previous forty hours and the rarely relaxed days and weeks and months before those forty hours. Remarkable, he thought. My toes and fingertips are dead, but the pecker is hard as a rock, never more alive, never more ready to go.

"Is something the matter?" she asked.

"What do you mean, the matter?" he said, his voice scratchy and unfamiliar to him.

"You're shaking. And not sex-shaking. Something-else-shaking."

"It's freezing in here."

"No, it isn't. The room's like toast. But would you feel better under the covers?"

"No, I'm fine," Weber said, and lay back and guided her head. The pains at his temples became more intense, and sensations of tingling skipped back and forth across his lips, but he was determined to concentrate on the joy Gloria was giving him. He could feel the light, lovely pressure of her breast on his leg, and the dryness in his throat, and the dancing heat of her, and then a barrage of brief constrictions in his chest. They hurt and frightened him, and he pushed her away and leaped to his feet.

"What—" she began.

"Nothing! Nothing, I told you! Nothing, goddammit!" he roared, profoundly alarmed, and hurried to the bathroom to drink some water, which would help, which would steady him. The pains receded as he turned the faucet on full force, yet an extravagant sense of ungovernable panic engulfed him, and he closed the door lest she see him, and cupped water into his hand to drink because the glass he was holding slipped from that trembling hand and made a fearsome sound as it broke on the tile floor. He could not stop drinking water, and then he could not bear another drop of it. An opened pack of Parliaments and a book of matches from Pavillon were on the bathroom stand and he quickly lighted a cigarette, guiltily remembering that a month ago he had formally given up smoking. The panic grew, the certainty that he must flee—to somewhere, anywhere, somewhere. He blinked in awe at his reflection in the mirror, at the pastiness, at the furious twitchings of muscles and nerves over his face.

His upper arms throbbed. He had been cold, and now he was suffocating. His breathing was hard, labored, and once again his chest felt unendurably heavy.

It isn't a heart attack, he thought, prayed, staring at his reflection. My face wouldn't be so white. I watched my father in his first and last heart attack—my God, he was my age, forty-four, exactly forty-four—and his face was vermilion.

"What is it? What's wrong?" He could hear the voice and the knocking on the door in spite of the running faucet he couldn't summon the will or the strength to turn off. Could hear someone. Someone? Gloria. The whore whose apartment I'm in. How did I forget?

Am I going to die?

Here, in a whore's john at midnight?

Don't finish me off so young, God. Hear ye, O Lord, King of Israel. Let me clear out of here first, in my pants and my socks. Punish me if that's what's on Your mind—but don't punish Karen and our children. Have the *Times* run the story, not the *News*. Don't hurt my family. Dignity, God, dignity. It's more dignified to drop dead on a street corner than in a whore's apartment.

"Unlock this door!" the whore called. "Should I get a doctor?"

Yes, a doctor, Weber said, but silently. He fell against a wicker hamper and tried to get up to unlock the door by clenching one hand around a sink leg and pounding the tile floor in fear and anger and helpless frustration with the other. Then pain and panic left him as he managed to unlock the door, and a glittering haze circled in front of him and he saw a swirl of neat and patterned dots.

He wakened in Gloria Barclay's bed. An elderly man wearing an Indian bathrobe and a stethoscope asked him how he was.

"Alive," said Weber. "Is that a good sign?"

"Try to sit up," the man ordered, and Weber did, with effort, surprising himself by his slowness. "Feel more than normal exertion?"

"Yes, considerably more," Weber admitted, pretending he wasn't frightened. "Wait—now that I'm finally up, it's not so bad."

"Let's check you some more."

"This is Dr. Burchill," said Gloria, wearing a gratuitously modest ankle-length dressing gown and looking worried. For some reason she had washed off all her makeup, and the usually urbane, blasé face now seemed very innocent and very young. "He lives in the building."

The elderly man asked questions briskly as he made his examination. "How old are you?"

"Forty-four."

"Any history of heart disease?"

"No."

"When was your last physical examination?"

"Let's see—about a year ago," Weber lied; it had been closer to two since he'd gone to Mel Hebranck's office. "I was told I was in excellent condition," he lied again; Mel hadn't liked his blood pressure reading and had been after him, as both doctor and friend, to come back for periodic checkups. There had, of course, never been the time.

"Parents living?"

"My mother is."

"What did your father die of?"

". . . heart attack."

"At what age?"

Weber sighed the sigh of a man caught, trapped. "Forty-four."

"What's your line of work?"

Now what the hell, Warren Weber thought, and shot an anxious glance at Gloria, who knew what his line of work was and who might already have told the doctor. Who, in turn, might enjoy telling Mrs. Doctor and the butcher and the world that Warren Weber had got sick in a call girl's apartment. "I'm in insurance," he said. "In Rochester."

The examination was long and seemed thorough. Then the doctor injected Weber with Seconal and began to replace his portable equipment in his bag; for a physician with this East 76th Street address, even a fossil of a physician, the cracking leather bag looked inappropriately seedy.

"We can rule out an actual heart attack," he said.

Thank you, God, Weber breathed, and said, "That's very good news, Doctor. What caused the fit? Exhaustion?"

"In part. The Seconal ought to sedate you, for the time being."

"I've been working hard lately, without much sleep. Do you know, I feel a hundred percent better, now that you've given me a bill of health. I'll—"

"You listened a bit too quickly, sir," the doctor said, stern for the first time. "I've given you nothing except a necessarily superficial examination, which tells me you have a coronary occlusion pending."

The abruptness was shocking. "A—"

"I could be mistaken. Only a series of hospital tests—X ray, blood test, cardiogram, urinalysis, and the rest—can really yield a complete picture. But I don't think I'm mistaken."

"Wait," Weber said hoarsely. "I feel all right now . . ."

"Then let me scare you. Your pulse rate is two-ten over one-eighteen. Your heart rate is one-sixteen, with far too many extra beats. You're extremely tense. You are not a healthy man, sir, and you should accept the fact seriously. When were you planning to return to Rochester?"

"In the morning. I'll get a plane early."

"I would strongly recommend you have a full examination here before you board that airplane. I'm in semiretirement but, if you like, I could refer you to one or two excellent physicians right here in Manhattan."

"I'll take care of it myself, Doctor Burchill. Thank you."

Weber paid him in cash—twenty dollars; no, don't bother with a receipt—and surreptitiously motioned for Gloria to usher him out. By the time she returned to the bedroom, still looking innocent and young, the pains and the panics were little more than distant recollections, and his shirt was on, he was knotting his tie. It was important to discount the old doctor's hysteria. It was terribly important, for now, to pretend that the doctor was a fool.

"You scared the bejesus out of me," said Gloria.

"I apologize," he said, smiling, liking her concern, liking her, wondering if he should push his luck a fleck farther and complete what he had come for; oddly, she was sexually more appetizing now with her unpainted face and chaste robe than when he'd arrived, ostentatiously horny. "And I'm grateful for your quick thinking, my tall heroine—you're a true Jeanne d'Arc at the top of the stairs. But where did you dig up that refined dressing gown, in a road company of *Mother Courage?*"

"It was all for Dr. Burchill. He knows my—profession, I think, but he gives me these sweet little churchly homilies when I go to him for flu shots or whatever and, well, he's sort of like a nice grandfather I don't want to embarrass."

"It's charming, but now you can take it off."

The concern showed itself again. "For the reason I think? If I heard the doctor right, you're not supposed to exert yourself."

"You heard him all wrong."

Gloria was a superbly efficient fire horse, clearly sensing the moment they met in bed that Weber needed her more as a receptacle than as a woman, and she seemed as amused as he that she was being used in stag-movie style, by a man wearing a shirt and necktie. "Soon," he whispered, and Gloria whispered, "Yes, love," and roiled obediently as it happened for him. The climax was disappointing, not because it was too fast but because Burchill kept crossing his mind, and he knew he owed Gloria nothing except money, yet he kissed the whore's cheek and told her it had been wonderful. Before he left, he tucked her fee, one hundred dollars, into the top drawer of her living room breakfront. He thought for a moment and dropped two additional fifties in. What the hell.

Rudi was dozing in the black Cadillac in the usual waiting spot, one block north of Gloria's apartment house, and came awake to drive him to Sutton Place. The Seconal had begun to take effect; Weber felt almost pleasurably weary. The madman conniption hadn't happened.

But it had.

All right, it had. But that antique of a croaker was an idiot, an alarmist idiot. I'll see Mel Hebranck, first thing in the morning, Weber promised himself; Mel doesn't hop around setting off alarms. A rest is indicated, sure; I don't need Old Kid Hippocrates to tell me that. And I'll take it, Karen and I will take it, and maybe take the kids with us, just as soon as some of the desk clears.

Don't drag me, God. Please. I have too many things to do.

It wasn't quite two o'clock when Rudi delivered him home and said good night, but the full moon and the blankets of brilliant white snow everywhere in sight made the street look as if dawn were on its way. Ben, the night elevator operator, jabbered the whole distance up to the top floor, some tiresome soliloquy about what more did the colored people want now that they owned New York City lock, stock, and barrel? And Weber felt lonely and once again frightened, even after he let himself into the dimly lighted penthouse. The apartment was still as he paused at the threshold of the foyer to take off his overcoat. The living room, to his left, was not dark but, rather, drenched in light. All the furniture—the white sofa, the graceful chairs, the mile-long phonograph, the tables, the lamps—everything seemed excessive, and the carpeting vulgarly thick . . . a depressing surprise, because he had been the one who had enthusiastically chosen the carpeting over Karen's carefully phrased misgivings. The imaginatively decorative touches, marks of Karen's splendid, unerring taste, the subtle blends of greens and blues, everything so richly comfortable and inviting, retreated from him now into detached possessions.

He stepped down into the room, where the dawn that wasn't dawn was pushing cold early morning light in at the windows whose drapes were not fully drawn. An image of the river and sky awakening to the day compelled him to walk to the drapes and draw them far apart.

Once he had opened himself upon the river, he could not get himself to leave. What peace and calm there was on the river now, the brush of sky gradually warming the sharpening outline of the barges, the beads of light bright in the high buildings far away.

After a long while, he went to the bedroom. Karen was asleep. He showered himself clean of Gloria Barclay, and the other whores, and the applicant whores, and toweled his body dry and slipped into bed beside his wife. He embraced her with tenderness, and she stirred and greeted him. The Seconal had him, and he was a middle-aged man who had experienced an orgasm scarcely an hour before, but he became hard again and entered his wife. Within moments, the hardness was lost. Karen asked if there was something she could do.

"Hold me," he answered. "Put your arms around me."

Karen did, and he slept.

By midafternoon of the following day, Tuesday, Dr. Melvin Hebranck's tests were done. His findings were even more oppressive than the whore's doctor's had been.

"Everything, but everything, comes to a screeching halt, do you understand, Emperor Napoleon?" declared Mel, who had been Weber's undergraduate roommate at Yale. "With complete rest, starting today and preferably in bed, you can begin to beat this thing in a couple of weeks. Go back to your normal insane pace, and I can guarantee Karen and your kids will be marching to slow organ music. It's a simple choice."

"Simple, my coronary insufficiency," Weber complained. "A couple of *weeks?* There are twenty-one million dollars involved in this season's TV shows alone!"

"What do you have a partner for?"

"To take out the garbage," Weber snapped, immediately regretting it; he knew, perhaps even more keenly than Phil Simms, how vital Phil was to GWS. "Christ, Mel, none of this is fair . . ."

"Neither is leaving a young widow and three orphans."

The too-quiet remark was sobering. "I couldn't stay in bed, though," Weber said after a cold moment. "I'd go nuts with the telephone nearby, even if it was turned off."

A compromise was finally made. Mel forbade any air travel but conceded that an ocean cruise to the Caribbean would do, on condition that the attaché case and all scents of work be left behind. Weber, who flew more than 100,000 miles a year because flying was the only way to get anywhere, complained that boats were things ridden by tired Methodist ministers and thick-ankled stenographers out to land husbands, that conceivably death was preferable to shuffleboard. But he saw his friend's exasperated expression, and heard the impatience, and agreed, with a sigh, to take the trip.

He taxied to the office, having phoned Jeanne Prescott earlier with an invented itinerary, and instructed Jeanne to reserve a suite on the first available cruise ship going to the Caribbean. "Going to the where?" she asked, eyebrows raised.

"I'm working up an idea for a series with a cruise ship setting. I want to get a first-hand feel of it," he said evenly. Her gaze told him she didn't believe him, that illness was the only thing that could stop his kind of man and put him on a ship, but she said she would get right to work on the reservation. Purposely avoiding the mound of messages on his desk, he walked to Phil's office, asked about the California trip, and then, swearing him to secrecy, told him the news.

Phil, who slept eight hours every night, played golf every weekend, and jealously guarded his health, looked shaken. "Am I supposed to be surprised? How long have I been after you to slow down at the red lights, and I don't mean cathouse?"

"You and everybody else," Weber acknowledged grimly, pouring himself a small Scotch; Mel had okayed liquor, in moderation, but had ordered him not to touch another Dexie for the rest of his life. "All right, I'll rent me a rocking chair and a shawl. Little by little I'm accepting the storm warnings."

"Maybe you will, at long last, because Charlie didn't."

"Because Charlie didn't," Weber nodded, and looked at his partner and friend. "You know something, Phil? All during those tests today, I was waiting for Hebranck to read something bad and tell me I'd be lucky if I lived through the day. And I kept thinking of Charlie. Not that he worked his ass into the grave before his time, but that he got so much done before he checked out. I saw my obit in the *Times,* clear as day, and it just barely remembered that once upon a time I had something to do with 'The Gundersen Journal.' Isn't that a lousy thing to be remembered for, that I had so much to give and what I ended up with was 'Champ the Chimp'?"

Phil nodded and folded his arms. "You say the word and I'm ready for us to start 'The Journal' again. We could sell it in a minute."

"By God, that would be something, wouldn't it? Let's go, Phil! Let's show those bastards they can't give us snotty obits."

"It would be great if you meant it this time."

"I do, baby. The second I get back, we go to town. There must be a hundred issues we could tackle. And son of a bitch—" He brightened and snapped his fingers—"do you know who we'll sell 'The Journal' to? Atwood! *Der* Caleb *Führer* Atwood!" He chortled. "Oh, baby, wouldn't that be sensational, putting together a show with meat on it and making Atwood swallow it! How could he ever explain himself to his redneck mother?"

Phil grinned, infected by the sudden enthusiasm. "Here's a notion to chew on for starters, while you're away. Do you know about this guy Jesse Nash?"

"From the papers and the newscasts, sure. What about him?"

"An hour show, tracing the two years from the time of the killing of that kid in Harlem, tracing Nash's rise along with it. Make a hell of a show if it's done right."

"Could be. Could *be!*" Weber agreed, humoring Phil, whose gift was business management, thank God, not show ideas; Phil had been loudly convinced that "Spy for Sale" would never sell, let alone go into an unflagging fourth season. "Mr. Shimolovich, suh, I promise to chew."

They discussed which projects could be postponed during the cruise, which ones could be entrusted to others to shepherd. And eventually Weber grudgingly conceded that New York, Hollywood, Chicago, and London just might be able to survive his brief retreat from each of them. Jeanne came through. All the cruises were booked to capacity for this Christmas and New Year season, but she had contacted someone who had contacted someone, and there was a suite on the *Stalwart*, which would leave on Friday, three days away.

Back in his own office, Weber phoned his wife and told her to pack. Karen, with her annoying genius for spotting trouble when he was most intent on hiding it from her, asked what was wrong. "I feel like a cruise, that's what's wrong," he maintained. "Let's take the kids with us."

"I don't think we can. They have their hearts set on skiing with the Lawlers in Stowe over the holidays."

"Then we'll make it a honeymoon. Ten minutes after we leave port, we can lock the stateroom door and perform certain lascivious acts."

By Friday, the day of sailing, Weber felt well, too well to fritter away eleven valuable days with Karen and no one else. After twenty years of marriage he still needed Karen, pretty Karen of the good intentions, those things you paved Hell with, but their marriage was as much an undiscussed grudge fight as it had ever been, and, try as they occasionally did to right a compendium of wrongs, they shared little and, more often than not, they bored each other in bed.

He would go, though, and the trip might even turn out to be productive. Something had happened to him since the years with Charlie, somehow he had changed from a man he respected and often liked to a shallow half-man, thirsting less for truth than to soul-kiss the Caleb Atwoods, men Charlie Gundersen rightly considered beneath contempt. He knew he had changed, knew it and hated it, knew character had drained from him drop by ugly drop and hated that, too.

Character, he thought. A man mustn't be buried until he's reclaimed his character.

I'll get it back. I'll work like hell to get it back. I'll begin by making love to Karen as though it meant something.

At 6:10 on that frigid Friday, ten minutes after they left port, he was in a foul mood, a mood of having been betrayed; all the sober resolutions vanished. The elegant but cornball ship *was* full of retired Methodist ministers and thick-ankled stenographers out to land husbands. No one had come to see them off because he wanted as few people as possible to know where he was, and therefore suspect he wasn't in perfect health; the official word at the GWS offices, both in New York and Los Angeles, was that he had impulsively flown to London to scout talent and to oversee the first anniversary in England of the Broadway hit comedy he had produced, *Serpent Dancing*. The image of a sea voyage suggested passivity, spiritual infirmity, not Warren Weber, the Brahmins' Barnum, America's most creative, active, and envied producer. Physically he felt fine, bursting, bridling with energy. He had followed Mel Hebranck's advice and left his work load behind, including even a bag of unoptioned, possibly buyable television, stage, and movie scripts he could, should, have brought to read under the sun.

The weather turned warm on the second day at sea, as the ship moved past Cape Hatteras, but Weber's restlessness grew and, with it, his irritability. Karen was not to blame for the cruise, and she was uncommonly patient with his impatience, but he was short with her and, he was aware, unnecessarily surly. He encouraged her to seek out her own amusements, and she went, not knowing he was ill because he had not told her about Mel, and he spent much of his time alone, thinking about the imprisonments of illness and finality of death, thinking about the noble promises he had made to Charlie and to himself and had not kept, might never keep. "The Gundersen Journal" could be revived, sure, but Weber wasn't sure if he could revive himself.

The *Stalwart's* first port of call would be St. Maarten. There surely would be a plane there. Karen could do as she liked, but he would hire a pilot if necessary and fly back to New York, where a busy desk awaited him, where he would look through the drawers of his mind and find purpose. This enforced idleness, the first in his life, was infinitely more dangerous than a backbreaking work schedule would be. Being idle impelled him to examine Warren Weber. It highlighted his emptiness.

Then, on the third day at sea, Christmas Day, he saw the Negro girl.

One

H*E WAS SITTING* beside the vast, crowded, kidney-shaped pool, sipping a gin and tonic, trying to follow the rhythm patterns of *The Waste Land,* which he had borrowed from the ship's library, trying to divine how Charlie Gundersen would have approached the Jesse Nash story, trying to ignore an unignorable, bad-breathed old man who sat next to him without invitation, who introduced himself as Irving Popkin from Great Neck, announced he was in the foundation garment game, and proceeded to detail the history of his angina and bursitis. The thick-ankled stenographers were in swim suits and in abundance, wearing invisible signs that advertised for companionship in screeching block letters; most of them struck Weber as a forceful argument for homosexuality. The afternoon sun blazed down from the cloudless, limitless sky like fire. Karen, who didn't like sun, was at the hairdresser's.

The girl walked past Weber and Popkin in a short-sleeved white terry robe that contrasted strikingly with her smooth caramel skin. She appeared to be looking for someone, or maybe for just a place to sit and put her large beach bag. Men's eyes fastened on her, including Popkin's, who interrupted his advice on how to live with angina and bursitis to mutter something about bleck ess, and Weber, closing T. S. Eliot, imagined it might be interesting bleck ess indeed. She was a lovely thing, probably in her early twenties, although Weber, who had fought hard to flatten the hypocrisy of tokenism and successfully integrate Negroes in television plays, caught himself entertaining the cliché that it was impossible to guess a Negro's age. But early twenties seemed about right.

She found an empty deck chair nearby, and Weber, watching from behind the protectiveness of smoked glasses, was angrily certain that she would have sat in Popkin's chair if Popkin weren't in it. She removed the terry robe, an exquisite young woman with high cheekbones and profoundly wise eyes and incorruptible mouth, not tall but standing tall, standing like a novitiate queen. Popkin said that he and Mrs. Popkin had seen her and another colored girl in the nightclub show last night singing very nice songs. He was surprised, he added, that the ship people allowed her to mingle like this with the passengers.

"Mingle?" said Weber. "She's by herself."

"Coming here, sitting here, I mean. You'd think they wouldn't allow it."

"Why not? Because she's an employee?" Weber asked, knowing exactly what the man with the bad breath meant.

"Listen, what are you, a keed? Look on what color she got."

"It's dark."

Popkin shrugged and nodded. "Listen, I got nothing against them. They work for me and I say like this, live and let live, I treat them very good. But mingling, that I don't see. You agree?"

The man was tiresome—not vicious so much as tiresome—and there seemed no purpose in sustaining a pretense of tolerance. Evenly, Weber said, "Mr. Popkin, why don't you get up and go away?"

"Huh?"

"I've mingled with you long enough and you bore the crap out of me."

Irving Popkin's jaw dropped. But he got up and went away.

The girl took a towel, a copy of *Mademoiselle*, and a bottle of sun lotion from her bag, and began to apply the lotion to her skin. Her one-piece Kelly green swimsuit was more conservative than the skimpy bikinis some of the thick-ankled stenographers were pathetically parading in, but it could not hide the fact that she owned a remarkable figure, vibrant and discreetly voluptuous. There was an aura of great class about her, and she demonstrated that class, Weber observed, by anointing her body modestly, without dramatics, as though it were a private act and not a public showcasing of her spectacularly displayable assets. It was a special body, very special, yet she did not seem aware that it was—a fact that captivated Weber, who wondered how she had escaped being signed up by the big-money show business boys long before this and who was determined to meet her.

Getting up to go to her, practicing his opening line, he saw a slender man in a ship's officer uniform bending over her from behind her chair, startling her with suddenness. Weber could hear nothing, but he could judge, by the officer's officer-type briskness and the girl's obvious fluster, that she was being ordered to scram. And she began to, after a few more moments of subdued argument, looking wounded and helplessly insulted. Before she had quite gathered her belongings together, Weber strode up to them and addressed the officer sharply. "Is something wrong here?" he asked.

The officer blinked. "Wrong, sir?"

"My name is Sanders. My brother is the president of this steamship line. Is there a problem here?"

"Oh, no, sir."

"This young lady appears to be upset."

The girl said, "It's all right," and started to rise, but Weber motioned her back.

"There is a company rule, sir, as you—ah—possibly don't know," said the officer. "No member of the *Stalwart* staff is ever permitted to use any of the facilities used by passengers. That's a strict rule."

"Well, it's a stupid and archaic rule," Weber snapped, "and I intend to contact my brother at once on the ship's radio and have a talk with him about it. That will be all, young man."

"Sir—"

"I'll take full responsibility. That will be all."

Dismissing him, Weber took off his smoked glasses, smiled, and sat on her footrest. "One more peep out of Captain Bligh and I would've had him flogged at the yardarm."

She looked worried, and beautiful. "Are you really going to contact your brother?"

"Why should I? My brother's in the furniture business in Philadelphia. His name's the same as mine—Weber."

"Then you're not—" Her eyes widened and she laughed. "Well, now . . . I thought I was the one with all the *chutspah*, coming up here, but you take the cake. *Chutspah* means—"

"I know what *chutspah* means. My brother and I belong to the chosen people. What's your name?"

"Robin Hamilton," she answered, her voice smoky but not sultry, the whole of her delectable yet curiously innocent, a knockout he imagined could interrupt her active participation in an orgy to inquire when the coconut cookies would be served. "I . . . maybe I'd better get going, after all. I knew I wasn't supposed to be here in the first place. It was crazy of me. I could get fired, and I want to hold onto this job."

"Who got you the booking? You're a singer, I understand. I haven't seen you work yet, but I hear you're good. Who's your agent?"

"Do you know anything about show business?"

"A little."

"The Fieldmont Agency booked us for this cruise. Have you heard of them? They're in New York."

"Yes." Ernie Fieldmont, a nickel and dimer, specialized in booking colored acts and pocketing more than his legal fee. To be handled by Fieldmont was to be very hungry black. " 'Booked us,' you say. Who's 'us'?"

"Grace Hamilton and me. The Hamilton Sisters. We're not sisters—we're not even related—but we have the same name."

"I'll catch you tonight. Wait, don't go yet. What are you supposed to do on the boat when you're not working, sit in the galley and peel onions?"

"No, sit in the galley and sing colored spirituals to ourselves, is more like it."

"Uh-huh, then the strict rule Captain Bligh was trying to enforce did have an ounce or two of racism in it, right?"

"Look at that man in the cowboy hat," she said softly, and indicating an oafish-looking animal in an outsize Stetson, bathing trunks, and flamingo polo shirt who was regaling a cluster of passengers by waltzing vigorously with a clearly embarrassed older woman. "That's Frankie Brand, the MC in our show. It's just coincidental that he's Caucasian, but he has the run of the boat. And see the white couple at this end of the pool—the man's handing the lady a cigarette? They're the dance team, Tony and Clarice, and nobody's telling them to go below deck. Yes, I'd call it racism. And I resent it. I've always resented it. But that's a long, weepy story and now I *am* going to go back to my room because I feel people are staring at me," she said, and stood. "That shows I'll never get very far in this business—I get nervous when people stare at me, and performers are supposed to want people to stare at them."

"People stare," said Weber, rising, too, "because you're so pleasant to stare at."

She smiled and met his eyes so directly, so frankly, that he half expected her to invite him to go down to her room with her. "Aren't you sweet! Thank you for being such a nice knight in armor, Mr. . . . Weber?"

"Weber, yes. Warren Weber."

"Warren Weber. I've heard that na—" She stopped, and the sudden flicker of recognition was the same flicker he had witnessed time after time in the past in young women on the professional make. "The television Warren Weber?"

"Guilty. I also talk back to ships' officers on the side." He waited for the predictable, the inevitable—for her to convey to him either outright or by deafening hints, that eventually her stateroom was his stateroom.

He was both disappointed and pleased that she chewed on the enlightenment for only a moment and then let go—or seemed to.

"Does Frankie Brand know you're on board?" she asked. "We had a famous manufacturer in the audience last night, and Frankie called him up on stage and made a big fuss."

"Miss Hamilton, I am registered on the passenger list as W. R. Weber, New York, New York," said Weber, carefully avoiding any mention of Karen. "If you so much as whisper a hint to that cretin, Frankie Brand, that I'm on board, I will personally strip you naked on that nightclub stage and beat you to death with the blunt end of our friend Captain Bligh."

Her laugh was like her voice, smoky but not sultry. Female. A child's, a hip child's. "It's a deal," she said. "I always hated to be stripped naked on a nightclub floor. Thanks again."

The show began at ten o'clock. Frankie Brand opened it with a perspiring volley of cheesy gags that kept alluding, for some incomprehensible reason, to the intricate art of anal intercourse. The audience, incredibly, laughed and even applauded. The dance team of Tony and Clarice followed; they had stolen all the steps and none of the talent of Veloz and Yolanda, and their turn was interminable. Even Karen, whose tolerance of the weakest performers could be excessive, began to draw ski marks on the tablecloth with her fork. Then Frankie Brand returned. His roaring river of gags about frontal intercourse were a relief, if only because of the change of position. And then he rasped a demand for a great big hand for the nifty, swifty Hamilton Sisters an' let's hear it, folks, and at last the two girls were at the mike.

Their first number, "Sisters," Irving Berlin's witty and disarmingly simple standard, was rousing, and they caught the audience at once, in spite of basic show business flaws immediately obvious to Weber. They were built differently—Grace Hamilton, a broomstick, was at least a head taller than Robin Hamilton—and someone should have advised them never to wear twin lamé gowns and twin hair styles. They moved uncertainly. Their makeup was a cosmetic disgrace. Their songs after "Sisters" did not build solidly because the sequence of the numbers had not been properly thought out. Yet the audience liked them, and Weber did, too. They had reached nowhere near the top drawer as entertainers, but they were fresh, and bright, and when they were through (leaving the stage awkwardly) Weber asked Karen what she thought.

"Well, I may be unfair," answered Karen, whose evaluations of acts were instinctive and often right on the nose, "but I think they'd do better, and go farther, if they didn't work together."

"How do you figure?"

"The tall one seems to have had more experience, but there's something a little grating about her—she's all show biz tricks and gimmicks, and it shows. The other one is softer, fresher—what would the phrase be?—not yet through the mill. They don't mesh. The contrast is too great and it gets in the way."

Weber nodded and nibbled at his lower lip.

"Oh-oh," she said, smiling.

"What?"

"I thought this was supposed to be a pleasure trip—no work."

"It is."

"You're chewing your lip, and that always means Pygmalion."

And again Weber was impressed by her uncanny mind-reading, this sheltered Radcliffe mother of his children, this gracefully graying, comfortably attractive *shiksa* who was only intermittently sensitive to his personal needs but who had a perpetual, sometimes aggravatingly incisive knowledge of the sum of his parts. He did enjoy playing Pygmalion because he frequently did it so well. He had made stars of kids with less talent and looks than the Hamilton kid had, and there was little doubt now that, if he put his mind and energy to it, and if he survived his forty-fourth year, he could turn the Hamilton girl into one hell of a Galatea.

"Let's get out of here," he said, motioning to the red-jacketed waiter for a check. Karen went with him to the Promenade Deck, and they stood at the rail and watched the diamonds of light glitter on the water.

"When are you going to talk to me, Warren?" she asked quietly after a while. "Or do we spend the remainder of the cruise like two strangers at a cocktail party, conversing but not communicating?"

"Oh, Christ," he sighed. "No Jung jargon, Karen, please."

"What's happening to you? Why are we on this boat if you have nothing to say to me? Why are you so removed?"

"I got worn out. I wanted a change. I'm not removed."

"You haven't said more than a dozen words. We have a double bed and you haven't come near me."

"Is that what's upsetting you, that you haven't been touched?"

"Shouldn't it?"

"Since when has not having sex been upsetting to you?"

Silence. Then, in a tone far too civilized: "I'm beginning to get the idea, Warren, that in some clumsy Machiavellian way you had something very definitely in mind when you decided we should take a cruise. I think you were even relieved that the children didn't come along because you wanted us to be alone so you could prove how little we communicate."

"I've told you a hundred times, Karen—I can do without your sounding like the lead article in *The Psychiatric Quarterly*. Climb off my back. I'm tired," he said, and realized that he was indeed tired; it was barely eleven o'clock—a time of night when he normally was wholly awake and bustling with vigor—and he ached to get into bed and go to sleep. The realization, dredging up an image of Mel Hebranck's wagging finger, disturbed him. The fact that he could not bring himself to tell Karen about Mel's diagnoses and cautions disturbed him. The mounting awareness since he had boarded this ship that he had no real feeling for Karen, or for much of anything, disturbed him. "I'm sorry," he said, not looking at her. "I'm not letting you have much fun, am I?"

"Please tell me what hurts, Warren."

"Nothing."

"Are you tired of being married to me?"

"No. Let's not have that periodic second act curtain again."

"Then what shall we have? How about honesty? I'm sure a divorce would be terribly painful to the children and me, but living with you for the rest of our lives without having you is an even more painful prospect. If—"

"What in hell are you baiting me for?" Weber flared. "Divorce . . . you're the one who always opens that can of succotash, never me. Maybe you want it. Maybe you're the clumsy Machiavelli around here. Maybe you're jockeying me, egging me to duck out of the contract so you can be free of your miseries and at the same time play the grieving homemaker whose heel of a husband deserted her."

"This is all so ugly. I loathe this cheap squabbling."

"So do I. The simplest way to end it is for you to leave me alone."

"Warren . . . don't send me away . . ."

"Then I'll leave and you stay here. I'm a crude Jew from the other side of the tracks, but I always try to be obliging to you rich, refined Gentiles."

He watched her leave, aghast that he hadn't the character, the guts, to call her back. They had had fights over the past twenty years, some of them so wounding that he had recoiled in awe at his capacity for inflicting such blows. But when had he last been this— cheap; yes, that was the word, this gutter cheap? The ethnic crap was an unforgivably low blow and a stupid one, because the intermarriage issue hadn't been an issue at all between them in years.

Am I going to go nuts all at once, or piece by piece? I don't recognize myself. I don't understand myself. I was always so sure I did. What's happened to all the juice, all the caring?

He walked aimlessly for many minutes and then, abruptly, hurried to the cabin to apologize. Karen wasn't there. He waited for nearly an hour and she still did not come. Resentment at desertion gradually replaced worry, and he picked up the ivory telephone and asked to be connected with Miss Robin Hamilton.

"Hamilton, Hamilton . . . I don't see any Hamilton on the passenger list, sir. Do you know what cabin she's in?"

"She's not a passenger. She's one of the entertainers."

"I—see. One more moment, sir, and I'll try to locate her."

"Call me," Weber said, and placed the receiver on its cradle. If Karen came in before the phone rang, he would decide then how to handle the call. Ten minutes passed, and the phone rang, and Karen had still not returned. He snapped it up, and Robin Hamilton said she and Grace were between sets with the band in the Coral Room. "What time are you through for the night?" he asked, close to the receiver.

"Two. Why?"

His watch read five past one. "Meet me on the Upper Promenade, where they keep the lounge chairs, at a quarter after two."

". . . All right."

Karen came in, looking chilled but contained, just before he hung up. "I was about to have you paged," he said. "Where were you?"

"Making love," she said, removing her wrap and stepping out of her pumps. "He was a nineteen-year-old coal stoker, with vine leaves in his hair. I told him I was a rich, lonely, Gentile divorcee, and that did the trick. All I have to say are two words—'rich' and 'Gentile'—and the young men fall all over me." She yawned. "Or they used to. No, I was walking, and thinking. I was going to stay up all night, anywhere but here, but that seemed silly, and the air turned cold."

"Karen . . ."

She glared at him. "Well, here I am, Warren. You were going to have me paged, so you must have needed me for something. Let me guess what. You want to deal with your own inadequacies by lecturing me on what an inadequate wife I've been. Or you're in the mood to empty some sperm in a hurry and call it lovemaking. Which of those two functions were you going to have me paged for? They're the only two functions you've ever wanted me for, aren't they?"

"Keep this up, and I'm leaving."

"That's the door, Warren, there on your right."

He drank Scotch at the Coral Room bar until two o'clock, feeling almost unbearably weary and disgusted with himself, but his spirit partially revived when the Hamilton girl and her broomstick partner appeared at the microphone, and wholly revived when the broomstick stepped away and Robin Hamilton did a solo. It was "Summertime," an almost impossible number for a novice to pull off, but she did the worn classic with genuine emotion and exquisite precision. Heart, that elusive and outdated extra dimension, was in it, Negro heart, Yiddish heart, sincerity, knowledge of the lyric and respect for it. Yiddish, yes, that's what she was putting into the number, thought Weber, a passionate voice with tears. And where had she learned those odd tricks of timing that made the words her own, as if she sang from some private sadness? She got a good hand when the number was done, mostly from Weber, who was enchanted by the promise in her.

At two he signed his tab and at two-fifteen she came to him on the Upper Promenade. No one else was around, which was marvelous luck. She looked radiant.

"Well, I made it," she said, and they sat together on the chairs nearest the rail. "Should I be here?"

"Why not? Is Captain Bligh still after you?"

"No, I mean if your wife wakes up all of a sudden and you're not there, will she come looking for you? I wouldn't like it much if she saw us together."

Weber pretended to be amused. "Who told you I'm married?"

"Grace. She knows everything about you. She's been in show business a long time and she knows everything about everybody in it."

"Did she say anything nice about me?"

"Oh, plenty of nice things. And she also said you chase every girl under eighty."

He laughed. "You're an extremely direct young lady, aren't you?"

"Uh-huh. It gets me in a whole lot of trouble sometimes."

"Did your friend happen to mention whether I catch many girls under eighty—assuming, naturally, that she's an expert on Warren Weber?"

"Grace heard you catch a lot."

"Then I'll ask another question. Knowing this, why did you agree to meet me here, in the dark, in the middle of the night?"

"Because Grace said she hears you're not a wrestler. I wouldn't come to meet the Pope if he was a wrestler."

"Well, I'm grateful to Grace for the character reference. I suppose the first thing you'll do when you leave here is fill her in on everything that was said here and everything that happened."

She nodded. "Pretty much, I guess—we tell each other things. Not that anything is going to happen, though. I'm a very slow starter in *that* department, you ought to know. And more often that not, I don't even start at all."

Again Weber laughed, refreshed by her. "I'll make a note. Actually, I asked you to meet me because I'm curious about something besides whether you're a fast or slow starter. You're lovely, and you sing well—you need training and more experience, but you can sing. What I'm curious about is, why are you still working out of the Fieldmont office when girls with a tenth of what you have to offer are billionaires?"

"Well, I'm nineteen. I haven't been at it very long. And you may have noticed that my complexion is beige . . ."

"No, don't cop out with that," Weber objected. "Maybe too many Captain Blighs are still running around loose telling you where you may and may not sit, but they can't keep you out of show business."

The girl frowned for the first time. "Mr. Weber, you sound like a pretty dumb fella. They can't keep me out but they can damn well make it a thousand times harder for me to get in. And they do. They sure do, and if you don't think so—*you*, of all people—then you're a pretty dumb fella."

"Maybe I can do something to help you get in."

Her smile was impish and delicious. "All right. Then you wouldn't be a dumb fella any more."

She talked about herself because Weber invited her to, yet, for all her attractive ingenuousness, he had the feeling he wasn't learning very much, that there were deep pockets of her past and present that were none of his, or anyone's, business. She told of her ambitions, and Weber listened, and then he talked to her, and he was frank. He detailed everything she did wrong or, equally serious, not professional enough, at a microphone. He told her he could help her get that first big break, but only if she had the stamina to work harder than anyone had ever worked before. He told her she would have to get rid of her partner, and fast, if she really cared about developing her individuality.

She listened. She listened well.

Then, impossibly, it was twenty minutes of four and of course it was time to go. Weber got up with her, and she did not back away when he took her arm, or when he brought her to him, or when he kissed her, but her grin when the kiss was done declared that she had accepted it willingly but not seriously. "That was nice," she said. "Would you mind if you did it again?" He kissed her again, and it was more deep-drawn this time, but she gently took his hand from her breast. "*Genug,*" she said good-naturedly, the Yiddish word for "enough," and as gently freed herself. "That's the only thing I have against kissing: you can't trust it. It starts off so harmless and then, first thing you know, it's not harmless any more unless you stop it quick."

"Let's do some harm. Some irreparable harm."

"I explained to you: I'm a slow starter. Especially with a man like you."

"What's a man like me?"

"If we end up in bed, I want to be sure I'm there because I want you, not because you can maybe make me famous and rich. It'd be *ichhhh*-y otherwise, and I hate it when it's *ichhhh*-y. I mean, you not being a wrestler and all, you can understand what I'm saying, can't you?"

"Against my better judgment, I suppose so."

"Sure. Well, good night now—or it's good morning, isn't it? I'd better find my way to my room by myself. Grace and I have this room about thirty floors below sea level. I had a very nice time with you, Mr. Weber."

Watching her go, uncomfortably conscious of the excitement in his loins, Weber warned himself to survive till he saw her again, and went to his cabin, where a table light was on and Karen, her azure eyes red-rimmed, was sitting up in bed, smoking a cigarette and gazing at the porthole. There was silence until he undressed and his teeth were brushed and Mel's nightly yellow capsule was swallowed. Then Karen looked at him and wept. She dove into his arms the instant he came to her and she mourned, "I can't breathe without you, darling. I can't bear it when we act this way, like two animals who don't love each other, and we do, darling, don't we, we do . . ."

The light was switched off and Weber held and comforted and kissed this woman he would never leave, this woman he would love if he could love. He wanted to talk love to her but the words would not form, so he kissed her mouth with his tongue and moved his hand over the warmth of her leg and wondered, as he had wondered so many numberless times before, why he could be a tender lover with other women who hadn't faces or names or meaning, an aware and sensitive lover with a whole man's knowledge of how to play a woman, and why he could not bring quality and caring to this woman who had borne his son and his two daughters, this Karen who was a barbed wire of involuntary restraint and who would die for him. Yet her supple forty-year-old body quivered at the touch of his hand as it had done almost equally numberless times before, and then her breathing became labored as he wakened her, and she gasped at the wonderment of what might have been an honest climax, and was still and tolerant for him. Weber reveled in his own lonely culmination because the fantasy this night was specific. Karen was a colored beauty named Robin Hamilton this night, and the electricity between her splendid legs was turned up to its highest voltage. He cried out his joy and, in the dark stateroom lighted by the full moon at the porthole, Karen smiled the contented smile of a woman who has pleased her man.

Weber had never understood Karen's, or anyone's, preference for going to sleep early and rising early; he had always been convinced that nighttime was the logical time to be awake. So when, at midnight on their fifth day at sea, she asked if he would mind her turning in, he assured her he would find something to do on his own.

Robin Hamilton met him. And met him again the following night after her last turn with the Coral Room band. Sex was out of the question, she made clear, because its proper place was in a bed, not in an open-air deck chair, and because neither of them had a bedroom that guaranteed privacy, and, mostly, because she meant what she had said that first night: she needed to be sure she wanted to make it with him, not The Warren Weber. When he kissed her, though, he observed that she trembled. She would not allow the kisses to get out of control, but he knew he had met someone he had cynically come to believe no longer existed: an uncomplicated woman with honest appetites. Not a Karen, who intellectualized sex and therefore distrusted it. Not the hordes of Gloria Barclays, who bartered it and therefore cooperated in corrupting it. He kissed Robin Hamilton and tried to remember when he had felt this alive, this young, this eager to happily anticipate the next days and years of his life. He wondered if the enthusiasm would continue once the pants were finally off, and knew it would.

"Thank you," he said before they parted.

"What for?"

"For making me happy. I like being with you. I haven't liked being with anyone in an awfully long while. Quick, see that falling star? I'm so happy, I can't think of a thing to wish for."

It was a line straight out of *Serpent Dancing*, but it obviously reached her. She looked at him, and touched his cheek, and said softly, "I'm going to beat it and run right this minute. That kind of sweet talk knocks me for a loop."

She didn't run, but she did leave quickly. At the Promenade door, she pursed her marvelous lips to kiss him from thirty feet away, and disappeared.

In St. Maarten the next afternoon, strolling the busy strip of beach with Karen and a gabby couple named Ahearne whom Karen had picked up on board, Weber saw the girl. She was in her Kelly green swimsuit, and splashing in the water with the broomstick and a young Negro Weber had seen at the piano with the band in the Coral Room. She saw Weber and waved, then turned away to splash again. He hoped she had turned away only because Karen was near, not because she was more interested in her own company of friends. He wondered if she was balling the Negro, and discovered he was jealous.

At dinner that evening on the ship, Karen confided that she wasn't certain she wanted to see Guadeloupe, tomorrow's seven-hour port of call. The Ahearnes had been there on other cruises and had advised her to forget it, it was a filthy place whose gutters were lined with dead rats and markets crawled with vermin, a reeking port whose inhabitants were grossly hostile to Americans. "Let's all pass it up tomorrow," she suggested. "It's just possible we may have met our match in Binky and Chet Ahearne, as far as back-gammon is concerned. They say they're sharks, and they may be."

He didn't see Robin that night, because it was a night Karen chose to stay awake late, but he telephoned her and told her to ditch everyone, drop any other plans she might have, and ride with him in the first tender going to Guadeloupe in the morning.

She joined him on the tender at 9:15, wearing a flared skirt and brightly colored peasant blouse, carrying her beach bag, and complaining cheerfully that she was getting too old to go with so little sleep. They landed, and the Ahearnes had been right: the initial view of the island was indeed unappetizing. Weber summoned a taxi driver and asked him, in French, which beach would be least crowded at this time of day or, for that matter, throughout the day. Grosier, said the driver, and took them there, leaving with the understanding that he was to return at half-past three to drive them back to the four o'clock tender.

The day was lovely and Grosier was a lovely beach, white and lonely and uncommercial; the other passengers would go to the conspicuously glamorous beach at La Caravelle, as simple and as French as Las Vegas, Nevada. Weber and the girl changed into swimsuits in separate dressing quarters and walked at the edge of the steely blue water until they reached a high, protective dune and simply fell to the sand.

Weber brought her into his arms and kissed her mouth. She responded, more fervently than on the ship, and she flinched but did not struggle as he gently squeezed the wondrous flesh of her thigh. "The past few nights, after I left you, have been murder," she confided. "It isn't supposed to be nice for a refined girl to thrash around in bed all night long so—hot. Can I use that word?"

"Perfectly refined word," Weber muttered unevenly, and his breath drew in, and the sight of her, the knowledge of her in his arms, attacked all his nerve ends. They were the only two people in the world, and she was on her back, and he slowly lowered the straps from her shoulders, and her eyes were closed as he regarded her rounded breasts and felt an electric shock at the beauty of them, at the youngness and pride of them, at the luxurious splendor of the erect pink nipples. "You're gorgeous," he breathed, and held her breasts in his hands and began to kiss them.

She suddenly drew away, onto her side away from him, and he heard a sharp intake of breath.

"What's wrong?" he asked, instantly concerned.

"Please . . . don't touch me . . ."

He sat back on his knees, puzzled, excited, peeved, worried, bewildered, and watched her right the shoulder straps. This was the golden girl, the uncomplicated girl, the woman who wasn't all the other women. This wasn't the girl who held you off when the moment was exactly right for not being held off. "Robin? . . ." he said, uttering her name for the first time.

"No good," he heard. "It's no good . . ."

She turned to him, her eyes wet, her faultless face now all the more expressive because of the pain in it, and she tried a brave smile that faltered. "You poor, nice man," she murmured, facing him fully. "The very last thing I've ever wanted to be was a tease," she said, "and that's what I am, just a lot of noise. I've been terrible. I didn't mean to lead you on, but I did. You must be either ready to climb a wall or kill me, the way I've treated you."

"You're crying."

"No, I'm not. Ashamed of myself, but I'm not crying."

"Why ashamed?"

"Because I hate that type of girl, that gets a man all worked up and then doesn't go through with it. I . . . I wanted to—I want you to know that, for what it's worth. I'm—I must be crazy when it comes to sex. I'm not a tramp and I'm not a virgin, but sometimes I think I'm maybe a little bit of both. I . . . oh, this is all so mixed up. *I'm* mixed up, and you should tell me to get lost."

Weber sat in the sand next to her and held her hand. The fingertips were ice. "I'd be a pretty dumb fella if I did that," he said tenderly. "I'm mighty hot, and not from the sun, but I'll survive. I *think* I will." He smiled. "Tell me about yourself, Robin Hamilton. Tell me what mixes you up."

She shook her head. "No. I like you and I trust you, but no, not yet, anyway. It's a whole long *megillah*, and I'm ashamed of most of it."

"Then censor it when you feel like it."

The girl sighed. "You really dig punishment, don't you?"

"A red-blooded glutton, that's me."

"Can we walk?" she asked, and they did. "Let's see, where do you start telling your life story when you're too ashamed to tell all of it? I guess two years ago, when my brother was killed. That's—"

"Killed? Was he in the Army?"

"Not likely, not at fourteen. Fourteen years old, shy and kind of runty but a wonderful kid. My mother worked two jobs—a maid and in a laundry—because she had this one big dream, that

Roland Lee was going to go to college and make us all proud. I was seventeen then, and my older sister Lula—"

Weber stopped and took her arm. "Wait a moment. Roland Lee Hamilton? The Stuart White thing?"

She nodded. "That's us. Two years ago, New Year's Eve."

"Oh, Lord, honey, I'm sorry! Yes, of course I know about it, but I had no idea you were his sister!"

Again she nodded. "You don't get over something like that. My mother's still alive, or so I hear, but I don't know how she keeps going."

"What do you mean, 'or so you hear'?"

She paused and knelt to pick up a twisted shell. "That's what's wrong with trying to tell a story I'm not ready to tell, that I just don't want to tell," she replied after a while. "Honestly, I don't want to go into it. I was doing something I shouldn't have been doing while my baby brother was getting killed, and my mother kicked me out of the house, and maybe she had a right to. I don't know. I don't know anything—that's why I should never talk about myself. I sometimes think I understand this crazy hang-up I have over sex—it's great with the right man and I go all out and at the same time it scares me—and then I turn around and realize I don't understand a thing. I don't know why I can't play it smart like any other girl in my shoes would and sleep with you because of all you could do for my career. I don't know why I let you half undress me like a whore and then acted like a scared virgin. I don't know why I'm talking all this *meshugaas*, not making any sense, not even trying to, I suppose." Weber kept still, and she stood, staring at the shell she was bouncing in her hand. "See? I'm a weirdo. I sound like I'm looking for pity, or sympathy, or whichever is which, but I'm not. I mean it, Mr. Warren Weber . . . I'm pretty, I guess, and I have a good shape, but I'm not worth your time, or anybody's time. I'm sorry you're stuck with me till that Frenchman taxi driver comes back."

She looked at him without expression, as though daring him to be kind. Weber regarded her silently for some moments, and then smiled, pointed to the sea, and said, "Come on, I'll race you to the water. Last one in's a rotten weirdo."

They swam, furiously and jubilantly. Weber disappeared and made her shriek by zooming up from the floor of the sea and grabbing her legs, and she disappeared and made Weber holler by zooming up from the floor of the sea and pushing him, hard, so that he lost his balance and fell. They chased each other. They scooped water at each other. Weber, who could not sing, became a baritone Enrico Caruso and belted out an atrocious but spirited "Vesti la giubba," and she joined in with an equally spirited belting of "Hello, Frisco, Hello." When he had had enough of the water, he lifted her in his arms and carried her, gaily pummeling, pretending she was being assaulted, to the beach and dumped her, making sure not to hurt her.

They laughed, and panted, and for no reason laughed again. They lay in each other's arms and talked little, only happy talk, the comfortable, casual talk made lazy and warm by a lulling sun. She was the first to lower gradually into a light sleep, and Weber regarded her, the perfect lines and angles of her, and thought, I've got to have her.

But not now. She's much too special to be rushed.

Warren Weber speaking. Warren Weber saying there was a woman too special to be rushed.

They dozed, and wakened to walk some more, and dressed—again in separate quarters—and found a tiny café that contained two tables and four chairs, a clucking, cadaverous proprietess with no teeth, and some foul-looking, foul-smelling beef that the woman offered to serve them but which made Robin's nose wrinkle. They settled for packaged Camembert and a surprisingly good red wine. The day was moving far too quickly, and the taxi driver would call for them at the meeting place they had agreed upon far too soon, but Weber was sure that today was just the beginning. And they held hands under the table, and Robin told him, without words, that she was sure, too.

In the taxi that returned them to the tender, he could not restrain himself from mentioning Jesse Nash, whose consuming mission for the past year, according to the papers and newscasts, was to avenge her brother's death. "That fellow intrigues me," he declared.

There was a beat, and then she nodded, and replied, almost coldly, "He manages to get himself into the newspapers, all right."

"Do you know him?"

"I—used to."

"You heard he was shot."

"Yes. I read that."

"Who do you think did it? He claims it was the New York police."

She gazed at the back of the driver's neck. "Baloney," she said quietly after a moment. "That's Jesse jumping off the deep end again. A colored man could have done it. More likely, in fact. A white man probably wouldn't be stupid enough to make him a martyr, not even some crazy redneck cracker."

"You don't sound especially friendly toward Nash."

She looked at Weber sharply, and spoke sharply. "Look, I don't want to talk about it, any of it," she declared. "I said that before. Will you please just cut it out?"

". . . Sure."

The silence was heavy, onerous, and long seconds passed and then she shyly reached for his hand. "Please don't give up on me, okay?" she murmured. "I mean well—at least most of the time." Before he could speak, or even form a reassuring smile, she kissed his mouth and whispered huskily, "God, I wish that driver wasn't here. I wish right this very instant we could make love."

His own voice suddenly husky as well, Weber gently protested, "Lady, we've got to do something about you. I can take one of your flipflops, and maybe a couple, but keeping up with you is mighty hard."

"I bet," she said cheerfully, and moved away from him. "There's the little boat we take to go to the big boat, right up ahead."

The tender reached the *Stalwart* gangplank thirty minutes before sailing. "The Promenade," Weber said. "Don't go there at a quarter after two. Be there one minute after. Half a minute after."

She shook her head, no longer cheerful. "No. I think I better not."

"Now wait—"

"No," she repeated too firmly. "Just don't—let's us forget it, all right?" And she moved quickly into the crowd of passengers.

Weber watched, flabbergasted, frustrated, enraged. She was executing a very carefully orchestrated ploy. Or she was a kook, the queen of kooks. Or a certified lunatic.

But none of it mattered, for she had brought him alive again. Mel Hebranck was all wet. Weber wasn't dying. The trade papers would have to keep their obits on him locked up under *W* for years to come.

Two

GRACE DEMANDED to hear everything—*everything*—about the private day with Warren Weber. "Nothing special happened," replied Robin Hamilton. "It was pleasant. We talked. Nothing special."

Dressing for the evening's first show, she bitterly reflected on the shocking, unforgivable way she'd behaved, not with the man who could give her the career she needed so keenly she could taste it, but the man she liked, liked very, very much, and yet manipulated, put through hoops and wringers with all the shamelessness and cruelty of a hussy.

Hussy . . . old-fashioned word, Mama's word to describe a bad and thoughtless woman. There was a more vivid, more direct word, and it was "cockteaser"—an ugly, repulsive word, and completely accurate.

Why with him, the first good, kind man after an assembly line of bums, weaklings, half-men? She had so desperately wanted, and wanted now, for him to be inside her, not just to feel just the surge of him but his warmth, his strength, his sincerity, his goodness. Then why the flipflops, as he called them?

Maybe because of his goodness, she thought. Maybe because she was still dirty from the thing—no, things—that had happened on New Year's Eve, two years ago, almost to the day.

That violent New Year's Eve, the night of coincidences and mazes, the night she had first known Jesse Nash. . . .

By lying about her age (seventeen) and her professional experience (none), an agent named Tommy Rexford got her a one-night
singing spot at Rigley's Lounge. He told the club's manager, Buck
Sinclair, that she had played a string of clubs through the Midwest,
and mentioned some names of clubs. Mr. Sinclair, a stocky man
with a dark brown face and poached-egg eyes, knew the North
and the South but not the Midwest, and hired her for the night
because she was good to look at and, he admitted to Tommy, because there was so little quibbling over her working for scale.

To Robin, who had never dreamed she would be inside it, Rigley's Lounge on 126th Street was a show business pinnacle, not a
place for frightened beginners, even talented ones, and as late as an
hour before she was to arrive there she worried aloud to Tommy
Rexford that she mightn't have the nerve to make it. But she did,
and she was helped by her best friend, June Fletcher, the only
girl friend Mama approved of because her father was Reverend
Fletcher. Robin was able to get out of the apartment by telling
Mama she was going to spend the night at June's place; June was
having a small New Year's Eve party, which was true, and the
boys who were invited were boys from the church and Reverend
Fletcher had personally okayed all of them.

Tommy took her to Rigley's for rehearsal in the afternoon. The
room, with its red walls that featured panels of brightly painted
unicorns and murals of kissing birds, was elegant, yet frightening
as well, for the length and depth of it seemed endless. Mr. Sinclair
examined the midnight blue gown she would wear, the gown she
had sewn when Mama was out, and suggested, seriously though
not in the form of an order, that she get rid of the material that
covered the cleavage between her breasts. She did not answer him
because she was scared of him, but she asked Tommy when they
were alone to deliver her decision: the gown was skintight, tighter
than any clothes she'd ever worn before, and she would feel naked
and might not give a good performance if she had to be any more
exposed. Tommy delivered the message, and Mr. Sinclair didn't
pursue the point.

Soon after the four-piece relief band began its first set that night, nearly every table at Rigley's Lounge was filled with people in splendid evening clothes, and the long circular bar was three and four deep with customers. The first show started at eleven, and the MC was Jesse Nash, a popular Harlem comedian, called in for replacement duty because Rigley's regular MC-comic, Corky Bailey, had come down with the flu the day before. Robin stood, trembling, in the narrow dressing room she shared with a beefy exotic dancer whose real name was Josie Raines and whose professional name was Bella DeBall, a tough, immediately friendly woman who advised her to relax and for Christ's sake to quit hiding those boobs under all that cloth, and who left the room when she heard her introduction, "Runnin' Wild."

I'm going to make a fool of myself, Robin thought, inspecting herself in the table mirror for surely the fiftieth time. I shouldn't have agreed to this, not yet. I wish there was somebody here with me. I wish Tommy Rexford didn't have to go off somewhere. I wish I was dead.

There was a knock at the door and she heard, "See you, darlin'? This's Sinclair."

"Just a minute," she called, and, righting the gown's left shoulder strap, admitted Mr. Sinclair, who terrified her, who would find out how much she and Tommy had lied to get her this job. She was relieved that he left the door open. "Old Buck is aces," Tommy had told her, "but you'd best put on your roller skates, anyhow, if you're alone with him. No more harm in him than a robin, Robin, but he sure do like the ladies."

"You'll be on soon, darlin'," Mr. Sinclair said. "You ready to knock them off their chairs?"

Her smile was assured, she hoped, and she spoke yet another lie. "I wouldn't be here if I wasn't ready."

He spotted the mess on Josie Raines's table, the wads of tissue and the single long mesh stocking with the run and the cigarette stabbed into the opened jar of cold cream. The sight clearly annoyed him. "Pigsty Josie," he complained and fussily picked up all the tissues, one by one, and dropped them into the wastebasket. "The thing I can't stand is mess, clutter." Then he smiled. "You don't want to be nervous, darlin'. Do your best like everybody out front's named David Merrick, but don't let anything or anybody throw you."

"I'll do my best, Mr. Sinclair. It means a lot to me to be playing Rigley's Lounge after all those clubs in, ah, the Midwest."

"Sure, you'll be a smash. Now let's gander how you look." He quickly studied her hair and makeup, muttering in affirmation, but he frowned at her bodice. "Run you just a sec to take off that overcoat, darlin'," he said, again not in the form of an order.

She was prepared to say no. He wouldn't have argued.

"How—much time do I have before I go on?"

"About five minutes. Josie's finishing up now and Jesse Nash goes back on. If you need a minute or two more'n five, Jesse knows how to vamp it."

"I won't need that long," she said lamely.

His big smile announced that she'd pleased him—which, she recognized without pride, was all she had meant to do. "Swell," he declared, and his kiss at her forehead was almost fatherly. "Everything's gonna be swell," he said, and strode out.

Robin's shoulders dropped, but she hadn't the time to reflect on her turnabout. Within seconds the extra fabric was removed, and scarcely more than the nipples of her full breasts were covered, and the pretty girl who looked back at her in the mirror was a fake temptress. I'm doing this, she thought, so that Mr. Sinclair will like me and maybe keep me on and pay me more. And isn't that why prostitutes do what they do?

The band finished "Mood Indigo," and there were the sounds of applause and whistles out front as she applied one final coat of lipstick. Josie, her hard beige face coated with perspiration, her silk sequined costume slung over a strong shoulder, padded into the dressing room. "Whew-w-w," she breathed, letting the costume fall to the floor and taking a cigarette from the pack she'd left near the cold cream jar. "Fifteen minutes out there with the organ grindin' and I'm ready for an oxygen tank." She retrieved a bottle of whiskey and a tumbler from a dressing table drawer and looked at Robin's new bodice just before she poured the whiskey. "Well, now, there's been a change in the weather and a change in the sea, looks like. You paid heed to Auntie Josie's good advice, after all."

"I feel like a nudist."

Josie guffawed. "Anything that helps the act, sweetie, is cookin' with the right and proper gas. I told you you shouldn't hide them pretties under a bushel. Like show what you got, like me." She cradled her own fleshy melons in her hands in a gesture too extravagantly lewd to be meant seriously. "You and me can be a team. Mine may not be as pretty as yours, but they're sure's hell lower." She lit the cigarette. "You want a loan of some glycerine? Rub some in around the valley there and the lights pick it up fine. Gives them old mothers at the table somethin' to think about."

"No, thanks. I—I'd better get going. All I hope is that they like me."

"Pete Gumbo sure will, the way you're stacked. Him and his gorillas're at ringside, and they're gettin' juiced to the eyeballs and mumblin' around how they wanna get fixed up tonight. Just make sure you steer clear of him and he won't bother you."

"Pete Gumbo? The trumpet-player?"

"The *ex* trumpet-player. Used to be the biggest and best, and then he went bughouse. He don't get any gigs any more 'cause he's such a commotion man, a real nasty mother, nobody wants him and them gorillas of his around. You should dig them gorillas—they look like they come right out of the George Raft pitchers."

"Then why are they here? Does Mr. Sinclair know they're here?"

"Does he ever! He's been givin' hell to Stan, that's the guy who took the reservation. But you can't blame Stan. He says somebody called today to reserve a ringside for four, and the party's name was Randall or somethin' like that, so what can you do?"

"I don't know, but I do know I'll watch my step," Robin said, and started uncertainly for the door.

Josie offered her the tumbler. "A little guts for the trip?"

"No. Thanks, anyway, Josie," Robin answered, and smiled.

"Miss DeBall, if you please. Star of the Waldorf Astoria—the Waldorf in Astoria, don'cha know. Good luck, sweetie. Go out there and kick 'em all in the butt."

Robin smiled again, liking Josie Raines and hoping never to work with her again, and walked down the cool corridor to the lip of the club and stood in shadow halfway between the stage and the first ringside table. The room was dimly lighted because the spotlight was on Jesse Nash, who was effortlessly making the people laugh, and she looked to see if she could locate Pete Gumbo, whose gross, ugly face she knew from pictures in *The Amsterdam News* and album covers. She didn't see him and decided there was too much on her mind to look for trouble. The stage up ahead, on which she had rehearsed this afternoon, scared her. The very real possibility that she might not find her voice in front of all these people tortured her. Let me be a hit, she prayed. If Mr. Sinclair finds out I lied, let him find out after I go over big and the audience likes me. I've got to be a success. I can't stay in Harlem any more. . . .

". . . the Great White Way," Jesse Nash was saying up there at the microphone. "I'm sittin' in my *shall*-ay in Mississippi, readin' etiquette books with one hand and rubbin' the head of Mississippi's governor for good luck with the other . . ." Laughter. "And this soul brother of mine, he hears I'm headin' soon for New York City, and he say to me, 'Massa,' he say—" Laughter. "He say, 'You'll love the Great White Way.' Now what happened's, I thought what he said was, 'The white way is great.' "

Laughter.

"So I cuffed him around a little. You dig, not too hard, just a little, just to keep in practice."

The audience liked him, loved him, because he was a professional, because he had been in the business long enough to have ironed away every amateur's mistake. Robin wondered why he hadn't gone farther in show business. She had always known there was a Jesse Nash, talented, funny, head-and-shoulders better looking than the other Negro comedians, and her sister Lula said that one fine thing about him was his race pride, that no amount of fame or money could make him join the ofay world except to take their money for services rendered. Robin had read about him in *Ebony* and *Jet*. Once she and June Fletcher had seen him at the Apollo, and they'd waited for him at the stage door and he'd talked with them just as normal as anybody and given them his autograph. Today she had been briefly introduced to him; he hadn't acted as though he remembered her and it would have been plain silly and juvenile to remind him of the stage door of the Apollo. She was sorry he didn't have a ritzier place than Rigley's to work in on New Year's Eve. Rigley's Lounge was Heaven, just about, to her, but for Jesse Nash. . . .

"To tell the truth," he was saying, "I don't cuff around as many Uncle Toms as I used to. Used to be many's twenty a week. Now it's three or four—eight, tops." Laughter. "Problem is, I can't keep up with the mass production."

Listening to his wonderful timing and delivery, working to quell her butterflies, Robin didn't realize for a moment, perhaps several moments, that the mild pressure at the back of her thigh was the pressure of a hand. The hand raised to one buttock, and she whipped around. The man glowered at her and kept his hand on her until she instinctively, angrily slapped it way. The man still glowered. He was Pete Gumbo, fat and towering, with a seedy, shapeless mustache and nasty eyes, and the lights were dim but someone must have seen what he did, the way he was looking at her, someone, a waiter or Mr. Sinclair or someone, yet no one did anything.

"Seems how's there's as many Uncle Toms rollin' off the conveyor belt these days as Cadillacs. Now you non-Toms in the audience—how many of us is there with us tonight? Let's see . . . there's one, there's another, I think . . . You know what a Cadillac is?"

Robin moved away, outraged. Waiting to go on stage as Jesse Nash finished his monologue and began to introduce her, she was furious, and the fury supplanted her nervousness. The three other men at the table—gorillas, Josie called them—sat staring at her without expression. This was the time for no distractions, and she had been distracted, upset. Even if she flopped miserably tonight, she would complain about Pete Gumbo to Mr. Sinclair.

"—young lady that looks more luscious every day, and tonight she looks like tomorrow," Jesse Nash was saying. "Ladies and gentlemen, sit up and say it good for Miss Robin Hamilton!"

Then there was no Pete Gumbo. The applause warmed her, dizzied her, and Jesse Nash's hand was helping her up the four steps to the stage as the band played a bar of "Lovely to Look At." She kissed Jesse Nash's cheek—impulsively, gratefully. The kiss surprised him, as it surprised her, and he could have stolen this moment from her limelight by clowning, and got away with it. He didn't. He whispered, "You're the star tonight," for only her to hear, and stepped off the stage.

The nervousness that was unmanageable disappeared with striking speed. Robin sang "Love Me or Leave Me" and was well into "Sing, You Sinners" when the fact hit her that there had been an ovation after the first number—not just clapping, but enthusiastic clapping and stomping. She sang "The Boy Next Door," wishing she could keep her eyes trained from Pete Gumbo for longer than seconds at a time, wishing he wasn't staring at her as though his fly was open.

"The Boy Next Door" was supposed to be the third and last number, with "Heat Wave" ready in the bullpen in case the noise for an encore was really justified. It was, and she tore into "Heat Wave" with the gathering certainty that she could go on all night, all year, that Mr. Sinclair couldn't help but offer her the moon after how she was getting through to the audience.

Then she was done, and Jesse Nash, applauding along with the others as he came back on stage, congratulated her. He said something private that she couldn't hear, but the tone said it was something good, and this time he kissed *her* cheek. She wafted rather than walked off stage. She had proved herself. Mama didn't know she was here in a nightclub ("Saloons is where Satan keeps his office," Mama claimed), but it would be all right. Now Mama would have to come around to agree that Robin Beverly belonged in show business. There would be lots of money. She would get Mama a new apartment, maybe buy her a house, and some of the money would put her brother Roland Lee through college.

In the corridor, Rick Sills, the tap dancer, was waiting to go on, and congratulated Robin. "Tomorrow night it's Broadway for you, doll," he drawled. Robin thanked him, giddy with joy, and headed back toward the dressing room. But she heard, "Say," and turned to see one of the men she had seen with Pete Gumbo.

"Mr. Gumbo, he wants you to come sit with him at his table," the man said. It didn't sound like an invitation. It sounded like an order.

Rick Sills disappeared.

Robin's anger returned. "He does, does he? You go back to Mr. Gumbo and tell Mr. Gumbo he can go fry ice."

The man's expression didn't change. "I wouldn't want to tell him a thing like that. You'd be makin' a big mistake, kiddo. Mr. Gumbo, he's Mr. Show Business. You have a drink with him, he can put you where it's at."

"I'd throw up first," Robin snapped, and opened the dressing room door and slammed it after her. A middle-aged man in a shiny, lapel-drooping tuxedo was sitting and drinking with Josie, who hadn't put another stitch of clothes on. "Your pipes sounded great from what we could hear, sweetie," Josie acknowledged, and introduced the man, who half rose, as Ed. Robin nodded but had no desire to stay and talk. The Gumbo thing bothered her. Josie lounging nearly naked in front of a man bothered her. She wanted to talk with someone, someone clean. She took a dime from her purse, excused herself, and left the room.

The Gumbo man wasn't in the corridor. There was a pay phone on the corridor wall and she called June Fletcher, whom she had promised to call right after the first performance.

"Don't leave out a *thing!*" June cried excitedly now from the other end of the line.

"It's all just fabulous!" Robin exclaimed, her enthusiasm renewed. "There are *millions* of people here and they all clapped their heads off! I didn't sing one note flat!" She babbled the news, exaggerating only here and there. June told her the party was squaresville, but everyone was covering for her and rooting for her to be a great big hit.

"You ought to see how my gown looks. I look like a real stripteaser!" Robin declared, and giggled. They giggled together and interrupted each other until the dime was almost gone. Robin promised to take a taxi to the Fletchers' after work and to come in quietly so that June's father wouldn't be wakened and start asking a bunch of questions. June promised to stay up. "I want to hear every detail, *every* detail!" she emphasized.

Jesse Nash was on his way to his dressing room, having introduced Rick Sills, as Robin replaced the receiver. He invited her to tag along, and she did.

His room was draftier than hers and Josie's, and just as drab; the walls' light green paint was peeling in the most conspicuous places and hard dirt caked the pipes. "Welcome to the Harlem Hilton," he said, letting the door close behind them, though not deliberately. Robin trusted him. Maybe it was because of the eyes, always just a trifle suspicious yet always kindly. Maybe it was the slow, sure way he walked—tall and straight, like a man in control of himself. She sat in the wicker armchair he waved her to and she couldn't imagine his ever getting out of line with her, or any girl like her, unless there was an invitation. He wasn't as handsome as he seemed to be on stage or in the photograph of him they had out in front of the club, but there was a gentleness about him that breathed through his skin.

He took two cans of beer from a small cooler and offered her one. She thanked him and accepted it, although she did not want it. She shook her head when he offered her a cigarette. He lit one, sat in the wicker armchair opposite hers, flung a long leg over the armrest, and said, "You may make a name for yourself one of these days in this business."

Robin brightened. "How was I out there? Did I do anything wrong?"

"Ask it another way. Ask if you did anything right."

She bit her lip. "Well, I—"

"How long've you been singing professionally?"

"Not very long."

"How old are you?"

"Nineteen."

His gaze was steady. "How old are you?"

She paused. "Going on eighteen. Can that be a secret?"

Jesse Nash put his long fingers over his eyes and then one finger over his lips. "We lock it up in the tomb. How long've you been singing professionally?"

"I started tonight. Only Mr. Sinclair doesn't know that."

"You want a thousand words of advice from a top-notch successful star like me?"

"Of course."

"Nobody top-notchier than yours truly. Thirty-one years old comin' up and I look like an old-timer. I *am* an old-timer. I've been in this dodge since Pluto was a pup. I've played in every state of the union except two, in every tenth-rate gin mill so run down they have to be remodeled before they can be condemned. Everybody's seen me work and nobody knows my name. Hey, there's a title I might give Baldwin for his birthday: *Nobody Knows My Name*. Now isn't that a ridiculous thing—that an old-timer of thirty-one can miss the boat as long and as often as I've missed it?"

"Oh, I can't believe that," Robin said, sorry that this tall, strong man was whining. "You're well known. I read about you in *Jet* and *Ebony* all the time."

He snorted. "Yeah, no doubt about that—in your press, I'm the crown prince. I show the landlord what they write about me in our press and he hands over the keys to the Presidential suite." He took a long drag from his cigarette and his expression softened. "Let's see, how'd I get off on the Nash sob story? Oh, yeah, I was trying to tell you I know a few things about show business even if I haven't been running very fast. Where are you in school?"

"Senior year high."

"How are your marks?"

"I have a B average. B minus, maybe."

"B average," he repeated, and showed he was impressed. "What about college? You wouldn't have too much trouble getting a scholarship with a B average."

Robin shook her head. "I've thought about it. Even if I wanted it, it wouldn't be fair. My mother and my older sister and my kid brother and I live together—we don't have any relatives that we could call on if we needed to. My sister's a saleslady in a department store downtown, but she doesn't make very much and, anyway, she'll be getting married and moving out one of these days. My mother works as a laundress, and some of the money she makes she gives to her church or to what she calls 'the poor folks,' as if we were rich. I have this wonderful kid brother, Roland Lee. He's the one who's important. No matter what, I'm going to see to it that he gets to college. He's the one who counts. I want to earn enough so he can go when he's old enough."

Jesse Nash sighed. "I don't buy that, that you're not important. An education's important for us—the black us, not the show business us. The more schooling we go after, the less we have Charley on our back. I've made thirteen tons of goofs in my time, but the biggest goof by far was that I didn't finish college. I can't even blame Charley for that—the goof was mine, all mine. Oh-oh, there he goes again—sob-story Jesse." He sat up. "Look, what the hell, we were talking about you as a performer. You want the straight goods? You're suffering from a bad case of Lena Horne phonograph records. Maybe that's because you're a kid and you haven't really tried your wings yet, but you're good enough to start developing yourself as you, not Lena's eight hundred and eighty-eighth impersonator. You don't know how to stand at a mike and you act like you're embarrassed you have hands. Now what else? Oh, yeah, that outfit you've got on. It's not my business if you shack up with the whole Senegalese Navy every Thursday night, but you can be a sexball singer without dressing like you're posing for dirty pictures."

It hurt, even though there was not a fleck of cruelty in his voice. She was about to put the blame on Mr. Sinclair, and changed her mind. She listened.

"None of these sins're your fault," he said. "You're a kid, you're just starting out, you learn by sticking close to the grindstone. But you need someone to steer you right. Everybody does, or you wind up in this racket like your whatzername roommate, Miss Aristocrat, the shake dancer."

There was a tap at the door. "Two, three minutes, Jesse," someone called.

"Gotcha," Jesse Nash called back and lit another cigarette. He hadn't touched his beer. "I go out to California day after tomorrow. Where do you go?"

"Well, just back home, I guess. I've been sort of dreaming, like a little girl. I sort of expected I'd go over big here and, you know, talent scouts and people like that would see me and have me make records and go into the movies. I know how it sounds when I say it out loud . . ."

He smiled for the first time since they had come into the room. It was a nice smile, nicely agreeing that she *was* a little girl. "Is anything holding you here in New York, besides your schooling and your family?"

"No. What else would there be?"

He shrugged. "Maybe the cultural progress of the black race could bear having you go to college a little late. Tell me something, honey, and this is Jesse talking, not the devil." He spoke quietly, slowly. "How would you like to go to California with me? Or meet me out there in, say, a week or whenever?"

The question was asked calmly, without the trace of a leer, yet Robin sensed that this funny man wasn't being funny.

He held up his hand. "Wait," he said. "My character leaves a whole lot to be desired, but, if I do have to pat my own back, I'm about as honest as any cat I know. I'm traveling single-o these days and that's always a pain in the neck to me. I'd like you to travel with me. Not only because I'm a part-time sex maniac, but maybe because I could teach you a couple ropes about this business."

"Mr. Nash . . ." she began hoarsely, and her heart was unendurably heavy in her chest.

"Mr. Nash the name dropper," he cut in. "I'm flying out to a place they call Hollywood or something like that, with all expenses paid by Marty Dickson. Somebody out there thinks there's a chance I can do a show with Dickson if Massa Marty digs my stuff. I suspect it won't come to anything—not much of anything ever does, really—but they're paying me pretty good and hoteling me fine for the stay there, and you'd at least see the Technicolor sights, and will you think about it while I'm doing my act?"

He got up but kept talking as he strolled to the door. "I close this first show. I'll be back in fifteen minutes and we can talk some more about it. If you don't feel like talking about it, I won't bring the subject up ever again and we can talk about normal things, like Booker T. Washington."

Robin sat alone, almost numb, for many minutes and even drank some of the beer. It tasted awful.

Was he a nice man, after all?

He knew how old she was. Had she said or done anything, besides wearing this stupid, show-off gown, to give him the idea she was a pushover? The other boys and men, so many of them, too many, acted surprised when she said no. ("Why'd you give me that hot eye, then?" "What hot eye?" "You're begging for trouble, girlie.") Jesse Nash wasn't like those men, those boys . . .

Marty Dickson . . . He was maybe going to work for Marty Dickson, who was the most famous comedian in the movies and television and night clubs. If he got in solid with Marty Dickson and those big people, he could write his own ticket. And if he had a pretty and talented girl with him who was with him at just the right time . . .

I've got to get out of Harlem.

I'm behaving like I *am* a virgin . . .

No, it's wrong to be thinking like this, all wrong, she told herself, and rose from the wicker armchair; I make fun of Mama's psalm singing, but I love her and she'd die if she found out I got anywhere good in the world by doing the wrong thing. I love her and I respect her and I've got to respect myself, or all Mama is and stands for won't mean anything. It will be like she never lived.

The door was still closed when she heard, "Hamilton! Robin Hamilton! Where'd that Hamilton kid go?" being bawled in the corridor. She opened the door and one of the waiters saw her and pointed to the pay phone's receiver, which dangled down the length of the wall. "For you," he declared. "Don't hold up the line too long."

Robin stiffened. Some of the kids knew she was here tonight, but no one but June would call her, and June would call only if something was terribly important.

"Hello?"

She could hear June Fletcher sobbing. "Oh Robin, oh Robin . . ."

"What's wrong?"

The sudden silence was petrifying. "June," she said, closer to the mouthpiece. "What is it? What's the matter?"

Still silence, and then another sob, and then in a strangled voice that sounded as if it came from under water: "Ro—Roland Lee . . . Roland Lee, Robin, why couldn't somebody else've told you, Robin honey, maybe they killed him, they think Roland Lee is dead."

Her knees buckled, but she gripped the receiver with man's strength. "Not my brother, not my brother Roland Lee, June, somebody made this up. June . . ."

A policeman had shot him in the alley behind Keever Place, had thought he had a gun and shot him. He was at Sydenham Hospital now, and nobody knew if he was alive or dead. His mother, Robin's mother, had been called out of church. No one knew where to find sister Lula.

"Robin . . ."

Robin looked at the telephone mouthpiece and, after a while, placed the receiver with extravagant care on its cradle. Then no time passed and Josie with the silver pasties was forcing her to drink something that made her cough but brought her up from a cot and Josie was asking why she'd conked out, was she knocked up, and people were crowding into the narrow dressing room, staring at her. What had happened? An instant ago she'd been on the telephone and now she was in the dressing room. All these people—

"Brother! Baby brother!" sprang from her lips, a crazy thing to say because everyone looked at her. She could not cry, she could not take the time to cry. Sydenham . . . where was Sydenham Hospital? 122nd Street, 123rd Street. Where was this? 126th. An hour away, a minute away, an hour away. A taxi . . . a taxi could take her there fast. Money, you need money to pay a taxi driver. Where was her purse? In her coat, but where was her coat? People were crowding, and Josie wasn't making jokes any more but acting concerned and asking what did baby brother mean. Out. She had to get out of here. No time for the coat, the purse, Mama was with Roland Lee, with strangers in a hospital, but why can't I move from here, why can't I answer them, why can't I say anything, where is the door I go through?

Then she was in the corridor and running toward the back door, but when she got there she had run the wrong way and she was inside the club and Jesse Nash was up on the stage, making everybody laugh. Her knees buckled again and her legs were water and she fell across a table, knocking glasses over, and the men at the table sat up. There weren't any ladies at the table, only men. Her shoulder strap coursed down her arm and she meant to weep but giggled instead, and got up, babbled at them, and ran backstage again, through the corridor and into the street. Someone had told her to wait there, that he would bring his car around and take her to the hospital faster than a taxi could.

Then she was outside, alone, and the cold air braced her back to sanity. She had apologized for knocking the men's glasses over. She had said her baby brother was maybe dead and she had to find a taxi. Then a car pulled up to the curb, and a man jumped out from the back seat to let her in, and she got in, and the man got in after her and slammed the door shut, and the car pulled away. "Please hurry," she said, and told them to take her to Sydenham Hospital, told them maybe more than once, maybe half a dozen times. She told the kind man who had opened the car door for her and who sat beside her that maybe her baby brother was dying, and the man who sat at the other side of her in the big car patted her breast and told her to relax, that nothing was that bad, that she was too pretty a kid to be acting like a nut.

A third man was driving the big car. She wasn't sure if he knew where the hospital was, so she told him, and she remembered that Roland Lee had been shot and she wondered if that hurt very much and she sat back and wept.

Then too much time had passed to ride from Rigley's Lounge to the hospital, and the car wasn't anywhere near it but in a dark place she could not recognize at all. The windows were up and the car's heater must have been on because there was heat, but she was freezing. Then the big car slowed down and the man at the right of her was Pete Gumbo, the man who had felt her in the club, the man she was going to have complained about to Mr. Sinclair and hadn't, and he was saying to the man who drove the car, "Over a ways, near them trees," and the man at the left of her, the kind man, tied some cloth over her mouth so that the cries she made made noise only in her ears.

Both of her shoulder straps had been pulled down by the time she was brought to a small, cold area of woods surrounded by trees, lighted only by the moon. A soft layer of snow was on the ground. Robin's eyes darted from one man to another, trying to determine which of them could help her, which of them had ever known pity, which of them would stop this thing, whatever it was to be, from happening. She could see the men, moving silently about. They had eyes, but she couldn't see their eyes.

One of the men laid a heavy blanket on the ground and another man trained a flashlight low, toward Robin's feet, while the third man hovered inches from her in case she got an idea to run away. She thought of Roland Lee, and of their mother without Lula, who couldn't be found, and Pete Gumbo waddled to her and made an *ummmm-phhhh* sound as he tried to bring her gown off easily. It would not come off easily, despite the flashlight trained higher, and Gumbo growled and cursed and, grabbing the gown's bodice into his fist of powerful fingers, tore at the gown until it was a collection of shreds.

"You gonna like this," he told Robin, not looking at her. "You gonna en-joy Gumbo."

She could not run because she could not see where to run to. The other men were close by. Gumbo was enraged that she wore a slip under the gown, and a brassiere and pants, and he ripped at them as the other men watched and he roared, "What you wearin' all them shittin' clothes for? Gumbo don't like to see you wearin' all them shittin' clothes," and she did her best to cover herself with her hands. He took his overcoat off before he pushed her down to the blanket and he fell hard on her and guided her hand away from her breasts to the heat of the thing that was hard and small and throbbing. "Gimme," he ordered, breathing heavily. "Gumbo says gimme."

The suddenness of it plunging surprised and shocked her, and she made herself think of Roland Lee as alive because to have this hateful thing while Roland Lee was dead was a horror beyond horror. She punched him as he emptied himself into her, even though she knew the punching would do no good. The horror beyond horror, she knew as he withdrew and as she would always know, was that this despicable man had stirred her.

The men watched her lean on her elbows as she vomited, and she heard one of them chuckle. Then one of those men leaped on her with his loins bare and Gumbo was instructing, "Don't you boys take too long 'bout it, I want to get home. *Music* I gonna write tonight. Best music I ever write."

The man on top of her paused to fondle her, almost tenderly, almost as though he were telling her she was a person, not an object. The moon let Robin see his face. He was grinning. He was lying a little to one side and grinning. She brought up her leg and hit him so hard in the groin that she was sure his cry of pain could be heard for miles around.

He punched her with his fist. He did, or someone did, and then she was not awake any more but introducing Roland Lee to the bigwigs in Hollywood who bowed low when they called her Miss Hamilton and who watched her smoke a cigarette through a long gold holder.

Poor, darling Roland Lee, Robin thought as she began the *Stalwart's* second evening show; he would have been well into high school now, he would have made Mama and all of us so happy. . . .

Robin did not go to the Promenade Deck to meet Warren Weber because this night, or some other night, there would be sex, which she had learned a great deal about since the night of the Pete Gumbos. But woven into the sex would be love, or something like love, and she was paralyzed at the prospect of learning about it.

Nor did she agree to see him alone for the rest of the cruise, although he called repeatedly. Then, as she and Grace were leaving the bandstand after their first set in the Coral Room on the evening before the *Stalwart* was to dock in New York, she saw him. Grace skipped off immediately to have a drink with a newly met importer who was traveling alone and who, according to Grace, was loaded with money. The second she was gone Warren Weber sprang up, all welcoming smiles, and invited Robin to join him and Mrs. Weber at their table. He even extended his hand. The eggs on the floor were hard to walk on, but she went, because the lady who had to be Mrs. Weber, a stunning lady smack out of *Vogue*, gave the welcoming smiles, too. A fleck frosty, maybe, nice-dowager frosty, but welcoming.

The introductions were made, and Robin was seated, and Mrs. Weber complimented her voice and her looks, and Robin asked for soda rather than liquor. The awkward formalities were done, and then Warren Weber, terribly awkward, spoke.

"Mrs. Weber and I have talked it over for several days, Miss Hamilton, and we're in full agreement," he said. "We feel you have the makings of a star." He gave her a gold-embossed card. "Will you call this office tomorrow, before you're unpacked?"

Robin kept blinking at the card. "I . . . thank you. Yes, I guess I will."

"You sound a little breathless, Miss Hamilton," his wife said.

"Yes," Robin agreed. "I guess you'd be, too."

"Yes."

They talked to her. She heard little. She nodded a lot. She smiled a lot. The call came for her to get ready for the next set, and all she took back with her to the bandstand was the memory of his having pantomimed for her to meet him on the Promenade Deck.

She planned to go. Until two o'clock she planned to meet him because he wanted her to, because she wanted to.

But at two o'clock she went down to the cabin she shared with Grace, and stayed in it.

In the morning, huddling inside her too-thin coat on the frigid pier, waiting for customs to get around to her luggage, she saw him and he beckoned her away from Grace. His wife was making a telephone call in a booth. "Why didn't you come to the deck?" he asked. "I waited nearly an hour, and got pneumonia."

"I figured I shouldn't," she answered.

"Did I say or do something that's kept me off limits since Guadeloupe?"

"No. Believe that."

"Where do you live?"

"On 44th Street."

"Where—East? West?"

"Very West, near Ninth Avenue. It's a little hotel and pretty depressing, but it's cheap."

"Let me come there this afternoon."

"No."

"I've got to see you, Robin."

"I'll come to your office, if you still want me to."

"Why wouldn't I want you to?"

She shrugged, ever so slightly. "Because I've been giving you such a hard time. Why would you feel like doing anything for me when I give you such a hard time?"

"That's ridiculous. One thing's got nothing to do with the other. But the office is teeming with people and—"

"I'll be there. Here comes your wife."

The customs man finally arrived, asked Robin to open the larger of her two bags, and barely glanced at the contents. He chalked both bags, and she thought about returning to the grind, to the New York that was a dark apartment, dark prospects, promises that never were kept, Jesse who would hang up on her, strangers, strangers she solemnly and compulsively greeted.

She wanted to run the other way. But Warren Weber would see her.

Three

ON THE MORNING the fanatics and the departmental Judases finally had their vengeful way and kicked him off the police force, almost two years to the day after the Harlem alley incident, Stuart Curtiss White drank a reflective beer in the first side-street tavern he came to and then rode the Uptown A Express to his home on Bennett Avenue. It wasn't quite noon and the somber, gritty train was nearly empty; two priests were talking and a fat jig lady was asleep. The ride was long and lonely, but he wanted it that way. He buried his face in the *News* and even pretended to read.

The whole mess had been, was, so goddam unfair. He was thirty-two years old, young and in perfect health, and he was washed up. Lucille, his wife, kept telling him that was the wrong way to think, that he had his life ahead of him, but the solemn fact remained with Stuart White that his life was police work and there was nothing else going for him. Lucille kept reminding him that it wasn't as if he'd been fired outright, that he would be getting three-quarters of his annual pay for the next year; and she kept reminding him that he always had at least a part-time job waiting for him in her brother Al's East Bronx liquor store. Well, three-quarters of an annual pay that was lousy to begin with wasn't four-quarters. And Al could stick that phony charity up his right nostril; they had never got along as brothers-in-law, and it would be only a matter of weeks before Al Petrie would start making noises like a charitable employer.

Nothing about what had happened was fair. Stuart White was a good man and a good, dedicated, honest cop, almost never on the take. There were four kids and four million bills. The TV set, his one enjoyment, stayed on the fritz because he couldn't bring himself to get it fixed with so many other things to pay on. Lucille needed to have her uterus scraped. She'd kept putting it off when his hospital benefits would have paid most of the operation because she was scared of the knife. One of these days she would really have to have the scraping, and then what? He would get the bills. The cops wouldn't. Her big-shot, poor-mouth brother Al wouldn't. He would.

The train approached 181st Street and he again recalled what maybe was the most unfair hurt of all. The rotten little bastards at Tommy's parochial school had given the boy a rotten time of it, taunting him with that "Your old man's a kid-killer" shit. They had quit after a while, but the taunts had been replaced by something as bad and maybe even worse: they excluded him; they treated him like some germ, some outcast. And, because of them, the once warm closeness between father and son had turned cool, tricky, somehow impossible to start up again. Lucille had stood by him for the whole distance, and their three younger children knew Daddy and loved him. And there were friends in the neighborhood who called Stu White's treatment exactly what it was: a bum deal. But his son Tommy's respect for him had gradually, definitely chipped away, and that knowledge was what made the bum deal so rough to endure.

What was he going to do now, at thirty-two, too young to toss in the sponge, too old to begin a new trade, a trade that paid money, not dribs and drabs but solid money, a trade guaranteed to buy the groceries when he was fifty, and sixty, and older? He had been twenty-one when he'd gone on the cops. The plan had been sound. He would stay on for the thirty years, doing his job without breaking his ass, he would earn eight grand a year eventually and derive all the cop benefits, and then, when it came to be pension time, he would have enough salted away in savings, plus the lifetime pension, to invest in a cushy little business in some sunny climate anywhere away from Jew York. It wasn't going to happen, goddammit, none of it was going to come off. The three-quarters annual pay he would begin receiving now would stop in one year from today's date. He had a little less than six hundred dollars in the bank, and no prospects, and neither education nor courage to drum up prospects on his own, and Lucille would have to have her goddam uterus scraped.

He stopped in McLeod's Bar for a beer before going up the block to the apartment, glad that Tommy and Eileen would be in school and that Brian and Stuart, Junior, home because they weren't old enough yet for school, were too young to read or to sense his defeat. He considered getting good and loaded today, because he had a perfect right to, but he remembered that his big-shot brother-in-law Al with the big rich liquor store hadn't brought any free samples to the apartment in months. Christ, he couldn't even afford to get drunk.

Cliff, the day bartender, wouldn't let White pay for the beer and, indeed, served him a second one on the house. "Since when are you so generous?" White asked the nice old guy with the sparse salt-and-pepper hair parted in the middle and the clicking store teeth.

"Today's special," said Cliff, who had known that today was the kiss-off day, who in one way or another had offered condolences over the past week and made White feel that he had a real friend. "They give you a hard time down there?"

"A buster," White conceded. Actually, he admitted to himself as he drank, the kiss-off, fully anticipated and without a single surprise, had been a grim experience but not a brutal one. To save him and the Department embarrassment, the newspapers had been told that Officer White was resigning because the effects of an old foot injury had returned, making his beat-patrol duties too difficult. He had been advised, and had agreed, to avoid reporters. The Commissioner had rapped his knuckles with a few formal, canned words, and outside in the hall the buddies who had been quietly in his corner all along shook his hand and wished him luck, and that had been that. Maybe he'd just been numb, and maybe tomorrow he would wake up and decide to go after the sons of bitches downtown who'd worked so hard to wreck his life. But, as of now, the kiss-off hadn't been too bad.

"You'll wind up a prophet in your own time yet, don't think you won't," Cliff said. "The boogs are getting wilder in this town with every tick of the clock. And why? You and I know why. Law and order's out and the bleeding hearts are in. The situation'll start righting itself when the right people get off their rumps and risk losing votes to say they've had a belly full, and that don't comfort you right now, I know, Stuie boy, but you wait and see. You'll have statues named after you."

White grinned, touched. "You're a gentleman, Cliff," he said. "Thanks for the suds. I'd better get on home now."

He went home, to the cramped flat with the linoleum on all the floors and the living room window with a view of the next building's living room window and the bowl of waxed fruit and the TV that was on the fritz and the smell of mustiness. Lucille, skinny, titless Lucille, wearing curlers and that faded print housedress he despised because he had seen it a hundred thousand times, greeted him in the kitchen with silent concern. The just-scrubbed kitchen floor was covered with newspapers. Diapers were clothespinned down the entire length of the kitchen clothesline. His favorite sport shirt was at the top of a basket of wet wash; it wasn't on the line, but the diapers were. Lucille took a clothespin out of her mouth and watched him, not moving, until he said he wanted some coffee. "I'll heat it up," she said, and went to the stove.

"Never mind. I'll have a beer—*if* you remembered to put one on ice," he grumbled. He rummaged a Schlitz from the too-small refrigerator.

"The coffee'll just take a minute, Stuie."

"I don't feel like waiting," he said, opening the can's top and scratching his thumb on the sharp edge of the tab. "You knew I'd be home around now. You know I like to have a hot cup of coffee waiting when I come home. But it's all right. I don't have any rights around here any more, now that I'm not the breadwinner any more."

"Stuie, you just quit that! I know how you must feel about today, but don't take it out on me. The coffee just needs heating up. It only takes a min—"

"I said I want this beer, didn't I? Anybody call?"

"Oh, yes, just like you said there'd be. One newspaper person after another. One even came to the door, about an hour ago. Wait, the coffee won't take long. I told them all what you told me to say—that I don't know anything and you won't have anything to say about anything when you come home."

"I'm going to sleep," White said, holding the Schlitz in one hand and taking a second Schlitz from the refrigerator to carry in the other hand. "If anybody else calls, tell them to go to hell."

Lucille's pencil-thin eyebrows lifted. "Sleep? Now? Stuie, I've been waiting here on pins and needles to hear what happened."

"Yeah, you must've been upset," he said calmly. "So upset you couldn't have hot coffee waiting. Or dry my sport shirt and iron it. Yeah, you were so upset you didn't have time to stop and think maybe one day in my life I wanted to come home to a wife, not a slob with those goddam curlers and not a drop of lipstick on or a little perfume. How would that kill you, for once in your life, to wear a little perfume when I come home even if I don't have a job? And you couldn't change that goddam dress I'd like to rip off you and sell to the ragpicker." He raised his voice because he had no idea of how to apologize to her. "I'm going to SLEEP, that's what I'm going to do, YOU GOT THAT message through your UGLY, EMPTY HEAD?"

She was alarmed. "Stuie, shhh, the baby's sleeping—"

"SCREW the baby!" he shouted and stormed out of the kitchen. The damp corner of a newspaper stuck to the heel of his shoe and, cursing, he kicked at it until it was freed.

In the darkened bedroom he set the two cans of beer on the dresser and stood over the crib where Stuart, Junior, eleven months old and beautiful, was sound asleep. He crossed himself to beg forgiveness for his blasphemy and kissed the baby's knuckles. Then he stripped to his underwear and socks, lit a cigarette, and lay on the squeaking bed with his opened Schlitz. And wished, as he had wished countless times over the past two years, that he had stayed here, home, on that New Year's Eve.

Lucille had wanted him to, because Roy and Myra Crosby had offered to drop by with a load of six-packs to help see the year in right. He had wanted to, because the thought of working Harlem on New Year's Eve had been a damned unappealing one. But his partner, Ike Lindstrom, was scheduled to work that tour, and that December 31 had a lot of patrolmen at home on their backs with the flu, so White had little choice.

Roy and Myra had come by at seven, though, and he'd polished off half a dozen festive beers with them and Lucille by nine, when he had to leave for work. He had a pleasant glow on when he met Ike, and the glow increased over the next several hours as he made spot checks at this nigger bar and then that one, for there was always a cordial dinge to beckon him to a dim corner of each trap and give him a Happy New Year snort.

The snorts of rye and Scotch and rum and vodka were free, of course, little gifts furnished in the trust that he, the fuzz, the white fuzz, wouldn't choose to rock any boats on this money-making night in Harlem. He experienced occasional instants of fleeting guilt through the long, freezing-outside evening, the least of them being his acceptances of freebies, which the Department continually said it had no patience with. White's uneasiness had to do with his being a beer man, not a liquor man. Some men could handle liquor fine, but the hard stuff always seemed to make him edgy and quarrelsome. This night, though, he was determined to control himself, keep the warming hootch from screwing his personality around.

He knew some mean white cops who got their jollies by cuffing dinges around because they were dinges, but he didn't see that. You had to watch the dinges, naturally, had to keep that extra eye on them at all times because they were what they were, welfare chislers and addicts and illegitimate children and foot-long dongs and lazy and always looking to boff white women and all the rest of it. Hell, those were documented facts. But he was not a bigot, never had been, never would be, couldn't be because he was a decent man, a religious man.

He was feeling just swell by eleven o'clock, and everyone he met became his friend. The boogs at the crowded bar at Shovel's Café were singing "Down by the Old Mill Stream," and he joined in with them, singing louder and purposely more off-key than any of them, and they were laughing and buying him drinks, and he put his arms around them. Then he was out on the sidewalk, trying doorknobs, and felt a pint bottle of whiskey in his coat pocket, and remembered that Shovel had given it to him as a present. When no one was looking, he uncapped it and drank from it, feeling warm and contented. But little by little the contentment faded, and the loneliness began to set in, and he realized that those spooks hadn't been so chummy with him because they liked him. They'd been putting him on, making fun of him. The goddam spooks had been conning him.

Everybody was always conning him. The whole goddam world. Because he let them walk all over him, he knew, because he never spoke up for himself when he had a right to. Every other grown man was taking it easy tonight, having fun with friends, celebrating the New Year. And he was out in zero weather, walking niggerland, all alone, and it wasn't fair. He drank. His watch read a quarter of twelve, and he was surprised that he'd had to squint his eyes into focus so he could read it, surprised he was weaving. And surprised that he remembered he was supposed to have rejoined his partner Ike but couldn't remember where or at what time. He knew he shouldn't touch the bottle again, and he drank some more, because the whole goddam world was conning him.

He paused at the lip of the alley near Keever Place because he saw a colored kid standing on the deserted sidewalk—standing in front of an apartment house and looking up at a third-floor window where the light was on and the shade was up and a black gal was walking around in a slip. The kid was little, maybe about sixteen years old, and there was something fishy about him. White grabbed his arm suddenly and squeezed hard.

"What you got in mind, boy?" he demanded, surprised that the words slurred.

The kid was scared as hell, and Stuart White knew he had a damned good right to be. What was he doing, alone on a deserted street, except brewing something? "Nothin'. Let go . . ." he said, trying to squirm free.

"Uh-huh, nothin'," White nodded, enjoying the kid's squirms. "A little heist, maybe, right? We see who's home tonight and who isn't, and we shuffle on in and help ourselves to a few trinkets— that's what you mean by nothin', right, boy?"

"Please, mister, let me go," the kid pleaded, and damned if he didn't begin to cry. "I live a couple of blocks away. I'm not supposed to be here . . ."

"That's for *damn* sure, sonny boy."

"I mean I promised my mother I wouldn't go out of the house tonight and I did, I guess it sounds funny, I did because I was all alone in the house and I wanted to be outside for a couple minutes on New Year's Eve, and I didn't mean anything, mister, please let me go and I'll go right home and—"

"Quit your goddam bawlin', boy!" White snapped, half believing him but then how could you really believe any of them? "What's your na—"

And then the kid did a very wrong thing. He wrested himself loose and ran.

Oh, let him go, White thought, and then drew his pistol and ran after him into the alley because you couldn't let these sons of bitches get the upper hand. The alley was dark, and White called, "Where are you, nigger?" Then he saw the kid, crouched, maybe thirty feet away, and heard the phony bawling, and heard the squeaky voice rushing words together, something about all he was doing was looking at that lady getting undressed and please please please don't let his mother know. White was going to give in because maybe the kid was telling the truth, after all—Stu White had nothing against anybody, no matter what color—but then the kid was holding something that suddenly glittered, and White knew it was a gun, and he fired two shots because the little son of a bitch would have shot him first.

And then there was quiet, and the kid toppled and was still, and White blinked and hurried to him, surprised that he might have grazed him because he had purposely aimed above the kid's head. He reached him, and turned him over, and the drink left him and the boy didn't have a pulse. Clenched in the boy's hand was a rock.

"*Holy Mother of God,*" Stuart White whispered. He shook his head to clear it, but he could do nothing else for many minutes except look at the boy in awe. Then bells clanged from somewhere and lots of voices were shouting Happeee Noo Yirrrrr from somewhere, and Stuart White lumbered to find a phone box. He came to one and called his precinct with the news, first making sure that his voice sounded sober, and he suggested an ambulance, just in case the boy was still alive. Then he remembered the bottle in his pocket, and carefully placed it in the gutter.

The boy was pronounced dead half an hour after he was taken to Sydenham Hospital.

One great break, as White told his story, was that no one suspected he had been drinking. Another break was that his story was believed. He had caught the boy breaking and entering, had given chase, had warned him to halt, had fired because he had assumed in the tricky darkness that the boy's rock was a gun.

He was temporarily suspended from all duties, pending further investigation. Privately he was assured by the precinct guys he trusted that there would be a stink but there was nothing to worry about—*if* the bleeding hearts and the coon leaders could be controlled. And it was quite possible that they could, because New York had a pretty fair administration for a change and at long last City Hall was on the side of the police. Dan Travers, the Mayor, talked a fancy civil rights line, but he was careful to avoid any significant boat rocking; the same was true of the Police Commissioner, Barney Gaines; and Manhattan's DA, Marshall Fellows, rarely bothered to push very hard where a case involved coons and cops.

Lucille stuck by him. His friends did, too.

Yet Stuart White was not appeased. He had not meant to, but he *had* killed the kid. If those spooks in Harlem hadn't drowned him in all that liquor that night, he wouldn't have gone crazy in the head and fired those shots. But that was no excuse; he *had* killed an innocent kid. He was stunned, and for a while inconsolable, when he learned that the boy, Roland Lee Hamilton, was fourteen years old. *Fourteen.* That there was no rap sheet on him. That he came from a good family, that he had never been in the slightest trouble, that he was smart and a hard worker in school, that his mother slaved at a back-breaking job so that he would go to college and be somebody.

Lord forgive me, thought Stuart White as he waited for the fur to start flying. I'll never take another drink as long as I live.

The fur did fly, and quickly. A grand jury was called. It was strictly a local incident, yet newspapers all over the country covered it, not only the New York papers, and they carried on as though it was some kind of major world event instead of what it was, the unfortunate shooting of one colored kid. Colored people who didn't know any of the facts were screaming for his blood; their leaders, even the so-called moderate ones, were against lynching, they were always saying, but they were ready to lynch Stuart Curtiss White. His name could have been Brown, or Black, or Green, or Purple. It happened to be White, and they were snide as hell over the fact.

He was sorry, deeply sorry, and he told everybody he was sorry. What more could he say? He was shocked by the way the school kids made life miserable for his son Tommy, and he explained to Tommy that it had been an accident, that the last thing in the world he was was a murderer. Tommy listened and believed him, and went back to school and came back home confused, and gradually it became clear, though never put in words, that he believed the kids and not his old man.

"Tommy will understand in time," said Lucille. "You're a good, decent man, Stuie. He'll come to see that."

The grand jury decided that a trial on the charge of criminal negligence was not indicated. A police departmental trial found him innocent and he was reinstated. His friends gave him a beer and sandwich party at McLeod's, and their kindness helped him shake off a large chunk of the depression that had plagued him since the accident.

He'd thought the ordeal was over then, but it wasn't. Some gung-ho colored organizations—White could never keep their names straight—talked the Hamilton's boy's mother, one of those Scripture-quoting types who had struck White as a colored woman with no hate in her heart, into filing a whopping damage suit against New York. Which, in effect, reopened the case and many of the wounds. The newspapers and television played it up big. They might not have, if not for some far-out kook group of coons led by a noisy, dark ape named Jesse Nash, whom White had known of as a second-rate comedian who worked in Harlem cabarets and who somehow had taken over the protest reins from left field and was all of a sudden manipulating everything. What bewildered Stuart White, watching and listening to Nash calling him a killer on what seemed to be just about every TV newscast, was that so many people obviously were taken in by the ape or at least paying attention to him.

Nash knew how to talk, how to get your ear and hold it, but he was wrong in everything he was saying, very, very wrong. He was calling the accident a brutal crime. He was making Stuart White out to be corrupt, callous, the symbol of everything rotten in the United States of America. He was demanding—not asking, but demanding—a fresh examination of the case, demanding that the sweepings come out from under the white-man rug. He was whipping everyone up, demanding that Stuart Curtiss White, who was a decent man and who had never knowingly hurt a decent man in the whole of his life, be brought to trial for murder.

The cops kept White on because, as Police Commissioner B. N. Gaines told interviewers, "A New York grand jury and the New York Police Department found Officer White innocent of wrongdoing. That's good enough for me. As long as I man this desk, I will serve the best interests of the city of New York. I will knuckle under to no pressures from whatever source." And because, as Mayor Daniel C. Travers told interviewers, "No one can discount the enormity of this terrible tragedy. My own personal opinion, after having studied the incident, is that Officer White should not have acted so hastily, but I am convinced that Officer White, whose conduct as a police officer for the city of New York has, I have been informed, been exemplary, knows better than any of us this day and for many days to come that he acted in haste. Concurrent with this, I must agree with Commissioner Gaines—due process of law has seen fit not to pursue this matter, and I am honor bound as your mayor to respect due process of law, the touchstone of democracy." And because, as Manhattan District Attorney Marshall Fellows told intimates, "There's no case. The cop was doing his job. He honestly thought the boy was going to shoot him, and his instinct told him to protect himself, as your instinct would tell you and mine would tell me. It was an awful thing—I have a fourteen-year-old son myself—but it's over. What's to be gained by ruining a young man's career?"

Stuart White watched himself become a tug of war. The more the fanatics like Jesse Nash, whom he had never even met, let alone harmed, worked to keep the incident alive (and he did, he sure did, everywhere; strong rumors were making the rounds that Commie money was keeping him going), the more B. N. Gaines was riled and determined that the force would not be intimidated. Gaines personally and quietly transferred his beat from Manhattan to Queens, where he would be less in the spotlight, and that meant endless travel to and from tours, but it also meant he was still on the force. *Thursday* Magazine offered him five thousand dollars for the privilege of ghostwriting his side of the story. He was ready to jump at it, not because he wanted to profit from a sad incident but because five grand could buy a lot of needed dental work and the thirty-six-inch color TV set he had always longed for and clothes that Lucille deserved and maybe a nice vacation, first class for a change, for her and the kids. Gaines's office vetoed the whole idea. White stewed, but privately. Lucille reminded him he still had a job. And, of course, that was something.

If you were suddenly a big shot—five thousand dollars' worth— and willing to settle for going on being a little shot, then that was something.

The pressures from the lynchers grew. There would be an election next November, and so the word was handed down: Stuart White would have to be bounced. The ones who handed him the news were the same ones who had reassured him over and over that he would be taken care of on the cops till long after he started tripping on his beard.

Bounced. As clean as that. No five grand, no job, no nothing.

The bedroom door opened timidly. Lucille still had that crummy housedress on, but the curlers were gone. "Are you all right, Stuie?" she asked, barely above a whisper.

And suddenly he loved her again. "Come here," he said, with the confidential smirk he used to announce that he was ready for a time.

She blinked. Lucille, who once in a while enjoyed a time and who always blinked when he announced he was ready for it, motioned to the baby, and told him, as she had told him a dozen times before, that she felt uneasy doing it when the baby was in the same room, especially during the day.

"The other kids are still in school," he said, sitting up. "Where's Brian?"

"Playing, upstairs. But—"

"Then come here," he ordered. Lucille looked alarmed, unsure, but after a moment she soberly nodded. She lowered the blind as far down as it would go, and, as she came to the bed, where White was busy taking his shorts off, slowly brought the dress up over her head, as though she considered the demand foolish but something she was prepared to obey because her husband had lost his job. White brought her to him by grabbing her skinny arm so that she fell across his loins, and he guided her head to the throb of him. There was a great need, as always, to squeeze it between two huge cushions of breasts, but Lucille had no breasts full enough to squeeze it between, and so he directed her to the next best thing.

She began, as he had carefully trained her, in spite of her silent protest that she hated doing it. But she didn't, he knew, and almost before he was aware of what was happening, without missing a single mechanical stroke, her body twisted around so that he was forced to do to her what she was doing to him. She began to whimper, and in no time at all she called, "Yeah!" and there was nothing left for Stuart White to do but to plunge himself into her and keep moving until he achieved some small semblance of what had started out to shake the walls.

Lying beside Lucille, he couldn't figure it. He'd never been able to. He always called the shots and somehow she always came out top dog.

"You're the best man there is, Stuie," she whispered, "no matter what anybody says."

"Yeah," he agreed. "Just you wait. Just everybody wait. I'll be special yet. This whole goddam town's gonna make it up to me some day for what they did to me. They're gonna know there's a man named Stuart White."

"Sure, Stuie," Lucille said.

Four

As soon as she got to the small hotel apartment she shared with Arbutus Harker, Robin phoned Arbutus at her office to say she was back and to ask about Jesse.

"Well, all I hear is from the papers," said her friend from high school days. Robin and Arbutus had little in common, but sharing cut the rent at this interracial, overpriced fleabag, whose only virtues were that it was located fairly near the show business activity and it was not in Harlem. "He's out of the hospital. They still don't know who shot him, but he's raising a rumpus, like you'd expect, accusing every honk under the sun, including the President of the United States."

He's all right, thought Robin. Thank God for that.

"Something else was in the paper, Rob. The cop was let go today, official."

There was no need to explain who "the cop" was. "That's good," Robin said, feigning conviction, caring only that Jesse was all right. "Listen, Arbutus, I'd better not hold you up. Maybe I'll see you here later."

"No problem—Simon Legree's out sick today. Tell me, you old globe-trotter—how long'll you be in town this time?"

"I'm not sure. It depends on an audition, I guess you could call it, this afternoon. See you, Arbutus. Got to go now."

She undressed before she unpacked, weighing the impulse to call her mother up on Amsterdam Avenue and tell her she loved her, to tell her a very influential white man had just about guaranteed that she was going to be a big star. Showering, she weighed the impulse to call Ernie Fieldmont, the booking agent who took a superior and patronizing attitude toward Negroes but who wasn't above sleeping with them, to tell him he could go fly a kite now that Warren Weber, the big leagues, was interested in her. Drying her body, she weighed the impulse to call Jesse Nash, to tell him he was the only man she had ever loved.

She didn't call Mama, because she hadn't dared call her in two years. Because Mama would call her bad names again. She didn't call Ernie Fieldmont because it was completely possible that Warren Weber could lose interest. She didn't call Jesse Nash because Jesse hated her for not being colored twenty-four hours a day.

Instead, wrapping the towel around her, she transferred clothes from the bags to the bureau and closet, and considered the day ahead. If the waves did part today, if Warren Weber wasn't simply a shipboard Casanova curious about putting her in his trophy room and nothing else, then her whole life would indeed be changed. There would be money. There would be heavy, luxurious Turkish towels, not raggedy ones. There would be recognition in glamorous hotel lobbies. She would be looked up to. People wouldn't look at her color. They would look at her, at Robin Hamilton.

"You're the worst kind of nigger there is," Jesse had once suddenly snapped, crippling her, scarcely minutes after love-making. "You want to wake up some morning and find all the black's been washed off!"

Jesse was proud to be Negro. All the Negroes she respected were proud of what they were. And that was fine with Robin Hamilton; if they viewed being Negro as a cause, that was their business and more power to them. But she resented, and had resented from as far back as she could remember, the lectures of those people, white as well as black, who told her she must be Negro before she was anything else. She had never been able to make people she cared about understand that her determination to see herself as an individual had nothing to do with shame at being colored or with indifference to the trials and joys of her people, and this inability to make herself clear was a continual frustration. I'm me, she would say; I don't want to be anybody but me. And they would not understand. They would accuse her, in shock or in sorrow, of wanting to run out on her race.

That's not true, she thought now.

And she chose the clothes she would wear today to meet the white Warren Weber in the white office on white 60th Street, and wondered, as she had wondered at other lonely times like this, if she was entirely honest.

There was shame. A little. Shame and impatience with Negro men in particular, too many of them, who gave up and stopped being men, as her own father had done, who hurt the race through weakness as much as white men hurt it through strength. She was ashamed when a colored man admitted defeat. She was ashamed when a colored man robbed a liquor store, when he shuffled, when he deserted his family.

Take pride in your race, Jesse said. Take pride in your race, Mama said. Mama, who was old long before her time because she was doing most of the things a colored man should have been doing for her. . . .

James Lonny Hamilton, a man with no education and no trade, deserted his family and responsibilities because he couldn't get a job that paid even half of a living wage and because Mama had had to go back to work in the laundry only one week after she gave birth to Roland Lee. He would have had to stay a baby-sitter, a six-foot, strapping baby-sitter, and his pride couldn't bear that. And so James Lonny Hamilton, who talked big and laughed deep and prayed hard, took his pride and walked away, leaving a wife and two small daughters and a month-old son in a rat-trap apartment that never had enough heat.

A remarkable thing to Robin, when she was old enough to understand why he wasn't coming back, was that Mama wouldn't allow her or Lula or anyone in the neighborhood to criticize him to her face; other fathers in the neighborhood had jobs and lived at home, other fathers didn't leave, but she defended James Lonny, took his part, still loved him. When Robin was eight and Lula was twelve, Mama received a postcard from him in Detroit. It read *Am fine be good. Jas Lonny H.*, and on the other side there was a color picture of a park. "Praise God he's alive!" Mama cried, and she saved the card and took it out from time to time and clucked, "Ain't you daddy got a beautiful hand!"

An even more remarkable thing was that Mama, who had had four years of substandard education in Georgia and who worked eight hours a day as a laundress and four more hours a day as a maid, would limp home and have Lula, and then Robin, teach her how to read better. She was absolutely determined that her children would get not only decent, basic schooling but would go to college—the problem of money would be faced and solved when the time came—and she raised as much dust when one of them got merely passing grades on a report card as she did when one of them was late for church. She, who came from so little, who had so little, who could hardly read a newspaper or her beloved Bible, who had every reason to give up, taught her children to strive. Not to be good in school, but to excel. Not to go to church to be Sunday Christians, but to learn the power of love from the Word of Jesus. Not only to do well for themselves in the world, but to do it with character and self-respect and charity.

At last Lula did enter City College on a partial scholarship, and Mama was delighted. But before the semester was over, when the money squeeze was tighter than it had ever been, Dr. Cochran checked Mama's heart and blood pressure and warned her to quit work as a domestic, preferably to quit the laundry, too. "It's not right," Mama protested to Lula, cutting her work and her income in half. "You needs your schoolin' ."

"Now you just settle your feathers, Mama," Lula soothed. "I'm not the first girl to postpone her education a little and I won't be the last. We want you to get to Heaven, but not yet." Lula, intelligent and pretty—all three children were fine looking like their father, Mama boasted—left school and got a saleslady's job in a fancy department store downtown in the East Fifties. It paid fairly well—enough, along with Mama's salary, to move the family into a somewhat better flat in a considerably better neighborhood on Amsterdam Avenue. It was home, warm with love and concern for one another—but it was manless.

Robin, at fourteen and fifteen, would go to the department store downtown, never bothering Lula, and walk through its clean aisles and pretend she was a lady customer who could buy anything that caught her eye, with no concern for price. She would see well-dressed ladies with their husbands, sometimes with children, too, shopping, and she loved seeing families, and envied them, and belonged to them. Then she would ride the subway back to Harlem, and come out of the station on 145th Street, and the sharp, drastic differences would never fail to crash around her. There were ladies, and men, and children, but all too rarely together. To get home, she would have to pass dark bars, rowdy and obscene music blaring from them, where men, who should have been at work or at home with their families, sat and wasted their hours and their lives. One big, embarrassing sign read Evil Eye Removed, embarrassing to Robin because the childishness of it seemed to represent Harlem. The community was colored yet most of the stores were white—colored-directed but white-owned. The supermarkets featured fatback and chitlins, the chain stores prominently displayed plastic shoes with pointy toes, and all the prices were higher than they needed to be, Robin knew in disgust, because colored people hadn't the gumption or courage to rebel against the prices. Instead of a community of bright, pleasant shops, museums, pretty parks, greenery, order, she saw saloons, pawnshops, dirty clothes, loafing, the resigned acceptance of deterioration and defeat.

It was Mama who heard her complain and who angrily told her that, for a clever girl getting honor marks in school, she was a ninny who should hang her brown head in shame. "Sure, black folks can't git their footin', and that's why some of 'em look and ack like they ain't tryin'," Mama agreed. "But Harlem's poor for the same reason all poor folks is poor—there ain't no money. A man wants to build, wants his own business, the banks won't lend him no money 'cause he's poor, and he's poor 'cause the banks won't lend him no money. Don't you *never* let me hear you, nor none o' my family, jabberin' high tone and superior. The black man's still a man, don't no matter how much, how often he's cut down and made to look less'n a man. You hear me good now, Miss Fancy. The secon' you git to feelin' superior to another of God's children without first you take the time to try to understand what you doin', that's the secon' I lose respeck for you. And I want to die and head for the fiery furnace 'fore I lose that respeck."

At fifteen Robin was popular, but Mama scrupulously monitored her comings and goings. She was allowed to go to parties and even a dance, but only if Mama's church was the sponsor and only in a group of young people who belonged to the church. When she discovered she had a better than average singing voice and asked permission to audition for the American Negro Players, Mama finally granted it, but only after Reverend Fletcher assured her that upstanding people were associated with ANP, the showcase for young talent headed by an honorable Christian, George McKee. She sang "Glowworm" and "Motherless Child" for Mr. McKee, who was casting for a series of single performance revues to be given on Saturday evenings. He was enthusiastic and hired her, on the spot, to sing a solo on the very next Saturday night.

Mama and Lula and Roland Lee and even Reverend and Mrs. Fletcher came to see and hear her. She heard the applause and knew she was whole. The cast congratulated her, and so did people she'd never seen before, and Mr. McKee told her he wanted her in more shows.

On the understanding that her school grades would be kept high, and that her church attendance and interest wouldn't flag, and that she wouldn't build any highfalutin ideas about seriously going into theatricals, Robin became a member of ANP—with the additional understanding that she and Reverend Fletcher's daughter June, who was already a member of the troupe as a prompter and prop girl, would never be out of each other's sight, especially after dark. Robin went to the old building, entranced, as often as possible. She listened to Mr. McKee lecture young actors easily and with wit on what the dusty classic dramas were all about. She watched, rapt, as performers more experienced than she moved expertly about the magic stage, this one practicing an intricate dance step, that one speaking lines, these two and those four clowning and getting laughs, Negro people and a sprinkling of whites active in the business of expression. These people seemed genuinely alive, and she could feel her own stage presence improving with each appearance before audiences, and she heard the applause, the bouquets of love, and there was no question in her mind that she had at last found herself.

Boys found her, too, Negro boys her age and young Negro men older than she. There were boys at school, and she had necked with some of them in dark school corridors after the last bell, and during intermission at the one school dance she'd gone to she had let Scott Haines walk her to the unlighted schoolyard and allowed him to put his hands on her covered breasts for a minute because he'd been so anxious to and because she'd wondered how it would feel; it had felt marvelous, and she had tingled and surprised herself by coming awfully close to letting him slip his hand inside.

The boys here at ANP, though, weren't gawky, nervous teenagers, but young men who seemed wondrously sure of themselves, and when they gave her meaningful, sexy looks she returned them. Everything stopped at flirtation, however. There were girls in the company with varying reputations of being free with their favors, and Robin didn't want to be one of them.

Then Mr. McKee announced that ANP would put on a new play, *The Winds of Change*, and introduced the playwright. Jerry Sorin was white, in his mid-twenties, with hair the color and texture of blond Brillo and a breezy, almost cocky manner. At first Robin disliked and resented him; too many members of the group fawned over him, and she suspected he was a white man deigning to let Negroes have his play because it wasn't good enough for Broadway. But she tried out for a part and got a small one, so she read the play. She admired it without understanding it, but she tried hard at rehearsals. And he began to pay more attention to her than to any of the other actors.

June Fletcher noticed the attention. "You'd better watch your step, if you want my advice," she warned Robin. "You don't want to get mixed up with a white man."

"Who the heck's getting mixed up with anybody?" Robin argued. "He's nice and intelligent, that's all. If I was going to get mixed up with a fellow, wouldn't I pick a colored fellow?"

"I sure hope so. You know what they say—a white man's only got one thing on his mind. And you know what that thing is."

"You stop that! He's not interested in me *that* way, and I'd never let him, anyway. What's the matter with you, June? Can't two people like each other without you thinking there's something dirty about it?"

He was Mr. Sorin, and then he became Jerry as they met for sandwiches in the cafeteria near ANP, at first with the other actors and, before long, alone. Robin was flattered that he thought she was mature enough to talk to, grown up enough to discuss the state of the theatre and the world with. He was sincere about being the kind of playwright who would help to break down all color lines, everywhere. He was a feeling man, a thoughtful and reflective man, and she loved being with him. In time she was not black nor was Jerry white; they were simply a young woman and young man who enjoyed solving the problems of the universe in a cafeteria rear booth.

The Winds of Change opened, with Robin speaking exactly four lines, drew only eight customers at the second performance, and closed after the third. Jerry was outraged, and Robin agonized over his disgrace. "What are you going to do now?" she asked.

"I'm not going to lie down and die," he declared. "I'm going to fight this lousy system. I have six more plays cooking in the oven, *truthful* plays, maybe too truthful for bubblehead American audiences to understand and accept, but that's not going to stop me, I'm not going to sell out to the system. This flop was the best thing that ever happened to me. I'm going to fight the money changers all the harder."

A week after the closing, he casually invited her to his place to hear him read his new, best play. They were in the cafeteria again; it was understood that he was never to call her at home, much less ever go there. Robin told him she wouldn't go to his apartment because it wouldn't be right, even though she knew he was an honorable man. He didn't press it, which surprised and disappointed her.

The next morning she went to her Saturday job at Gilley's Bargain Store and telephoned him at her first break from the cash register. "If I can get off work early, I could—come by for a little while," she said. "If it's all right."

"You bet," he said, and told her how to get there. "I'll have some dustcloths ready. This place hasn't been cleaned in a month."

Mr. Gilley let her leave early when she complained of a cold coming on, and she stood at the downtown subway for many indecisive minutes before she walked down the stairs and through the turnstile. She was afraid. And she could barely wait to get there.

Jerry lived out of Harlem, though not far away; his building was on 113th Street and Broadway, three blocks from Columbia. The apartment was tiny and a mess, and it was very definitely a man's, but Robin's conflicts about coming dissolved almost as soon as he admitted her. June would have been shocked. Mama would have smacked her and then spent the night praying in church. But Robin belonged here.

"Welcome to the gourmet's paradise," Jerry said, taking her coat and dropping it on a chair. "You haven't lived till you've tasted my canned Franco-American spaghetti."

Robin cleaned the apartment as he sat on his lumpy studio couch and read her the first act of his play, an anticapitalism drama that he predicted would earn him a million dollars, and she wondered if she could survive if he kissed her.

When he finished the first act, Robin, who had understood little of it, told him it was wonderful and began to walk past him toward the sink, where she could pretend to be busy, where he might not see that she was trembling. "I'm forced to agree," he said simply and, just as simply, caught her wrist and brought her down beside him. "I'll bet my can of spaghetti you've never been kissed by a great playwright."

He wasn't letting go, but he wasn't rough. How am I supposed to act? she thought. Bold, ready? He wouldn't like that. Be a tease? No, that's all right for boys, but this is Jerry. Admit how scared I am? No, never . . . Her smile was tentative and worried, and all she could think about as he held her and began to kiss her was that her hands were dirty from cleaning his apartment. The kiss was chaste, gentle, without pressure or urgency, and, grateful for his gentleness, she put her arms around Jerry because she loved him and trusted him.

He flipped a wall switch without needing to move much, but the room was still lighter than she wanted it to be and, at the same time, darker than she wanted it to be. Robin said nothing, yet Jerry seemed to sense some of her fright. "Relax," he said.

"I'm relaxed."

"Tight as a drum. And there's no reason to be. All my violence goes into my plays. Away from the typewriter, I wouldn't hit Hitler."

"My hands are dirty," she said helplessly.

"Mercy sakes alive," Jerry said, and kissed her again, and this time she could feel the tip of his tongue on her lips and she was afraid to make him stop. She waited for him to touch her breast, and he didn't, and she became alarmed when she realized that his hand was already over the top of her stocking, alarmed because she had been only distantly aware of that hand on her knee. She pulled away from the kiss, breathing hard, and brought her arms away from him, too. "What's wrong?" he asked.

"This. This is wrong," Robin said huskily, and yanked his hand away. "I'm sorry, Jerry. I can't go through with this."

"What are you sorry about?"

"That I let you think I was—ready. I'm not. You're not to blame —I am. I'm crazy about you, I guess, but I'm so full of goose pimples I could die and I'd better go home now, all right?"

"If you want to."

"I don't *want* to . . ."

"Then calm down and keep saying to yourself, 'Jerry is kind, Jerry is good, Jerry will never harm me.' Yes, my little African queen?"

"Yes. All right, Jerry. Yes. But I've *got* to wash my hands."

In the closet-sized, musty-smelling bathroom, Robin washed her hands and bathed her face with cold water and wondered if it was going to hurt much, wondered if he would stop when he found out she was a virgin, hoped he would, hoped he wouldn't, cursed herself for having started it all, blessed her luck of having her first man be the man she loved. When she returned, the studio couch had been turned into a bed, and she observed that Jerry, for all his displays of masterliness and self-confidence, seemed almost as nervous as she. That helped. It helped a lot.

Then, in the room's semidark, Jerry was kissing her and bringing the cotton dress up over her head and kissing her again as they both stood. There was no shame at being seen in her slip, nor was there shame or even embarrassment when the slip was gone and she saw Jerry's eyes on the swell of her bra and the upper mounds of her breasts, on the firm and bare midriff. And then he was cradling her in the bed, whispering love words.

"Ohhh . . ." she breathed.

"You like."

"Oh, yes, I like. Oh, yes, I love . . . darling."

"A marvelous body. Such a beautiful body."

"Kiss them. Oh, please don't stop, please don't talk."

And he kept on, and on, and she heard his voice. "Are you wearing anything?"

What kind of odd question was that? He knew she was naked. "Wearing? Wearing what?"

"Do you have a diaphragm?"

"A what?"

He grunted and left her. He came back and Robin watched, fascinated, as he rolled the transparent rubbery thing down over the first penis she had ever seen, red and unreal. And she felt abruptly revolted when he rolled on top of her because this wasn't at all the way it was supposed to be. The gentleness had gone out of him. There was supposed to be sweetness, wasn't there—sweetness and . . . reassurance? The depth and breadth of the act was supposed to be a sky filled with the rushing wings of birds and white gulls in the bright afternoon, and the act was strange, strange and unloving, and she loved him and did not dare to tell him she was sickened by it.

It took so long, and he was hurting her. He was trying to be kind, he was saying he hadn't known this was her first time but the pain would go away, and she clutched Jerry—Jerry, Jerry, Jerry—and kissed him as he worked at this hateful act, and ached for him to be done. And then he was, and much of the pain and the indignation was forgotten because she knew she had pleased him. He asked her if she was all right, and Robin said yes, yes, heavenly, and she marveled at how disgusted she had been moments before and how supremely happy she was now. Jerry smoked a cigarette and asked, "Any regrets?"

"Oh, no!"

"It gets better, my little African queen. Believe me."

"I believe you. I'd believe anything you told me."

"That's my loyal Nubian princess."

"What's 'Nubian'?"

"A native of Nubia, an old African kingdom. Your great-great grandpappy was emperor there. Emperor Koochiehoochiebooboo." She giggled. "I love you even when you talk crazy."

"Come to think of it, I have a big case on you, too."

After that day, Robin went to Jerry's apartment every time she could find an excuse to get away from her own home. She was a liar, and she knew Mama abominated liars; she would say she was going to the George Bruce Library, or ANP, or to choir practice at school, and she would hurry to be with Jerry, who let her cook for him and clean for him and who loved her. He was right: sex did get better, less strange, more natural. But sex didn't bind them together; love did, warmth did, happiness did. Jerry was nearly ten years older than she, and a thousand years smarter, yet they could talk with each other with ease. He talked about what had shaped him to become a writer, about his grim childhood in Baltimore with an uncommunicative Jewish father and neurotic Presbyterian mother, the mother who ranted against Negroes and Catholics and, eventually, Jews. He loathed his mother, he said. He loathed all people who hated in plurals.

Then Robin went to his apartment one afternoon and the door was opened by a middle-aged, plain-looking woman who stood in the doorway and asked her what she wanted.

"I'm—is Mr. Sorin here, please?"

"Are you the maid? My son didn't tell me a cleaning girl was coming in today."

"I—"

Jerry appeared, looking troubled, and said, "Ah—I'm sorry, miss . . . I forgot to call your agency this morning to say my mother came in from out of town and I wouldn't need the place cleaned today. I'll call when I need someone, all right?"

He closed the door.

It didn't happen. It couldn't have happened; it was a joke or a misunderstanding or something, and Robin waited at the door, motionless and aghast, for him to come to her. He didn't, and at last she left.

She walked home because she couldn't find the subway she had found so easily so many times before, walked in a sodden daze, not believing it had happened, believing it and feeling the hurt like a snakebite, believing it and weeping without tears, lost and naked.

No one was at home when she got there. She wept, and swore at Jerry Sorin, and loved him.

Two mornings later, Saturday, a blustery October day, she went to her cashier job at Gilley's. Jerry was waiting for her at the corner and led her to Briggs's Coffee Shop. "I'll be late for work," she said.

"No you won't."

He ordered two coffees and didn't look at her till the waitress went away. Then: "What can I say?"

"I don't know," Robin said mournfully, staring at his knuckles. "Nothing, I guess."

"She never comes in from Baltimore without phoning or writing first, but she did on Thursday, and there wasn't any way for me to reach you, to tell you not to come. I'm sick about it, Robin. She's a nervous, psychotic old bat. She would've had a fit if she knew about us."

"Why?"

"Good God, what do you mean 'why'? She's my *mother!*"

"And I'm the cleaning girl."

"Oh, hell, don't be so damn sensitive. What else could I've said on the spur of the moment?"

"Anything else, Jerry. I thought you cared about me."

"Christ, but you're talking like a fool. Of course I care. I care a lot. But it isn't as though we had any real future ahead of us—you know that." The coffee came and he was moodily silent till the waitress left. "What was I saying?"

"You were saying we don't have a future. I'd like to know why not."

He blinked at her. Softly he said, "My God, Robin, wake up. Hasn't anyone told you you're *colored?*"

Robin sighed. "No. Not for a long time."

"Look, you're worked up," said Jerry, who was worked up. "I don't want this thing to finish like this. We've meant too much to each other. Look, ah, don't go in to work. We'll go to my pad and straighten this thing out."

"What about your mother?"

"Oh, she left that same day. She stays with my married sister in Queens. Come on now, what do you say? Don't show up for work."

"What will we do?"

"Do? We'll talk. Jesus, will you stop looking at me like I'm a bigot?"

"You're ashamed of me."

"No, I'm *not*, dammit! Is that all you know about me? *Me*, the guy who feels and cares, really cares about your people? Would I have started an affair if there was an ounce of prejudice in me? I can't be responsible for my psychotic mother and the whole damned prejudiced world. Most of the guys I grew up with, they're true-blue liberal, but you'd never find them anywhere near Negroes on any intimate basis. You know I'm not like that. I've proved it." His voice was heavy and he looked terribly flustered, and Robin felt his hand on her knee. "I need you, Robin," he said. "And you need me. I was your first man, not just in bed but in every important way besides. You love me. Say you love me."

He was hunching forward and Robin slapped his face, so hard that the waitress and the customers turned. She slid out of the booth and ran to the cold sidewalk, in tears and in shame. She ran past Gilley's, mortified, degraded, sick with knowledge and consumed by confusion. She bumped into people and kept running, through the Harlem that was hers and was not hers, the Harlem that did not take her in, the Harlem she would never escape.

She ran as though she were being chased.

Robin refused to believe she was pregnant, even eight weeks after she failed to have her period. Fifteen-year-old girls didn't get pregnant. He had always put something on to protect her, hadn't he? Hadn't he? Of course she didn't have a baby inside her. She vomited in the mornings and she wasn't getting her period yet because Jerry had lied when he said he loved her, and she was upset about that. Her period had come late at other times when she'd been upset about something. Not eight weeks, and then ten weeks, but late.

Then at last she knew she was pregnant, and she was too afraid to go to a doctor, or a library where there would be books to tell her what to do, or even to tell June Fletcher. She could feel the baby, and she knew Mama would kill her, and she strapped heavy tape across her belly to keep from gaining weight.

In the middle of the fifth month a stabbing pain wakened her during the night. It left and she went back to sleep, and it wakened her again. It became excruciating, and the knowledge was overwhelming that her baby was about to be born.

She put on a robe and tiptoed to the kitchen, where she reached for Mama's pair of scissors on the sideboard, and took the scissors down into the cellar of the apartment house. She tiptoed in her bare feet to the coal bin at the rear of the small, damp cellar, pulled the chain that lighted the dull bulb, and lay down to lessen the pains and to wait.

When it was time, she gently brought one of the tiny feet out and, perhaps a minute later, the other foot. Within half an hour, her body bathed in icy sweat, she had pulled the baby out and cut the navel cord, praying she was doing it right, with the sharp scissors. The baby was a girl, and white, and it was dead.

The blood would not stop, nor the panic, nor her urge to cry out for Mama, for anyone, but she lay as still as she could for hours, holding her baby, until the afterbirth was passed. Then the panic and the pain disappeared, as though by magic, and she lost consciousness.

The morning had not yet come when she was conscious again, and she staggered up the stairs to her apartment and gently shook Lula, and told her, and fell into bed unconscious. It was bright afternoon when she came awake, and the sun poured into the room like liquid gold. Lula was sitting on the edge of the bed, gripping her hand.

"Does Mama know?" she asked.

"No," said Lula. "She left for work early."

"You didn't go to work?"

"No."

"The baby . . ."

"I buried it."

Robin sobbed and Lula, holding her, wept too. They held each other, rocking. "I'm so ashamed," Robin whispered.

"I know," said Lula. "Rest, honey."

Lula made her stay in bed for two days. Lula told Mama it was a cold. Lula waited on her, served her broth. Lula did not condemn, did not criticize, did not even ask questions.

Shame stayed. Shame, and the face and the body of her baby, and the fact of her baby's white skin.

She went back to school, carrying the shame within her. She moved through the halls of her fifteen years of life, as dead as her dead white baby.

Four years ago—*Lord, only four, not four hundred and four?*—and Robin searched for the suede pumps she would wear to East 60th Street, and clearly heard June Fletcher's fifteen-year-old voice warning, "*You know what they say—a white's man's only got one thing on his mind. And you know what that thing is.*"

White man, yes, and colored man, red man, purple man, plaid man, agreed Robin, more melancholy than outraged by her wise-guy cynicism. The towel's knot came undone as she knelt to retrieve the suede pumps from under her bed, and she paused to regard her image in the three-quarters-length mirror as she stood. Her body was beautiful because so many men had told her it was beautiful. She had learned how to use it—as an instrument of defense and a weapon, as a ticket to quick acceptance and resounding contempt. She had taught herself how to receive fondlings and caresses with a semblance of passion. With skillful deception she could moan as lips made love to her, she could whisper, "Yes, yes," and make it sound like a plea when she felt the weight of a man on her; she could move with him; she could twist and writhe; she knew how and precisely when to arch her back, precisely when to fake ecstasy. With a soul most scornfully dead, she had become an expert on how to play the game.

Except with Jesse, where no fakery was necessary.

Except with Warren Weber, the first man since Jesse who had stirred her to genuine craving. The first man since Jesse she had run from.

Mr. Straitjacket, come and get me, she thought. I'm ready for you.

Five

At GWS, WEBER, looking and feeling fit, went into action. He phoned Lou Patterley, the best man in the East at evaluating whether a vocalist had the goods or not, and ordered him to the office. "Not today, Warren," said Patterley. "We're winding up rehearsals on the Talbott show."

"Give me one hour. Three o'clock. This is important."

"I can't spare one minute, I'm trying to tell—"

"Spare it, Lou. For five hundred in cash, from me to you, spare it. Three o'clock."

". . . I'll squeeze it in."

Weber summoned Jeanne Prescott and told her about Robin. "You be on deck," he directed. "I want a full report—what you figure she needs in wardrobe, hair style, makeup, the works. Oh, and get me Larry Endicott's home number."

"For when?"

"For now. I'm going to call him."

"Is that wise?" asked Jeanne. "He's never up this early. You'll only make him cranky." Larry Endicott, "The Midnight Son," hosted the hottest late night gab show in the country, ran a tight ship, and ran it live.

"That's very possible. Come on, come on, snap it, baby. Pa's in a hurry."

Larry was reached and raised expected hell at being wakened in the middle of the night. "This better matter," he grumbled.

"It matters so much you'll kiss me," said Weber, crossing his ankles on his desk and shaking a Dexie out of a vial he kept in a desk drawer. "Lawrence, me bye, I'm giving you first crack at a chick vocalist who'll send Streisand into exile and who'll send your Nielsen through the roof. She's—"

"What? Is that why you woke me up, you son of a bitch, to sell me an *act?* You arrogant son of a bitch, what the hell'd you do, mislay the agency's number? You couldn't call Max or Lambert?"

"Sure, but they'd snow me with the job about how your show's booked solid for a month, and I can't wait that long, Lawrence. This girl's going to take off like a comet. Her name's Robin Hamilton and she'll make your crusty mouth water—and I want you to introduce her in a week."

"The *gall!* The goddam friggin' *gall!* . . ."

Weber chuckled. "Jot that name down, Lawrence, so you won't forget it. In a week everybody'll know it. Robin Hamilton." As Larry Endicott sputtered, Weber chuckled again and replaced the receiver gently. Jeanne was blinking in awe. "The trick in this dodge, my last duchess," he told her, "is to do things in a somewhat unorthodox manner."

"You're insane!" she cried. "That's no way to sell an untried act!"

"You are absolutely correct. And it will work. Now pick up your pad and your pencil and take all this down." He dictated a Robin Hamilton ad Jeanne was to place for a week from today, full page and without pictures, in every trade paper on both coasts. She was to get after Ronnie Haley, who was to see that Robin Hamilton's name appeared, starting tomorrow if possible, in the columns. She was to alert the record people, the picture people, the money people, that a great new star named Robin Hamilton Robin Hamilton Robin Hamilton Robin Hamilton was on the way.

"Are you jumping the gun?" Jeanne cautioned. "What if Lou Patterley says she's not ready?"

Good-naturedly, Weber sighed, "Oh, ye of little faith. When has the sahib ever misgauged? Now get off your tail and go to work."

"Speaking of tail, Miss Hamilton's must be sensational. I've never known you to go this all-out," she said dryly, and rose.

He laughed and watched her leave, watched the slender rump and the clean long legs, the polished, sophisticated female. Jeanne had been his private secretary for more than a month before he'd made his first play, and he'd scored about a week later. It had all been so intriguingly casual. They had been working late on over-due dictation, and she had easily, smilingly stepped aside when he'd first sent up the subtle red flares, but then she put her pad and pencil down and her smile was cool and agreeable. She seemed to take forever in the john, but when she came out she was clearly ready, and it happened on the office couch that became a bed by pressing the magic button, and there was no more dictation that night.

The sublime thing was that there *was* dictation the next day, business as usual, or almost as usual; they referred to the night before calmly, without regrets or promises. It happened again a week or so after, and then not for several months, and then it did, and then not. Weber was sure the relationship was unique. Friends sniveled to him that their secretaries invariably changed, invariably got sticky and emotional following the first bang, and he was grateful to Jeanne for her equilibrium.

Alone now, he suddenly realized that he had neglected, through some perversity rather than absentmindedness, to tell her—or any-one—that Robin Hamilton was colored. He grinned. And wondered what Jeanne would make of that neglect.

He went to Phil Simms's office and Phil, obviously pleased at the sight, told him he looked himself again. Then they discussed what had happened and not happened in Weber's absence, and then Phil, pouring coffee, asked how much thought he'd given to reviving "The Gundersen Journal."

"Not much, frankly," Weber admitted. "I've been thinking of something maybe fresher, more interesting and salable."

"Here we go," Phil grunted. "Daddy Warbucks Wins Again."

"Oh, hold that Trotsky fire for a minute, will you, and hear me out? I've been making a few notes," Weber said, tapping his forehead, "for a series that just could work and make us all proud. You film the entire thing in Harlem. The basic set is a social work agency in Harlem, and the hero is a Negro caseworker."

Phil shook his head. "Susskind tried something like that with 'East Side West Side.' It ran a season, but it sank."

"Will you *wait* a minute? We get us a name—a black actor who sells tickets. We get us writers, not hacks, and they pound it out with the gloves off. One week, a white slumlord keeps refusing to give a tenement heat and a baby dies of the cold. Another week, the dope problem. Another week, a sepia Romeo and Juliet. But *truth*, Phil, not just schmaltz. Stories about the poor, the disadvantaged, Negroes mainly but we won't forget the Puerto Rican market. *Real* stories—warmth and struggle to make it with the American dream." Weber paused. "*Nu?*"

Phil shrugged. "I'll buy it in a second. But who'd pay for it?"

"Vanguard, sight unseen. And you know why? Because every week we'll give them a guest star they otherwise couldn't land for all the money in the bank. We'll start with Brad Hammond for openers, and then Margalo and Kev, and then just watch everyone jump aboard!"

The seldom smiling Phil smiled and sat up. "Jesus, could you pull it off, Warren?"

"Lead-pipe cinch," Weber nodded, and supposed he meant it, unwilling to confess that he hadn't come up with the idea until he had entered this office. Of course it could be pulled off. Except for a couple of fat money specials, Brad Hammond, the most sought-after singer-actor in the world, never went near television. Margalo Wells and Kevin Beaumont, the most sought-after husband and wife acting team in the world, consistently rejected fortunes to say even Hello Folks on the tube. And there were others, all good people, white people on the good line in the cause of civil rights and civil liberties, and they were friends of Weber or they had been friends of, and indebted to, Charlie Gundersen. They would appear, at sensible salaries or, hell, for scale, and the avalanche would go into effect. The other untouchables would scramble to join the parade.

Even Vanguard's Caleb Atwood, who got his nocturnal emissions from dreaming that all blacks were herded back to Africa, would salivate at the lineup.

Weber saw and heard Phil's growing enthusiasm, and the adrenalin flowed. "And Mr. Shimolovich, suh, a capper just occurred to me, a gorgeous capper. Guess who we get to play the lead."

"Poitier? Belafonte?"

"Where the hell's your imagination?" Weber scoffed and paused for a moment. "Jesse Nash," he said.

"Jess— Where's my imagination? Where's your head?"

"On these strong, manly shoulders, as always. Would that make news or would that make news?"

"Couldn't you have thought up someone a little more controversial?" Phil asked sarcastically.

"That's exactly the point!" Weber said with relish. "You were the one yammering for us to clear the dust off television, weren't you? Well, here's the chance, and in a big, luscious bowl."

"My God, Warren, it does sound exciting, I admit that. I'm not even thinking about whether a sponsor or a network would sit still for it. Would that crazy Nash sit?"

"If the mighty Warren of Weber tells him to, he will," Weber replied with outsize regal disdain, and stood. "Mull on it, Mr. Shimolovich, suh. I'll get back to you."

Phil shook his head, but this time with *qvelling* pleasure. "That cruise did wonders—*wonders*," he emphasized. "You're clicking a mile a minute again."

"Salt air can overcome anything, even saltpeter," said Weber. "I read that in a bottle that was swept up to shore." He returned to his office, in relaxed control. Not even the Dexie he had been forbidden to take would key him up today. Robin was coming.

"Why didn't you tell me your new acquisition and I share the same delightful ancestry?" Jeanne scolded, as a way of announcing that Robin had arrived.

"How does she look?"

"Yummy. And cul-luhed. Is that what I'm drumbeating—anothah cul-luhed stah?"

"Once there was this famous Jew in Nazi Germany. His name was Staadtmann. He wanted to get off the hook, so he asked to be made an honorary Aryan, and Hitler gave him the job."

"Bullshit. You could have told me, Warren."

"It slipped my mind, which demonstrates to you bigots how successfully the darkies have woven themselves into the fabric of modern life. Show her in, Ilse Koch."

"Up yours," Jeanne said with flinty dignity, and turned on her heel.

Robin, dressed all wrong in a loose, heavy-knit turtleneck sweater, short skirt, patterned stockings, and square-cut, bulky-heeled shoes, entered, and looked more than yummy. She looked delectable—and frightened. Weber greeted her warmly. "Am I really here?" she asked.

"You certainly are. What have you been doing since this morning?"

"Pinching myself."

"That's more than you've let me do."

It was a mistake, for she glared at him. "Now it's my turn to say I'm sorry," said Weber, taking her coat. "I'm also sorry that you're nervous. You mustn't be. We're the good guys here. Everyone's on your side."

"What's going to happen?"

He yearned to hold her, and restrained himself. "You'll sing, and you'll meet some people, and they'll love you. Not the way I do, but they'll love you. Now stop fidgeting. You're acting as though you've never performed before." He flipped the intercom and instructed Sam to come in. "Sam Dawes is on his way," he told Robin. "He'll accompany you, but he'll do more than that. Sam's not only a first-rate piano man, he can advise you in five split seconds what numbers will show you off best."

At last she smiled. "I'm ready when you are, I guess."

"Atta girl."

Sam Dawes arrived, a young man with an elderly face and wholly a pro, and the introductions were made. Weber told him to spend some time with her alone in Room J till Lou Patterley came, and see what they could come up with. They left—Robin walking as if she were being escorted to Death Row—and Weber forced himself to concentrate on other matters until three o'clock.

Then it was three, and he went to Room J to join a set-jawed Jeanne and the rangy, perpetually worried-looking Lou Patterley. He nodded to Robin and Sam, and sat. The number was "Time After Time," and, after a slight clinker in the very first bar because she wasn't breathing right, Robin was into the song and the voice sounded fine. Weber furtively watched the others as much as he watched her. They were listening, and they seemed to be liking. The voice was a little of Ella, a lot of Lena, and a drop or two of Diahann Carroll, but she had merchandise of her own to sell and she was selling it, the Negro hurt and the Yiddish heart, and she grew more relaxed and in charge of herself as she repeated the bridge, and she sailed toward the finish line like seven-tenths of a pro. Weber's toes wiggled inside his shoes.

There was no applause when she was finished because there wasn't supposed to be, and she appeared a little dazed, and she did "Bewitched," and "Just One of Those Things," and the ambitious, nearly impossible "Summertime" she had done on the *Stalwart*, and then it was enough and Weber went to her, smiling. He thanked her and asked Sam to take her to his, Sam's, office. She went, still looking dazed. But Sam winked at him.

"Well, Lou?" he demanded.

Lou nodded.

"Is that why I called you over here—to nod? I realize you're not normally given to extravagant enthusiasms, but can't you do better than that?"

"That's a hell of a set of pipes she has," Patterley finally conceded. "I agree—she looks like a winner."

Even Jeanne nodded, and Weber was jubilant. "You see?" he exclaimed. "The master's never been wrong yet. Let's get her ready. I want to put her on public display in a week."

Lou's eyebrows raised. He seemed stunned. "A week? Make *sense!* That kid's not nearly ready for any important exposure yet. Basically the voice is true, but she's shaky on the high registers and the low registers, especially when she goes for broke, and—"

"But basically the voice is true."

"Hell, yes. She's got plenty riding for her already, along with her looks. She can pack a lot of guts and feeling into a song and her sense of phrasing is unbelievable for a youngster who's obviously had as little professional training as she's had. But make *sense,* Warren!" Lou repeated. "In a week's time you can't teach breath control and all the—"

"You can do anything, Louie boy," Weber interrupted. "I want you to go to work right away. I want her nationwide a week from today."

Lou Patterley reddened and frowned. "It's impossible. Even if I had the time, it's impossible. I'm knee deep in the Talbott show. There are only twenty-four hours in—"

Again Weber interrupted, this time softly. "Don't say 'impossible,' Lou. Anything's possible, because you're the one man who can make anything possible. There aren't twenty-four hours in a day. There are forty. Ninety, if necessary. And you'll swing it because you'll be depositing two extra grand in your fat account a week from today. Okay, Lou?"

"Warren—"

"Thanks for coming by, Lou," Weber said, and motioned for Jeanne to get up. "We'll be in touch with you later today and work out a schedule."

"Warren . . ."

Back in his office, Jeanne read Weber the notes she had made, on coiffure, on clothes, on posture, on grooming. "What do you think of the package, bigot?" he asked.

"You may have something, after all."

"Boy, you and Patterley can barely control your excitement, can you?" Weber said, grinning. "This is *it*, Jeannie! We do have something. I feel it, I know it. Now I want you to contact the pros, the best consultants in town—grooming teacher, wardrobe expert, whoever, but the best—and tell them to be ready to roll up the sleeves the second we're set." Jeanne left and he noticed, as he flicked the intercom to summon Robin from Sam's office, that Robin's coat was missing.

"Goofiest thing," said Sam. "The minute we got here, she busted into tears and ran out. I figured she was in your office."

Weber checked. Yvonne, the receptionist, had seen her get into an elevator about ten or fifteen minutes before. She was wearing a coat and she looked as though she was in a big hurry.

At five that evening, Robin timidly phoned Warren Weber.

"Good Christ, girl, you almost turned me into a basket case!" he roared. "Where the hell are you?"

"In my apartment. I got scared."

"I haven't been exactly soothed, either. What's your address? I'll be right over."

"No!"

She could hear him mutter "Goddammit," and he said, after a heavy sigh, "Quit already with this weirdo-shmeirdo, will you? Two dozen people are busy right this minute manufacturing a new product called Robin Hamilton. There'll be time for the hide-and-go-seek games later. Or maybe you'd better clue me in, here and now—how really scared is scared? I can get on my knees and beg to make you the biggest name in the business, but if you're going to keep this up, if you're going to conk out once the machines are turned on at full blast—"

"I was so sure nobody liked me today."

Again she heard a heavy sigh, and a pause. "I won't come near you for a while, not till the machines start. Will that help?"

"A little."

"All right then. Now follow me closely. You're to be in this office tomorrow morning at ten on the button. How much stuff do you have in your apartment—can a cab carry it all?"

"I don't have many things. But I don't understand—"

"Then listen. There's a furnished apartment in your name at The Havilland, on East 6oth, less than a block from here. You're to move in there tonight. Hold on a minute." She heard him talk with someone, and then he came back. "You met Miss Prescott here today. She'll be at The Havilland at eight o'clock, and the two of you will spend the evening going over everything you'll need in the next few days in the way of clothes and whatnot, and she'll give you an itinerary. Are you following me?"

"I'm trying to. Do you mean just move out, bag and baggage?"

"No, only absolutely essential things, like a toothbrush, until your shopping spree begins. Now don't give me any argument. Time's a-wastin'. I can count on you to be moved into The Havilland by eight?"

". . . Yes."

"All right. Just don't hand me any more run-out *tsores*, do you hear?"

He didn't wait for an answer. He hung up.

The East Side building was sumptuous beyond belief, but this whole day was like a movie you weren't supposed to believe. The white man at the lobby desk greeted her as Miss Hamilton, and a bellhop took her and her three shabby bags to a compact but elegant apartment on the fourteenth floor. There were seascapes on the pale green walls, and a large television set, and a commanding view of New York from the wide windows in the living room and bedroom, and plenty of rich, nubby towels in the bathroom. She gave the bellhop a dollar and hoped that was right.

She remained numb, even at eight o'clock when Miss Prescott, chic and efficient and guardedly friendly, arrived and asked her if she'd had much trouble in finding a taxi to carry her belongings.

"That wasn't so hard," Robin admitted. "What was hard was looking at him when he brought me here. He was a white driver, and I'm sure he's still scratching his head."

Miss Prescott grinned and lit a cigarette. "The poor man's world probably came to an end."

"I . . . well, I sort of feel the same way. I don't know what I feel."

"The end? It's the other way around."

"All this is happening so *fast* . . ."

"That's how Warren Weber operates, dear. You'll get used to it. Let's get cracking now, okay? You're going to be a busy girl, starting now."

They sat in the living room, her own living room, and she strove to dock herself to all the unreal things she was being told. Larry Endicott—yes, *the* Larry Endicott—had personally phoned the office this afternoon, and she would be on his show next week, as his testament of faith in Warren Weber, who had never let him down, had never sold him a bad apple. She and Miss Prescott would go on a tour of the stores and buy her clothes. There would be singing lessons, between tomorrow and next week. And conferences on music arrangements. And posture lessons, and grooming, and wardrobe, and rehearsals, and there might be time for a sandwich on the run.

Miss Prescott talked, and Robin tried to take it all in, and then there was everything more to talk about and nothing more. At the door, Jeanne Prescott turned to her and smiled. "Can you use a bit of advice, dear?" she said, not asked. "Treat Warren good in the sack. He doesn't go this red-carpet route for every girl, I can guarantee you that."

She was still smiling as she left.

Robin returned to the center of the unreal apartment that was very real, hurt by the easy assumption that she was Warren Weber's mistress because of all he was doing for her. But the hurt soon lessened, for she could be practical, too. Of course the dirty minds of people would go into action. How could she stop them?

And, if there was going to be a successful career, why would she want to bother to stop them? At the top, at the peak, where you owned everything that mattered, you could ignore them all because you were better than them all. Colored or white, you had proved yourself.

She walked from room to room, again and again, as she undressed, gradually making herself believe that today had taken place, that tomorrow would take place, and days after tomorrow. When she had her bearings, she would call Arbutus Harker and recount the Cinderella story. She would have to call Grace Hamilton, as well. Grace would understand. Grace wouldn't hold a grudge for having been the one who was passed over.

She ran the deep, long tub. The water rushed into it, and she stripped and stepped in, and reveled in its warmth. Tomorrow, reality would be real again. Tomorrow, she might even be able to call Mama.

Mama . . .

Six

MAMA NEVER DID find out about Jerry Sorin and the baby, but Lula, who had been so surprisingly comforting, said to Robin a month later, "I'll always be your sister. But I'll never care for you again."

It was a wounding thing to say, because there was no way to argue it. Robin devoted herself to keeping her marks in school as high as possible, because of the joy on Mama's face when the report cards were excellent, but otherwise she withdrew from all activities outside of schoolwork and Mama's church. She avoided boys. She retreated even from most of her girl friends. They were puzzled by her change, as she knew they had a right to be, but she could confide in none of them.

Then she was seventeen, and the dream of being somebody, of using her looks and what she was convinced was a better-than-average singing voice to get somewhere in the entertainment world, drove her out of the numb lethargy she'd lived in. She met Tommy Rexford, who listened to her sing and who promised he would see what he could do for her, even after he patted her hip and she slapped him.

Tommy came through with the Rigley's Lounge job for New Year's Eve, and she giddily told June Fletcher about it, and June giddily told the other kids. On New Year's Eve she sang at Rigley's Lounge. She sang, and met Jesse Nash, and her brother was shot, and she was raped in a wooded area of Harlem.

In that wooded area, she came awake in a bed of snow, her clothes torn beyond repair, her body numb with cold. There was no one, no car, nothing except the twin realities of Pete Gumbo and Roland Lee. She fell when she tried to get up because her legs, naked legs in cold dawn, would not hold her. She tried again, this time embracing the trunk of the tree near her, and she stood, surprised that she had any circulation left, now shivering at the cold, now perversely immune to it in her determination to be anywhere but in this place.

She didn't know where she was, nor how she could get home to Mama and Lula without clothes or even a dime to make a phone call, nor what time of day it was, nor whether there was anyone else alive in the world. Yet she carried herself, staggering, stumbling, over mazes of snow-covered ground, until she came to a road. The sky was gray and unsettled overhead, just entering daylight, and when she finally saw a car approach she instinctively retreated behind a tree because her gown was all torn up and the driver would see her.

Then she wanted a car to stop and she stood in full view of the road, holding what was left of the front of her gown over her breasts, but no car would stop. One car slowed down, but then sped away.

Her legs weakened again and she sank to the side of the road. She heard a car, and heard a door open and close, and she looked up through bleared eyes. A man was walking slowly toward her, a big man, colored, Pete Gumbo maybe, moving cautiously and holding something in his hand. She was about to cry out, and then all consciousness drained from her.

She came to, enveloped in warmth, in the rear seat of a taxi. There was a heavy overcoat and a blanket over her, and the car was heated. The man was beside her, rubbing the cold from her hands with his own strong ones. "I'm afraid you'll live," he was saying. "But we better get you to a hospital to take a look at that frostbite. You're one brown lady that's blue."

"No, I—I'm all right," Robin said quickly, wanting to trust the man yet worried that he was so close.

"What happened to you?"

"Are we anywhere near 150th Street?" she asked.

"Not too far."

"I have to go there. I live there. I don't have any money, but if you'd help me, if you'd take me there—"

"Yeah?"

"I have some money there, or my sister would pay you."

The man squinted his eyes as he surveyed her, as though trying to decide if he was letting himself in for trouble. "You're all banged up. Sure we shouldn't find you a doctor?"

"Please . . . take me home. I want to see my mother. . . ." Mama couldn't still be at the hospital. And she couldn't go to the hospital looking like this.

She huddled under the overcoat and blanket as he drove. He didn't talk much for a while except to apologize for maybe having scared her with the tire iron he'd carried in his hand when he'd gone to her; he'd had no way of knowing whether she had a bunch of friends nearby, waiting to roll him. Then he asked her again what had happened, this man whose taxi card read John M. Stover. The question was a reasonable question and Robin told him the truth, or enough of it, because the talking helped.

"So you went and learned something for yourself," he commented. "Nighttime, unless you have a beau, you stay home. I was born and raised in this city, and it's never been a jungle like it is now. I have a daughter older'n you, and she got strict orders she's not to step a toe out of the house after dark unless her mother and me know who she's goin' out with, and where, and what time she'll be back. Safer that way all around. I'm right sorry about your brother, miss. I hope he's gonna be all right."

The street in front of Robin's house was still almost empty—the clock in the window of Bixey's Bar across the street read half-past seven—and she prayed no one would see her getting out of a taxi in a man's overcoat. John M. Stover said he would take her to her door, collect his coat, and leave. It was only now that Robin noticed he hadn't put his meter clock down, and she mentioned it. "No charge, this trip—you got enough troubles," he replied. "Just call me a friend and that settles the bill. What you have to do is have your mama patch you up, the second you get in, hear?"

At her apartment door Robin balked for a moment, but then she knocked, softly. Finally she heard, "Who is it?" from the other side of the door—thank God it was Lula, not Mama—and the door flung open.

"Robin, where on earth have—" Lula began, and her hand shot to her mouth when she saw her sister. She stayed speechless as Robin asked Mr. Stover, "Will you wait one minute till I put on a robe?"

"Sure, miss, but be quick, okay?"

Inside, Robin whispered, "Where's Mama?"

"Asleep. At least she's in bed," Lula answered. "Lord have mercy, will you tell me . . ."

Robin hurried to the small bedroom she and Lula shared, shucked off the coat, got into Lula's robe because it was nearer at hand than her own, and hurried back to the front door with the coat. "I don't know how to ever thank you," she said to Mr. Stover.

"Just as long as you're home safe and sound," he said, and started for the stairs.

Back in the parlor, Robin began to flood her sister with desperate, disconnected questions about Mama and Roland Lee, but Lula insisted on knowing where she had been. "As if Mama didn't have enough to contend with, we called the Fletchers where you were supposed to be, and June Fletcher told us about that nightclub," Lula complained. "Mama finally got to sleep—Dr. Cochran gave her some kind of a pill—but now you're home and . . . oh, Robin, where *were* you? What're you doing half naked like that? Who was that man that brought you home?"

The situation was impossible because each sister needed to know too many things too fast from the other. And then, suddenly, neither spoke a word because their mother, in her flannel robe and looking a century older than she had looked the day before, was framed in the doorway to the cramped, immaculate parlor.

"Your baby brother is dead," she said, her voice deep and strangely relaxed, her heavy body straight and dignified.

Robin burst into tears, for herself as well as for Roland Lee, and ran to her, the robe sash flying open.

Mama slapped her. Robin reeled back, shocked, stunned.

"No Jezebel's stayin' in my house blessed by the Lord Jesus," Mama declared, the voice still oddly free of emotion. "Look at you. Hussy clothes, and you bosoms hangin' out like a sideshow. Whore-hussy from the cabarets, from the houses of sin, you ain't welcome in this house no more. Now you hear me, you hear you mother, you pack what you own in a satchel right now and you clear out of this Christian house."

"Mama, let me explain—"

"Explain to whores an' hussies an' scum o' the earth like you, come prancin' in here actin' like you wasn't a Jezebel when you baby brother, Mary rest his b'loved baby soul, was layin' dead. You leave this Christian house, mind, you leave and you spend all you days beggin' fo'giveness of the Almighty in Heaven for what you done."

Then Mama turned and went back to her room—Mama, whose love had filled this home, who had taught her children to judge not lest they be judged, wonderful Mama who would not listen.

Robin told Lula about Pete Gumbo as Lula watched her pack some clothes, and Lula told her the little there was to know so far about Roland Lee. None of this was happening . . . it was still a dream—Roland Lee, Pete Gumbo, Mama . . . but then she was out of the apartment that had been her home, and her cheek still stung from Mama's slap.

With her suitcase, and the $8.35 she had been saving and hiding in her bureau drawer, and the two ten-dollar bills Lula had pressed in her hand, Robin walked the early morning streets of Harlem, without a notion of where she could go. Harlem was the only place she knew, and she marveled at how little she knew of it, how few people in it she could phone.

With nearly thirty dollars, she could have subwayed downtown and moved into a hotel, but she reminded herself that downtown was white and unwelcoming to colored girls who carried cardboard suitcases and looked lost. She thought about phoning Tommy Rexford but decided against it; he would want the last thing in the world she felt like giving.

She walked the subdued New Year's Day streets as far as 125th and Lenox, and at last she phoned June Fletcher's number. She hung up when she heard Reverend Fletcher's voice.

She thought of Jesse Nash, but didn't know where to reach him.

When the awareness of being totally adrift became intolerable, she phoned Tommy Rexford, waking him. Tommy told her to come ahead.

He had hot coffee waiting for her in his warm flat, and he was sympathetic as she poured out her story. He had big plans for her, Tommy said, and he would be her guide and friend as well as agent from now on. He would get her bookings better than Rigley's. But the first order of business was to have a hot bath and a good day's and night's rest.

There was a sofa and only one bed in the flat, and Tommy made her take the bed. She was just about asleep in the darkened room when he slid in beside her. Her body stiffened and her stomach contorted in disgust, but she had the strength only to ask him not to touch her.

"I'd never do anything to hurt you, honey," he muttered, and his hand was gentle on her shoulder. "I'm not no pig like that Gumbo pig."

She was startled that she wasn't fighting him, and she was startled further that she liked his warmth near her and on her. Her hips began to churn within seconds after he started, and what she was allowing, encouraging, wasn't only whorish but sinful and sick because she could see Roland Lee watching her. Yet her breathing grew as labored as Tommy's, and she was sorry that he didn't wait for her to match his peak.

Three days later, it became clear that Tommy's big plans for her included turning her into a professional whore. That wasn't the way he said it, of course—he suggested they earn some pin money until decent bookings came through by lining her up for evenings with some gentlemen friends who would shell out a proper dollar to be shown a good time, and the minute he had a ripe club date ready, and so on and so on—but the suggestion revolted her and she moved out.

There had to be somewhere to go, somewhere that she could look at herself without seeing dirt. Yet dirt was all around her. The newspapers and the news on television over these three days were convincing her that everybody cared about Roland Lee's murder but nobody was going to do anything about it; Roland Lee could have been a stray cat rather than a boy, a human being, shot in that alley, and he was buried like he was dirt, too, because no one who could do anything cared enough.

She phoned her home. Lula answered and said that Mama was holding up pretty well but that the mention of Robin's name was forbidden.

Robin remembered Bea Russell, her father's niece who lived in Philadelphia, her only living kin except for Mama and Lula, and called her at six o'clock in the evening, when the cost was cheaper. There was no special reason why Cousin Bea should be nice to her —Robin had met her only twice, because Mama considered all of Daddy's side of the family a pack of shiftless heathens—but Bea *was* nice to her on the telephone and invited her to come.

Bea, a cheerful, buxom lady, and her husband Chick lived a block from the small luncheonette they owned off Susquehanna Street, in an apartment that was crowded even for them, but they took Robin in, with the unspoken understanding that she wasn't to make it her permanent home. Chick Russell was a surly man who scarcely glanced at her, but Bea assured her she was welcome, and even talked Chick into letting Robin work a few hours a day behind the counter.

On the day the white policeman was cleared of criminal negligence in New York, Robin and Chick were alone in the lunch-eonette when the report came on the radio. "They didn't take very long, did they?" said Robin soberly.

"Wha'd'you 'spect?" Chick grunted, shifting his toothpick from one corner of his mouth to the other. "It's like that Orville Sanford fella's been a-hootin' and a-hollerin' all along—'If you black, step back, we never gonna git a fair shake in these Yew-nited States till we start doin' some shakin' up ourself.'"

These were the most words she had heard Chick speak, and she looked at him. "This Orville Sanford—he hates all white folks, or says he does," she said.

Chick frowned. "Uh-huh. Somethin' wrong in that?"

"Why, of course! It doesn't make any more sense than some of them hating all of us!"

The toothpick shifted again and he shook his head. "Dummy. That's what you are, a dummy, chatterin' like that. You, 'specially you, chatterin' like that with what they done to your brother. I don't want none of 'em around me, *none* of 'em, and if you'd grow a little brain in your head you'd see the only way to respeck your-self is to keep clean of 'em, and that means all of 'em."

"I—can't agree with you, Chick," she said, uncertainly.

"Is that a fack?" he teased. "Why'n'cha chase over to the War-wick, then, or the Barclay, and meet up with some nice blondie-head white guy and see how fine he treats you. That what you anglin' at, to git in with the blondie-heads?"

"That's plain silly. All I mean—"

"Listen, I didn't go but four years in school, but I'm a college p'fessor when it comes to *them*. That Sanford fella's right as rain—the whites don't want you nor me for nothin' 'cept to mind their babies and empty their trash, no matter how fine and fancy they talk. You take my advice and stay with your own. White man's just waitin' to chop you up seven ways to Sunday."

Robin didn't answer. She was uncomfortable with this man who was so quiet when Bea was around.

A customer came in for two containers of coffee, to go. When he left, Chick had more to say. "You're not a bad-lookin' colored girl," he declared. "What you got against us colored men?"

"What do I have *what?* Chick, you're talking crazy . . ."

"Not so crazy. I been lookin' at you since you got off the bus from *Noo* York City. You're not some innocent lamb like you try to ack. You go for me, I can tell." And then he was telling her that Bea was a good woman but a cold fish when it came to loving, and he was a lonesome colored man looking for a little affection, not just fooling around, and colored had to stick with colored, and he would buy her presents and treat her fine, what did she have to say about that?

Two customers came in. Robin took their orders, gave the orders to Chick, and went to the little room behind the diner, where she put her coat on. She told Chick she was going home because she had a terrible headache. Chick left the hamburgers unattended on the grill to order her not to breathe a word about anything to Bea.

That was the night she read, in the *Philadelphia Bulletin*, that Marty Dickson was enthusiastically predicting nonstop stardom for his newest "find," Jesse Nash. The item quoted Marty Dickson: "We're about to release Jesse's first comedy LP, and we have fat club, television, and movie assignments on the fire for him. This is the kind of talent that doesn't come down the pike more than once or twice in a show business lifetime, and I'm tickled pink that Jesse Nash is on board with us. Mark my words: a month from today the country's going to throw pearls at his feet. Come to think of it, what's his feet got that he hasn't got?"

And that was the night Chick came home from the diner to find her alone; it was Bea's evening out to play bingo. Neither greeted the other; the parlor television set was on, and Robin, her hair in curlers, pretended to be concentrating on it. She could hear Chick rumbling about in the other room. She wished there was a room for her to go to and hide in besides the parlor, but there was none. She wished she had the nerve to write to Jesse Nash.

Chick came back in ten minutes, carrying a bottle of Seven-Up, and sat at the opposite end of the room and watched the screen with her for a while. Then he asked, "How's the headache?"

"Better."

"I keepin' you up, sittin' here? Maybe you wanna bunk down for the night."

"Well . . . pretty soon."

"You give a thought to what I said before, 'bout the two of us bein' friendly?"

Robin stared solemnly at the screen. "We are friends," she said. "But that's as far as it's going to go."

"High-hattin', that's what you up to. I take ya in and feed ya, and you go high-hattin' on me."

Annoyed, she said quietly, "I won't go to bed with you. Kick me out if you want to—tonight, right now—but I won't go to bed with you."

"Who's talkin' 'bout kickin' anybody out? I'm talkin' 'bout bein' friendly, that's all."

There was, she decided, only one way to deal with him. "How long are you going to keep this up, Chick?" she said. "Because if you don't quit now, for good, I'm going to Bea."

She still didn't look at him, but she knew she had reached him. Presently he muttered, "You're a fresh-ass."

"When I have to be," Robin answered, nodding.

There was another silent moment, and then his chair squeaked as he got up. "You're a fresh-ass, awright, but you'll come aroun', and you won't go blabbin' outta school about nothin', neither," he promised. "What you got waitin' on ya if you leave here, if you git noisy and git kicked out? You think it over. You won't git a roof over your head an' three squares a day so easy somewheres else. I can blab a li'l, too. I can let Bea know you been makin' eyes at me, and who's she gonna believe, me or you? Think it over good."

He lumbered out of the parlor, leaving his empty soda bottle on the floor beside his chair. Robin reread the *Bulletin* item and rehearsed what she would write or say to Jesse Nash if she ever got the nerve.

Cousin Bea came home shortly before eleven, after Chick was asleep, and brewed tea for herself and Robin. They sat at the kitchen table and Bea, stuffing herself with gooey cakes, gossiped harmlessly about her friends at the bingo club, and prattled genially and endlessly about the simple pleasures that made up her life with Chick. She trusts her man, Robin thought, afraid for herself and for Bea, recognizing that there would be trouble if she stayed here, certain she could bear no more trouble. She listened to Bea, and loved her, and marveled at her cousin's apparent acceptance of a life that would never improve, never go beyond bingo games and fattening cake and cramped, segregated walls and a bleak diner.

I've got to find a home, she thought. This isn't my home.

When Bea turned in for the night, to get under the covers with her man, Robin read the newspaper item yet again and then suddenly put on her coat. She went to the public telephone booth at the corner and asked the operator if there was something in Hollywood, California, called Marty Dickson Enterprises. Yes, there was. Struggling for calm, she placed a person-to-person, collect call to Mr. Jesse Nash. He wasn't there, said an answering service voice; who was calling?

She gave her name, and Cousin Bea's number. She said it was an emergency and asked that Mr. Nash call her as soon as possible.

She went back to the apartment and sat near the telephone, which was in the parlor. The call came in two and a half hours later, waking both Bea and Chick. She assured them it was for her.

Jesse Nash listened to her for less than a minute. Then he repeated the address she gave him and said that her air fare to Los Angeles was on its way.

Robin got out of the Havilland tub and reflected on how far she had come, if it had been far at all, since Harlem and Susquehanna Street in Philadelphia and since 44th Street. She dried herself with not one but two fluffy towels, and set her hair in the curlers she had been collected enough to remember to bring from 44th Street.

Sleep eluded her, but she hadn't expected to sleep much, anyway. There was a television set in the living room. There was one here in the bedroom, as well, and this one had a remote control button. She watched *Marie Antoinette* and tried to empty her mind of everything, everyone.

You leave this Christian house, mind, you leave and you spend all you days beggin' fo'giveness of the Almighty in Heaven for what you done, Mama said.

You're the worst kind of nigger there is. You want to wake up some morning and find all the black's been washed off, Jesse said.

Quick, see that falling star? I'm so happy, I can't think of a thing to wish for, Warren Weber said.

Let me grow up, she prayed. Let me be somebody nice.

The next day and the days that followed were feverishly hectic. Robin broke down twice and wept that she couldn't possibly be ready for such a big debut on Wednesday, if ever. But there was a calming influence, and he was Warren Weber. "You're doing fine," he would say. "You're doing just fine. My God, can't *you* see that?"

There somehow was a free moment and she called Arbutus, who was thrilled and who wished her the best. There somehow was another free moment and she called Grace, who spat, "You plotted behind my back, you stinking bitch! I'm the one who deserves a break after all these years starving, not some plotting, newcomer bitch like you. I only hope you fall on your ass, that's all I hope!"

Then it was Wednesday night in a cavernous television studio, and a man with puffs and an eyebrow pencil was chewing gum and making her up. And she was briefly introduced to Larry Endicott, "The Midnight Son," a dapper man with a blond pompadour who barely nodded to her and who yelled across the room, "Get your goddam friggin' hands off that boom mike!" and stormed away from her.

Hordes of people darted about her, even after the show seen by millions of people went on the air and Larry Endicott had an opening monologue of jokes that was thoroughly nice-guy. And then it was Robin's turn, and she heard the introduction, and a man near her raised his hand and pointed a long finger at her, and she was in front of television cameras. She sang. She knew she was bad on "You're the Top." She knew she was disastrous on "My Man's Gone Now." And then the applause was thunder, and she was supposed to smile and get off, but Larry Endicott came stalking at her, and she couldn't hear what he said but he put his arms around her in full view of the audience and the camera and kissed the top of her head.

And then it was past one o'clock in the morning and she was in the rear seat of a long, black automobile, and Warren Weber was holding her and telling her she had been flawless. "Tell me everything that happened!" she exclaimed.

"Weren't you there?"

"Oh, not within a million miles. Tell me, tell me!"

It all came back as he talked, the acceptance, the love, the waves of love. The talk kept bubbling, all the way up in the elevator and for moments after they were in the Havilland apartment. He brought a bottle of champagne from his overcoat pocket, and popped the cork in the kitchen.

"Go get two champagne glasses, Robin," he directed. "They're on the bureau in the bedroom."

"The— What would champagne glasses be doing there?"

"Because I said so. I had your door lock picked and put them there. Hurry and get them, before this wine goes flat. I'll be out here somewhere."

Crowding the bedroom were red roses, all over the place, and she counted seven baskets with a dozen in each. The card in the first one read, *I love you. Grumpy.* The second read, *I love you. Sneezy.* The third read, *I love you. Doc.* And she moved giddily through the rest of the dwarfs. On the bureau there were indeed two champagne glasses. Plus a diamond bracelet, which was clearly the most expensive diamond bracelet in the world and which had a small cardboard tag attached that read, in pen, *Woolworth, $.39.* Plus a white box with the legend *Bonwit Teller* printed across it.

In the box was a black, sheer, almost transparent, discreetly beaded, breathtaking negligee. The card read, *I love you. Warren.*

To support herself against the delicious weakness in her legs, Robin propped her elbows on the surface of the bureau and regarded Robin Hamilton in the mirror above it.

It was time. It was very much time.

With tremulous, uncertain fingers, she took off her clothes, carefully placed them out of sight, and brought the negligee down over her head and her arms. She brushed her hair, and touched her mouth with lipstick, and regarded herself in the mirror again. The face that suddenly was someone else's face looked appealing. The shoulders looked good. Her breasts were rounded and pretty, and part of her was surprised and a little bit embarrassed that the nipples were so stiff with desire.

Working to bring her breathing into some semblance of order, she went to him, smiled shyly, and said, "I couldn't find the champagne glasses. I guess I'm not very thirsty."

He enfolded her, and she tingled. His kiss began tenderly, almost chastely, and then he was holding her closer and foreign sensations shot through her loins as his hands cupped her buttocks and she felt him growing hard against her. Each breath was a sharp pain in her lungs, and he parted her lips and his hands roved her thighs and all intimate places.

In the bedroom, the negligee gone, watching him free his own clothes, she knew for the first time in her life that she was not worried about whether she would disappoint a man. He came to her in the partial dark of the room, and she was instantaneously responsive. He kissed her body as though famished, but she was impatient with preliminaries, and then she was burning and she clung to him and whispered, "Will you? Now?"

She received him eagerly, her hips churning, embracing him hard with her arms and legs, and all of it was so completely right. With Jesse, she had felt Jesse and love. With this man, she felt Warren Weber and love, and the sharp-edged hairs of his strong body on her chest, and the hard, hot, velvet instrument she was squeezing and burying but not really taking from him, and she felt it, felt it, felt the plunge and the prick of it, suddenly knew why it was called a prick and wanted to share her discovery with the world. He was stroking her slowly, with certainty, with man's certainty, and she bit his chin with her teeth, wanted the velvet to burst inside her, wanted it to velvet her forever, wanted it, wanted it O God I've never had it like this, wanted it, I'll die if it doesn't happen now, I'll die if you stop, want it, want it, deeper, fuller, slower, need it, faster now, the sweat, we're in a bath of sweat, deeper now, deeper, yes that's right, it's coming, it's swirling all through me and I'm going to come, lover, my dearest lover, O dearest God it's all so completely right and it's beginning to happen, I've never had it at exactly the same time, not even with Jesse, oh baby oh daddy it's getting ready, and her body jerked and twisted insanely and he flooded her and she cried out in her ecstasy.

They held each other for a very long time, because words would not form. Then he asked, "How are you?"

"In love," Robin said, and suspected she meant it.

"We're just beginning," he said. "Everything's just beginning."

"Yes," she said.

Seven

ROBIN'S FIRST REVIEWS were more than favorable if less than plentiful, and Weber immediately arranged for her to do "The Curly Custer Show," a high rater and at prime time, and to make three additional television variety show appearances, all within a period of three weeks. Larry Endicott wanted her back. He squealed on hearing that her price had doubled, and called Weber a thief and other names that reflected on Weber's sex habits, and agreed to pay it.

After the Custer show, two major record companies offered to sign Robin, but Weber, normally a man who believed in striking irons while they were at their hottest, took Lou Patterley's advice and rejected the offers. Lou's point, and Weber allowed it was a sound one, was that her voice and delivery were getting better all the time, but that no record could show her in physical action. "She comes across fine on the tube," said Lou, "because if the breath gives out and she hits a note on the cheek instead of the head, she can get away with it with that great face and shape. All she can bring to an LP are voice and delivery, and I think you'd be smart to hold off till she's absolutely ready."

"How long will that be?"

"Well, she's learning faster than any kid I've seen and heard in a damn long while. She seems to gain more confidence every time she goes to bat. I'd say, all things being equal and if she works as hard as she's working now, another month or so could do it."

"All right, I'll settle for three weeks," said Weber. "I don't want anything to muff this." Besides, the money would be better if he made them sweat a little.

The good reviews grew plentiful by the time Robin had made her fourth television appearance, and Weber reveled in the unexpected gravy of seeing her, on her second appearance on Endicott's show, do a minute and a half comedy bit with Endicott before her spot, and do it with charm and ease; he had not considered the possibility that she was an actress, or could be made an actress. Others did, though; Hollywood called, with cautious but very real interest.

To Hollywood as well as the record companies, to nightclubs and even to some television people, Weber replied from the driver's seat, "No, not now. I'll get back to you." He spaced her appearances carefully; simultaneously, he pressed Ronnie Haley and Ronnie's staff to keep telling every man, woman, and child that there was a star named Robin Hamilton.

When he wasn't with her—and that was often, damn it, because the hired pros took him at his word and worked her almost around the clock—Weber kept his own vow to Phil and himself: he assigned to others most of the GWS projects that didn't really, after all, require a tenth of the mothering he had given them before the cruise, and divided his time between coordinating Robin's career and conferring on the Negro caseworker series with nonhack scriptwriters he had rarely had occasion to approach in the past. Men like Bob Penniman, one of the few black writers Weber knew whose novels and short stories weren't concerned almost exclusively with race, and Gene Trowbridge, a white man who had won a Pulitzer for an eloquent, feeling play dealing with race. Both men were excited by the idea. He assured them, at their first meeting, that he planned to see the project down to the wire, and he guaranteed that he would allow no one to tinker with, tamper with, or water down a single script.

"I want to call the series 'Moore.' Moor—get it? The lead's name is Jim Moore," he said. Then, with rehearsed casualness, he dropped the bombshell. "Jesse Nash used to be a comic, so with any luck that could mean he's an actor, too. I want Nash for the lead."

Both men caught the bombshell smack in the middle of the forehead and, when they came to, protested. "Hell, that's a transparent gimmick, Warren, and nothing else," argued white Gene. "I'm all for controversial issues and controversial people, but from everything I hear, you shouldn't go near that guy even if he could out-act Olivier. He's supposed to be off his streetcar. Unpredictable. Strictly from a practical view, who needs unpredictable actors?"

"That's where you'd lose me in a minute, Warren, if you went through with it," argued black Bob. "Even if a sponsor and a network sat still, which they wouldn't, and even if Nash agreed to work for you honks, which he wouldn't, you'd still be nuts to even think about it. He's a wild man."

"Oh, look—"

"No, you look, Warren. For all of Jesse Nash's crazy words and acts, and in spite of the fact that I dislike him personally, there's a lot to be said for him. He's a feeler, not a thinker, but with all the dramatics he accomplishes something no other Negro today comes close to accomplishing half as well. He reaches the kind of Negro who's been trained from the cradle that he's not really a citizen and therefore he's inferior. Jesse wants those Negroes to be proud of themselves, and somehow, despite the histrionics you'd imagine would be a cinch to see through, he succeeds. I admire him because he's somehow able to show even the Al Lingos and Bull Connors that black people *hurt*. And if he's good for nothing else, he somehow manages to keep that cuckoo outfit, FREE, from going all-out cuckoo."

"So what's your beef? A minute ago you jumped at me as if I'd lined up Attila the Hun for the part."

"The effect would be about the same. In too many people's minds, Jesse Nash is associated with violence. Oh, as far as I know no one has ever accused him of actually being violent or even of preaching violence, but for some reason I can't fathom he won't shake loose from FREE, and from his boss Orville Sanford, who *is* a psychotic. I like your Jim Moore character," Bob said, and Gene Trowbridge nodded agreement. "I can see an exciting series, and a useful one. But the Jim Moore you're talking about and the Jesse Nash I'm talking about are poles apart. Jim Moore can help my people, and your people, too. Nash has too many hang-ups, in his public image and probably the private one. In the long run, maybe the short run, Nash is a destructive man, and I wouldn't write him a postcard, let alone a TV show."

Gene concurred, and began an oration, but Weber was interested only in Bob Penniman. "You admit there are seeds of good in this fellow Nash," he said. "If the core of what he's saying has value, if he's identified as a man who cares deeply about Negro people and the bettering of their lot, isn't that more important than the company he keeps? A series with Nash—"

"Wow, but you have a genius for tuning out what you don't want to hear," Bob interrupted. He shook his head. "Warren, I'll tell you something. We've known each other for a hundred years, and I'd stand up for you till I drop, but for a supposedly brilliant white man you have some big blind and deaf spots. Nash won't leave FREE, which means he won't leave Sanford, and Sanford pulls the strings of FREE. Nash's central purpose seems to be to change the crushed-down Negro's picture of himself as an intruder in Mister Charley's land, and Orville Sanford's central purpose is to turn every black man against every white man. Collusion, my friend, collusion somewhere in the woodpile. Nash talks about white exploiters. Sanford and every high-echelon member in FREE *except* Nash talk about Jewish exploiters. Nash tells the man in the ghetto that the grocer and jeweler and druggist and shoe-store owner who screws him is a white man. The Sanfords press down hard on Epstein and Cohen. Nash says, 'Make Whitey open the door.' The Sanfords say, 'Get ready to kill Whitey.' The facts are, there are no facts at hand, and that muddies the waters, and Jesse, for all his good, is a willing or unwilling victim of something deadlier than guilt by association, and all I can say is, you take that ten-foot pole of yours and don't touch him with it."

"My sentiments exactly," said Gene Trowbridge.

After that meeting there were several more with Penniman and Trowbridge, and they were constructive ones. Weber said, with sincerity at the time, that the notion of Jesse Nash playing Jim Moore had been merely a notion, not a declaration from On High. He granted, to himself, that Penniman and Trowbridge had been quite correct in their warnings: Nash, according to the latest news reports, *was* a wild man. His assailant, the white man who had shot him on orders from the New York Police Department, was tracked down by the New York Police Department and turned out to be a young Negro crackpot named Clinton Ramsay, who quickly confessed. Ramsay belonged to a rival civil rights group that believed in prayer as the sole way to overcome oppression, and he had been directly instructed by the Lord God Jehovah to destroy Jesse Nash because Jesse Nash did not worship the Lord God Jehovah.

On hearing of the confession, on being shown the indisputable evidence, Nash was quoted as saying, "All Ramsay did was pull the trigger—*if* he did. But who put that religious fanatic stuff in his head in the first place? No soul brother did. Your lily-white structure did. Going back three hundred years, your structure started keeping Ramsay busy by teaching him to pray to your white-structure God. You did that because otherwise he'd have the time to begin asking questions about his rights as a man, and that would naturally interrupt business as usual."

It was an infantile rationalization, Weber decided with mingled delights, and a perfectly gorgeous fast-on-the-feet display of impishness.

This could be one hell of a coup, he thought, because it's so beautifully daring. If it's done right, and I'll see to that, it can reap benefits for both colors. And it can force people in the industry to talk long and excitedly about Warren Weber, mighty Jew.

Despite her merciless schedule, despite the seemingly perpetual appointments and constant challenges that stimulated and drained her, despite the increasing numbers of professionals accumulated to professionalize her, Robin remembered to look over her shoulder for Weber. And Weber, proud of her magical improvements, proud of her steadily growing presence in public, was right there.

And in her bed at The Havilland, whenever it was at all possible. He was grateful that Karen was not a wife who kept close tabs on her husband, grateful to be in the kind of business that could legitimately take and keep him away from home at any hour of the day. If Karen was a jealous woman, if she suspected that he got into beds other than hers, the subject was not raised, nor, for that matter, had it ever seriously been raised as an issue in their twenty years together—uncommon good luck, he realized, for apparently everyone except Karen in New York and all points east and west knew he enjoyed other beds.

The growth in Robin in the scant short weeks since she had first sung for GWS was stunning and, to Weber, profoundly gratifying. She, Robin Hamilton the star-to-be, had been created, but surely by herself almost as much as by Warren Weber and the tutors and groomers and the fuss of pros. She knew she was good and would be great, though she knew it in a continually refreshing way; she obviously knew precisely how and when to distinguish between her contributions to the development of Robin Hamilton and the contributions of others. She thanked people, always the right people, and she took instructions and suggestions with grace and intelligence, and they liked her, and there was not a vestige left of the girl who had fled to the GWS elevator in terror.

Weber saw growth in the Havilland bed, as well, observed how instinctively and joyfully she took instructions and suggestions, marveled at how inventive she could be on her own above and beyond the instructions and suggestions. She was playful and passionate, an imp, a hellion, a demander and thanker. She was skillfully evasive and certainly less than frank when it came to accounting for unexplained pockets of her past, Weber was aware, but lovemaking made her frankness positively glow.

"What's the name of those zones, I think they're called, that's supposed to get women worked up the most when they're touched?" she asked one night after he brought her to the hotel from a long taping session at NBC and they had completed history's most flawless act of sex.

"Erogenous."

"How many are there supposed to be?"

"Seven, with normal women. With you, we'd need a scorecard and plenty of pencils to record them."

She laughed. It was girlish and free and utterly wonderful. "Three hundred million, at least," she said, cuddling close. "And I'm not even ashamed!"

"Why should you be?"

"Because when something is this good, a girl is expected to be ashamed." She guided his hand to her flat stomach, looked at him with a shining smile, and said, "Even this, for heck sake—who would've thought a girl could get all aroused just having her belly button touched?" Her lips were close to his ear. "My belly button," she whispered, "and my eyebrow, and my big toe, and, gee, anything, any place. I've never called you darling before except, you know, well, you know when I say it. Can I call you darling now?"

"Sure, darling. But only if you say it three hundred million times."

"Darling, darling, darling, darling, darling, darling. I'm so proud of me."

Weber laughed. "Proud, all of a sudden? What brought that up?"

"I'm proud that I don't feel like some sort of a tramp, doing these things with you. I guess that's what they mean by love. I don't put on any act with you, never once from the first time. Everything's so—*real* with you. I couldn't pretend anything."

He swiftly, instinctively raised his hand, away from her, but she did not appear to sense the meaning of the reflex. "Love, yes, love," he said, more jauntily than he meant to, and, after a decent interval of moments, slowly moved his body away from her. He left the bed and said, more gravely than he meant to, "The hour, she waxes late."

Robin sat up, bringing the bedsheet over her breasts, and there was alarm in her eyes. "What is it?" asked Weber.

"I said something wrong."

"Wrong?"

"I did, didn't I? A second ago you were here, and now you're there. What did I say wrong?"

"You're demented, child. You didn't say anyth—"

"Was it those things I said above love? Is that why you moved away?"

"Of course not, you dope," Weber lied, and strode to her and kissed her mouth. "But it *is* late."

"Warren, let's . . . please let's make love again."

He tightened and thought fast. "Demented is the word for you, all right. You're barking up the wrong stallion. What did this old man finish, not fifteen minutes ago?"

"That never stopped you before."

"Possibly, but—"

Aggressively, abruptly, Robin whipped the bedsheet and blanket away, exposing a bright blaze of caramel flesh. Weber was immediately riveted, not so much by the sight of the wondrous body, which he had memorized, as by the shock of its clear demand, a demand almost audible. He saw her eyes, Robin's almond, young eyes, and scarcely recognized them: they were hard, less inviting than daring, less pleading than insisting. A queer noise rose from her throat, a noise that was invitation and desperate need, and Weber, who had never known this Robin before, who had not been this quick to second excitation for the past half dozen of his forty-four years, quickly felt the blood pound in his gut and at his neck, in his brain and in his loins.

He fell upon her but could not invade her, for there was next to nothing to invade her with. "Old man, old man," he muttered. Robin, smelling clean and sweet and of lust, gently teased, "Yes, yes, old man," and held him between hot palms, working to restore him, to restore it, it which was beyond restoration. And presently it began to grow, indefinitely, indecisively, and then very decisively, and they slowly rocked back and forth and from side to side, and she whispered, "This isn't an old man," and rode him as though he were a carousel, then a roller coaster, now both conquering and submissive, now the hoyden, now the lady, now the hellcat. He could sense, feel, see the beginning of subtle, voluptuous convulsions, could see her contorted, beautiful face, heard her beg, "Do me, darling, do me, do me . . ." and listened with almost indolent detachment to her moans of pleasure.

He went home that night to Karen. They drank a small brandy nightcap and Karen told him, quietly but with obvious concern, that she had just this day learned, during lunch with her friend Sally, Dr. Mel Hebranck's wife, why the cruise to the Caribbean had been taken. "It's a peculiar feeling," she said, "to learn about the state of my husband's health from Sally Hebranck, over a Caesar salad."

"I've been back to see Mel twice," he declared. "He says I'm topnotch."

Karen nodded. "Yes, I learned that, too. And I'm as relieved as you are. Do you remember, years ago, when we didn't keep secrets from each other?"

"I didn't want to upset you. As it turned out, I was right. I'm feeling better than I have in ages," Weber said, and believed he meant it. He hadn't been this eager to waken in the morning since the exciting years with Charlie Gundersen. He carefully guided Karen off the track of his health and the secrets spouses kept from spouses, and they discussed GWS's progress with Robin Hamilton, as though Robin were a property and not a special person he was bedding. He discussed "Moore" and his mounting enthusiasm over it. Karen was an excellent, supportive listener, and the occasional comments she offered were germane and acute, and he was surprised to remember the many times, like now, when there was no one he was more comfortable with.

They continued to talk, even after they were in bed, about his health, which he vowed to guard; about their children, who were constant sources of exultant pride; about their cook, who was thinking of retiring and going back home to Copenhagen—subjects a successful man and his wife of twenty years talk about after midnight. Weber felt so close that he had a perverse urge to tell her about Robin. He wanted to confide that the affair was more crush than romance, that he recoiled at the word "love," that he wanted only Karen to love him, that he would never touch Robin again because it would lead nowhere good.

He had much to be thankful for. He was most thankful that Karen indicated, in the unspoken yet decipherable way a long-married wife can express herself, that she could do without sex if he didn't feel up to it. He held her, though, and even kissed her.

It was Ronnie Haley's emphatic recommendation, as the important newspapers, magazines, and television talk shows began to clamor to interview Robin with some degree of depth, that the gloves come off; he knew about her brother from Weber, but she had instructed Weber to instruct Haley that the matter was something she would not discuss in public.

"Okay, Warren, I can agree with you up to a point," the press agent admitted. "She figures, and you figure, that the public'll think she's using the kid's murder to help her up the ladder. Gorgeous—very thoughtful, very sensitive. But you know the game's not played that way. The public's bound to make the connection sooner or later, and the longer you hold off, the more alibis you're gonna have to come up with to explain why you kept the lid on. And, as it is, I don't have much to work with. She went to school in Manhattan and you discovered her singing on a boat. That don't stop no presses."

Weber nodded. "You're right. I'll get back to you."

For days after he seriously broached the subject, Robin was adamant. "It was a terrible thing, it won't ever stop being a terrible thing, but I won't talk with anybody about it."

"Why not?" Weber gently asked. "If you have so much feeling about it, and you have, and I help you with what to say, then why not?"

"Because once I start talking, they'll want to ask me questions about my mother, and why my mother isn't with me, and about Jesse Nash and that policeman White, and what I think about everything. I don't know *what* I think. I'd cry, that's all I'd do, it wouldn't be phony but it would look phony and I couldn't stand having people think that. I'd be all tongue-tied and, no, I won't do it. If you order me, if it's either do what you say or give all this up, then I'll give all this up. I mean that, Warren. I honest and truly mean that."

"No one orders you to do anything," Weber said, and needed a full week of lavish displays of understanding and tenderness, of loving her in bed and telling her he loved her, to get her to agree to let Ronnie Haley pull out all the stops.

On the morning of the day she was to fly to Chicago to open at the elegant Prentiss Room and also tape her first panel appearance on "Paul's Place," a hugely popular television talk show that was seen in thirty-eight states, Weber discovered he could not go with her because a 103° fever had hit Phil Simms and the New York shop could not go unattended. He arranged for Jeanne Prescott to fly with her and stay with her until he could join her. Robin wanted to cancel the trip, but he rushed to her apartment, where he soothed her and promised to take her and Jeanne to the airport. That was the morning, as she dressed, that they carefully went over every question she could conceivably be asked and the answers she would give.

"What are your opinions on Jesse Nash, who appears to view the case of your brother's death as his own personal crusade?" asked Weber, playing Paul Rand, the Chicago columnist who hosted "Paul's Place."

For the fourth time since they had started, Robin balked. "Do I have to talk about him?"

" 'I appreciate . . .' " Weber patiently prompted.

"I appreciate the efforts of everyone interested in seeing justice done," she parroted, and recited the rest of the generalized answer he had prepared for her. It went fine, and the show would go fine, he assured her, and then he asked, as Warren Weber, how well she really knew Jesse Nash.

Unexpected anger flashed. "I've talked enough about Jesse Nash!" she snapped.

The sharp retort was puzzling because the anger was inappropriate. "What gets your back up every time his name is mentioned?"

"Nothing!"

"I'd call it a fair question," he said cautiously. "When we go to the nit-grit, Robin, when we tell each other things about ourselves, I always come away with the stubborn suspicion that there are important little items you leave out. Maybe not purposely, but you do hold things back."

Defensively, even waspishly, she turned on him. "Look who's talking about secrets! I ask you about your wife, your family, and you back away, you act like they're in some special gold case, do not disturb, like they're nobody's business but yours."

"That's a strident voice, Robin."

"You bet it is, you just better believe it's supposed to be! You sit up there on that high mountain and you make me sick!"

"You're all wound up because of Chicago. You wouldn't be behaving like a fishwife otherwise." He touched her arm and she sprang away, as though burned. "This is no way for us to separate, dear," he said. "Come here. Let me hold you."

"No! Leave me alone! If you're going to take me to the airport, then go downstairs and wait in the car. If you don't want to do that, then I'll ride a bus or something."

"I don't have any car to wait in," said Weber, sorry he had hit a nerve on a day that was surely nerve-jangling enough for her, yet amused by her little-girl tantrum. "Rudi parked me here to go and collect Jeanne. It's cold outside. Would you want it on your conscience that you put me out in the snow up to my crotch?" There had been no snow in Manhattan for nearly a month.

"Don't talk dirty! Just get out of my bedroom!" she cried. Chuckling, Weber went into the living room, where he drank some Scotch he had brought to her weeks ago and which she had not touched, using it to wash down a Dexie. Mel had given him rigid orders against Dexies, even after the last physical, two weeks before. What the hell did Mel know?

Rudi called from the lobby to say he was back and that Miss Prescott was in the car. "Come up and get Miss Hamilton's bags," Weber instructed, resigned for the time being to the fact that Robin wanted no hired servants, although he had done his best to insist that she have at least one, if only to carry her luggage; her curious explanation was that she wouldn't feel right giving orders to a Negro servant and certainly wasn't ready to give orders to a white one. Weber had offered to dig up an Apache, a mulatto, and an albino for her to pick from. She hadn't liked the joke.

She emerged from the bedroom, chic in a simple sheer wool no-color dress, regally pulling on gloves, groomed and coiffeured to perfection, looking like a natural-born queen with the kingdom's loveliest face, firmest bust, and shapeliest legs. She greeted little, impassive Rudi as he fetched her luggage, but she ostentatiously ignored Weber until the chauffeur preceded them out of the apartment. Weber helped her into the Autumn Haze mink he had directed Jeanne to buy for her, and said, "I know I'm a ruffian beyond belief, but will you at least give me a hearty handshake ere we part?"

She seemed to be struggling to keep her eyes trained away from him, but then she looked at him, and he was smiling, and she burst out laughing. They were in the apartment foyer and the front door was open, but she willingly entered his arms, and not even their bulky coats could impede the fluidity of their embrace and surprisingly prolonged kiss. "Come get me soon, darling," she whispered.

"I feel you're not leaving me with much of an alternative."

"Is that what you feel? Guess what I feel," she said, still whispering, and pressed the heel of her hand to the covered bulge of him. "Can I take this with me to Chicago and sleep with it till you come for me?"

"Robin . . ."

"Oh, gee," said Robin, the little girl again, and quickly searched the entire foyer for the purse she had placed on the bureau right next to the door. "Let's go. Let's go now, or I'll miss the next fifty flights to Chicago."

Jeanne sat in the Cadillac's jump seat on the way to Kennedy. Weber and Robin sat in the back. The talk was pleasant, trivial, strained. At the terminal, as Rudi hurried off to a reservations window, as Jeanne scooped up an armful of magazines at a newsstand, Robin complained, "What gets into me?"

"Not I," said Weber, wishing he had not given up smoking cigarettes.

"That kind of talk, back in the apartment, I mean," she said. "That you-feel-I-feel kind of talk. It's the way bums talk. I hate it when I talk like a bum." The waiting room was bustling with people. She looked at him and said, "I wish everybody here would suddenly disappear right this second. I want you so much, Warren. It's not just sex, I—oh, darn it, yes it's the sex, I'm dying for us to do it, but it's—I mean it's more than that, I want you right this second so much that I want to say it's impossible to love you any more than I do but I want to show you I—oh damn you it's your fault I sound like some sort of a lunatic, all I mean—"

"Hey, there, Warren!" they heard. They turned and Weber recognized Jack Dickson, dapper as always, the good-guy older brother of the lousy guy Marty Dickson. It was an evil moment to be interrupted, and they grinned and greeted each other and shook hands, and the evil moment became a bewildering moment because Robin was instantly stark and embarrassed and because Dickson, whose terrain was the West Coast and who had no reason to know Robin, obviously knew her and said, his smile broad, "And hello,

Miss Hamilton. You've certainly come up in the world, haven't you?"

"You two know each other?" Weber asked.

Robin nodded, seemingly preparing to stammer something, and Jack Dickson said, "Some time ago, yes, in passing, you might say. Which one of you is flying to Chicago, or are you both going?" he asked, pointing to the door ahead of them. "There's where I'm headed, and I could use some company."

The announcement for boarding was made as Weber replied, "Miss Hamilton is going, with Jeanne Prescott," and beckoned to Jeanne. "You know Jeanne, don't you, Jack?"

"I certainly do," Dickson declared, and kissed Jeanne's cheek. Weber motioned that he wanted a moment with Robin, and Dickson said, "Of course. I'll be talking with you," and walked through the door.

"How do you two know each other?" Weber asked Robin.

"We met in California a few years ago," she replied, and he glowered at the way she said it, which was nervous and unreal. "Just once."

"When were you in California?"

"A few years ago," she repeated, and seemed anxious to leave, not so much to board the plane as to escape last-second questions. "I'll talk with you on the phone, all right?" she said, and moved much too rapidly through the door.

Weber took Jeanne's arm. "Listen in," he ordered. "Find out what gives and call me at the office the instant she's in another room."

On the ride from Kennedy to East 60th, he spoke memos into the rear-seat Dictaphone but kept seeing Dickson, kept seeing Dickson's white body and Robin's caramel body rolling together a few years ago. A few years ago. Robin had been one year old, a few years ago. Robin hadn't known anyone, hadn't learned to wave bye-bye or say Ma-ma and Da-da, hadn't had teeth or hair or eyes or soul or gender till Weber had found her on the *Stalwart*. So what was with California? What was with Dickson?

He had nothing against Jack Dickson, an intelligent, nose-to-the-grindstone man caught in the money trap and loyalty trap of helping to orchestrate the career and kiss the keester of his trillionaire brother Marty Dickson, whom Weber loathed with a consummate, articulate, singularly pure loathing.

What was Robin's embarrassment all about?

No, thought Weber, forcibly brushing the filthy pictures away. No. I was her first white man, her very first.

Eight

THE JET TO CHICAGO took off exactly on time. Robin held her breath until she was airborne, hating flying as much as ever, vowing she would never fly again. She was polite to Jack Dickson, handsome, attentive, his close-cropped hair grayer than it had been two years ago, polite because he had been polite to her in Hollywood and because she sensed he was as decent a man now as he had been then, but she was careful to say as little as possible without sounding rude or, worse, indifferent. She asked about his brother. Marty, he said, was fighting a maybe losing battle with arthritis—don't breathe this to a soul—an implausible and cruel disease to visit on someone thirty-eight years old, but otherwise Prince Marty was going great guns, bigger and better than ever. Robin asked about Jack Dickson's wife—what was her name? Stella?

"Estelle. We're divorced now."

She told him, when he asked, that she and Miss Prescott would be staying at The Prentiss, but made a point of adding that she would be up to her ears in work from the time she stepped off this plane till the time she boarded another one.

"I'll be at Executive House," he said. "That's only blocks from The Prentiss. I'll be busy, too, but if you have a sudden yen to see the sights, just pick up the phone."

A limousine and reporters met Robin and Jeanne at O'Hare. Robin, donning dark glasses and a fixed smile, spoke as an animated automaton, as Warren and Danny had trained her. "I adore Chicago!" she exclaimed and, at Jeanne's subtle signal, showed a discreet-saucy few inches above the knee. "I've never understood why they call it the Second City. I'd call it the First. The First even before the First."

Flowers were waiting in wasteful, copious abundance when she and Jeanne were shown into the wide, high Prentiss suite. Robin dropped her Autumn Haze, her heart beating fast, and asked Jeanne Prescott, "What if no one comes to the opening?"

"That's not too likely," Jeanne answered. "The first two shows are sold out."

The dozens of people involved in putting the Prentiss Room opening together—from the club's manager to the men in the orchestra—were friendly and unhurried, and the rehearsal and the first show in the spacious, glass-walled room went extremely well; the applause was generous, the compliments wonderfully flowery. Robin phoned Warren and told him how nicely she had been received, but, when he asked about Jack Dickson and California, she grew impatient because the whole story would have taken too long to tell. "I've met a lot of people, and Mr. Dickson is one of them," she said, aware that it was a silly answer. Warren seemed to think so, too, for he wanted to know more. "I'll tell you everything when you get here," she promised, certain she would not.

"Okay, Madame X, lady of intrigue and mystery," sighed Warren. "I may find out you were a rumrunner and a bag woman and an ax murderess and your name is really Typhoid Mary. But in the meantime, I miss you like crazy."

"I miss you, too, darling darling darling. I mean that."

Replacing the receiver, she wondered, as she had wondered since Guadeloupe, why she hadn't told him everything, the entire story, in the first place. Now it gets more complicated, she thought. He'll find out about Jesse, everybody will, and that means explaining all the more.

Before the second show Jeanne brought the morning papers, and together they glowed over the Prentiss Room ads. Warren, or someone, had gone all out: the *Chicago Sun-Times* carried a full-page ad with a head and shoulders and decolleté shot of Robin, the name "Robin" in bold letters and the name "Hamilton" in small, and nice things *Variety* and the *New York Times* had written about her quoted below. "Now do you believe you're in business?" Jeanne teased.

"I'm trying to," Robin affirmed, liking her; at the beginning and for some weeks after, Jeanne Prescott had been rather stiff, a bit distant, but gradually the thaw had come and the affection was real. "It still isn't easy. This picture isn't me, but I guess it is."

"It is, honey lamb. It sure is."

Several pages beyond, there was a photograph of Stuart Curtiss White, and Robin, jolted as she always was when she came upon his name, reflected on how relieving yet how odd it was that she had never seen this terrible man in person. The small item beneath the picture said that he had joined the national office of Soul of America, the controversial, patriotic, educational organization headed by wealthy pharmaceuticals manufacturer Willard Chase Cunningham of Helena, Montana. Part of the article quoted a statement by Willard Cunningham: "Mr. White is a welcome addition to SOA and we are most fortunate in having him with us. A Christian, an American, an exemplary husband and father, he has been vilified, crucified on the altar of foreign ideology, left to see his name destroyed because he stubbornly rejects the sin which is atheistic leftism. We are dedicated to not permitting that to happen."

At the "Paul's Place" taping two afternoons later, Robin, scared despite the tranquilizer Jeanne had fed her, met Paul Rand, a gentle man with the face of a wrinkled teenager, and the other guests who would be on the two-hour show: Johnny Wood, the tap dancer who looked half his fifty-seven years because he lived on health foods and had never eaten butter, which was the direct cause of at least eight major diseases; Bruno Eisendorf, a former university professor of ethics, now a motion picture producer and director, who was in Chicago to plug his new movie, *Lust for Three;* Porter Blair, star of the wacky television series "Frontier

Freud" and a staunch advocate of ending the military draft; and Frieda Monroe, a psychic who had accurately predicted the outcomes of the last three presidential elections, each within 50,000 votes, and who had helped the Chicago Police Department solve a number of murders. The guests sat around a square table. Paul Rand didn't get to Robin until the show was half over, chiefly because Eisendorf and Wood hogged much of the conversation and because she was quite content to keep silent. When Mr. Rand did get to her, after he asked her how she liked being the most prominent singing star of the season, and after he identified her as the sister of Roland Lee Hamilton, he momentarily stupified her with a question Warren had not anticipated: "What are your feelings about the report the other day that Office White has teamed up with Soul of America?"

"I—to be truthful, I don't know very much at all about Soul of America, except that it's supposed to be—well, what's it called? Right wing? I don't know anything about politics," she replied, amazed that her voice sounded so steady.

Luckily, Porter Blair, who sat beside her, jumped in with an impassioned attack on Soul of America. "You may want to cut this out of the tape, Paul," he declared, "but I've watched those buzzards up close, and a better name for Soul of America would be Soul of Fascism. It sells bigotry, ignorance, fear, distrust, and has absolutely nothing constructive to offer, and if this guy Stuart White's connected himself with it, he's either mighty hungry or he's got some bigotry of his own on the brain. I suspect it's both, don't you, Miss Hamilton?" Johnny Wood said, "Now hold your horses a minute, Porter. I'm a liberal just like you, but aren't you liberals the ones who're always hollering, 'Don't judge anybody till the facts are in'? Till we know just—" Porter Blair said, "If a fish smells bad, you can be pretty sure it's a bad fish. SOA—" Paul Rand said, "Easy, gentlemen. You're not letting Miss Hamilton speak." They said they were sorry. The focus was squarely on Robin, and she scrambled to recall sentences or even wisps of sentences Warren had drilled into her. "I really can't say much on the subject yet," she announced weakly. "I—well, for the time being, I'd rather not discuss it."

She did discuss Roland Lee, briefly, at different times during the remainder of the taping, because she was asked to and because there was no way to avoid it. She remembered him as a good, shy, kind boy, and recalled how proud he had made Mama by mastering the multiplication table when he was seven years old, and prayed she wouldn't look or sound weepy, and then she confided to Paul Rand at a break that she didn't want to talk any more about Roland Lee. He nodded and the show eventually ended: Mr. Rand thanked her for being a charming guest, and, in the corridor, Porter Blair told her he was stopping at The Prentiss, too, and maybe they could have a drinkie before he left town. "Maybe," she said.

The show was emotionally exhausting but Jeanne, who never flattered falsely, assured her Mr. Rand had been right, that she *had* been charming. "Warren and Ronnie would've liked you to do more with the civil rights stuff, but you were better this way," she maintained. "The others were so windy, you were refreshing. You came across real and genuine. And, damn you, you may show up like Dracula's grandpa when they run the tape tonight, but there in the studio you looked like a dream."

"I was so nervous!" Robin squealed. "I'm all right when I'm singing at a microphone, but that thing just about killed me."

"It didn't come through, which is what's important."

Warren phoned and promised he would be in Chicago before the week was out. Jack Dickson phoned and invited her to dinner. She thanked him and explained that she hadn't a free minute. Porter Blair phoned and reminded her of their drinkie date. "What time do you finish work tonight?" he asked. "About one o'clock," she answered. "Then why don't we watch Paul's show together?" he suggested. "It plays between twelve-thirty and half-past two. We could see at least half of it."

"Who else will be watching at that time of night?" she asked, sure that he wanted to sleep with her and, remarkably, aware that the prospect interested her.

"Probably two insomniacs and four burglars."

"And all your fans."

"No, I'm including all my fans," he said, and she laughed. "So what do you say? I'm in 3007 and I'll be having a small party here."

"Well . . . all right, it's a date," she agreed and was unaccountably relieved to hear later that Jeanne would be out on the town tonight with an old beau from Evanston and wouldn't be able to watch the show with her. She bathed for her own show, and marveled at how persistently she was holding onto the fantasy of sleeping with Porter Blair, whom she had often seen on television and whom she had barely met. I went to bed with those other men between Jesse and Warren because I didn't have a Jesse or a Warren to love me, she thought. Now I have Warren. At least I think I do. I love him. At least I think I do.

I think. I'm not sure. And maybe that's what's wrong, maybe that's why I'm supposed to be walking on air and I'm not. I don't have Warren Weber, not really, and I never will have. Because he's married. Because he's a king-size riddle.

Because he's white.

Because he's white, thought Robin Hamilton, and no white man will love me for long.

Which is no excuse for Porter Blair, for being intimate with him, which of course I won't be, and maybe I will, maybe I just will. He's not even all that attractive—he can't be more than thirty but there's a kind of prissy something about him, and he's losing his hair. Still, he wants me, and—

Stop it, she told herself sharply. Stop acting like a bum. There's no reason to any more.

Jesse had called her some terrible names, but never a bum. I wasn't one while there was Jesse, she thought. When he sent me that money in Philadelphia—was it only two years ago?—when I left Chick and Cousin Bea to go to him in California, I was still a good girl, sort of. . . .

The shabbiness of her coat and suitcase embarrassed Robin, much more now as she came off the plane in Los Angeles than when she had boarded in the East. But Jesse Nash, looking marvelously successful, squeezed her moist hand and seemed entirely approving.

"How'd they treat you up there?" he inquired.

"Hello," she said, hoping she didn't look quite as out of place as she felt. "I'm never going up again in one of those things, I can promise you that, not a million dollars."

"First flight?" he asked, and nodded for a porter—a white porter—to take her suitcase.

"Uh-huh, and the last. We had those—what do you call them?—air pockets, and I thought I'd jump out of my skin."

"Next time you fly, I'll see to it that air pockets are made illegal," he said. "Come on. Car's over this way."

The car was a beauty, big and new and shiny, and her eyes widened. "Snappy, huh?" he remarked, opening the door for her. The porter put her bag in the rear seat and Jesse Nash gave him some money. "Very," Robin agreed in a weak voice, dazzled by the rushing realities of the big car, by her first palm tree, by a January that was hot, by the expensive sports clothes Jesse Nash was wearing, by the absolute fact that she actually was here.

"I would've given it to the junkman by now, but I'm waitin' for the ash tray to get full."

"Is it really yours?"

"Well, in a manner of speakin'. Marty Dickson runs a kind of free rent-a-car service. He owns nineteen of these babies, and anyone on the payroll who wants to get somewhere just pretty much helps himself."

"I'm awfully impressed."

"You and me both, ma'am. You and me both."

On the brightly sunny ride away from the airport, with no idea of where they were headed, Robin thanked him for having come to her rescue and congratulated him on his success. "Don't call it that yet," he corrected, driving easily through relatively easy traffic. "I have a ways to go. I did an LP that could fall on its face, and so could I. But I *am* opening at a ritzy club tonight, and I got to admit I wasn't driving any Impalas when I met you at Rigley's."

"I think it's wonderful, what's happened. You must be terrific or Marty Dickson wouldn't be so excited about you."

"Oh, I'm terrific, all right," he said, grinning, and then, speaking casually but as though ready to burst with good news, told her good news. Jack Dickson, Marty's brother—business manager, bottle washer, and occasional talent scout—had caught Jesse Nash's act in Omaha and had that night made a firm offer: an all-expenses-paid trip to the Coast to repeat his act for Marty. If Marty was half as enthusiastic as Jack, a contract with Dickson Enterprises would be immediately signed and sealed; if not, there would be a thousand-dollar guarantee for the time spent. Marty had flipped. The comedy album Jesse Nash had cut for Dickson Enterprises' own record company was called *Color Me Colored*, and it was about to come out. It was being pushed hard in general by Dickson Enterprises and harder by Marty Dickson in particular, even though it contained essentially the same material Jesse Nash had been paid peanuts to use in one sewery joint after another over the country. Marty, an always-on comic who was a perennial hit in pictures, television, and cabarets but who was big enough, man enough, to share a spotlight, was taking him to parties and loudly raving for anyone who would listen (and everyone listened to Marty) that Jesse Nash had a whizbang of a future ahead of him. Marty had arranged for him to open tonight at Phideau's, a class club on the Strip. Marty was going to have him do a featured spot on his television show next week. Marty was taking him to Miami Beach in the next couple of weeks to open there with him. Marty was talking about putting Nash in pictures.

"I could be wrong, but I don't guess I'll need my tin cup for at least a week," he said drily.

Robin, never seated this close to success before, strove to control her giddiness. "Marty Dickson must be a wonderful man. I've seen him on television a lot, and in the movies, and he can always make me laugh. Is he like that in person?"

"More or less. Yeah, he's funny. Hey, I'm a fine one! I've been blattin' on so much about myself. Let's talk about you. Bring me up to date on what's been doin'. I couldn't follow you so good on the telephone. All I knew was you were hurtin'."

She paused. "Can I tell you everything later?"

"Sure. Why not?"

"I'm awfully nervous, Mr. Nash, and not just from the airplane trip. I never dreamed I'd be in *Hollywood*, and riding in a big car like this, and with *you*. I'm just praying I won't embarrass you in any way. Where are we going?"

"There's this little shanty I had set up for you. You can stay there for a time till we figure out what to do with you."

The spectacular hotel was named The Starfire, and Robin remained speechless in the spectacular lobby and spectacular elevator and for moments after she entered the spectacular hotel room that he insisted was hers. It was one of the half-dozen rooms and suites at The Starfire that Dickson Enterprises paid for the year round whether occupied or not, he explained; he had told Jack Dickson that she was coming, and Jack had ordered him to bring her here. When the white bellhop left, she apologized for her cheap clothes and ugly suitcase and confessed that she'd felt like a washwoman in the lobby full of swanky people. "Too bad about those swanky people," Jesse Nash scoffed. "You pick out the ones that glanced at you snooty and I'll have them dispossessed. Look, you want to fresh up and change. I'll head on back to my digs— I'm right down the hall, in 12-A—and you phone me when you feel like it."

Scared, she hastily said, "No—please don't go. Unless you have something to do, I mean . . . I don't want to be alone."

It was a dumb kid thing to say in daylight, but she watched his eyes narrow in understanding, and she stood immobile, at the broad window that overlooked a mammoth swimming pool, until he had lit a cigarette and settled into the blond armchair near the bed. The drapes were partially drawn, yet there were sun patches on the gold carpet. He was looking at her, waiting for her to talk.

His patient, steady attention told her to begin, but there was no right place to begin, not in this rich room so far away from home. Hold me, she wanted to say, comfort me, make me safe.

But there was no way to say it, and so Robin sat on the bed and told him the story that started with Pete Gumbo and ended with Chick Russell. She tried to tell it without calls for pity or blame, and she was warmed by the extent of his patience and the concerned questions he interrupted with, by his telling her he had attempted to reach her as soon as he'd read about her brother in the paper. When she was done, and he had shaken his head in disgust and cursed Gumbo and all the Gumbos in the world, she wanted, needed, this strong and good man to rise and touch her, to kiss her lips sweetly and assure her she would never have to be scared again.

He didn't. He continued to sit, as though waiting for her to give him some sign. The sun patches were retreating and this strong and good man, who had invited her at Rigley's Lounge to be his girl friend in California, had her in California now and was waiting for her to make the first move. "I'm grateful to you," Robin affirmed, smiling wanly and carefully crossing her legs. "Starting now, I'm going to stop acting like a sad sack. Nobody likes a sad sack."

"Oh, I do," he kidded. "Whether I'd want any kid of mine to marry one's a different matter, but the best friends I got are sad sacks." Then he sat forward. "Say, you want to go out and see a little of L.A.? I don't have to show up at the club for a couple hours yet."

He wasn't catching on, and Robin was surprised that a gentleman swinger like Jesse Nash was being so slow on the uptake. The hem of her dress came back slightly and a little less discreetly, and her look became serious and she said, in a smoky voice that was not hers, "Wouldn't you rather—stay?"

"Ma'am?" he asked, the eyes narrowing again.

"You paid for me to come three thousand miles. It's only right I do something for you besides cry over myself." She couldn't look at him any more, and all the dirty, unloving hands on her made the thought of sex repellent, but she found the courage to ask, "Do you want to—make love?"

Jesse Nash cleared his throat. "Let me get this straight," he said carefully. "You sittin' there dyin' for my body?"

She blinked. "I thought . . . Well, I want to show my appreciation . . ."

The quiet word seemed to quietly outrage him. "Your mama called you a whore. Was she right?"

"Mr. Nash . . ."

"Don't you talk slutty to me again," he warned. "You got no respect for yourself? Then have some for me. You had my mouth waterin' for you that night at Rigley's and it's still waterin', but if the two of us hit the hay together, it won't be because somebody owes a bill. You dig?"

Robin nodded, mortified, and instinctively uncrossed her legs.

"That's good. That's very, very good. We got to get you some clothes, that's the first thing on the menu. You go fresh up now and we'll go pick you out a dress somewhere."

"You don't have to spend any money on—"

"I don't have to do anything," he broke in, and got up. "Nobody has to do anything they don't want to do. Have your shower bath and call me when you're ready."

He left the room without looking back.

A shamefully expensive Moygashel was bought, and some other too-expensive clothes over her gasping, palm-to-her-mouth objections, and she went with him that night to Phideau's, a glossy, chromey nightclub that was a million miles and a million years removed from Rigley's Lounge in Harlem and that had a big photograph of Jesse Nash near the canopied entrance. Tonight was a very special night, he dourly admitted in his dressing room. He puttered at his mirrored image with an unwavering steadiness that was too extreme to be anything but nervousness; Robin, dressed for the opening in the Moygashel, sat and sewed a cuff button he had pulled off his white dinner jacket. You didn't play Phideau's unless you were somebody, he said, somehow more to himself than to Robin. Dickson Enterprises controlled fifty-one per cent of Phideau's. Marty Dickson had personally engineered tonight, had personally generated the excitement in this unexcitable town. The club was sold out tonight because of Marty's newspaper and trade paper ads, because Marty had personally called the columnists, because Marty had personally goosed the important people into viewing tonight's opening as an event.

For the fourth—or was it fifth?—time in the hour they'd been here, Jesse Nash abruptly charged to the bathroom that adjoined the dressing room, and Robin heard the lock on the door click after him.

This time the dressing room door opened and the bushy-haired man she immediately recognized as Marty Dickson stalked in without knocking, called, "*Oy Jesseleh!*" looked around, saw her, and grinned. "You're not Jesseleh, are you? No, *you're* not Jesseleh!"

The thread and needle dropped. "You're Marty Dickson . . ."

"Last time I looked," he nodded and paced, snapping his fingers, this famous Marty Dickson with the large green eyes and jutting jaw, shorter than he seemed on the screen, maybe forty years old instead of the thirty he seemed on the screen, not at all handsome but immediately electric, thoroughly alive. "Now, don't just sit there, honey. Bow down and tell me twenty times how great I am. Or I'll settle for knowing where the star is and you can bow down later. Is he here or did he chicken out and head back for the plantation?"

Scrambling to retrieve the thread and needle, she pointed to the bathroom, wondering if she should apologize for being here. "He'll be right out, Mr. Dickson," she said, doing her best to sound poised. "I'm—very pleased to meet you."

He wouldn't stop pacing, wouldn't stop snapping his fingers. "Yep, yep, yep. What's your name, honey?" he asked, pausing only to screw a cigarette into a holder.

"Robin Hamilton."

"Robin. My favorite bird, next to the albatross." Her eyebrows lifted. "That's the bird I keep around my neck for kicks. Too bad Jess saw you first—I'd like you around my neck and then *you'd* be my favorite bird." He grinned and lit the cigarette. Robin didn't grin back. She couldn't decide how to act.

Jesse Nash appeared, dressed for the show except for the white jacket, and his normally expressionless face brightened a bit. He extended his hand and said, "Well, there's the man now." Dickson, a full head shorter, seized his hand but instead of shaking it suddenly began to wrestle with him, ferocious-ape-playfully, and then vigorously waltzed him around the room, singing "I'm in Love with Vienna" in a shrill soprano. Robin laughed, in embarrassed surprise as much as appreciation. Jesse Nash, freeing himself, smiled but, oddly, seemed a trifle irritated. "Leggo, Daddy," he directed. "I promised this dance to Grammaw here." He straightened his sleeves and introduced Robin.

"We just met," she acknowledged in a soft, timid voice and finally smiled, a timid but welcoming smile. "But hello again, Mr. Dickson."

"Hello again, Robin-Bobbin," said Marty Dickson, and, to Jesse Nash, "How they hangin', white hope? Off-white? Off-off-white? Need anything?"

"No, can't say's I do. I'm a touch more jittery than an old warhorse like me oughta be, but I'll get by."

"You'll mutilate 'em," Marty Dickson proclaimed, fingers snapping. "I'll be back after the first show. I just wanted to see how you're holding up. Cream of the crop's out front."

"Yeah, I wish you would come back. Let me know what places I laid down and died."

"Don't lay odds I won't, sweetheart." Robin was aware of the man surveying her. "What about Robin Bobbin here? Where's she seeing the act?"

"We'll find her a place somewhere."

"You bet your blue booties we will," Mr. Dickson said loudly, and his full attention made her uncomfortable. "She'll sit with me and my party, ringside, all agreed? Yep, it's all agreed!" He checked his wristwatch. "I gotta git now. You should *see* the class at my table tonight! You ready? Abe Weinfarb—how does that grab you? Abe Weinfarb, only a California State Supreme Court judge! Only hobnobs with the intellectual elite—they'll eat any-thing—only judges and deep thinkers, and he and his missus, they're *our* guests tonight!" To Robin he declared, "When it's time, Robin Bobbin, have somebody bring you to our table—they all know me here." He bear-hugged Jesse Nash and declared, "You'll mutilate 'em, blackjack baby, *mutilate* 'em!" To Robin he declared, "Snap it up with the star's button, honey. You're keeping history waiting."

He marched out of the dressing room, singing in the shrill so-prano, "Every time I tint my hair, I dye a little . . ."

Jesse Nash, no longer smiling, was shaking his head.

"Whew," said Robin.

Jesse nodded.

"Is he always like that?"

"No, usually he's pretty lively." The button was sewn and he took the jacket. "Go sit with him. It'll be all right—he behaves when his wife's on deck and she's on deck tonight—but don't sit right next to him. In the dark, Charley'll find a way to climb up your leg."

"Charley? You—"

"Charley, Marty, what's the difference?" Jesse Nash snapped and donned the jacket. "They're all honks. They're all swell fellas, give you their eye teeth, and where black women are concerned they're all honks. Don't pay me mind, doll—the butterflies are ridin' herd. Scat. I'll see you later."

"Well . . ." Robin began, tentatively rising.

"What we'll do, we'll arrange some way for you to get back safe to the hotel, and maybe I'll peek in on you. I won't be leavin' here till two or thereabouts, and that's late."

"I don't mind wait—"

"You want to bug me?" he snapped. "Do what I tell you."

"All right," she said. "I— Well, good luck tonight."

"Yeah."

A waiter escorted her to a long, crowded table near the stage, and Marty Dickson jumped up to bear-hug her and introduce her to the well-dressed party of, at swift count, a dozen people as Jesse's lady friend Robin Goldberg. She felt strange, uneasy, inexplicably unwelcome, in spite of his smiling liveliness, in spite of his drawing attention from nearby tables by whistling between his teeth and calling to a waiter for a chair for Miss Robin Goldberg.

She heard only a few of the names at the all-white table. Here was Mrs. Dickson, a surprisingly unglamorous, surprisingly plain but smiling lady. Here was his brother Jack, older, huskier, more serious and better looking than he, and Jack Dickson's wife, a stunning, frozen-faced young woman with albino hair. She heard the name of Judge Weinfarb of the California State Supreme Court, and retained the name only because Marty Dickson, bobbing up and down, unable to sit still, pointedly repeated it twice within a minute. Long after she was seated, she tried to unfreeze her own smile, and failed. No one seemed to be making a point of ignoring her, but no one paid much attention to her, which both relieved and disturbed her. Even Marty Dickson turned away, though she caught him from time to time eyeing her with a peculiar scrutiny. He kept snapping his fingers and exclaiming, "Sensational! That black cat's gonna be sensational!" She agreed to a ginger ale with lemon peel when somebody, Jack Dickson, asked her if she would have a drink, and wondered why it was necessary for Marty Dickson, in the dressing room and here, to refer so often to Jesse Nash's color. There was certainly nothing mean about it, of course, nothing unfriendly. His closest friend, the columnists were always writing, was Coley Dennis, the famous entertainer, and Coley Dennis was black. But what was the point of all those references?

Then the nightclub's overhead lights suddenly dimmed, drums

rolled, and Marty Dickson scampered, to applause, to the microphone and told a string of gags in a hurry and gave Jesse Nash a
grand, warm introduction. The applause was great because he
whistled between his teeth and ordered it, and then Jesse Nash
shambled out. He seemed startled that Mr. Dickson took him in his
arms and pretended to kiss him passionately, but for only a moment, and then Mr. Dickson stepped out of the spotlight and Jesse
Nash stepped into it.

After a nervous, faltering first minute, he found his stride. He
got the audience and held them. Robin expected he would merely
touch on race as a topic because this was Phideau's, not Rigley's
Lounge, and at least ninety-five per cent of the audience was
white. She was wrong. He talked about politics, and people in the
news, and rich people, and poor people, and he was funny, but he
spoke as a black man, a quietly seething black man telling the
white folks, with jokes, what was wrong with them. Robin was
uncomfortable. The audience was laughing and was with him, even
as he rubbed their noses in his charges of inequality and dishonesty,
and in the darkness of the room she could see Marty Dickson
beam, yet she felt she belonged anywhere but here, felt the audience was looking at her and accusing her of subscribing to all the
insults that were being tossed so easily from the microphone.

The acceptance of Jesse Nash grew, and he was on for more
than half an hour. The final applause was spontaneous and, here
and there, thunderous, even after the lights went up and he shambled off. The guests at Mr. Dickson's table were clapping hard and
loud, all of them except Jack Dickson's frozen-faced wife, who
clapped, Robin observed, because Jack Dickson nudged her hard
and angrily with his elbow. "What'd I tell ya, what'd I tell ya?"
Marty Dickson cried enthusiastically, jumping up and away from
the table to hop to another table and another, pausing at each to
bear-hug and kiss and slap shoulders. "Oh, the wildest, sensational!" he bleated, back for an instant, and ran in the direction of
the dressing room, weaving in and out of the narrow aisles. Jack
Dickson excused himself and followed him.

"Your name isn't really Goldberg, is it?" asked Jack Dickson's wife, one dark eyebrow cocked.

The sudden attention startled Robin, but she formed the awkward smile again. "Oh, no," she replied. "That's Mr. Dickson's sense of humor. I'm Robin Hamilton."

The young woman nodded. "Yes, my brother-in-law sure has a sense of humor. Everybody around here's got humor. Mr. Nash—it's Nash, isn't it?—he's got humor, too. What are you, his girl friend? His wife?"

"Friend."

"Good. Let's everybody be friendly. Let's all sit together at the same table and everybody in the world be friends." She pondered her drink, and suddenly Robin realized that the unfriendly young woman with the albino hair was a little drunk, maybe a lot.

Robin waited for Jesse Nash to send for her, to come to her. He was the only person in the world she trusted.

Robin went to the dressing room but stayed in the background for more than an hour as people, singly and in pairs and clusters, drifted in and out with congratulations and suggestions, as a solemn Jack Dickson sat in a corner and wrote continuously on a long yellow pad, as a tobacco-chewing man took random, candid snapshots of Jesse Nash, as Marty Dickson danced about, as most of the people were eventually cleared out and Marty Dickson hit Jesse Nash on the back and barked cheerfully, "Come on, come on, sweetheart, don't sit there like a stick. Move *around!* Look *alive!* What the hell's the matter, you rupture yourself out there?"

"I guess I'm still a little numb. I feel like I'm just home from diggin' the Suez Canal with my teeth. I need a breather."

"Breathe later, you *schlemiel!* I can't understand you! The *woods* are on fire!"

"I'd rather hear what I loused up."

Marty Dickson ceased his excited pacing, sighed, winked at Robin, and shrugged. "Prima donnas we got here already," he complained, without bite, and took five minutes to evaluate the act, remembering all the major jokes and where they had been situated. He explained why bad timing had made one joke fail and why smart timing had made another one click. He analyzed the act as though he knew every word of it by heart, and at moments of seemingly deepest concentration his eyes suddenly found Robin's body and fastened on it for long seconds at a time. The act's analysis wrapped up, his fingers started snapping again and he said, "You'll have it all worked out for the second show. By to-morrow night you'll be clean as a whistle, right? Right!" He fired up his thousandth cigarette. "Now Ah saddle Ol' Paint and go home to beddy-bye. You're on Easy Street now, sweetheart, but I gotta get up early and go out and make a buck." He directed himself to the outline of Robin's breasts. "Take good care of Hot Lips here, Robin Bobbin," he said. "A month from today, he's gonna own this whole cockeyed business." His grin was broad and he scampered out.

Jesse Nash looked sullen.

"Who's the sad sack now?" Robin teased. "This is the biggest night of your life, of anybody's life, and you're acting all gloomy."

"I know," he agreed, nodding, inspecting the coal of his cig-arette. "All I keep thinkin' is, I'm beholden to that white man. I'm not proud of myself, but that's all I keep thinkin'."

"But he's doing so much for you!"

He nodded again, vigorously now. "Sure is, sure is, no argument. He's treated me straight, right from the beginning, knocked him-self out to build me up, more than any guy's ever done, black or white. So why can't I relax and groove with him, let him know he's a great guy? He wants me to say thanks. He doesn't say so in so many words, but that's his right and why can't I say it?"

He paused. "Because he's white. Damn me, because he's white. Makes no sense. Looks from here like I *am* going to be a big shot, and I owe it to Marty Dickson, and I hold back from showing him I like him. I hold back because he's white."

Robin said nothing.

"Marty didn't bring my people here on slave boats. Marty didn't have my granddaddy lynched in Texas because my granddaddy was an uppity nigger who rapped at the wrong doors, callin' for better than outhouse schooling for black kids."

He looked up, and at her. "Makes no sense. And I can't help myself." His chair made a scraping sound as he rose, and for a moment Robin thought he was going to break down, thought he was going to embrace her and start to weep. He didn't. He smiled, a vague, sad smile, and said, "I'll look in on you at the hotel, okay? Marty's brother Jack offered to drop you off—the Starfire's on the way to his house. Estelle, that's his missus, the one with the Swansdown Flour all over her head, she's a first-class pain, but Jack's an accommodatin' sort. I'll be tied up here for a time."

Robin didn't want to leave, but slowly and obediently got ready. "I'll wait up for you," she promised.

"Do that, doll. And don't mind me. I'll be talkin' and actin' like a sane man before you know it."

Jack Dickson drove the shiny mauve convertible. His wife sat beside him. Robin sat beside her.

"That was an evening to remember," Estelle Dickson was muttering, and the whiskey fumes were strong. "Mingling with all the royalty, oh boy, that was a red-letter evening."

"All right, Estelle, knock it off," Jack Dickson said quietly.

"Why? Because the royalty followed us to the car?"

"That's enough," he warned, icily, and there was no question that he was acutely embarrassed. "Is New York your home, Miss Hamilton?"

"Yes, I was born and raised—"

" 'Born and raised, born and raised,' " Estelle Dickson mimicked in a hateful singsong. "Who gives a crap? You never ask me where I was born and raised. Royalty you ask, royalty sitting right next to me, I can smell it, all that royalty has the same smell, who gives a crap—"

They stopped for a red light and Jack Dickson raised his left hand and slapped his wife, hard, across the face. Robin gasped. His wife gasped, too. "I apologize for my dignified wife, Miss Hamilton," he said. "Please stay in the car. We're only about five more minutes away from your hotel and my dignified wife has given me her word she will be completely silent. Because she knows that otherwise I will break her arm."

Robin was delivered to the hotel at midnight on this first day in Hollywood. Jack Dickson slid out of the convertible and opened her door, waving the doorman away. "This ride must have been awful and endless for you," he said. "I'm terribly sorry. The whole thing was unpardonable."

"I'm all right," she said. "Thank you."

"I'll—be seeing you again, I hope," he said, standing close, and Robin nodded. She was halfway into the lobby when she recognized, or thought she recognized, the special tone in his voice. Maybe he hadn't simply been polite. Maybe he really was hoping he might see her again—away from the others, away from his brother and Jesse Nash, away from his unspeakable wife. The possibility was flattering and—

No, she thought resolutely. One white man for *that* reason was more than enough. One man like Jerry Sorin was more than enough.

She was here because of a beautiful man named Jesse Nash.

In her room, she bathed and waited. She felt the textures of the expensive clothes that had been bought, touched the walls of this splendid hotel room, thought about the distance she had come and where she had come from, thought about Pete Gumbo who didn't exist and Roland Lee whom she could do nothing for, thought about Mama who loved her, and waited. She slipped nude into the double bed because her one decent nightgown was too washed out of shape to be right in this fine bed. Jesse—Mr. Nash—had bought her clothes but no underclothes. In the same situation, she reasoned, a man on the make would have led her to the bedclothes department. He hadn't.

She waited, but after a while her eyes would not stay open. It was daylight when she wakened, and she was alone. Her watch—

the wristwatch Mama had saved up to buy her for her last birthday—read ten minutes past eight, California time; much too early
for Jesse Nash to be stirred from sleep, she knew, but she phoned
him nonetheless. He wasn't cranky, but neither was he cordial. He
had tapped at her door at around three-thirty, he said, and there
had been no answer, and so he'd turned in. He would get back to
her, he said, and hung up.

I'll go to his room, thought Robin. If I go in my coat and with
nothing on underneath, he won't send me away. I'll get into his
bed and he'll hold me.

She did none of these things. She waited.

The days and nights after the Phideau's opening were almost cease-
lessly busy one. Jesse Nash taped "The Marty Dickson Hour." He
sat for rounds of interviews. Business at Phideau's boomed. The
columns were sprinkled with his name. His album, *Color Me Colored*,
was rushed into release amid much ballyhoo. Plans were made for
him to go to Miami Beach, where Marty Dickson would direct and
star in a movie by day and headline a club show at The Waltham
at night. Jesse would appear in the club show. A role in the picture was being hastily written in for him.

He became Jesse to Robin, not Mr. Nash, and when his rigorous
schedule allowed them to be together he was unfailingly kind to
her, yet she found the purpose of their relationship bewildering.
What was entirely clear to her was that he had the right to come
to her bed any time he chose. What was becoming clear to her
was that her feeling for him was growing more and more sexual
—a realization that frightened and delighted her.

What was not at all clear to Robin was why he seemed to view
himself as something close to a father figure. He insisted that she
wear a coat if the evenings were chilly. He ordered her to steer
clear of strangers, and he gave the order as though she were a
child. He invariably came up with excuses for staying out of her

room, and she was invited to his suite only when other people were there.

It was understood that she would fly to Florida with him, understood that eventually he would have more time to spend with her. She tried to use her lonely hours profitably. She wrote a very long letter to her sister Lula, rewriting it endlessly, detailing her life since New Year's Eve, taking pains to explain that her association with Jesse Nash was platonic. She began a Jesse Nash scrapbook. At his request, she carefully read newspapers and magazines in search of items he might convert into material for his act. She swam a lot, walked a lot. In one week she received four phone calls from Jack Dickson, asking to see her. Each time she was pleasant, and each time she said no. She wasn't sure if she should mention him to Jesse. She accepted spending money from Jesse. At first she felt odd about taking it. Soon it was natural, for she was not his mistress but his daughter.

That status changed ten days after she had arrived in Los Angeles, on an evening Phideau's was closed. Jesse took her to a small cocktail party at Marty Dickson's home in a place called Bel Air, a small party that turned out to be not small at all. Looking up the long driveway to the estate—it had fifty-one rooms, Jesse told her—she was nearly blinded by a torrent of lights. Special police had been hired to handle the cars in the driveway, which curved around the Georgian house in a complete, glittering circle. Every light was on in the vast house because, Jesse remarked, Marty probably owned stock in the Electric Company.

Robin, awed, breathless, was admitted to the house with Jesse by an elderly, magisterially dignified Negro in a white coat. Her wrap was taken, and Jesse sighed and said, "Let's wander into the valley of the shadow." The party was in noisy and heavily populated progress in an immense, high-ceilinged living room that immediately struck Robin as a harum-scarum hodgepodge of beautiful things and crazy junk. Guests stood or sat in groups among the fifteen-foot-high pink lamps, chatting and poking forefingers and drinking. Some of them she recognized from movies or television, and most of them she guessed she should recognize. There was a crowd gathered at the far end of the huge room, where Marty Dickson and a colored man were involved in some hectic pantomime that was making people laugh.

"That's Coley Dennis, isn't it?" she asked.

"Yeah," Jesse nodded, obviously not pleased. "The cat that used to be black." A waiter in a red jacket came with a tray of drinks, and Jesse took two and gave her one. "Dig the conked hair and the suit tailored by Caucasian Brothers," he snorted. "Figures." Jesse had talked with her several times about Coley Dennis, the dancer-singer-actor-musician who was a big talent and a total disgrace, a black ofay. Not because he kept marrying white, Jesse had complained. Not because there wasn't a single Negro cause that could bank on him for a benefit, much less a buck. But because his hatred of everyone and everything he'd come from was expressed by him in public, with honed-to-perfection subtlety, in ways that made the Eastlands come on like Dred Scott.

Jesse drank. Robin did not, though she held her glass and tried to look sophisticated. She was impressed that people came up to Jesse and treated him like a celebrity, impressed by his ease, impressed that he seemed so much surer of himself than he had only a week ago. She was impressed by the gigantic house, the people who were bigger than life, by the wealth, by Mrs. Dickson who came to her and remembered her name and treated her as though she belonged here. She wished, as she moved about the room with Jesse and met people, that he would quit looking daggers at Coley Dennis, because she wanted everything to be pleasant.

Mrs. Dickson was telling her how pretty she looked when a great screeching roar was heard and Robin and everyone turned to see Marty Dickson, kicking and flailing, being carried in the arms of a big man in a gorilla costume. "Help, help!" he was screaming. "No, I won't marry you and live in Africa! I'm a nice Jewish goil and we live in Flatbush with my folks or nothing doing!"

Everyone laughed, including Jesse, who had been talking with a bald, bulgy man Robin dimly recalled having been introduced to at Phideau's. Coley Dennis sprang to the gorilla as Marty Dickson was being let down and ordered loudly, "You heard the lady, Umgowa! How many times I got to tell you these mixed marriages never work?" Dennis and the gorilla began to wrestle. Another man romped to them to referee the match. Marty Dickson called, "Don't hurt him! I can't thtand gorilla blood! Rosalie Fink tellth you boyth to thtop thith inthtant!" and the wrestling stopped as he stamped his foot and minced to the piano. Suddenly, in a different voice, he cried, "Buy Liberty Bonds!" and raised a large flower bowl from the piano and held it aloft, like a torch. "Hang the Kaiser and bring our doughboys back home by Yom Kippur! Let's get out there and win one for the Gipper, chappies. While we're at it, let's win one for the chappie, gippers!"

People laughed, and Mrs. Dickson, smiling but shaking her head, excused herself and seemed to be swallowed up in the crowd. The man at the piano burst into "Over There" and Marty Dickson pitched the bowl to Coley Dennis and limped away, like the Spirit of '76, playing an imaginary fife. The limp became a normal, masculine walk and he took a cocktail that a waiter gave him and greeted some people, bussing a few cheeks and shaking a few hands with his own left hand. He saw Robin, and his face lit up, but he did not go to her. He greeted a heavy woman Robin recognized as a character actress with, "Gorgeous, what say you and I play some bridge to see who gets the rubber?" and she giggled, and the giggle became an embarrassed but affectionate peal when he pinched her corseted acre of a backside. Presently he got to Jesse, who was about ten feet away from Robin, and he waved to Robin, but gave no indication that he planned to acknowledge her any further tonight. His arm was around Jesse, and they huddled in conversation for a few moments, and then he loped away, alone.

Music was piped in from somewhere, a warm and syrupy "You'd Be So Nice to Come Home to," and more guests arrived, and the party got noisier and smokier. Jesse beckoned to her, and there was apology on his face. "You won't like this, doll, and I don't much like it," he said, "but I got to go to work somewhere in one of this fifty-one rooms for a little while. Marty wants it, and I guess I can't say no. There's an important newspaper guy here—Eric Knapp, his name is—Marty wants the two of us to jaw together for maybe half an hour. You be okay while I'm gone?"

"Of course, Jesse. I'll be fine," she said, meaning it, not meaning it, wishing she could lose the sinking feeling of desertion she almost always experienced at times like this. She sipped her drink, despising it, and accepted a cigarette someone offered her because most of the ladies in the room who were smoking cigarettes looked sophisticated, but she only pretended to smoke it. She moved about, listening to the talk. Someone was saying, "So he told me the public would hold still for one more Western series if it was different and I just laughed in his moosh," and someone else was saying, "—offered her a flat ten grand to sing just one song, and the agent said the figure was insulting. *Insulting*, yet! Six months ago she was hanging salamis in a butcher shop and all of a sudden she's Jenny Lind!" Then one white man attached himself to Robin and talked to her about Ralph Bunche and Jackie Robinson and George Washington Carver and Lena Horne. Then another white man squeezed her bare forearm and winked and asked her if she didn't agree that, in the clinches, liberals and reactionaries were kissin' cousins.

Then she felt a hand on her shoulder, and it belonged to Marty Dickson. He held her hand and said, "Take a walk with me, Robin Bobbin. I want to show you something."

He led her out of the crowded living room and down a long corridor, wordlessly, even grimly, without a smile or a semblance of the finger-snapping, into a room on the ground floor that was all red leather and bookshelves and knotty pine walls with plaques and photographs and pictures of sailing ships, and a sudden worry occurred to her that maybe something was bothering him about Jesse and he wanted to confide in her.

She heard the lock at the door snap and, turning, seeing the serious face of this least serious of men, knew that Jesse wasn't on his mind. "What—what did you want to show me, Mr. Dickson?" she asked.

"The moon," he said. "Best place in the world to see the moon is right here from the window. I've had experts in from the four corners of the globe—well, three and a half corners—and they took a secret ballot and it was unanimous. This room is the best place to I think we better have a great big kiss on the lips, Robin Bob-bin, Robin Brown Breast."

Her impulse was to run—he wasn't holding her all that tightly—and go and wait for Jesse, because being here was very wrong. She was fearful of him, fearful that Jesse would find out, fearful of being with sophisticated people and out of her depth, and she began to struggle, not too hard but enough to let him know she didn't want him to think she was some pushover, and she felt his mouth on hers and realized she was being kissed by a famous movie star. She let him kiss her some more, careful not to show she liked it. But the kiss got intense and she did like it, and she began to kiss him back until she recognized that that extra sensation was his hand zigzagging into the bodice of her cocktail gown. She quickly broke away, flustered, shaky.

"Where you going?" he asked.

"Back to the party," Robin said, near the door but not unlocking it.

He looked tired, and she heard him sigh. He switched the overhead light off and began to pour some whiskey at the small bar she had not seen till now. "Anything special you have against me?"

"Against you? Of course not—you're a wonderful man. It's just that I don't understand this—well, what you were doing a second ago."

"No kidding. I was starting to get us comfortable," he said measuredly. "We can still get comfortable for twenty minutes or so, right over there on that couch. If we don't talk about anything else, we can talk about a test I can set up at the studio. Jesse tells me you sing. Is that right?"

The hideous thing was that he wasn't even looking at Robin as he was making his cold, obscene proposition, as though he knew it was obscene and was ashamed. Robin reached for the knob, and this seemed to shock him, and he put his glass down and grabbed her, and his greedy hands hurriedly went everywhere. "No," she warned sharply, fighting him now. "I'll scream . . ." He was muttering something about soundproof, and the Pete Gumbo of him was petrifying but only for a moment, and she pushed him with all her strength.

He glared, but he stayed where she had pushed him. "All right. Out!" he exclaimed. "A man tries to do you a favor, you spit in his face. That's gratitude? Yeah, yeah, gratitude. All right. Get the hell out."

In the living room, praying that her upset wasn't printed on her face, Robin saw Mrs. Dickson and turned away. She accepted a drink from someone, and drank it hastily. She was introduced to Coley Dennis's wife, a beautiful woman with a heavy accent that sounded Spanish and whose name was Felícita. She talked with the woman, and with others, and ached for Jesse to come. He did, eventually, and suggested they get ready to cut out. "I'm ready now," she agreed.

Jesse asked the Negro butler for her wrap and was thanking Mrs. Dickson for the nice evening when Marty Dickson came barreling into the room, once more the jolly comedian in furious action. He sang "Daisies Won't Tell, Dear, but Don't Trust a Pansy." He saw Robin, and pretended he didn't. He bear-hugged Felícita Dennis, faked a passionate kiss, and exclaimed, "Chiquita Banana, Pancho find you moocho poocho. You are star from right out de Pampas. You are magnifico, you are spiktacular!" Coley Dennis's wife shrieked happily. He seemed hurt that Jesse was leaving so early but, ignoring Robin, thanked him for coming to the wienie roast, and galloped away, dancing across the room with a waiter.

In the car, they agreed on a hamburger at a drive-in. Riding there, he apologized for being a party-pooper but then admitted he had barely been able to wait to leave. Something about Marty up close, something he couldn't yet define, smelled diskosher. Being called Blackjack-baby was tolerable the first dozen times, but when was it supposed to let up? That tight palship with a scum ofay like Dennis had a sewer smell to it. Something was out of kilter. Something to do with hiring not a talent but a house nigger, to show off liberal-style, to salve Whitey's conscience. Something, something that was getting honkier every day . . .

"You sound more and more like my cousin's husband in Philadelphia," said Robin. "If you listen to him, every white person in the world is our enemy, and all they do all day long is cheat colored men and rape colored women. That kind of talk is ridiculous, Jesse." But she privately wondered if Marty Dickson would have been quite so insensitive, quite so hateful, if she had been white.

"Who said 'hate'?" Jesse asked patiently. "That's an interesting remark about rapin' colored women, though. The night Marty first met you at the club, he comes slobberin' to me with questions about how are you in bed? And I tell him he's got enough to do mindin' his own business, but he doesn't quit, he wants to know is it true that all colored chicks are hot little maniacs in the sack. And he can't even dig why I finally order him to lay off."

I must never, she resolved, never tell him about tonight.

"Oh, I'm not singlin' out Marty, necessarily," he went on. "The fact just remains, doll, that white guys look at colored girls in a special way, not just because pretty colored girls are appetizin' to look at but mainly because they are colored. That's the difference."

"Are you such a noble character? When you see a pretty white girl, don't you get ideas?"

He shook his head. "Nope, I surely don't, and I don't expect I ever will. Isn't one white lady on the face of the globe can faze me that way."

Or colored lady, Robin avoided adding.

The drive-in was gaudy-bright and not particularly busy, but the carhop was taking forever to come for their orders. Waiting, Robin observed, "You're a strange person, Jesse. You're the most decent man I've ever met, and yet these things you've been saying . . . I don't know how to take you. Isn't it possible you might be partly wrong? Is it possible you're not being fair about a lot of things?"

The corners of Jesse's mouth went down and after a reflective moment he nodded. "Anything's possible. Yeah, I guess I do sound a little ornery and suspicious. It creeps up on me every now and again, and I don't like it, but I guess I've had just too much experience in my day puttin' trust in white folks and then watchin' that trust get slammed in the rear end. That carhop over there, for instance—what's takin' her so long to take our order, would you say? The place isn't that crowded."

"Maybe she's new here."

"Right. And maybe she figures colored customers can always come last. I could be wrong, but then again, that's how my mind works." He lit a cigarette and looked at Robin. "I think all I meant to say to you, doll, is you have to learn to protect yourself. You're a nice kid, with a lot on the ball, and I'd hate to see you get burned just because you trust everybody."

"Does that include you?"

He laughed, a trifle uneasily. "Me you can trust. Seems to me I've proved that."

Solemnly she asked, "Why, Jesse?"

"Huh?"

"Why haven't you even kissed me? Am I that unattractive?"

A pause. "No, ma'am. The mouth gets more watery all the time."

"Then how long do you think you have to treat me like something so delicate? I want you, Jesse—I'm sure I do. You were right in bawling me out that first day—I must have sounded terribly cheap—but I'm not the same girl now. I won't go to pieces."

A slight shifting of weight. "I was waitin' to be sure, doll," he said huskily. "You've had some rough deals."

Quietly she said, "That carhop's never going to wait on us. I'm not really very hungry, anyway. Are you?"

"No," he answered, and started the motor.

There was voluptuous silence as Jesse headed for The Starfire. Not far from the hotel, he pulled the car to a stop and brought her into his arms. He kissed her eyes and throat and her mouth, and gently pressed his hand to her breast. Robin's trembling fingers guided his hand inside the V of her gown, and a shudder went through her body as her flesh was touched. She responded with a wisp of a moan, surprised at her forwardness and immodesty and astonished that she could be ready so quickly, yet only fleetingly ashamed. This wasn't Marty Dickson, faceless, loveless. This was Jesse.

Jesse.

Still silent, his lips and hands left her and the ride to the hotel was endless. In the elevator, as he stood tall beside her and dropped his key and awkwardly retrieved it, she was sure the other passengers knew her secret and were disapproving. And soon they didn't matter, nothing mattered except that she and Jesse were in her room, and the door behind them was bolted, and the only light they needed was the soft one near the draped window.

His arms extended and Robin invaded them, less in passion now than in an overflowing hunger to be loved. Jesse's breathing was labored, and he said huskily, "Waited too long, baby, waited too long," and his kiss was loving, not just hot, and when he brought the wrap off her shoulders she discovered, in mute alarm, that the prospect of being unclothed before him was suddenly mortifying. She saw the wrap slither to the floor, saw the uncritical delight in his eyes, and hoped he would not touch her again.

He did. Gently, wordlessly, he guided her not to the bed but to the window, and he hurried nothing, but then the cocktail gown had disappeared and he was freeing the bra hook and kissing her shoulders and then her breasts, and she was afraid he would be able to tell that passion was gone, that maybe it had never been real, that she was dishonest, that she loved him but could not bear to do this alien thing with him. Desperately she wanted to cover her breasts, her body, herself, but she silently went with him to the bed and warned herself that she must not disappoint this man.

"Would you turn the light off?" she meekly asked just before he came to her a minute later, and he did, and it helped. In the dark's charade of safety he was no longer Jesse but a faceless man she could fool, and she received his fondlings and caresses as if she, too, were someone else. But then, without announcement, she was no longer enduring the weight of him but reacting to the man of him, to Jesse, to Jesse Nash, and she held him and moved with him at his pace and whispered names of endearment, true names, genuine names.

And without announcement, the knowledge of Jesse became almost oppressively blissful, and it was impossible, the whirling within her belly had never happened before, wasn't supposed to happen, surely not this fast, and it was about to happen. Jesse was moving slowly, firmly but slowly, and she was ready and could not tell him this for only sluts had it happen this fast. She forced her thighs and legs hard against the bed and trained her head toward the wall so that she would not see the silhouette of Jesse. This was passion, she had known about it and never known it, and she needed to stem the maddening tide of it, and all she could do was kiss Jesse's face repeatedly, and writhe the body that Jesse owned, would always own, and call him dearest and beloved, and then without announcement she shivered convulsively and the dam burst.

She could not stop shivering. She could not stop hugging Jesse —Jesse, Jesse—she knew love, knew all the corny songs weren't corny at all. She was whole.

On the day they flew to Miami, Robin received a letter from her sister Lula. It was a letter without blame but also without love. A lawyer had talked Mama into suing the white policeman for damages for wrongful death, and Mama, who at first had argued that she had no intention of getting rich on Roland Lee's being dead, was going through with the lawsuit. Some civil rights people were after the Manhattan District Attorney to demand a grand jury investigation of the killing. Maybe it would come about, maybe it wouldn't. The point was that there were folks who weren't satisfied to let the matter fade away.

Mama, the letter said, did not want Robin back ever.

On the plane, not apprehensive at flying because Jesse was beside her, Robin wished she could feel more guilty over being so secure, so rapturously happy. Jesse had sort of, kind of brought up the subject of marriage; not all that directly, not an offer to find a preacher—but, on his own, he had briefly talked about people being married, and said that marriage was something he sometimes thought highly of.

She was happy because her body delighted Jesse in bed. She was happy because she had proved to herself that shame was not a necessary ingredient in making love, not if the man was Jesse. No couple had ever made love before them, no woman had ever had an orgasm before Robin, no woman had ever pleased a man before she had pleased Jesse, so totally, so meaningfully.

They held hands on the plane, and Robin knew that only good things were ahead. . . .

And now, in this posh suite at The Prentiss, with the world waiting, she wept for Jesse Nash and all those good things that never happened.

When her second show in the Prentiss Room was finished, Robin considered going to the suite on the thirty-fifth floor to shower and change her clothes, but decided against it. "Paul's Place" was on, and she had promised Porter Blair she would go to 3007 as soon as her show was done.

"Thirty, please," she told the white elevator operator, and smiled and thanked the middle-aged white couple in evening clothes who rode up with her and complimented her on her singing; they were from Durham, the man announced, here in the Windy City for the podiatrist convention, and when it came to entertainment, her race had the other races beat a country mile. She found 3007 and knocked lightly. The living room was dimly lighted as Porter Blair, wearing an ascot and a foulard robe and holding a large, dark drink, admitted her with a lively smile and called, *"Entrez-vous!"*

The color set was on at the far wall, and she could see a medium closeup of Paul Rand and Frieda Monroe on the screen. "Where's the small party?" she asked.

"Right here. It consists of you and me," he answered, closing the door and, for all she knew, locking it. "Who needs a big gang around when you're admiring yourself on the boob tube? What's your pleasure in the drinkie department?"

Soda, she wanted to say. "Anything. Whatever you're having," she said.

She sat on the zebra couch, slightly more relaxed than she had expected she would be, and there she was on camera, looking, as Jeanne Prescott had claimed, like a dream, with her knees covered and her fingers laced, nodding at Bruno Eisendorf, who was saying that the art of motion pictures had the obligation to reflect the art of ethics. "Bruno," said Porter Blair now, handing her a large, dark drink and sitting next to her, "has all the personal ethics of a mongoose, but he's a sweet fella, wouldn't harm a fly. Unless it was open. I'm glad you came. I've been drinking alone and watching the boob tube alone. They claim that a male bachelor who does that three nights in a row has deep-seated problems of homosexuality, and tonight begins my third night in a row of drinking and watching the boob tube. So you see? I probably won't have to commit suicide, after all."

Robin laughed. "I think you're a little high, Mr. Blair."

"Canard, a base canard!" he snorted, and laughed, too. He was a trace too pretty for a man, at once too breezily self-confident and too unsure of himself. "No, all seriousness aside. I *am* glad you came. I was making bets with myself that you wouldn't."

"Why? I said I would."

He shrugged, and motioned for her to drink. She did. It was strong and made her cough, but she raised the glass to her lips again. "Story of my life," he said with an elaborate frown. "Women have the most insolent habit of finding me obnoxious."

"That's awfully hard to believe," Robin said, wanting to see the show and not wanting to offend him, wishing he weren't so close because suddenly, inexplicably, there *was* something vaguely obnoxious about him, and suddenly she realized that this was the very last place she wanted to be, here with a stranger, a Marty Dickson-type stranger who could give her no warmth, no love, nothing that had even transient meaning.

Yet she drank the awful liquor, in the hope that it would coat her senses quickly, in the hope that it would help make her appealing to this man who was Porter Blair, John Doe, James Lonny Hamilton, Jerry Sorin, Joe Doakes—this man, this appreciator. He talked about the women who found him obnoxious—latent dykes, latent butches, the whole caboodle of 'em but they had a right to their religion and their opinion—and she saw herself on the screen, touching the tip of her nose with her forefinger, hearing herself say, "—land Lee mastered the multiplication table when he was seven years old, his teacher sent that home in a note, and we had to help our mother stand up, she was so proud," and felt him closer, and was dazzled to discover that she had finished her large, dark drink and the glass was empty except for the ice cubes.

"Let's freshen that drinkie!" he cried, snatching the glass and jumping to his feet, and zigzagged to the shoulder-high mantel, which he used as a bar. He freshened his own as well, liberally, Robin saw, and she gazed at the screen, where Porter Blair, sober and polished and incisive, was saying, "The rights of man means *man*, not every third or sixth man, but every man, and if—" and the drunk Porter Blair was chortling at the mantel bar, and presently he zigzagged back to the couch with a large, dark drink in each hand.

But the silly ascot was askew and the sash of his beautiful foulard robe had come undone—purposely?—and he wasn't wearing anything under it. He kept up the constant, aimless, foggy, point-less chatter, and Robin, slightly ill, looked and then looked away. "One woman," he said, giving her the second drink, standing over her, grinning. "Let me find one woman who doesn't find me ob-noxious, and I'll die happy. Would you like me to die happy?"

I can't stay here, Robin thought. "I'd like for you to close that bathrobe, Mr. Blair. You're embarrassing me."

"Truly? But interested, too, I'll bet. Just a little interested?"

She placed her glass on the table near the couch and got up. His smile vanished and he immediately tied the sash. "What are you going to do?"

"Leave," she said, again amazed that her voice sounded so steady. "Please get out of my way."

"You just got here."

"I know. You shouldn't have been in such a hurry to be ob-noxious."

"Stay. I'll behave."

She walked toward the door, clenching her fists at her sides in fear rather than rage. He followed her and touched her shoulder, but she knew suddenly that he wouldn't hurt her. "Stay," he said, talking fast. "I'm lonely. I'm always lonely. If you go, you'll be lonely, too. I can't help the way I act with women sometimes when I drink too much. Stay. Let me explain. Let me talk. *Care* about me!"

"I'm sorry," she said as she shook off his hand.

"Are you scared of me? I'm scared of you—isn't that fantastic? I love women, really I do, and they always scare me. You be dif-ferent. Care. Please. Let me talk!" She saw his robe on the carpet as she reached the door, saw panic in his face. "*Look* at me! *Care* about me! Somebody for God's sake *care* about me!"

She hurried to the elevator and to the suite on the thirty-fifth floor, where she thought she would be sick and wasn't, where she poured some of Jeanne's whiskey into a water glass and drank it, hating it but drinking it all, where she stared at the telephone that rang and rang and rang.

Why me? she thought. Did he pick me out?

There's not a black man alive who would behave like that white man did, she thought.

She saw her reflection in the living room mirror, the caramel girl who was staying in the big hotel that was not run by colored men. The sickness rose, and she heard someone, everyone, cry *Care about me—me, me, me!*—and his beautiful foulard robe was on his carpet and she got to the bathroom just in time.

Nine

STUART WHITE's money troubles were over.

So were his worries about what he was going to do with his life.

As a cop, he had been forbidden to accept a penny from *Thursday* Magazine, let alone the five thousand dollars it had offered him for an exclusive ghostwritten account of the Hamilton accident and its aftermath. As an ex-cop, he had gone to the *Thursday* offices in Rockefeller Center, to the man named Mr. Beale who had made the offer, with the announcement that he was a free man now and ready to work on the magazine article and take the five thousand. Mr. Beale had as much as told him to get lost: the story had been hot news at the time; it wasn't hot news now.

That had been a low day. But everything turned out for the best. Just when he had been about ready to resign himself to a lousy job as clerk in his brother-in-law Al's liquor store, he received a visit in his Bennett Avenue flat from a refined man with the refined name of Roger Kenworthy, who asked him how much he knew about Soul of America. At first White, suspecting a sales pitch, explained that he couldn't afford to contribute any money to anything, but Mr. Kenworthy hadn't come to get money. He'd come to give it. He produced a certified check for fifteen thousand dollars, made out to Stuart Curtiss White. Soul of America had been following his tragic case, the refined man explained, and was of the opinion that he was a Christian Dreyfus. This check, he said, was a means of rewarding Mr. White for the painful abuse he'd been subjected to by a powerful un-American system that every real American knew was morally bankrupt.

"Is this—well, what is this, a gift, like?" croaked White, his throat dry, blinking at the zeroes on the check, embarrassed that he wasn't wearing socks.

"Not quite," Mr. Kenworthy said, and smiled. "You're familiar with SOA, aren't you?"

"SOA?"

"Soul of America."

"Oh. Well, I've read about it a little, here and there, sure. It's against the Commies."

"In our overall design, yes, exactly. Though we prefer to call ourselves pro-freedom—that's more constructive. Our founder, Mr. Cunningham—and I'm here, by the way, to represent Mr. Cunningham directly—doesn't say, nor does he encourage us to go around saying, that there are Communists with black beards and time bombs lurking in every closet. He assumes that everyone understands by now that there is an international Communist conspiracy intent on burying us, and he knows, and we agree, that there are fine, patriotic organizations hammering that point home night and day. The enemy we're far more intent on warning Americans to guard against is in a way more dangerous because he cloaks himself in so-called respectability. I mean the so-called liberal element, the foreign doctrine apologists, the people whose hearts bleed for everything except their own country. The people who persecuted a good man called Stuart Curtiss White."

"Well . . ." said White, and his bare feet shuffled. "Listen, would you like a beer?"

"Thank you, no. I'll come to the point, Mr. White. I assume I have your strictest confidence?"

"Yes *sir*," White agreed, feeling important and inadequate. His wife Lucille came into the living room, and Mr. Kenworthy shot to his feet like a gentleman. White introduced her, explained that he and Mr. Kenworthy were talking business, and Lucille rubbed the heels of her hands at her sides and left them alone. "You sure you wouldn't care for a beer?"

"We have, in our files, documentary proof that by this time next year, perhaps sooner, major steps will be in effect from Washington which will in law, not merely theory, reduce every United States Christian Caucasian man, woman, and child to second- and third-class citizenship and, eventually, to outright slavery. For a start, the Negro people will not only control the streets, as they do now, but there is a master plan afoot, with the strings pulled by certain men in government whose names I'm not at liberty this moment to divulge, to replace every Caucasian chief of police in the large and small cities with Negroes, and to give them complete autonomy. And I can see your hair curling, Mr. White, as I knew it would, but I'm sorry to say there are a dozen additional such radical plans in the fire for our country."

"Boy."

"Indeed. Now you may have heard or read in the Hebrew-owned press that SOA is a racist organization, anti-Negro. Nothing could be further from the truth. No Christian—and we're all Christians here—has the right to preach superiority over any man blessed by the Son of God. We in SOA are fonder of the Negroes, and we have their best interests much more at heart, and much more realistically, than the bleeding-heart liberals who make all the noise. You wouldn't be against a man because of the color of his skin, would you, Mr. White? I could certainly sympathize if you were to say yes, because I know, and SOA knows, what you've been put through. But I can tell you're obviously not a bigot."

"Oh, no. Like you say, my religion wouldn't allow it, even if that's how I wanted to feel, which I don't."

"Good. I was hoping, on my way here, that that was what I would hear. Our position is humane. We specialize in informing the public that there are many patriotic, Christian, decent Negroes who know perfectly well that they can't rise above their station overnight. Those others, the ones responsible for the soaring crime rate, for the swelling relief rolls . . . we can't even blame them, not really. They act like wild animals because the liberal element has allowed them to, encouraged them to, *trained* them to. And it's the liberal element, Mr. White, that's taken over the reins of government, right from under our noses, the very same element that left you and your wonderful family to starve."

"Well, ah."

"What does your future hold, Mr. White, if I may ask a personal question? Are you financially secure?"

"Oh, no sir, not even close," White quickly replied, again eyeing the zeroes on the check. "The bills keep piling up."

"Then will you consider joining SOA? I brought a contract with me," Mr. Kenworthy said, taking a paper from a sleek leather case. "It provides fifteen thousand dollars a year—plus expenses—and a year from the date of signing, you and we may wish to renew it."

White was dying for a beer, dying to go tell Lucille about the money. There weren't too many words on the paper, but he was too dizzied to make head or tail of them. He recognized the word *lecturer*, though, and respectfully asked if it meant what he thought it meant.

"SOA is as much educative as it is activist," explained Mr. Kenworthy. "We conduct our own lecture bureau and send out speakers, such as yourself if you join us, to talk before schools and churches and patriotic groups around the country. By expenses, incidentally, I mean that SOA will pay for all your transportation, food, lodging, and every other reasonable purchase made away from home."

"Whoa here a minute," said White. "I never made a speech in my life, Mr. Kenworthy. I got through high school, but talking in public—that's never been my big thing."

The refined man smiled. "No one expects an orator fresh from the factory, Mr. White. You'll have all the help you'll need and, before you know it, I can promise you, the simple trick of it will be second nature." He offered White a gold pen. "On this line, Mr. White, right after the X."

Lucille would probably give him holy hell for signing something this important without reading it. But White thought of the check that might be withdrawn, thought of this man who was surely no con man, and signed his name. "What do I do now?" he asked, handing the gold pen back, wishing he could keep it.

"Within a few days you'll get a call, and you'll very likely be asked to go to our New York office in midtown, where you'll be given some literature to read and where you'll be shown several fascinating films." He stuck out his hand, and White shook it. "It's heartwarming to meet a man as intelligent and as concerned for his country as you, Mr. White. We'll meet very soon again, I trust."

"Lucille," White called, "go get Mr. Kenworthy's hat and coat! I'd be glad to interest you in a beer."

Lucille goggled at the check, and did give White holy hell for signing a paper without first going to a lawyer, or at least to her brother Al, who was a businessman. "Is that all you can say when I put fifteen thousand dollars in your lap, that I don't know any-thing about business?" argued White, who knew she was exactly right. "I'll tear it up then, is that what you and your genius brother want me to do? I'll go clerk for your genius brother and drop dead of a heart attack, sweating my ass for every cent he doles out, is that what you'd rather have me do?"

"But who pays fifteen thousand dollars for a speaker when you're not even a speaker? And not even some of it at a time, but the whole check all at once?"

"People who've heard about me, that's who. People who respect me, who have enough faith in me to give me fifteen thousand dol-lars because they figure I can deliver the goods."

"But what goods, Stuie? That's all I mean. Nobody respects you more than me, but you're no speaker. My goodness, what do you have to speak about?"

"The liberal element. The son of a bitches that left you and I and the kids to starve, that's what I have to speak about. And I don't just get this fifteen grand for the whole year, but whenever I travel, or you need new clothes or a color TV or whatever, this outfit, they pay for everything. You should've *heard* how Mr. Kenworthy talked me up like I was some real big shot!"

He got the phone call three endless days later, and within an hour he had hustled into his blue suit, rather than the slacks and houndstooth-check jacket he preferred, and subwayed to a snazzy reception room on Lexington. He was ushered in real VIP style into the snazzy office of a Miss Gardner, a six-footer with iron-gray hair who talked New England, like Katherine Hepburn only ten times tougher and faster, and who was obviously not a lady to waste time in small talk. Speedily, talking, talking, talking, reciting a speech as though she had committed it to memory years before, she filled his lap and his edge of her desk with a thousand pamphlets, papers, and even books, and the only times her diction was precise and slow were when she said "Lib-ber-als." He was to take the literature home and read every word of it, said Miss Gardner, the better to understand what SOA was fighting for. He was guided to a small projection room, where a fat young woman who introduced herself as Miss Smiley served him hot coffee and gave him a whole pack of cigarettes to keep, and where a bunch of movies were run off for him and nobody else, movies that showed the hammer and sickle, and parts of speeches by table-pounding men White did not know but did know were dangerous, and rolling wheat fields, and niggers rioting, and scenes of Midwest farmers and their families building America, and niggers rioting (the same niggers, in each movie, at the same storefronts). The narrator in each movie had a great baritone voice, the kind that gave even men goose pimples, and talked almost poetry talk about the sapping of the vitality of a special land, the land of America, that had been invented and constructed by Our Saviour.

Miss Smiley refilled his coffee cup. He had never been treated this special in his life.

When the lights went up, he waited for someone to come to him, but even Miss Smiley was gone. He went out of the projection room, where he waited a decent ten-foot distance from two executive-looking men who were talking, and then the shorter and younger of them, a crewcut, ruddy-faced guy in a black blazer, saw him and asked if he was *the* Stuart White. He nodded. The guy beamed and said "Well, *hi*. I'm Rod Jones," and squeezed his hand, and led him to an empty office smaller than Miss Gardner's, and lit his cigarette for him and told him two dirty Rastus and Mandy jokes. White laughed at each because Mr. Jones did, even harder, and then Mr. Jones straightened some papers on his desk and said, eyes twinkling behind black horn-rimmed glasses, "Well, now, fella, Rog Kenworthy's spoken very highly of you. I'm the friend in need you've been assigned to, or shall we say vice versa? Or which vice is versa? Ah ha ha ha ha ha. I'm the fellow who'll write your speech."

"Which speech?"

"The speech. The speech I'll write after we've spent a few bull sessions together and I pick up your ear and cadence. It'll fit you like it's been tailor-made, which it will be, fella, because it'll be yours alone. You'll memorize it, and it'll go with you everywhere, and you'll be so professional at it so fast that every woman in every audience will come running up to rip your clothes off. We have no claims on what you do on your own time, fella. Ah ha ha ha ha ha."

In little more than a week, after four long meetings with Mr. Jones, after hours on end of talking into a tape recorder that took some doing to get accustomed to, Stuart White was presented with his speech. It was natural as could be in the way it was written, a damned sight more natural and down-to-earth than the thousand pamphlets, papers, and even books he had pored over and struggled to understand while waiting for the speech. It covered all his recollections of what had happened from the moment he'd assumed the colored kid in the Keever Place alley had had a gun, through the constant harassment of liberals who'd labeled him a fascist thug when all he'd done had been to protect his life and limb as a police officer—as a man, and the husband and father of a loving, law-abiding, church-going family who depended on him—through the final humiliation of being busted because of the never-resting pressures from the outside on the Police Department. It wasn't completely accurate in every detail. It twisted things a little, here and there. Here and there it lied. He had twisted things and lied during the tape recordings, and Mr. Jones had done his own share of twisting things and lying, but the meat of it was true, and the speech was beautiful.

Exactly one week after he was given the speech, when Mr. Jones and some other men White met at SOA but whose names he could not retain were satisfied that he had the speech down pat, White was flown to Washington, D.C., where he carried his suitcase to a taxi that drove him to the snazzy hotel that he had been directed to check into, a hotel room that was ritzy and that disappointed him because the TV set wasn't color. A man named Van Sterling phoned him from the lobby, as prearranged, and drove him to a Soul of America chapter meeting in the ballroom of a fellowship lodge about ten minutes from the hotel. The place was crowded, and White was nervous, but he shook every hand that shook his, and he sat on the dais where a minister prayed into a microphone for the Almighty to save His creation, America, from the tyranny of the anti-Christs that would blight it. Then a barrel of a man, with a slight tic that suddenly jerked the corners of his lips upward and false teeth that whistled in the microphone, was embarrassingly flowery in his introduction of the persecuted Stuart Curtiss White.

The applause nearly bowled White over, and he stumbled on his opening words, but he started again and said Mr. Jones's speech from memory, and people stood in line, when it was done, to shake his hand. They told him they were praying for him, and one lady with bare arms that were all wrinkles and crevices near the armpits exclaimed, between hiccups, "You're our last hope, Ah-mair-ah-cah's last hope."

The advance understanding had been that he would submit to no question-and-answer period following the speech, owing to a busy schedule that would have to spirit him away immediately. Van Sterling drove him back to the ritzy hotel, where he sat in his hotel room, opened a can of beer he had left on the windowsill to cool, watched an East Side Kids movie on TV, and wished he had the nerve to go down to find some hatcheck girl and bring her back here and lay her.

After Washington there was Philadelphia, and after Philadelphia came Boston and then Baltimore and back to Washington—separate trips, all before SOA chapter meetings, all trial runs for the already committed, with no doubters or possible hecklers. Then, when they believed he had his sea legs, they spent another busy week while Mr. Jones and Miss Gardner and the others whose names he could not retain threw questions at him, and when he said uh and er, one or all of them leaped into the breach to supply him with the right, the only answer to the question. His first appearance with the speech and an open question-and-answer period was in a large church hall in Racker, Arkansas. He was met at the airport by a homely but shapely teen-aged member of SOA whose name was Debs Mayhew and who drove him to his hotel and thanked him for calling her a teenager but insisted she had reached her twenty-fourth birthday in January. She wasn't married, and she got less homely as they neared the hotel. White invited her up to the room for a cold beer before they were expected at the church, and she followed him to the room fifteen minutes after he went there because the desk clerk was her cousin Polk and it wouldn't do for Polk to see her traipsin' into the elevator with a man.

White half filled the room's plastic bucket with ice from the corridor cooler, buried two cans of beer in the bucket, and they were fairly chilled by the time Miss Mayhew showed up. They sipped the beer from water glasses, and she asked him all about the Great White Way, where she had never been yet, and he told her about the famous Stork Club and the famous Roseland where he was a regular, as were all New Yorkers on the In, and she went oooohh, not changing the tone of it, for moments after he sat beside her on the single bed and put his hand under her skirt. She slapped his hand lightly, but kept saying oooohh and kept smiling.

White brought her rimless glasses off and held one of her breasts. "That's naughty," she said, smiling.

His hand went all the way under her skirt, feeling the tingle of warm flesh, and that was when she really slapped him, still smiling, and said, "Now honestly, Mr. White, I'm with the *church!*" He kept grabbing, desperately now, and she got up, ambled away from him with her water glass filled with beer, and said, "We type of girls don't do that type of thing here in Racker, Mr. White. I can't speak for up in Nyew Yawk. You stayin' here overnight in our fair metropolis?"

"Yes."

"Well, then, if you cross your heart and hope to die you won't be naughty, I'll drive you back after the meetin', but you got to promise you won't be naughty, and you got to extra special promise you'll have somethin' better to offer a guest than this corny beer."

The Racker speech went fine, as did the question-and-answer period. Did he feel that his superiors in the Police Department had sided with him, or had they leaned harder on him because the victim had been colored? His superiors and his fellow officers had been generally Christian, White answered, in spite of the outside pressures of agitators. There had been a few exceptions on the force, like a colored officer and a Jewish-descent officer named Bernstein who had ridden him pretty hard. But he had not held, and to this day did not hold, any lasting resentment toward them, because it was possible he might be uncharitable, too, although he prayed not, if he were colored or if his name was something like Bernstein.

What about the statements in the Nawthrun newspapers and on the television, by gen'men like Jesse Nash, that the Hamilton boy was not a member of a hoodlum gang in Harlem but an angel child? A boy's death was a boy's death, and a tragedy to all, no matter his goodness or badness or color, White answered, but the fact did remain, and no one enjoyed bringing it up, that there was a stack of rumors and evidence that Roland Lee Hamilton had for a couple of years, unknown to the police, had his juvenile delinquency "treated" in a New York City hospital welfare clinic, paid for by the taxpayers, by a psy-chiatrist named Lefkowitz, who was later disowned or disbarred or something because he'd had these sexual relations with a number of female teenage patients, but maybe that was hearsay and where was I?—yes, the boy *did* have a neighborhood reputation as a thief and wheeler-dealer, the kind of clever kid who could always talk his way out of trouble by pinning the blame on the nearest Caucasian kid.

But all this, White emphasized, was what he'd *heard*. He'd been too busy defending himself to check out the many Roland Lee Hamilton rumors, some and maybe all of which were true, but— shrugging—no one could be sure, because the Communists and liberals and social workers and columnists wanted Stu White's hide more than they wanted to investigate the truth.

Had he prayed after the shooting incident, had he sought the solace of Christ Jesus? Oh, again and again, without stop, White said with the break in his voice that Mr. Jones had taught him: "I got on these knees and I *never* stopped. I like to think I'm strong enough to face up to any situation, but I'm here to tell you ladies and gentlemen that I wouldn't have lasted very long if it hadn't been for prayer—and for the prayers of my family and friends."

Sweat was rolling off him during the coffee and sandwiches, and during the ride to the hotel in Debs Mayhew's seven-year-old Rambler. "You were swell," she said, skirt rucking back.

"Lousy, just lousy," he said. "And I don't know where to pick up a bottle of liquor in this lousy town."

"I took care of that. I got this catchall bag, and it's right here in it," she said, and patted the bag, the size of a beach ball, between them. "The bottle was four dollars and fourteen cents, cash on demand. You have four dollars and fourteen cents, Mr. White, don't you?"

He took the bottle of whiskey and went to the room alone, be-cause her cousin Polk was still at the front desk and it wouldn't be right for them to be seen together. He put plenty of corridor-cooler ice into the plastic bucket, and set up two double shots into two water glasses on the glass-topped bureau. He phoned Lucille, charging the call to his room, which SOA would pay for, and told her he was still going strong, that a multimillionaire in the audience had stepped up and pumped his paw and told him he ought to be either a minister or in the picture show. The children were well, Lucille said, and everybody missed him. He was watching the old TV, he yawned, nothing to do till the airplane in the morning, and yes, he asserted, all money and popularity aside, he might sound like a square but he had found the religious and patriotic spirit and he did believe the kids would grow up as better Christians and Americans because of what he was doing here in Racker, Arkansas.

The tap of knuckles hit the door almost as he hung up, and White, his yellow knit tie taken off and his shirtsleeves rolled up, raced to admit Debs Hayhew. "Bolt that good and don't be naughty," she warned. Scooping up one of the glasses, she pulled the cord that lowered the window curtain, removed her eyeglasses, and asked, "Are you married?"

"No," he said. A lot of his speech had dealt with his wife and children, and she had heard it.

"Oh, that's nice. I'd never have a drink in a married man's hotel room. Listen—it's hot and I've been drivin' you all over Creation. If I take a shower, and I don't lock that bathroom door, do you promise not to pester me?"

"I promise."

"All rightee," she said, and gulped and gulped her drink, and set it on the glass-topped bureau, and passed him with a smile. He heard the bathroom door close, and stripped to his Jockey shorts, and brought the bedcovers down, and stiffened her drink. He waited at least a minute after he heard the shower. The bathroom door opened easily. She screeched when she saw him, and covered one apart of herself and then another with the dinky washcloth, but the smile was as broad and inviting as ever. "You sashay right out of here pronto, you naughty man!" she cried, holding the washcloth in midair. White advanced and clutched her thigh. She slapped his face with the cloth and objected, "No fair! You head right on back to Nyew Yawk, here and now, hear?"

Still in his shorts, he got into the shower bath with her, and Debs Mayhew, chuckling and muttering, "Naughty, naughty, naughty," began soaping him, going from one side of his wide chest to the other and then over his wide shoulders. With a fresh bar of soap of his own he soaped the valleys and slopes of her, and the shower plastered his shorts to him. She pulled them down as she squatted on her knees, and asked, "What have we here?" and White was as mortified as he always was with a new woman because the impressive size of him did not continue below his belly. She gasped a little, though, and remarked, "Man, this is a *nice*, naughty shower!" and went to town until White pushed her back, just in time. She fell into the tub, not hard, still smiling, and said, "For dirty folks, we're mighty clean, right?"

They dried each other with the soft towels, and Debs Mayhew said, "I hope you don't think I've ever done naughty things like this before. My daddy's a man of the cloth. Reverend Mayhew— you met him at the church."

"You're fine."

"You like these?" she asked, and pushed her not especially nice breasts together. "They grow 'em prettier here or up Nawth?"

"Here."

The bed had the smell of starch and she opened her arms, suddenly looking both desirable and horrible, and her smile faded when White confessed that he'd thought *she* had brought some protection along, that he didn't have anything with him. "Well, now, you're a real big city slicker, aren't you?," she said. "What kind of a drugstore do you suppose *I'd* go into and buy those things?"

"I'll—you wait here and I'll go down somewhere and buy some," he said helplessly.

"They all close down at nine o'clock," she said, and sat up, now frowning at him. "Yes sir, some real big city slicker. Why, you're no different than the hayseeds right here in Racker! I supply the liquor, I supply the body. What do you supply, 'cept little Oscar? And little is right."

"Look, you don't have to talk like—"

"Oh, *bull*, I don't have to talk like! What *do* they teach you up in Nyew Yawk? Sixty-nine, at least?"

"No." That was out of the question; he could never face Lucille and the kids again. "I don't go along with that."

"Uh-huh. 'Cept it's okey-dokey if I do it to you, right?"

"That's different."

"Uh-huh. Different. Man, but I picked me up a real live-wire powerhouse." She got out of bed, went to the bathroom, and locked the door behind her. She was gone a long time, and when she came back she was dressed and wearing her glasses. "You owe me four dollars and fourteen cents," she said.

"Listen, don't go running away," he pleaded. "You don't want to leave me all worked up like this."

She gave a laugh that was pure mean bitch. "A real big city slicker like you, you'll figure out something. Come on now, power-house—four-fourteen. Or are you short in that department, too?"

Enraged, he took a five-dollar bill from his wallet and slapped it on the glass-topped bureau. "There!" he shouted. "Keep the change!"

And damned if she didn't. "Mercy bo-koo," she said. "Now y'all can go back to Nyew Yawk and tell all the other big city slickers what a big hit you made with the small-town gals. Maybe I'll learn, one of these days. Maybe I'll learn that a hayseed's a hayseed, doesn't matter where he comes from."

The door closed. White desperately wanted to phone Lucille, just to hear her voice, but Lucille would wonder about his calling, for no reason, long distance, twice within an hour. He considered easing the panic in his loins by himself, and didn't because that would be a sin.

With a zest and concentration of purpose that would have given pause to Charlie Gundersen, the original whirlwind, Weber immersed himself in "Moore" as though it were the holiest of television crusades. Bob Penniman bowed out of the project, sadly and even bitterly, because, at showdown time, Weber would not guarantee that the idea of Jesse Nash in the title role had ceased to fascinate him. Gene Trowbridge, who thoroughly agreed with Penniman that Nash simply would not do, had second faltering thoughts when Penniman bowed out, agreed to stay on because the series could strike a forceful blow for human rights and, not at all incidentally, because Weber offered him a generous percentage deal on the package. Carl Montgomery, an old-hand, slick Negro scriptwriter with almost as much talent as Bob Penniman and only a modicum of Bob's racial hang-ups, agreed to replace Bob.

While the two writers were locked in a GWS office, instructed to quickly but carefully come up with a sample script, Weber worked just as quickly and carefully. He worked closely with Phil Simms, still at home with a fever, on a budget he could take to Caleb Atwood at Vanguard. He placed a transatlantic call to Kevin Beaumont and Margalo Wells, who were making a picture near Rome, and told them that he wanted them to send a cable stating they would do a guest shot on "Moore"; Kev and Margalo, who had adored Charlie Gundersen, said they would, at once, if Weber would airmail them six Stage Delicatessen salamis. After nine telephone calls around the United States he located Brad Hammond in, of all unlikely places for Brad the incessant swinger, Fort Lauderdale, and explained why he needed him for a one-shot on "Moore." Hammond, show business's busiest, most gifted, and most independent cuss, had not forgotten that he had been singing under a rock until Weber had personally engineered his first solid breaks, and promised to send him a telegram of affirmation immediately.

With a detailed "Moore" budget, a detailed prospectus he wrote himself, a sample script, and signed pledges by Hammond and the Beaumonts that they would appear on the show, Weber did two things in the same afternoon: he made an appointment to see Caleb, and he summoned Red Barnes to bring him Jesse Nash. Red, known as "The Bringer," was a ubiquitous functionary in the upper and lower strata of the show business world, a man with no discernible profession except that of Applied *Chutzpah* who knew where nearly everyone in the world was at any given moment and who could, more often than not, for a fee or a favor, deliver them. Weber rarely knew how; he did know that Red delivered, and that was worth a sizeable reward.

On the next to top floor of Vanguard Broadcasting, on an unseasonably warm afternoon in Manhattan, Caleb Atwood greeted Weber with the predictable, self-possessed, good-looking, vaguely wary, deep-freeze smile he bestowed on his friends, whom Weber was sure could all be fitted into a gnat's eyeball, and his enemies, whom Weber was sure would cramp the Colosseum. Coffee was served—Atwood maintained a strict law against liquor in his elephantine suite of offices, for others as well as for himself, before dusk—and they traded trifles as they invariably did before bargaining, and then the soft-spoken dandy in charge of television activity at VBN commented, "I caught your young colored lady on a show a few weeks back. What was her name again—Jefferson, Washington?"

"Hamilton, Robin Hamilton," corrected Weber, who knew that Caleb knew the name perfectly well, for there was nothing about television that Caleb did not know. "Great, isn't she?"

"Oh, yes. Although my taste runs more toward Bessie Smith."

"Bessie's dead," Weber said, and wanted to kick himself for adding, with a smile, "But maybe that's your point, Caleb." He loved to give the needle to Superwasp Atwood, who referred to "nigras" because he had too much class to say "niggers" yet not enough to say "Negroes," and who, Weber hadn't a particle of doubt, referred to him behind his back as "The Jew Commie." But now Weber wanted something important from him, and this brief needle had been an adolescent, indulgent extravagance. "Anyway," he remarked hurriedly, "for the record, the Hamilton girl's career is going like a house afire. Now what I came to see you about—"

"Same old Warren," said Caleb, sounding more amused than perturbed. "We never meet but that you insist on calling me the Grand Dragon of the Klan. Why is that, I wonder?"

"Because I'm a japester, a very comical fellow. Because that's the glue that's held our love affair together over the years, Caleb—we like to needle each other."

"I've never been aware of needling you. I've never been aware of needling anyone. For one thing, sarcasm takes time, and time is something I always have precious little of."

"All right, then, let's lay that pistol down, babe, and start talking industry."

Atwood's dark eyes narrowed and were quizzical for a moment, and he seemed ready to keep the ball bouncing for just a little while, but the quizzical look vanished and he nodded. "A new project?" he asked, and Weber nodded. "This is an odd time of season to come up with one, isn't it? The summer's lined up and the fall season's tight as a drum."

"Vanguard will drop everything for this one, Caleb," Weber declared and handed him, across the desk, a single sheet of paper, double-spaced, telling in two paragraphs and eight crisp sentences, what "Moore" was about.

He watched Caleb, who read the paper slowly, expressionlessly. Caleb barely glanced up but said, "Okay, start selling."

Weber did. He proffered Phil's beautifully prepared budget, to be examined quickly now, and the sample script and notes for future scripts, to be studied later. He talked about dramatic impact. He talked about his enthusiasm and the fact, the indisputable money fact, that not one GWS show had ever lost a dime for Vanguard or, for that matter, any other network.

Softly, Caleb asked, "Who's going to sponsor this gem of yours on national television? A Harlem meat market?"

Weber talked about the change in the temper of the times. He ticked off random names of fat-pocket sponsors who were standing impatiently at the turnstile, ready to finance any smart show because they knew that smart shows moved the goods. He talked about the millions of white viewers who were always ready to sit for an unpreachy show that packed a wallop, and of how he was too smart a ringmaster to let any show preach. He talked about the burgeoning colored market ("Negro market" just might throw Caleb off), quoting statistics of their still unrecognized buying power.

He showed Brad Hammond's wire and the Beaumonts' cable, and said he was sure he didn't have to educate Caleb to the fact that with the unbuyable Hammond on the first show and the Beaumonts on the second, or vice versa, that those first shows would guarantee stratospheric ratings if only because of their names, and the other guest-shot untouchables would join the parade for scale.

And finally, because Caleb, a sonofabitch for remaining expressionless and immovable, was receiving him like an office boy in knickers come to request a half-dollar raise in pay, he shamed himself by sounding like the office boy's grandfather who has worked for fifty years and hopes the firm will give him a gold watch.

"Along with everything else, Caleb," he said, "I've been of value to VBN."

"No one denies that," Atwood conceded, and, for the fleck of a second, there was a smile that seemed genuine. "Have you been to the other networks yet?"

"No."

"You've made a lot of money for the other networks, too. They're always showing off their liberalism like some big erection, maybe they'd go for it. You may not like me, Warren, but you have to admit I'm a consistent man. I think this country started to go down the drain the minute liberalism took over, and some day you and I might want to have a philosophic quarrel about that, but I haven't swerved a jot from that conviction, in business or over a cocktail, and I trust you'll credit me with consistency, at least."

"I do."

"Very well. Then why come to me with this notion when you knew I'd turn you down?"

Measuredly, Weber said, "You haven't turned me down, Caleb. And you won't, and VBN won't. Forget—for just a minute, because it's bad business to forget it, and you're anything but a bad businessman—forget that 'Moore' has a dozen built-in potentials for earning us all a pot of dough. Why I brought this first to VBN, and VBN is going to take it, is simple. VBN knows I've stayed to mint money for it when I could've taken plenty of the goodies to the competition. You might say that VBN is going to reward me for having been a long, faithful, and money-minting servant."

Pause. The hard eyes again, examining the surface of the desk. "Maybe you'd better clarify that, Warren. I don't seem to hear a suggestion. I seem to hear a threat."

"We're grown men, Caleb, with years of business to do together ahead of us. Why would I threaten you? For Christ's sake, how could I threaten you? Threat isn't my style. That's what I keep telling Claude, every time I run into him—'threat isn't my style.' "

It was go-for-broke, either a master stroke or idiot stroke, possibly both, Weber thought. Claude was C. Harvey Rhodes. C. Harvey Rhodes was the aged but unquestioned head of VBN, ruler even of Caleb Atwood. You didn't mention Claude's name in testy company; no one did, ever. Weber had, just this minute, and he realized, with a lurch in his heart, that five years of graceful sparring with Atwood could end right here.

The hard eyes became almost invisible. "I'm disappointed," Atwood said evenly. "I always thought of you as a shrewd trader, bright, the type of man with the brains to see next week and next month and next year as well as the moment at hand. Now you're acting like a fool. And I can assure you that Rhodes doesn't respect fools any more than I do. He leaned forward. "Warren, at VBN *no* one goes over my head. It would be a mistake. Rhodes would be annoyed, and come to me. Profits or no profits, past or present, I would see to it that you would be barred from selling VBN as much as a shoelace, ever again. And I have a little influence around this industry, as you may have heard. I can assure you that if you try to rock my boat even a millimeter, I will sink yours, and everyone on your little pink crew, to the bottom of the deep blue sea."

His smile was, incredibly, sweet as he continued. "As you say, Warren, we're grown men. Situations in the real world aren't always wrapped up in a neat, pretty package as they are on your thirty-six-inch home screen. For the sake of survival, if nothing else, grown men must learn to understand each other, don't you agree?"

Rising, Weber collected the papers he had placed on the desk. "I'm sorry you didn't cotton to my series idea, Caleb."

"So am I, Warren. But you'll sell it somewhere."

"That's right. To VBN."

Atwood's smile clicked off like a lamp.

"Caleb, sweetheart," said Weber, "you're beyond question the first bona-fide moron I've ever met who pulls down half a million dollars a year. What do you earn it as? Certainly not as a psychologist. When I waltzed in here, I was all ready to take 'Moore' to the competition if you eased me out like a gentleman. Well, you didn't, Caleb. You took my baby threat and gave me a daddy threat in return. That was *your* mistake, Caleb, and VBN is going to do this show. I'll see you around sometime, sweetheart. Maybe we can castrate a couple of old niggers together."

"Weber—"

"*Mister* Weber, Caleb, it's *Mister* Weber," he said, and carried the papers out of the elephantine office.

He returned to GWS, afraid to tell Phil, who was still feeling lousy, that, as of this warm afternoon in Manhattan, Vanguard was blown. He was surprised to find Jeanne in her office. "Robin's doing fine," Jeanne asserted. "She told me to come back to work, which is where I should've been in the first place. How could you, or Gin, or Louise, or *someone* let such a mountain of work pile up for me?"

"You shouldn't've left her till you talked with me," Weber chided. Jeanne had phoned him, an hour after landing in Chicago, with the report that there was no real report to give; she'd caught a word here and there between Robin and Jack Dickson, heard Marty Dickson's name mentioned by them both but that was all, heard Jesse Nash's name mentioned by Jack but that also was all; she'd asked Robin about Jack Dickson, and Robin's answers had been evasive.

"Don't worry about that chick," Jeanne counseled now. "I've watched her in action. She's about as helpless as Sonny Liston."

Weber phoned VBN to ask for an appointment with C. Harvey Rhodes, but Rhodes wouldn't be back from Europe till the end of the week. He phoned Robin at The Prentiss, but she wasn't in. He left word for her to call him, and then he accepted a call from Red Barnes, "The Bringer," who gave him Jesse Nash's very private number in New York. He dialed the number and identified himself and his business to a woman who said Mr. Nash would be out of town for a few days, and he told her it was imperative that Mr. Nash get in touch with him. Then, on sudden impulse, because he had intended to fly to Chicago tomorrow for Robin's closing—Lord, how the time whizzed by!—but couldn't wait, he summoned Jeanne to make a plane reservation and a suite reservation at The Prentiss, and summoned Rudi to be on deck. He phoned Karen to say he could not make the Mary Martin opening with her after all, and tightened the office's most immediately loose ends, and Rudi drove him to the airport.

On the impulsive flight, Weber had three vodkas, neat, because they were impulsive, and considered the alley fight that was guaranteed with Atwood, and found himself thinking of Nora Gundersen, Charlie's pretty, peaceful, lady-brainy widow who lived in Skokie, near Chicago. Nora would be well into her fifties now, and her nice kids, Ross and Patsy, had to be well into their teens, maybe older. He would call Nora, who rightly shared in the GWS pie and whom he hadn't called in far too long. He would see her because he liked her, and because he was about to start swinging like Charlie Gundersen again.

Charlie had spent a busy lifetime battling, and besting, the Caleb Atwoods.

Would he have been proud of Weber for standing up to Atwood as he had, and would, for risking the entire sweetheart VBN account because of—all right, the word 'principle'? Don't be embarrassed by the word.

Charlie had been one of the very few men Weber knew who used the word 'principle' in normal conversation without sounding self-righteous, pompous, ludicrous. God, nobody used the word any more, not naturally.

I'll reclaim it, he told himself. I'll make it fashionable again.

At O'Hare Airport, Weber phoned Robin, whose squealing joy that he was in Chicago threatened to pierce his eardrum. "How soon can you be here?" she exclaimed.

"Well, from the airport to you, I'd guess half an hour."

"Sooner, sooner, make it sooner, darling. Five minutes. One minute!" He bought the Chicago papers and a skycap took his valise and attaché case to a waiting taxi. In the back seat, unfolding the afternoon *American*, he saw a front-page picture of Willard Cunningham next to the second of a three-part feature on Soul of America. He found himself wishing that freedom of the press did not involve giving loony hate groups a free publicity ride. No, God, Peter Zenger, and all you out there who fight for freedom of speech, I didn't mean that, he thought hastily. But the fact that Soul of America—*oy*, what a wicked name!—was current news, and therefore legitimate news, appeased him only slightly.

Not the *American*, but a wire service had prepared the story, and Weber, reading it avidly, had to admit it was reasonably balanced and reasonably fair, that although it didn't call Cunningham and his growing band of starched-collar hoodlums a peril to the real soul of America, neither did it confuse the excrement of the fascistic old psalm-singer and his moral thugs with ice cream. It detailed Cunningham's Horatio Alger background, the poor, cold, hungry Montana orphan who had turned his newspaper route into a thriving business, using orphan employees, by the time he was ten years old; who at fifteen had developed simple yet brilliant techniques for moving newspapers from the printer to the consumer with speed more revolutionary than ever dared before and, because of it, had become the richest self-made fifteen-year-old capitalist in the United States; who was a millionaire at twenty, a pauper at thirty, a multimillionaire at forty, and now, at seventy, the multi-multi-multi and et cetera king of pharmaceuticals, the gent who also owned most of the lumber, cotton, and tinplate in the land.

Probably because the details of SOA had run in yesterday's installment or would in tomorrow's, the story only sketchily outlined the avowed function of the organization, which boasted a paying membership of half a million citizens in its first year of formal existence, with the rolls growing. Soul of America's purpose, according to Cunningham, was not to beat the drums for white Christian supremacy, as the agents of demonology charged in the kept mass media, but to inform ethnic minority groups that they were being used by the Intellectual Agnostic Liberal Conspiracy, which was every bit as demonic, though not as clearly defined, as the International Atheistic Communist Conspiracy, and on, and on, and on . . .

It was wordy, and it could afford to be because of the money behind the cornball language, and a child, Weber knew, should have been able to translate the language simply. Black men, it said, had better shape up and learn that Willard Chase Cunningham knew what was best for them. And for Willard Cunningham.

Four Cunningham corporations sponsored seven shows on television, most of them innocuous and most of them popular. Six of those seven shows were on Vanguard. Caleb Atwood was in charge of all six. Okay, it was guilt by association, but—

"—'cha look where ya *goin'*, ya crazy mutt!" the taxi driver shouted at another taxi driver. Weber felt the suddenness of the cab's brakes and a jolt. He looked through the window and gathered that one driver had sideswiped the other. They were at an intersection, not far from The Prentiss, and the other driver, a Negro, saluted Weber's hack and zoomed away. "I tell you," Weber's driver complained, driving again after the additional indignity of a red light, "those niggers are *runnin'* this town! You see what his bus did to me? You see the snot-ass way he laughed at me? Jesus, it's never been like it is now! My family goes back in this country five generations, and it's never been nothing like it is today!"

Possibly because Weber was silent, the man went on with rumbles of anger about how They were having the crap coddled out of them, about how They belonged back in the jungle, about how They were the only people here who didn't even want to try to better Themselves, and about They this and about They that.

"Why are you a cab driver?" Weber inquired suddenly.

"Huh?" The driver half turned, frowning. "Why, Mister, I got five mouths to feed at home, four little ones and one big one, and I . . . Well, what do you mean, why'm I a cab driver?"

"I'm interested to know. You're white, and you've had a head start in this country of five generations, and you haven't done any better for yourself than that black man who sideswiped you. Doesn't that strike you as odd?"

"Whaddaya, a wise guy?"

"Yes, very wise, which is one reason I'm riding this taxi and you're driving it. And I don't know you, which is the nicest thing that's happened to me in weeks, but I do know that one reason you're not President of the Stock Exchange is that you have a big mouth and a weak brain. Let me off at the corner and I'll walk the rest of the way."

He found a five-dollar bill and tossed it into the front seat, not waiting for change, disgusted with the man and himself. He had the door open before the cab had come to a stop.

In his Prentiss suite Weber called Robin again to ask her what room she was in.

"What room are *you* in?" she asked.

"Twenty-seven twenty."

"I'll come there. I can't just pace around here waiting for you, I've got to keep moving." Softly, her voice close to the mouth-piece, she asked, "Do you think anybody's listening in?"

"No."

"Don't be too dressed up when I get there, okay?"

He barely had time to strip and don a robe when he heard the faint knock and opened the door. Robin, looking radiant and smelling sweet and wearing a plaid raincoat on this unrainy evening, stole in past him, not smiling, scarcely meeting his eyes. When he bolted the door and turned to greet her, she was half standing, half leaning at the mirror, her elbow resting on the top of the bureau, her fingers lazily threading through her hair. Her right leg and knee and thigh showed through the part in the still buttoned raincoat, and the leg was raised and cocked so that her foot rested on a hassock. Playfully provocative, burlesquing all movie vamps, she said, throatily, "M'sieur find Fifi desiraboool, *non?*"

Throatily, though not faking it, Weber said, "Girlie, I'm a retired truss manufacturer, eighty-one years old on my next birthday, and I'm in Chicago to attend the Loyal Order of Eunuchs convention. You can't tantalize me, you brazen whippersnapper."

She slowly undid the bottom button and the top button of the raincoat. "What zat mean, 'eunuch'? M'sieur cannot get eet oop?"

"M'sieur would not dream of considering such primitive tomfoolery," said Weber, feeling eet go oop. "I commit myself to the finer things of life, like shooting vicious deer in season and attending conventions. Now I must demand that you leave, you earthy temptress, or I shall be forced to call the manager."

"Ah, ze mana-jair, perhops he can get eet oop for Fifi," she said, and all five buttons were slowly undone, and the lovely, creamy brown breasts were glimpsed through the folds of the coat, and Fifi became Robin, and she said, "I must be in the wrong room. I don't fool around no old men. Takes too long, and I don't even get tipped proper."

Weber rushed to her. They trembled in each other's arms, at

each other's body, and their kisses were famished and uncontrollable. Later, much later, Robin gave in and explained how she knew Jack Dickson. She told a story about being rescued from Philadelphia by Jesse Nash, about going to him in Los Angeles and being his girl friend. She told a convoluted story that Weber suspected had crannies of make-believe as well as truth, and when she finished he asked why she had not been more forthright with him before this.

"I guess Jesse is a subject I want to stay buried," she said. "He was the moon and the stars, once upon a time. Right now he's a dangerous man. He used to try to understand himself, but he doesn't even bother any more. I don't want to be connected with him, even for a minute."

He told her about "Moore" and about the maybe ideal man to play the title role. Robin's quick laugh was surprisingly coarse. "You really must be off your rocker!" she exclaimed. "You wouldn't just be asking for trouble, you'd be begging to pay for it. Jesse's not the man I knew, or anybody knew, two years ago. He's turned into a crazy man."

"When was the last time you saw him?"

"A long time ago. But I know. Don't you be a crazy man, Warren."

"You still care for him, don't you?"

She blinked. "What makes you say a thing like that?"

"Just a hunch, listening to your tough talk. I could be wrong."

A little pause. "No, you're right. You're wrong and you're right. I can't hate anybody I cared about once, and I did care about Jesse, till I couldn't take any more of him and left him. He pleaded with me to come back, but I couldn't. But . . . I mean, what I'm trying to say is that I'd feel awful if anything bad ever happened to him, but I don't want to ever be in any position where I'd have to see him again."

While Robin dressed for her first show, Weber phoned Nora Gundersen from his suite. A housekeeper said that Mrs. Gundersen was with her daughter Patricia in Gloucester—Pat had just given birth to a girl—and was there any message? Weber asked Pat's married name and the name of the hospital, and wired little Patsy six dozen roses with the message, *Just heard the marvelous news. Stick to your Gundersens. Much love, Unca Warren.* He replaced the receiver, feeling like Methuselah's father. He had chain-smoked with Charlie while Nora was having Patsy. Had it all been that long ago, that unaccountably long ago, that many good battles ago?

The Prentiss Room tables were at a premium, but Weber wangled a ringside from the supper club's manager, Tully Nolte, and phoned the after-six numbers of Art Ducas and Doug Foster from GWS's Chicago office and Liz Hornaby and Perry Portieri from the Chicago papers to join him for the first show. Liz and Doug were free, or would make themselves and their spouses free, and they did join him in the club he hadn't remembered as being so gold-braid swank. Liz was one of the last of the really diligent gal reporters, intrepid but fair, and Doug Foster and his wife Edie knew Chicago inside out, and they all told Weber what he already knew but loved to hear—that Robin had the city in her little brown palm, that there could be no holding her back.

Perhaps a minute before Robin's intro in the jammed room, Liz Hornaby raised her third martini and inquired, "What's the scoop on our princess being once married to Jesse Nash, Warren? Why've you and Ronnie Haley kept the news under wraps? Did you great brains honestly think it wouldn't surface?"

His swizzle stick stopped swizzling, and he gaped at her. "Married?"

"Come on now with the coy-boy stuff, lover," she grinned. "You know better than to play dummy with Liz."

"My God," said Doug, looking at Weber, "you look like you *didn't* know!"

Goddammit, thought Weber. "No," he said, and cleared his throat, and asked them both how they'd learned it, and when

they'd learned it, and if they were sure it was true. *Chalmers'
Weekly* legmen had tracked the tip down on the Coast, they said,
and it sure was true, and *Chalmers'* was running it this Thursday,
even though Robin had refused them an interview.

Goddammit, Weber thought again, and sat dazed and silently
furious through the intro and the applause and through Robin's
first two numbers. He watched her at the mike, gradually telling
himself that it was a rumor without substance because she was a
funny kid but she wouldn't have kept *that* from him. . . .

He watched her, listened to her, saw the clean movements and
certainty, and realized he had been so close to the development of
Robin Hamilton that he had missed the exact moment when she
had become the Compleat Pro. The customers weren't goggling a
colored beauty; they were giving rapt audience to a pro, and a pro
was someone who made no mistakes. She understood the love
lyrics she sang, and she was heating up the place with those numbers, yet she was uniquely different from all the other hot-number
vocalists Weber had observed for seasons, unique in that the se-
ductiveness was somehow wholesome. She sang one number after
another, with the instinctive pacing of a genius, and Weber decided that her artistry lay in the elusive quality of her sensuality;
she was stoking up the droolers, yet somehow she would not have
offended Billy Graham.

Her last number before the guaranteed encores was the "Black
Star" ballad that Mossy Chaikin had written for the act. She
brought to the verse an authority and solemnity that stilled the
audience and the waiters.

> *Spring was always too far from sight*
> *I never seemed to do anything right*
> *I was the girl with two left feet*
> *Unloved, unnoticed, incomplete*
> *I was sure there'd never be a man for me*
> *I was sure that was the way it had to be . . .*

She was alone in the baby spotlight, and the slow two-four chorus was hers, not Mossy Chaikin's, not the Brill Building's. Hers.

I was born
Under a Black Star
Under a canopy of ebony
A Black Star.
Never imagined
I'd have the chance
To ever feel
Real romance.
  Then you came
  From a bright star
  And you brightened every corner of my
    Black Star
Now there's no Black Star
Above me
Look at me, now I'm free because you love me
You love me, you love me!
Hello, love
Good-bye, Black Star.

The song was repeated from the bridge, there was an instant of silence, and then the audience erupted in a mass fever of applause. Weber was deeply impressed and, when her encore was done and more applause followed her off, once again furious. He eased himself away from Liz Hornaby and Foster, promising Liz the scoop interview with the girl if one was warranted—he would have to check it out—and told the captain that his party was to have all the food and liquor it wished, and went to the dressing room with his news.

"Is it true or isn't it?" he demanded.

"Yes . . ."

"What the hell kind of patsy do you see me as, how many kinds of a sucker?" he thundered. "How many other tasty tidbits are there about you I can expect to learn from the Liz Hornabys and *Chalmers' Weeklys* and the chambermaid? God damn your arrogance, don't you figure you owe me *anything?*"

"It isn't arrogance. Please don't yell," she said in a tiny voice. "I can't bear—"

"Yes, arrogant! Arrogant and stupid. Forget us, forget we had this notion we mean something special to each other. Do you have even a sleepy idea of the time and sweat and money that's gone into making you, that's riding on you right this minute? We're not building you up as some hooker with a pair of boobs and a tin voice, we're trying to build a *star!* It's a careful job, not slapping a poster on a wall and praying, and there's publicity and there's notoriety, and one more of your hidden facts of life I can't control for the press because the press fills me in before you do, and I can assure you that's how you'll be remembered, as a pair of boobs. Not for the voice, not for the talent and the class, but for the closet skeletons. Now I want to know, here and now—what other choice whammies are you carrying around in your suitcase?"

"Nothing. Please don't be mad at—"

"Don't be *mad?* Lady, I'm so mad I could kick your butt from here till Thursday—when, by sweet coincidence, *Chalmers' Weekly* goes on the stands!"

He knew that something was making him overreact, that the sensible and mature thing would be to stay with her and calm down or meet her later and thrash out her past and future with her, but he felt deceived and hurt, and he took an elevator to his suite, where he phoned for a reservation on the next jet out of O'Hare and called the bell captain to have someone come at once and repack his bag. Waiting, he placed a person-to-person call to Milt Ashley, a *Chalmers' Weekly* editor in New York, but Milt wasn't expected home till around midnight.

He landed at Kennedy shortly after midnight, New York time, and placed the call again. *Chalmers'* was a top-circulation newsweekly rarely kind to him—or, for that matter, to anyone but King George the Fifth, he'd once remarked to Milt—and Milt was frequently the driver behind the wheels that crashed into Warren Weber. But Milt Ashley was also something of a friend, in a Toots Shor bar way, and he would level when asked to. Now Weber reached him and asked how rough the story would be.

"That depends on how much readers like Hamilton and don't like Nash, or the other way around," said Ashley.

"Oh, boy, typical *Chalmers'* double-talk, which comes out hatchet job. I can read the last paragraph now, where your noble rag will ponder on when the fast-rising sepia songbird will declare herself, pro or con, on the matter of the dusky anarchist."

Milt chuckled. "Something like that, only better written."

"Where did you get the story?"

"I didn't handle it. Barney Young did, out in L.A. But I know he didn't get it from your esteemed offices or from Haley's, which incidentally disillusions me, Warren. I was always under the impression that you and Ronnie Haley would gladly have carnal knowledge of each other in Woolworth's window if you thought it might see print. You two guys have been selling this Hamilton dish for all the three of you are worth, with every gimmick under the sun. What made you skip the marriage to Nash? You're a past master at pulling publicity strings the way you want them pulled, and here you leave an item like this for us happy archaelogists to pick up."

"I'm a careless clod. Do you have the proof nailed down, Milt?"

"No, we love to run retractions and invite libel actions," Ashley said. "Of *course* we have it, fathead! Now is there anything else I can help you lose sleep over? I have to go and catch forty winks of my own."

"No, you done real good, Milton. Thanks."

He went home, where Karen and the Palmers, Lowell and Judy, had just come from the Martin opening and were having drinks. Weber joined them for a short one and chatted with them, at one point answering Judy Palmer's demand to know what that gorgeous colored girl Robin Hamilton was really like by saying, soberly, "We've just learned at the office that we've been duped.

She's not colored at all. She was born and reared in Darien, where her father runs the eastern division of the White Citizens Council." Lowell Palmer laughed, and Judy didn't know what to make of the answer, and Karen flashed him one of her sharpest disapproving "Don't play your hostile games with our friends" glances, and he gave Karen one of his best "Get rid of them" pantomimes, and excused himself a minute later with the yawning alibi that he had a lulu of a busy day ahead of him.

He was in a pajama shirt and robe in the bedroom, with the door ajar, when he heard the front door close. He went to her and, as she was in the middle of asking why he was acting so peculiarly, held her and kissed her with an intensity that started as passion for Robin and became passion for Karen. "You are the *strangest—*" she began, not entirely receptive but not retreating, and he guided her onto the closed, heated terrace, where he did not flip the light switch on and where he kissed her until she became Raggedy Ann and breathed, "Oh, Warren, Warren . . ." They sat and then stretched out on the verandah, and he did not hurry as his fingers worked at her zipper. He faintly heard her mild protest that she wasn't prepared, and he kept on, and then there were no more sounds from Karen other than the sounds of questioning and then cordial and then eager response.

In the morning, at GWS, Jeanne told him that Sol Aaron had called from Hollywood the afternoon before and wanted to be called back. Other, and bigger, studios had begun to make firm contract offers for Robin over the past week, and Weber had disregarded Sol Aaron, who controlled Cambridge Pictures, as too small a fish to belong in the auction sale. But now he waited till one o'clock, when it would be ten A.M. on the Coast, to return the call, for Aaron had been the sole man to offer a one-picture deal with no right to option unless and until GWS chose, in its own time, to talk option. If Sol was still as agreeable today, if the tape recorder connected to Weber's telephone could record the verbal agreement, if Sol's New York boys hustled up contracts this afternoon for Weber to go over this evening, if Robin, returning to New York tomorrow, arrived in time to sign before the word about Mrs. Jesse Nash reached their corporate ears, Weber's instincts directed him to go ahead. The money would choke no horses, but the showcase of a Cambridge picture with Robin, over which Weber had insisted he wanted more than paper control, would be certain to charm many an influential critic and bring the real moneybags scrambling with offers that would choke plenty of horses.

At 1:15 P.M., New York time, Sol Aaron, who knew he wasn't paying as much as the biggies could be expected to pay eventually, agreed to every demand. At 1:20 P.M., knuckling under at Weber's even-voiced insistence, Aaron sweetened the original price by an additional $25,000. "This girl better come through a camera good is all I can say," said Aaron.

Replacing the receiver, Weber thought, And she'd better not blow up the world, is all *I* can say. Then he busied himself in a number of office projects, including the rehearsal of his opening words, when and if Jesse Nash agreed to meet him.

Ten

·

ROBIN FINISHED HER ENGAGEMENT at the Prentiss Room, not yet sure
if she had the courage to go back to New York and face Warren,
the only person except Mama and Jesse who could make her fall
apart by being mad at her; not yet sure she was ready to do with
her career what Jesse had done with his—ruin it before thinking
the consequences through. The applause and affection *were* good.
The money was unbelievable. Her seven-league strides as a performer were good and unbelievable.

There was no one to go to, to confide in. Even Jack Dickson
had left Chicago. Porter Blair had telephoned her, after the disastrous night in his suite, with a rush of gibberish apologies, the
central one of which was that he wouldn't, couldn't have behaved
so abominably, psychopathically, if he hadn't been drunk. On the
phone he had sounded drunk. Porter Blair had left Chicago, too.
She would almost have gone to Porter Blair. Not really, but almost.

Her last show done, she reluctantly attended a late party, spon-
taneously set up in her honor by the band and even the Prentiss
Room waiters. She drank two cocktails instead of one, and watched
what she said to strange people because one of them might be a
reporter, but the charm came through with polished ease, the
charm that had been awkward and forced when Jesse had taken
her to meet people, and she was lonelier than she had ever been but
she couldn't give up this life, she knew, because so many people
wanted to be so nice to her.

Mr. Nolte, the Prentiss Room's manager, saw her to her suite, and seemed to be waiting to be invited in, but she thanked him for all his kindnesses and went in alone. She poured a glass of the whiskey Warren or someone had brought her and drank it, understanding for perhaps the first time in her life why some lonely people like to get drunk, and sat with the glass and thought of Jesse, who hated drunks, who hated everyone who wasn't a responsible individual each minute of the day. Jesse, who had said, "The minute they know they got you scared, that's the minute they got you and that's the minute you might as well close up shop, because you'll never stand up on your feet again."

She sipped the whiskey and remembered the Waltham Hotel in Miami Beach, a hotel much like this one, where Jesse had pretended nothing could faze him, where he had been very scared, in spite of his happiness, in spite of his being the tallest man in the world. . . .

The Waltham lobby, Jesse remarked, could have used Burma Shave signs on the way to the front desk. It was an enormous balloon of glass paneling from roof to floor, its furniture slinky and extravagant, and even the squadrons of bellhops looked wealthy. The lobby had the look of hard, cold cash, and, as if to testify to this, its color motif was varying shades of green.

Robin and Jesse were assigned connecting rooms, preposterously ornate rooms, on the twelfth floor, but one went completely unused. She was almost unbearably happy, because of Jesse's happiness, because he was at last in total command of himself, sure, accepting of his success, more relaxed than she had ever seen him. All vestiges of doubt and suspicion seemed to have drained from him, to be replaced by a more certain step, by increasing confidence in Marty and the folks around Marty. On their first night in Miami Beach they made love on their private terrace, under the sky. On that night, Jesse spoke the word "love" for the first time, and Robin bawled.

Filming of *Kid Hamlet* began the morning after they arrived, on the Waltham golf course, and here a wide-eyed Robin, staying close to Jesse who wanted her close, learned that movies were not shot from beginning to end but, at least in the case of this movie, the other way around. The motion picture was, and would be, Marty Dickson's: story line by Marty Dickson, directed by Marty Dickson, produced by Marty Dickson, starring Marty Dickson. The "plot," Jesse told her as they stood in the hot sun and watched the little man scamper about shouting orders, was as formless and free-flowing as the plot in every other Marty Dickson comedy. This one was supposed to be about a dim-witted, well-meaning young man who inherits a fabulous but bankrupt Miami Beach hotel and, though unequipped to run it, determines to make a success of it; he is beset by mobsters who try to move in and take over; he innocently falls in love with a glamorous lady who happens to be the chief mobsters' girl friend; he is kidnaped and held for ransom; a six-year-old girl with golden curls helps him to escape and the two of them are chased all over scenic Miami Beach; and by being the world's dumbest man and having the world's purest heart, he singlehandedly captures the crooks, makes a great financial success of the hotel, turns it into a Disneyland, only more mammoth, and hands the keys over to children everywhere to run it and enjoy it, free. In the last scene he adopts the six-year-old girl with golden curls and marries a poor honest chambermaid who becomes ravishingly beautiful by the simple process of taking off her glasses.

"It sounds too crazy," Robin said.

Jesse nodded. "It'll take three weeks to shoot and it'll gross nine jillion bucks. Every picture he makes grosses nine jillion bucks."

"Where does the 'Hamlet' come in?"

"Who knows? Who cares? Marty said he wanted to make a picture of his version of *Hamlet*, and I guess this is his version of *Hamlet*."

Jesse did not work that day—he was to be in several big scenes later as an eccentric multimillionaire—but he was expected to be available, and he was, and Marty Dickson paid finger-snapping, affectionate attention to him during breaks, and even bear-hugged

Robin warmly, openly, with Robin Brown Breast jokes, as though there had never been a moment of tension between them. The nightclub show that evening was a sellout, formal and glittering, and Marty Dickson gaily butted into everyone's act, including Jesse's, but the hijinx were supportive rather than mean and Jesse was a hit. In their room later, they shared a turkey sandwich delivered by room service and Jesse mused, "Guess it was three years ago, I played a white club not far from here. I'd finish up two, three in the morning, bushed, sweat rollin' off me—plenty of empty rooms right near by, but I had to get dressed and cross the tracks over to the colored section." He sighed. "Never gonna forget that. Times change, though, little by little."

Marty Dickson seemed to thrive on the inhuman schedule, but Jesse managed to keep up with him. Work on the movie began each morning at seven and often ran till six or seven in the evening because Marty Dickson, highly organized, was determined to wrap it up well under schedule. The club show rarely ended before one o'clock in the morning. The pace was brutal, but Robin watched Jesse fall in with it, watched him walk on air, and walked with him.

On the sixth whirlwind day in Miami Beach, a Saturday, Jesse completed his third day of work, with an estimated five or six more to go. Because there was to be no shooting the following day, Marty Dickson insisted on doing two club shows instead of one, and jubilantly announced that the second show would be a swinger because today was his and Helen's wedding anniversary and a bunch of his oldest and dearest cronies were flying in to help celebrate. On that evening, shortly before midnight, Robin was with Jesse in his dressing room when Coley Dennis breezed in, surprising her and, she could quickly judge, Jesse, too; they had not been introduced at Marty Dickson's party in Bel Air because Dennis had made an almost ostentatious point of avoiding an introduction. Now he called, "Hey now, big fella, congrats, congrats, and put 'er there!" emphasizing heartiness that didn't seem genuine, in a strange dialect that sounded put on ("That cat's more Picadilly than pickaninny," Jesse had once said), and thrust out a smooth, manicured hand.

Jesse forced a sliver of a welcoming smile, said, "Hello," and introduced Robin.

Dennis glanced at her and said, "Hello," but clearly was acting like a man in a great hurry. He told Jesse, "Sorry we couldn't catch your act before tonight—been working like a madman lately —but I did catch the first show and I'm here to inform you, big fella, you were worth waiting for. Socko. The social conscious stuff, socko. Marty's been raving to me about you and, as usual, he knows what he's raving about."

"Well, thanks. I saw you yokkin' it up out there, you and your party," Jesse said and let a small pause sink in. "Where are your friends, by the way? Miss Hamilton here and I'd like to meet them."

He was baiting Dennis, Robin sensed. He had purposely come down harder than usual on the race stuff in the first show, he'd admitted to her, because he'd spotted Dennis and a party of five whites in the room; the whites had laughed and applauded only after Dennis did, as though they'd needed Dennis's consent. Coley Dennis, smelling of expensive cologne and looking fleetingly troubled, answered hastily, "Oh, they're gabbing and they still have the feedbag on. You know how it is. Ah, look, I don't want to take up your time. I just wanted to say hello and all kinds of *terrific* good luck. Ah . . ."

Robin sat mute, worried. Jesse's face was expressionless, but she could see the displeasure. "Wait, don't rush off, Dennis," he said, too evenly. "Fill me in."

"What's that? Fill you in on what?"

"On why you're here. Why you're rushin' away. You don't like me and I for sure don't like you. You didn't pop in to see me just because this is Be Kind to Darkies Week, now did you?"

Coley Dennis looked quizzical and uncomfortable. "What in the holy hell are you talking about, fella?"

"I read you as phony, fella, as phony as that conk in your hair. That's exactly and precisely what I'm talkin' about."

Instant fury brightened Dennis's eyes, and Robin was alarmed at the speed with which heartiness switched to hate. "You cheeky crud!" he hissed. "You *rotten*, cheeky crud! All right, yes, you're right, if it was up to me I wouldn't waste my energy taking a leak on you. You spout all—"

"Just watch that language in front of a lady," cautioned Jesse, not stirring in his chair.

"Don't give *me* orders!" Dennis cried. "Who are *you?* You go spouting all that second-class-citizen black man shit into the mike like you're some *expert*, and people listen to you because Marty picked you up somewhere, and maybe some of them will start believing some of your shit and you don't give a goddam that what you're—"

"This fine gentleman's language bother you?" Jesse asked Robin. She shook her head—and otherwise was numb.

"—you don't *care* that what you're doing is trying to knock down everything somebody like me has been building up over the years. You stupid cracker, who are *you* to talk about phony? Why don't you go march in some goddam civil rights parade if you're such a goddam expert on your goddam Cause?"

"You're gettin' red in the face, Uncle Tom," Jesse blandly commented, lighting a cigarette. "Becomes you, I must confess."

"I sat through your shabby act and I came back here to say hello strictly as a favor to Marty," Coley Dennis stormed, ignoring Robin, curiously not meeting Jesse's eyes. "He digs you for some reason I'll never dig, and he's been after me to be nice to you. *Nice!* If I thought I was going to be insulted by some upstart hillbilly, you can bet your ass I wouldn't've moved a muscle. And you can also bet your ass I'll have a word or two to say about you to Marty."

"Yassa, massa," Jesse drawled, getting up and performing an elaborate shuffle. "Gimme dem gallopin' dominoes an' dat switchblade. Gimme dat Rivuh Jordan. Gimme dem colla'd greens and dat mushmelon."

Coley Dennis charged out of the room. The cologne lingered.

"Oh, Jesse . . ." Robin mourned.

"I could've slugged him," Jesse said softly after a moment. "Oh me, but how sweet I'd sleep tonight if I'd pushed out two or three of his teeth." He took a deep pull on his cigarette. "Proud I didn't, though. This isn't the right and proper battlefield. I'll know when the right and proper one comes along. And so will Coley. A couple more black folks like him, and the Klan can go on the big board on Wall Street."

Tensely, Robin watched the second show. It began with the same careful construction as the first, but gradually became a formless free-for-all, with Marty Dickson as its raucous cheer-leader. A galaxy of celebrities was in rooting attendance, and Marty Dickson, rapidly swiping one drink after another from friends' and strangers' tables, whipped about on and off the stage, ad-libbed feverishly, commanded show business stars to the microphone, got more and more tastelessly risqué and then downright dirty, and some of the stars appeared embarrassed and some played along, trying to top him.

Then the stage was crowded, and Jesse had still not done his act nor had Penny Stone, the vocalist who was to have opened the show. Coley Dennis said, "Knock, knock," and Marty Dickson said, "Who's there?" and Dennis said, "Oz," and Dickson said, "Oz who?" and Dennis said, "Oz you' new neighbuh, man," and people on the stage and in the audience laughed with them, and they kept calling each other "Boy" and rubbing each other's heads. Robin couldn't catch every word of the growing bedlam of drunken frivolity, but she knew that the jokes were centering on smut and race, with Dennis every bit as disgraceful as Marty Dickson, and she felt shame and suspected that there were people at the tables, white as well as black, who were uncomfortable, too, who recognized that the race stuff was getting out of hand. There was music, and Marty Dickson and Coley Dennis sang "Me and My

Shadow," with Marty Dickson playing the shadow, and, one by one, the others on the stage got in line behind Coley Dennis and did everything he did, from shuffling to rolling their eyes to marching to shuffling again. And then Marty Dickson, near the wings, leaped out of line and out of sight for an instant and leaped back with Jesse on his arm, and Robin could see him grinningly place Jesse in the line.

But Jesse, anger distorting his face, was having none of it. He brushed the small comic's hand away and seemed ready to turn and leave the stage. Marty Dickson's grin froze. Over the blaring music, Coley Dennis cried, "Hey, come on, join the pack, soul brothuh!" and went to Jesse, grabbing his sleeve, and Robin gasped as Jesse jerked his arm back and shot a fist into Coley Dennis's head.

Dennis was flung backwards, off the stage and onto a ringside table. There were shouts, and someone screamed, and the music abruptly stopped. As people scrambled to help him, as others stood or sat horrified, Marty Dickson the most horrified of all, Jesse glared at Marty Dickson, as though daring him to be next.

There was, sharply, an eerie, pious silence in the great room. Marty Dickson, obviously outraged, obviously aware of an audience hanging in air for his response, blinked and said hoarsely, "In this corner, wearing purple trunks, uh . . ."

Dennis, brought to a sitting position, looked stunned, not quite conscious. Jesse took a single step to the microphone and said, in a voice that was quietly and surprisingly even, "I want to take this opportunity to thank you white folks for your swell sense of humor. I agree nothin's funnier'n watchin' us niggers havin' fun, long's you're all *liberal* about it. I wanna thank my white master"—he indicated Marty Dickson—"for helpin' to remind you all that us niggers just natch'ly got rhythm."

He paused. "I'm leaving this happy family this evening," he said, dropping not a single "g." "I'm leaving because I'm a black man and there's only room in Mr. Dickson's happy family for niggers." He faced Marty Dickson. "Got a suggestion for you, Marty. If the party starts losing its steam, why don't you set up a nice friendly lynch party? Your liberal family here might be a touch squeamish about it at first, but you know and I know they wouldn't miss it for the world."

He walked off.

Robin hurried after him.

"Do you have the least idea what the hell you *did* to me out there in front of everybody?" Marty Dickson roared in Jesse's dressing room. People, including reporters and photographers, were trying to get in. "You big-shot son of a bitch, do you realize you made me out to be a *bigot* or something? The joint's *crawling* with the press! Jesus, what *possessed* you to make a schmuck out of me?"

"Because that's a little bit of what you are, Marty," said Jesse. "Trouble with me is, it took me a whole long while to find it out."

"You crazy son of a bitch, talking like that, I'll *break* you! You hear, I'll *bust* you, I'll *ruin* you, I'll make you see who your friends are!" Marty Dickson cried. He stomped out and slammed the door behind him.

Jesse refused to see anyone. He dressed quickly and took Robin through the busy corridor, jammed with reporters barking questions and photographers popping flashbulbs, to the Waltham, where a sea of messages awaited him. He phoned the desk and left word that he would accept no calls, no messages. He stripped, yawned, scratched his chest, and silently got into bed. Robin was afraid to talk, and soon he was asleep, or seemed to be.

The next day, Robin sat by, her cold fingers laced in her lap, as Jesse agreed to a press conference. Had he and Marty Dickson been in touch since last night? he was asked. No, he replied. Did he know that Coley Dennis had suffered a slight concussion? No, he replied, and yawned. Did he know that Marty Dickson was talking a blue streak, to AP and UPI and anyone who called, about the Dickson record on civil rights, about ungrateful actors, about the need for Jesse Nash to apologize and set everything straight? No.

What were his plans now? Jesse crossed his legs and read from no paper. "I don't apologize for being a black man, ever, that's my first plan," he said. "I appreciate Marty's boost. I appreciate his faith. I've done some work on this *Kid Hamlet* picture and I'm sorry my part in it'll be scrapped—for his sake and lots of folks' sake that helped me. But I don't work for Marty Dickson, ever again. Marty doesn't mean I'm an ungrateful actor. He means I'm an ungrateful darky."

Wasn't there a contract between them?

"That's right," Jesse answered, nodding. "A generous one—and I haven't really checked, but maybe it's an ironclad one, too. Maybe Marty can hold me to it—maybe he's got an army of white lawyers slick enough to keep me from workin' from now till Doomsday. The point is, I couldn't care less. I could climb out from under by Tommin' it, but I never did learn the knack of Tommin'. If Marty can't fathom that he's the one should be makin' the apologies, then could be he's even more of a white man than I figured he was."

What now, if neither man chose to give an inch?

Jesse shrugged. "I sit tight. I check out of this hotel at three P.M. today because I don't want to be beholden to Dickson Enterprises for one more night's lodgin', and I fly back to L.A. to clean up some unfinished business and for the time bein' I sit tight. I enjoy where I'm sittin'. It's called the catbird seat, and most black men never get close to the cushion."

What was meant by that?

Toying with a cigarette, grinning, he said, "I mean, ma'am and gentleman, that my pride in black men and my shame in white men gets more swelled up every minute I sit here. Startin' today, I'm gonna be a black man like I never was before."

Robin flew with him to Los Angeles, where they registered at a Negro hotel in Watts as Mr. and Mrs. J. Nash and where they conferred with a Negro attorney named R. R. Brunswick. Brunswick listened to Jesse's story, examined every legal paper Jesse handed him, and said, "If you want to strike out on your own as a performer, it looks from here as if Mr. Dickson's firm has you over a barrel. But maybe not. I'll do some homework and let you know."

As Robin traveled the city with Jesse, meeting his friends, only a few of whom believed he was wise in meeting Marty Dickson's public attacks with more public attacks, and as they waited for something to break, the newspapers continued to report and editorials and columnists continued to analyze the rift between the two men. Jesse learned that Marty Dickson had been strongly advised to clam up, to refuse to discuss the mess with reporters, but Robin thought she could understand why he kept talking, kept defending himself: the weight of sympathy seemed to be not with him but with Jesse; no one was calling Marty Dickson a racist, but everyone in the press who dealt with the issue appeared to be in agreement that his over-liberated jokes at the Waltham—some of which were quoted, not always accurately—had been in atrocious taste. Marty Dickson remained steadfast: he would live up to his promise to make Jesse Nash a star, but only if Jesse Nash publicly corrected the bigot image and made a public apology. Otherwise, he would hold Jesse Nash to their perfectly legal contract, which meant that Jesse Nash could accept no jobs as an entertainer without the express permission of Dickson Enterprises.

"What *are* you going to do, Jesse?" Robin asked.

Jesse clearly was concerned but, for some perverse reason, pretended to be amused by the awesome fireworks. "Sit tight, like I said," he answered.

One of his friends Robin met, at lunch, was Orville Sanford, a bullet-bald, heavily mustached, obviously educated Negro of about forty. She knew of him, and she was a little frightened of him. Orville Sanford was West Coast coordinator for a civil rights organization that was considered moderate, but lately—especially since Roland Lee's death—he had been prominently in the news as a militant. After Roland Lee was killed it had been Orville Sanford, more than any other Negro leader, who warned New York City that black people everywhere would be following every step in the investigation of the killing, that they would search under every rug for sweepings. He had not struck Robin as the leader type—force was missing, despite the forceful speeches, and his voice was almost painfully high pitched—but he frightened her, nonetheless.

Now, sitting across from her in the Watts coffee shop, he was impressed that she was Roland Lee's sister. He asked her, point blank, how deeply she was involved in avenging her brother's murder.

To her relief, Jesse answered for her. "Miss Hamilton's not a scrapper, Orville," he asserted. "But we'll remedy that."

Mr. Sanford merely blinked.

"I'm glad you looked me up," he told Jesse. "I would've contacted you, but I didn't know how. You've been covering yourself with glory, friend."

Jesse's grin was wry. "That'll be dandy consolation while I stand in line for my relief check."

"Don't make me weep!" Mr. Sanford scoffed. "There's nothing you can't do if you have guts—and you've shown you have an ample supply. You're coming up in the world."

"So are you," Jesse said. "For a cat who's always stayed behind the scenes, looks like you're turnin' into a one-man band."

"That's the general idea," Mr. Sanford nodded. "I'm pulling out of the organization soon."

"Out of SPIRIT?" Jesse asked, eyebrows raised. "You been with it since it was a pup, just about."

"That's right, too long. It's become so respectable, so molasses-action respectable, that you can scarcely spot a dark face in the executive offices any more. Whitey's grabbed the reins—Whitey with the Jew know-how—and you know how long we'll be allowed to speak above a whisper once he's really entrenched."

"What's up your sleeve, soul brother? You plannin' to start a whole new civil rights movement?"

"Yes. That's exactly what I'm planning."

With gentle sarcasm, Jesse said, "We don't have enough roamin' the land now, do we?"

"More than enough," Orville Sanford said sharply, "and there's not a realistic one among them. In the long run, the clean-collar boys like SPIRIT just want to sit on Charley's lap. The nonviolence boys want to make ringing speeches for posterity and make believe Christ is still working down at the office. The Muslim boys say, 'You built this filthy country and died in all its filthy wars, now let's cut out and build a black little world for ourselves.' Who needs that daydream nonsense?"

"Um. Well, let's try to figure you out, Orville. If I catch you right, you don't want us livin' with Charley but you don't want us to segregate ourselves. No vanilla, no chocolate. What other flavors you got to suggest?"

"Race pride!" Mr. Sanford shot back. "The same thing I read you talking about in the newspapers. Talking back. Hitting back. Arming ourselves."

Jesse frowned. "You've lost your cork, cousin."

"Why? Because I want our people to climb off Charley's lap?"

"No, because Charley owns the store. The store's in his name, and until we can buy it off him you can't go choppin' him down. There's too many of him around, for one thing."

"Don't bother to read me statistics. Organize the smallest army properly and there isn't any store that can't be demolished."

" 'Demolish,' " Jesse ridiculed. "What happens when some hot kid listens to you and he takes what he hears literally? He kills Charley, and Charley walks him to the gas house and kills him back. What does that do for the kid?"

"For starters, it tells Charley that Hattie McDaniel's over the hill."

Jesse's eyes narrowed. "You know what you sound like, man? A dummy—you got your degree and you're a dummy. How in *the* hell is the establishment gonna get its back broke if yours gets broke first? Of course you don't hold up Ralph Abernathy's picture if some baby comes at you with a jack-handle. Of course you defend yourself and your property. But Charley has all the cops in his store, so why's a smart fella like you talkin' like a crackpot?"

A faint, bland smile came to Mr. Sanford's lips. "I talk the way

I talk, Jesse," he said, "because I'm fed up, up to my eyeballs. I don't sit behind a safe, shiny desk, not all the time I don't. I get out from behind it every now and again, and what changes do these crackpot's eyes see? Rosa Parks can ride up front in the bus, and my children don't have to sit in the balcony when they go to the movies and watch how savage the Indians were to the white man. Big deal. Black skulls still get cracked because they're black. For every token spook you see in Charley's store, there's a thousand of us who can't get near it. Fed *up*," he went on with mounting passion. "I'm fed *up*. Not for me personally but for the man who can't call himself a man, after three hundred years, because Charley keeps cutting his balls off." Hurriedly he said to Robin, "Excuse me, Miss," and as hurriedly returned to Jesse. "And don't tell me it's a grand country because my daddy was a tenant farmer who couldn't write his name and I went on to school and I can support my family. This rotten, corrupt country's going to know who I am and what I stand for very soon, Jesse. I have backers, backers with money. Call me a crackpot—go right ahead and help yourself—but it's only a matter of time before all our brothers join up with me. And that includes you, too, if you don't mislay your guts and sell out again."

"Don't hold your breath, Orville," Jesse said. "Who are these backers with all the gold?"

"I can't tell you, not just yet."

Shaking his head, Jesse smiled. "My, my, but this is a powerful lot of cloak-and-dagger for lunchtime. Orville the ebony conspirator. Can you at least give me a hint what your first official act'll be when you take control of the Army and Navy?"

The man didn't return the smile. "Is that considered a laugh line?"

"If you have to ask, I guess not. No, none of this is funny. I've always had a lot of admiration for you, man. I still do; you take a stand on an issue, and I admire that. If that Manhattan DA gets an indictment, it'll be because you more'n anybody else kept raisin' hell. That kind of thing's what you should be givin' all your talent to, not this takin'-up-arms silliness. You'll be washed down the drain in no time flat."

"Maybe. Let's compare notes, and tunes, in about a month, say. I'll be in New York then, at this address," he said, and scribbled an address on a paper napkin. "Where do you expect you'll be?"

"Maybe there, too. I don't know anything for sure right now."

"You'll know a great many things for sure by then," Mr. Sanford said with confidence. He insisted on taking the check. "You'll know that you're not free, and I'm not free, and—" pointedly— "Miss Hamilton isn't free, until all black folks are. And I mean all."

Outside the coffee shop, they shook hands and parted. On the walk back to the hotel, Jesse said, "Old Orville and I've known each other four, five years now. Never been what you'd call tight buddies—I played some benefits for SPIRIT when he asked me to. That's how we became friends, but never close. Funny, though—I thought I had him pegged up, down, forwards, and backwards. You see how you can be wrong. I never would've taken him for one of those wild-eyes. There's nobody smarter than old Orville, and a lot he says is right on the button. But I never would've figured him to go in for that gun talk."

"You stay away from him!" Robin ordered.

Jesse chuckled. "I'm gonna get me a Molotov cocktail—no, a whole case—and join the crusade," he teased.

"Will you *stop* jokes like that!"

He grinned and grew quiet. "Yeah," he nodded. "Oh, quit frettin', doll," he said and squeezed her hand. "These old bones tell me we'll come out of this Dickson jazz just fine. There's a whole lot about the U.S. of A. that smells, like Sanford claims. But I sure ain't licked yet."

R. R. Brunswick met at length with Dickson Enterprises' attorneys and reported that Jesse was indeed licked, that he was forbidden from practicing his trade for anyone other than Dickson Enterprises, that he could not work even for Dickson Enterprises until or unless he issued a public statement retracting all the damaging words he had uttered against Marty Dickson.

A settlement had been discussed, Brunswick acknowledged. The contract could be rendered null and void, but only for a yet-to-be-determined sum of money Jesse would pay, and only if he issued a simple but public apology to Marty Dickson and acknowledged the integrity of Marty Dickson.

"You go tell Massa Dickson," Jesse spat, "to take that settlement and stuff it up his lily-white behind."

He replaced the receiver and turned to Robin. "You feel like marryin' an out-of-work actor?" he asked.

"Jesse!"

"I'll buy you a teethin' ring for a weddin' present."

"Jesse!"

They flew to Maryland, simply because someone had once told Jesse that Elkton did not require a three-day wait for blood-test results. A white justice of the peace with the remarkable name of I. Percy Love married them in his tobacco-smelling study, and they spent their wedding night in a Negro motel named Motel. The bile-green walls were mottled, and the water that came from the shower's nozzle was skimpy, and the mattress sagged and the bed made obscene whining noises the moment it was touched, and Robin shamelessly bawled and bawled and felt like an idiot child, but the more she bawled and bawled the more convulsions of ecstasy she experienced, and she loved her husband, Jesse Nash, and loved herself for being Mrs. Jesse Nash.

They flew to Detroit, where she met Jesse's brother Rafe and sister Pearl, and Rafe's wife Fay and Pearl's husband Vincent, and his family kept circling her, turning her this way and that, and clucked congratulations at Jesse for having picked such a wow. In Detroit she met Archie Enders, a friend of Jesse's, who was a tax expert and investments counselor. Archie vowed to find a lawyer with more on the ball than R. R. Brunswick, and took the records of Jesse's financial picture to study.

By the time they reached New York and checked into a midtown hotel, and Jesse had phoned Archie to give him his new address, Archie had completed his evaluations, and the news was not good. The only monies Jesse could definitely depend upon were the royalties from the *Color Me Colored* album, which could be sizeable but certainly not enough to retire on. He chided Jesse for not having sought proper guidance before signing with Dickson Enterprises. He chided him for having banked so little of the original avalanche of income and for having sent so much of it to brother Rafe and sister Pearl and every civil rights organization under the sun.

Archie also directed him to a Manhattan lawyer named Emmett Briggs. Briggs's considered reply was not much different from R. R. Brunswick's: the shaky case could be fought, as any case could be fought, but Jesse should be prepared to spend a considerable amount of cash. And prepared as well not to work until the case was settled.

The change in Jesse was gradual. A month passed, a long month of waiting for Marty Dickson to get off his back and free him. By the end of the month, with the stalemate still in force, pretended calm changed to worrisome frustration, and frustration changed to increasing bitterness. And then, seemingly overnight, Jesse began to express his bitterness less toward Marty Dickson and more toward Marty Dickson's slick white attorneys. Soon he was condemning all white attorneys. And then most white men.

Robin suffered with him, and thought she understood the good man who was Jesse, but she could not be sure how serious he was. "You're starting to sound a little like that Orville Sanford," she cautioned.

"No I'm not!" he snapped, too quickly.

But he did, more and more, when he talked at all, and in time there were long hours in every day when he left her alone, and one evening she opened the *New York Post* and saw a picture of him and Orville Sanford. A new civil rights group, called FREE—The Federation for Rights to Education and Equality—had been formed, and Orville Sanford was its president and Jesse Nash its

vice-president. The purpose of FREE, the item read, was to protest—with a strict code of nonviolence and by strictly legal means—
the white power structure, which was clearly intent on maintain-
ing the status quo of second- and third-class citizenship for Negroes. In the picture, Orville Sanford was smiling. Jesse was not.

Robin had never seriously questioned aloud a single motive of
Jesse's. That night, when he returned to the hotel, she did. "Why
couldn't you have told me what you were doing?" she asked.
"Why did I have to read it in the paper?"

"Because you maybe woulda given me a hard time. And I have
enough folks standin' in line to do that."

"Jesse, it's all wrong! I don't want you to get in trouble!"

His jaw set. "Okay, I'll tell you what. Since Charley won't let
me earn a nickel at my trade, I'll go into another line of work,
'cause even niggers got to eat and pay rent, even Charley knows
that. Let's see now what I'm cut out for besides show business, let's
check all the choices. Polishin' shoes—there's a step to the top. Or
I could go for a chauffeur's license and drive Charley around in his
nice limousine." He frowned at her. "Just you butt out, doll. For
the first time in my life, I know exactly what I'm doin'. "

"But that man, that Sanford . . ."

Jesse waved his hand. "Sanford happens to know what he's
about, too. He's got brains, and money behind him, and he knows
how to get action where it counts. I spent a lot of time with him,
talkin', listening'. That jazz he was spielin' in California, about guns
and that, that was a crock of bull, just to hear his own voice. He
knows that kind of thing doesn't work—he says so now. Where I
come in, I stabilize Orville. I can handle him just fine. And we're
gonna make somethin' of this organization. I met some of the folks
that's tyin' in with him, and they're the smartest folks you'd ever
want to meet."

Robin did not argue, for she could not bear to argue with Jesse,
to question him for long. She believed him about the fine people
in the organization until she met some of them, a week after the
article in the *Post*, in a Harlem office that had the legend FREE

lettered on its glass door. They were well-dressed people, soft-spoken people, and they were polite to her and to one another, yet she sensed something sinister in the air, as though well-dressed and soft-spoken people were working up some unclear but treach-erous plot. There was talk about preparing a mammoth rally as soon as possible, to enlist new members and new money. There was talk about Jesse coordinating it and acting as its master of cere-monies, and someone said, with a cold grin, "Charley Hebrew may not look kindly on Jesse going back into show business, even if it's for a worthy cause." Jesse said nothing. There was general agree-ment that the first order of business, separate from the rally, was to concentrate all available energies on publicly playing up the prob-able whitewash of Officer Stuart White, and the slogan "Will Whitey Whitewash White?" was voted as a rallying cry to be quoted and posted everywhere until and after an indictment was brought against the policeman. Robin was nearly tongue-tied when Mr. Sanford made a point of announcing that she was Roland Lee's sister and that she was ready to do anything, go anywhere with Jesse to seek justice for her slain brother's memory. She looked at Jesse for help. Jesse said, "My wife's ready."

Alone, after the meeting, Robin complained, "I'm *not* ready! Why did you say that? Who gave your Mr. Sanford permission to say that? I don't like any of this. I don't like those people. I won't have anything to do with any of them!"

"That include me, too?" Jesse asked quietly.

"Oh, Jesse, can't you *smell* something bad in all this? I never said I was smart, but I do know you're not like those people. They're—I don't know how to say it—they're sick people. All this—this *hate*. I could feel it all over the room, it suffocated me, and it scares me, they scare me. Jesse . . ."

"Leggo the hysterics, doll. You don't know what you're jab-berin' about. You'll join up, because I tell you to. And because it's right."

She tried to go along, and could not. The oftener she met these same people at FREE, and met other ones, and heard the hate in their composed voices, the more revulsion she felt and the more frightened for Jesse she became. She went to the Harlem rally and listened to the loathing of anything Caucasian in Jesse's long and heartily applauded monologue. She went back to the hotel, alone, before the rally was over. That night, Jesse railed at her, and he was so angry that she thought for a moment that he was going to hit her. He told her he was a man at long last, genuinely respected as a man at long last, and she was deserting him. He told her he had been patient too long with her retreat from the reality of her brother's killing, that she owed it to herself as well as all black folks to stand up and be counted, that she was not better than the Coley Dennises unless she woke up in a hurry.

And again she tried, for Jesse's sake, and again failed. She endured his recitals of blame and charges of disloyalty for as long as she could and then, two months after the formation of FREE, she knew she didn't really know this new Jesse Nash, and she wounded them both during a furious argument when she suddenly shouted, "You're lying to yourself! You're not in this thing for Black Power, you're only interested in Nash Power, and you're a fake, that's all you are! Nash Power, that's all you're interested in, Jesse Nash Power!"

He was stunned, and so was she. After he was silent for a full minute, he said, very quietly, that the marriage had been a bad mistake. He was drawing a salary from FREE, not much, but he would give her a few hundred dollars in cash, more when he had it, and he didn't much care which of them should go for the divorce.

She remained dazed as he systematically packed some clothes and softly closed the hotel door after him.

When it was clear that he wasn't coming back, that he indeed wanted a divorce, Robin accepted twenty-one hundred dollars from him and gave some of it to a lawyer to start divorce proceedings. She lived through the next month as a sleepwalker, dismayed at having been cast out by the man who had spoken love to her, too dazed and rudderless to go to him or to anyone who mattered. She moved into an inexpensive hotel off Washington Square that didn't seem especially concerned about her color, and she spent hours of each day in her small room, shamed at having been cast out. She came upon a newspaper item that said Marty Dickson, expansive and forgiving, had decided to tear up Dickson Enterprises' contract with Jesse Nash, that Nash had been more trouble than he was worth and now was free to come and go as he pleased in show business. But Jesse was gone from her.

She read newspapers and listened to the radio in this city that was and was not hers, and learned that FREE was becoming more and more a civil rights group to be taken seriously, that its membership was swelling largely because there were Negroes in New York and in various other parts of the country who were proud of Jesse Nash and who wanted to be identified with him. She read, and heard, that FREE was attacking all those who were attacking it as a potential violent racist movement. She read, and heard, that Mama, incredibly, had agreed to appear at rallies and public meetings, to be pointed to on platforms as the grieving mother of Roland Lee Hamilton. What was incredible was that she could not conceive of Mama—shy, afraid to speak even to more than three of her church ladies at a time—allowing herself to be sucked into such grandstand razzle-dazzle.

She ached for Mama, ached to hold her. She ached for Jesse, for the Jesse who had been gentle.

By chance, one day, she bumped into Arbutus Harker, who had been the Hamiltons' next-door neighbor on Amsterdam Avenue and who had been a senior in high school when Robin had been a freshman. They had never been particularly friendly because of the difference in their ages, but they embraced each other now like very close and long-lost friends, and they had some coffee together in a luncheonette. Arbutus, still single and not even dating because of her crazy work hours, was a keypunch operator at International Credit Card, worked days one week and nights the next, and lived alone in a small flat on 44th Street. Robin discussed herself, fairly truthfully though not in elaborate detail, and they agreed before they parted that they both could save money if Robin moved in with her.

Robin did, and the arrangement was good, chiefly because Arbutus was a friend who didn't pry much and who was seldom in the flat. Her savings low, her spirits only intermittently restored, Robin forced herself to come at least partially out of her painful fog and look for a job. She felt ugly, and without talent or worth, and she had no show business contact except Tommy Rexford, who had gently taken her into his home and gently tried to turn her into a prostitute, but she found out where the second-rate agents and managers maintained their offices in Manhattan, and had her hair done and began to make the rounds.

The turndowns ranged from agents who refused to hear even her name, to agents who agreed she was a looker but short on experience, to one agent who openly, impatiently declared that colored acts were a drug on the market that season. In the corridor outside one office a middle-aged Negro wearing an old, once-gay blazer that was too tight for him, introduced himself as Happy Dan Van the Dancing Man ("Maybe you've heard of me?"), and suggested that if she was up against it, she might try the Ernie Fieldmont Agency, down on West 36th. "Ernie is white but he specializes in colored acts," said Happy Dan Van. "He takes more of a cut than he's s'posed to, ever'body knows that, but least he comes up with jobs. I use him when I'm rock bottom. If you can put your pride in your pocket, puddin', check in on Ernie."

The cramped offices were a three-flight walk-up, off Seventh Avenue. The reception-room walls were covered with faded photographs of stars like Bojangles Robinson and Ethel Waters, and a heavy mustiness was present. A fiftyish lady with brass-yellow hair gave her a card to fill out, almost absentmindedly, and Robin filled it out, writing her true maiden name and her address, but otherwise lying shamelessly, inscribing midwestern and southern nightclubs that had never existed. She was told to wait, and she did for more than an hour, and she recognized Ernie Fieldmont when he came in from the outer hall because she had had time to study wall pictures of him and Negro entertainers she had never heard of. Each of the pictures showed him with his arm around a different Negro, and each autograph read something on the order of *To my pal Ernie Fieldmont, couldn't have made it without you. Love always, Beans.* Or *Chloe.* Or *Daffy.*

He breezed past her, taking her card to his office, a stubby white man with a penciled mustache, preposterously long sideburns, and large space shoes. In a minute he called for her, and winked at her when she went in, and she sang "Come Rain or Come Shine" and he accompanied her on a cigarette-scarred baby grand. He asked her questions about her experience even though he was holding her card, and Robin lied, and she was sure he knew she was lying. He said he might have a spot for her on Saturday night at Chez Groovy in the Bronx, and mentioned a salary that was clearly below scale. "All right," she said. "The price isn't much, but I'm anxious to get started here in the East."

He winked again, squeezed her arm, and peered at her in a way that suggested he knew what she looked like with her clothes off. Escorting her to the door of his office, he patted both her buttocks and stated, "I'll get you started, baby-poo. They don't call me Starmaker Ernie for nothing, right?"

Robin worked at Chez Groovy in the Bronx on Saturday night. And at Tiny's Hideaway in Flushing the following week. And after that, at dreary clubs called Bunker's, and Hot Spot, and Tess & Mike's, and The Chatterbox, in the lonesome reaches of Queens and Long Island and even New Jersey. The pay was dreadful. The hours were grindingly long. The traveling was endless, and dangerous. Men with three or four beers in them assumed they had the right to paw her. Arbutus told her she was nuts, and she couldn't disagree, but she accepted any singing job offered her, at any price offered her, for she was gradually, surely learning how to perform for audiences, even audiences that looked and did not listen, even audiences that occasionally did neither. She slapped Ernie

Fieldmont when his harmless pats began to be more than harmless, not because he was a white man but because he was a loveless man. The slap was hard, startling him, and it could have ended their association. It didn't. He growled, but he continued to book her. And after that day he never touched her again.

She worked hard, improving, sliding back, improving, and, in spite of no strong urge to know any man besides Jesse, met several who seemed interested in her for more than pawing purposes. Alvin Wade, blacker than Jesse and demonstrating some of the qualities of sweetness that Jesse had once demonstrated, was a thirty-year-old trumpet man she got to know, and on their second date they went to the flat on 44th Street, where he lectured her on classical music and, because Arbutus was working all night, she let Alvin into her bed. She hated every kiss, every feel, every stroke and, by the time he had emptied himself into her, hated him. But she hugged him and whispered how wonderful he had been.

After Alvin there was Ben, and then Harry, and then Luther, and then Freddie, nice men all but transients all, men who emptied themselves into the cold brook between her legs because they wanted to and because she hoped that this one, this one, would be Jesse.

None of them was Jesse, and she tricked all of them by pretending she was the hottest and most pleasured morsel since the beginning of time, and each of them went away sated and quite unloved.

By the time the divorce became final, Ernie introduced her to a lanky girl named Grace Hamilton, older and professional, a vocalist who had also been working singles, and announced that a cruise line going to and from the Caribbean was willing to hire a colored duet for one tour, maybe more. Robin and Grace became the Hamilton Sisters, and remained the Hamilton Sisters on the *Stalwart* until Robin met Warren Weber. On the *Stalwart*, sailing away from Jesse and toward Jesse and away from Jesse, she met white men. Some of them were tender, or thought they were. None of them was Jesse. . . .

Now, in the fine hotel in Chicago, she thought of all the men since Jesse, many of them kinder, some of them stronger. Yet none of them was Jesse, either.

The whiskey Warren or someone had brought made her depressed and giddy, sweaty and rubber-legged and just a tiny bit hot, loving-hot. She did not bathe because she could not walk quite straight and she was afraid to bring her legs over the side of a tub, so she phoned down to round-the-clock room service for a chicken sandwich as she got out of all her clothes which were stifling her in the air-conditioned suite. She was brought out of sleep on the living room couch by a persistent tapping at the door, and she had risen to open it wide and see a bug-eyed elderly Negro man with a rolling tray before she realized she was naked except for stockings and garter belt. She slammed the door shut, crying, "I'm sorry, I'm sorry, nobody home!" and locked the door and locked herself in the bathroom, poising there and shivering until it was clear that no one was going to come and be mad at her.

She went to bed, unexpectedly and fully reliving the delivery of Jerry Sorin's baby.

Sunlight from the bedroom's undrawn shades wakened her. There was a memo pad on her night table, and she could not recall having written on it, but she recognized her handwriting. In script running downward, the top sheet of the pad read, *Send $$ to Mama. Send note—I will always love you, Mama. Robin Beverly.*

Eleven

C. HARVEY RHODES, President and Chairman of the Board of Vanguard Broadcasting, a gray-faced, gray-haired diabetic and survivor of three major ulcer attacks and one massive coronary, sat at his desk precisely eleven hours after leaving Berlin. He folded his arms across his chest, convinced as never before that excitement was a luxury belonging to the young and healthy, and listened to the events in his absence as described by the young and healthy Caleb Atwood. He had never invited Caleb to his home because he did not like him, but he respected him, at least that part of him that annually increased the network's profits. He had placed television autonomy in Caleb's hands, had watched and counted the revenue that gushed in, had led the Board vote that put a dazzling amount of VBN stock in Caleb's name, and—because there were no Rhodes heirs, heiresses, living business associates, or even a reliable messenger boy to leave VBN to—Caleb Atwood would own control of VBN. And soon, for the last doctor in the world, Bronf in Berlin, had leveled with C. Harvey Rhodes, had advised him to count on no more than a year at the outside.

Rhodes calmly listened to the adding machine that was Caleb, caught the deftly polite implications that the network would prosper beyond the most romantic projections if he, Rhodes, would gracefully retire and turn over all the responsible reins to dependable young adding machines. He was weary from the plane flight, weary from avoiding the remembrances of the good contributions he was going to have brought to broadcasting and had never quite got around to. He did not approve of Caleb's character this morning any more than he had on the morning he'd stolen him from the fat network across town. But he approved of himself even less because there had been a time when he could have stayed Caleb's cash-green thumb just a little, could have said, "The company's earning fabulous sums—let's work on some other things we'll be remembered for," and had not. That time had passed somehow, overnight. But which overnight? And he was very tired, too tired to talk back to the handpicked, young-blooded adding machine he had, with eyes quite fully opened, hired.

That same day, shortly after noon, out of curiosity, he agreed to receive young Warren Weber. He rather liked Weber more than most of the charmer-hucksters he knew—why, he had never been entirely certain except that Weber rarely pretended that any Gundersen-Weber-Simms product was anything but a consumer item—but he agreed to see him only because the charmer-huckster had never requested a private meeting before.

Weber arrived, breezy and confident and sensitive enough to avoid the hard sell Rhodes hated, and Rhodes listened patiently to his idea.

"Why have you brought this to me, Warren?" he asked quietly. "Why didn't you go to Caleb?"

"I did. Caleb rejected it."

Rhodes coughed behind his fist. "Well, then . . ."

"And I rejected Caleb's rejection." He smiled. "I realize what I'm doing, Mr. Rhodes. Caleb has turned down other ideas of mine—which I incidentally always sold to one of the other networks the same day and which, incidentally, went on to coin money. But this ball game is different. I've never smelled success the way I do with 'Moore.' And from every angle—it can move any sponsor's goods and, every bit as important, it speaks for mature social responsibility. Caleb turned it down because he wants plantation darkies dancing to banjo music, and that's the only thing 'Moore' doesn't have to offer. NBC, CBS, ABC—they'd gobble it up in a minute, but it belongs on Vanguard, with or without Caleb's blessing."

"Why?"

"I'll answer that bluntly, sir. Vanguard and I have been good to and for each other, and even though I needn't have any preferential allegiance to Vanguard I do have a special affection for it. But very bluntly, sir, I'm here because the other networks make some attempts to manufacture quality as well as pap and Vanguard makes next to none."

"And, possibly, because you wish to prove something to Caleb by going over his head and coming to me?"

Weber's smile was brief. "Now you're the one who's blunt. I didn't ask for this appointment, Mr. Rhodes, for any reason other than that Caleb is a genius at programming everything but quality, and quality is where his judgment is most vulnerable. I'm going to sell 'Moore,' sir, because it *matters*—not next season, not even next week, but now. And I want you to have it."

"Would you by any chance have a sponsor tucked away there in your briefcase?"

"I'll get you one. I'll get twenty to choose from. And if you and I draw up some preliminary papers of agreement by tomorrow at the latest, I promise to have a sponsor on the dotted line by Friday."

"You're trying to rush the period of gestation, Warren. Any first-year biology student will tell you—"

"Forgive me for interrupting, sir, but yes, I am in a hurry. And so will NBC be in a hurry, if I show them what I've shown you— these guest-appearance guarantees by Brad Hammond and the Beaumonts. I'm not trying to crowd you, Mr. Rhodes—I have much too much admiration for you to try that—but I would like to leave this copy of the 'Moore' package and check back with you, say, at noon tomorrow."

Rhodes summoned Caleb when Weber left, assuming that the charmer-huckster would have expected him to do just that. "So

St. George broke in on you, after all," said Caleb. "I warned him not to, Claude. I reminded him that the burdens of programming rest on my shoulders, not yours. I'm sorry you were bothered by his barging-in tactics, but in a way I'm glad, too. It gives me a good reason to bar him and anything he has to peddle from Vanguard. We can do without his pushy arrogance—the other networks can have the whole GWS gang, with my compliments."

"What objections do you have against this 'Moore' thing, Caleb, aside from your distaste for Weber? I've only glanced at what's written here, but it does show some promise."

Caleb raised his black eyebrows. "My Lord, Claude, are you *serious?* Is *this* what Vanguard's worked for, a Darktown Strutters' Ball, with Africans swarming over the screen, preaching how they're all slaves? With a Dean Martin show just a few channels away, who'd give few seconds to *garbage?*" Possibly because Rhodes's expression did not change, possibly because he did not answer, Caleb went on, seeming to sense something amiss. "Claude, let's drop Mr. Weber and Mr. Moore and the whole tawdry subject once and for all, shall we? We're all terribly busy. There really isn't time to waste detailing the thousand and one reasons why I won't have Weber and his ilk near Vanguard ever again. I—"

"Then take the time, Caleb. I like to think you're not wasting time when I ask you to explain something to me."

It was stated softly, it meant *I am C. Harvey Rhodes and I am still Vanguard Broadcasting*, and it worked. "Of course," said Caleb, smiling coldly. "In terms of dollars and cents, separate from the intrinsic ugliness of the idea, it would be a suicidal project for Vanguard for the season-after-season sponsors it would chase away. Every fall season we're several million dollars richer because of Willard Cunningham alone. I know Mr. Cunningham, and I know for a fact what his reaction would be if we carried a show like this. He'd cancel all his shows so fast that our heads wouldn't stop spinning for years, and he'd probably maneuver others to cancel."

"I am not in the communications business," said Rhodes, "for the purpose of masturbating Willard Cunningham."

"I know you're not, Claude," said Caleb, almost gently. "On the other hand—the masturbating hand, to use your phrase—you've never refused any Cunningham sponsorship either, have you?"

Rhodes paused, then nodded. "You've caught the emperor stark naked."

"Each man is placed on this earth for a purpose, Claude. Yours was to build a great empire called Vanguard Broadcasting. Mine is to keep Vanguard smooth and solvent. Let me do my job, Claude. The moment this company loses a penny because of a mistaken decision on my part is the moment you'll have my resignation on your desk."

Rhodes nodded, and was left alone. Contemplatively chewing rather than swallowing the Digitalis tablet as he had been instructed to do, he thought of his death and of what Caleb would do with it. The FCC demanded, and occasionally got, a reasonable number of hours a week on each network devoted to programs of an educational and/or informative nature. Not once but on five separate occasions, Caleb had recommended an hour special on Soul of America, allowing the leftists their criticisms in the interests of balance and free speech, but showing the aims, achievements, and aspirations of SOA, also in the interests of balance and free speech, in a positive light. "That outfit's full of screwballs," Rhodes had said. Caleb had said, "It's headed by Willard Cunningham—who's not a screwball, and who could be easily induced, after this special, to give Vanguard four or five new shows next season."

No, Rhodes had said, and no he would always say. Always. A year at the outside, Bronf had said in Berlin. What have I been doing with these old-fashioned rose-colored glasses? he thought. In a year ("At der outside, Herr Rhodes, at der outside"), I won't be Claude Rhodes. I'll be six feet under the surface of the earth, trapped in a box. They say the dead don't care. I'll care. I'll care if Caleb converts my store into a bowling alley, with Willard Cunningham controlling all the popcorn concessions.

With each appearance, the delivery of Stuart White's speech, his ease in the question-and-answer periods and, most of all, the persuasiveness of his sincerity, steadily improved. His picture was put on the cover of the monthly magazine, *Soul of America Speaks*, and Lucille was so proud, and so were the kids, and he was treated like a big shot whenever he was home in Washington Heights long enough to step into McLeod's for a beer or two. He began to receive invitations to be interviewed on radio and television shows —not in Jew York, naturally, but here and there around the country—and he balked, but Mr. Jones and Miss Gardner pressed him to accept and tutored him on what and what not to say on the air.

On one radio show in Savannah, he admitted that Soul of America paid his traveling expenses (Mr. Jones had instructed him to say, if and when the question ever came up, that his immediate needs were met though not generously bankrolled by SOA, lest the public think he was on his truth crusade for the money), but that he and his family were having a hard row to hoe, trying to make ends meet. "I've been offered a lot of jobs in private business and industry, at good salaries," he said, having memorized the statement written by Mr. Jones. "But that would mean I'd have to give up the fight, give up trying to show fellow Americans what can happen to their freedom, what happened to *my* freedom, when liberals organize a stranglehold."

He kind of hoped, though he did not really expect, that people would send him money. They did; by his fourth appearance at the lectern and on radio and television, after he made his original admission of near-poverty, money started to come in, a dollar bill here, a fifty and even a hundred-dollar check there—not a fortune, but nothing to sneeze at, either. He checked with Miss Gardner, who checked with somebody somewhere and who told him he could keep the money as long as it was clearly understood that he was hired by SOA to educate the public, not to make public appeals for gifts. Money continued to come in, presently enough to pay for Lucille's uterus-scraping or for the needed dental work on Tommy's bad teeth. White gave the needs a great amount of thought, and bought a twenty-six-inch color TV set in Times Square, instead. He explained to Lucille that it was necessary for his work: now that he was on television himself, he had to study the tricks of the trade up close.

The $481.36 set arrived without a repair warranty because he had forgotten to ask for one, and the set conked out completely two hours after it was installed. He assured Lucille that he had a guarantee, and the next morning went down to the Times Square store to get one, and the man who had sold him the set shrugged and said, "Tough, mister. We sell all our merchandise too cheap to go around handing out warranties in the bargain." He paid the local repairman seventy-five dollars out of his own pocket when the set was returned—in cash, for it would not do for his wife to come upon a cancelled check. "It's none of my business," said the repairman, "but I thought only out-of-towners bought anything from those gypsies on 42nd Street. I charged you fair, but those guys down there rooked the hell out of you, you don't mind me saying so. This'll play, but you bought yourself an inferior piece of goods." The repairman and Lucille knew each other, and White warned him that he was never to breathe a word of it to her.

White understood why SOA's New York office, and its home office in Helena, Montana, forbade his speaking out against Jesse Nash, who was publicly calling him every vicious name in the jig book, from liar to bonehead puppet. SOA's theory, and they were always right because they always thought things through, was that Nash made even the most gullible white Americans mad with his lunatic indictment of white Americans, and was therefore a valuable if unwitting ally of Soul of America and all the important things it stood for. So he swallowed his anger and left Nash alone. But his first serious quibble with the organization's highmindedness came on the day Miss Gardner showed him a large glossy photograph of Horace Denny, the colored justice on the U.S. Supreme Court, with his arm around Nick Stanton, the colored Commie who had been convicted of passing top-secret military installation information to the Russkies and whose case was, four years later, about to reach the Supreme Court. As soon as Miss Gardner identified the two men, he knew she was showing him dynamite; he was the first to admit to his friends at McLeod's that a newspaper to him meant the sports page and then *Dick Tracy* and *Blondie*, but he did know that Horace Denny had gone on the Supreme Court bench no more than a month before, and here was Horace Denny wearing a Supreme Court robe and being buddy-buddy with a convicted spook traitor whose case was about to be tried before the Court.

"Our esteemed President of the United States," said Miss Gardner in that New England voice, "was the anti-Communist who yammered loud and long for Mr. Denny to be put on the bench."

"Boy," said White. "Where'd you *get* this picture?"

"We got it. You'll be on William Burnham's TV show here in New York tomorrow night. His real name is Bloom, wouldn't you know it, and his technique is to attack, attack, attack, and let the guests wriggle out on their own. When he asks how dare you criticize the civil rights programs, you are to hold this picture up on camera. Bloom-Burnham doesn't have much of a viewer rating, but we've arranged to have some people in the studio audience who'll see to it that your bombshell gets all the national attention it deserves."

Miss Gardener carefully coached him on how to handle himself on the Bloom-Burnham show. He left her office with the picture in his hand, feeling watched and important, feeling as Paul Revere must have felt at Wherever It Was. He stopped in Rod Jones's office, and Mr. Jones certainly did know all about the picture and the plan to spring it on the Burnham show. "Phony as Burnham's professional name," Rod Jones chortled. "The picture's doctored."

"Doctored?"

"Well, now, don't *you* look like a crestfallen cub scout! Cheer up, Stu, and appreciate art when you see it. The photograph's a two-shot triumph. I happen to know something about photography, and, for my money, this is the best picture of its kind ever assembled. Diligence and dedication were involved, and they sure as shooting paid off."

"But . . . phony, you said? . . ."

Mr. Jones stopped being merry. "Is this when the tough Stu White starts going soft?"

"Oh, I wouldn't—"

"Wouldn't you? Wars aren't fought with velvet gloves at tea parties, fella. When you signed up with SOA, you signed up to help us fight a war. I never would've taken you for a cream puff, and I hope I'll never have to. We don't have any room here for softies."

"I . . . you'll never have to lose any sleep over where my loyalty is, Mr. Jones."

William Burnham was a flinty, sarcastic man who reminded White of a Jewish version of his father and who jumped on him before the live television show was a few minutes old. "Isn't it true, Mr. White," he rasped, "that you're a paid employee of Soul of America?"

"You say Soul of America like it's something that needs a bath," White joked.

"That was my intention!" Burnham snapped, and delivered himself of all the expected liberal-line charges against the organization: that it was anti-democratic, anti-labor, anti-immigrant, anti-intellectual, anti-twentieth century, and, above all, anti-Negro. White, meeting the abuse with careful calm, claimed it was unfair to expect him to defend every charge anybody under the sun might want to make against SOA, and added that no one at SOA expected him to go along with every one of its positions, and added further that if people took the time to really study SOA, they would find it wasn't any of those things Mr. Burnham said it was. He went into part of his speech, the condensed version, about the

family, and all of them never missing church on Sundays, and playing catch with the kids on free Sunday afternoons. He talked of
his pride in being a New York police officer. He told of the tragic
circumstances that had made him shoot the Hamilton lad, and his
grief, and being hounded out of his job by folks who had never
known grief themselves. No, he answered Bloom-Burnham, he
wasn't speaking against colored people when he spoke around the
country to patriotic Americans; how could he, when he was a
Christian? What he did speak about around the country was the
injustice of the hounding he'd suffered and the destruction of his
career—not because he'd been a bad or dishonest cop, not because
he'd made a mistake, but because the Negroes and the liberals had
ganged up on him and smeared him as a killer of Negroes. His point
in telling his own story to Americans, he told Burnham, was to
make them aware that they must never take liberty for granted.

Bloom-Burnham was a stuck needle. "What my viewers and I
still don't understand," he scolded, "is where Soul of America fits
into the picture, if you're using them only to pay your expenses
so you can get your lofty message across and if, as you say, you're
not anti-Negro."

"I'm not. And neither is SOA. Where do you get lying information like that?"

"Ah, where? I'll show you where," Burnham gloated, and fussed
with papers and held up a copy of *Soul of America Speaks*, the one
with White's picture on the cover. "May I read you a section of
a sterling editorial on page three of this sterling house organ, *Soul
of America Speaks?* Yes, I believe I will. Here we are. After the
typical patronizing bromides about the goody-two-shoes niceness
of the black-skinned folks, this grand editorial says, quote: 'Yet the
indisputable fact remains that, as the most respected anthropologists
have proved beyond the shadow of a doubt, the Negro brain is
smaller than the Caucasian brain. This insufficiency contributes
not only to Negroes' sloth and lack of ambition, but also leaves
them constitutionally vulnerable to exploiters. The Negro, repeatedly told that he is downtrodden in this land of golden op-

portunity for all, soon finds himself in the unenviable role of hand-maiden to the pie-in-the-sky promisers, who themselves are dedi-cated to a single end—the communizing of the world.' " He made a twisted face and slapped the magazine down hard, so that the microphone would be sure to pick up the sound of contempt. "There's more, but I have a queasy stomach." Glowering at White, he snarled, "So the word has descended from your heroic organi-zation up there on Mount Olympus. The Negroes are not only simpletons, but you can put 'em on a conveyor belt and they come off Commies. *Truthfully* now, friend, do you subscribe to a hun-dredth of a hundredth of this trash?"

Now, thought White.

"Well, I'm no egghead, so I'll be truthful and admit I didn't follow all you read," he said, and produced the photograph. "But you and your viewers might be interested in this." The photograph was shown on camera, and he identified the two men, and would not tell Bloom-Burnham where had got the photograph, but as-sured him it was the real McCoy and added that he was no ex-pert on government or politics but this sure looked like somebody was cooking up something down in Washington, D.C.

The interview and the photograph made news, big news, the very next day. But the exposé backfired almost as fast.

As White was to understand it, Horace Denny went straight to the office of the U.S. Attorney General. The Attorney General, Herbert Graham, went straight to the Department of Justice, which went right on twenty-four-hour duty and located a photog-rapher named Marvin Emory, who took four hours of grilling to confess that he had been paid four hundred dollars in cash by a woman named Maude Gardner to assemble two photographs—one of Justice Denny with an arm around his wife, the other of Nick Stanton with his arm around a Polish Communist functionary—so that the Justice's wife and the Polish Communist functionary could be excised and the picture made to show the black judge and the black traitor in smiling cahoots.

Attorney General Graham released the facts and the two undoctored photos at once, and they flooded the news media, exonerating Horace Denny and, presumably, changing some citizens' attitudes on Soul of America. White locked himself in his apartment, refusing to answer a single one of the constant phone calls, even though one or more of them might have been from SOA. He kept trying to call Miss Gardner for guidance, but the secretary, who knew him, did not know where Miss Gardner was. He finally reached Mr. Jones. Mr. Jones ordered him to sit tight and talk to no one till the dust settled, and hung up.

The hanging up, the fact that no one at SOA thought enough of him to guide him, even to comfort him, wounded White, and he drank eleven cans of beer and half a pint of rye, and collapsed into bed. He was jerked from sleep by the phone, which he answered because it might be Miss Gardner or Mr. Jones calling. A guy from the *New York Clarion* asked him for a statement. "What the hell're you after me for?" he complained fuzzily, mad at SOA for deserting him when he needed them most, impressed in his partial stupor that a big paper like the *Clarion* was interested in him, anxious to be let off the hook. "What'd I do? They gave me this picture to hold up, gave me these things to say, and I did what I was told," he said, sorry he had started because he wasn't sober or awake enough to weigh his words. Angrily he said, "Go see SOA. Leave me alone. I get paid when I talk, mister. Name's White, Stuart White, don'choo forget it, mister. I'm a decent man, a Christian. Go to hell, y' know? All right?"

Charges were brought against Maude Gardner, and White was presently advised that some district attorney would be wanting to have a talk with him. Waiting to be summoned for questioning, White drank heavily in spite of Lucille clucking that liquor was the worst thing in the world for him, and he watched and listened to the bastards attack him on the twenty-six-inch TV set with the muddy colors, and read about himself in the papers. He wasn't too hurt by the growing number of attackers who were the nuts, or jig or Jew or even Protestant spokesman. He was keenly hurt, however, when the Catholics took out after him. He had been born and raised a Methodist, had taken Lucille's Catholic religion, at her pleas, just before their first son's baptism. He never felt peaceful with the acquired religion because it awed him, because it seemed to paint him into a corner whenever he had a bad or immoral thought—and he had, and always had had, bad and immoral thoughts, thoughts that the awesomeness of the Church could not erase or ease—yet it was his religion.

And so he experienced an end-of-the-line feeling when Sean Cardinal Patrick, whose credentials as an anti-Communist no sane man could question, issued a statement from his New York diocese. It was brief, minced no words, and it went: "For the Stuart Whites to defend unbridled character assassination by calling themselves Christian is a blasphemy not to be tolerated. Christianity is *for* something, infinitely more than it is *against* something. True Christianity loves, while jingoistic postures of the faith hate, and corrode the heart of that which is love. The religiosity of Mr. White and his cohorts is spurious, to say the least, and an affront to the concept of Christ's Divinity."

White went to McLeod's Bar oftener than ever, and stayed longer, but stopped buying rounds for the house. Still waiting for that district attorney to summon him, he had three—or was it five? —drinks with Harry Weaver, a highly intelligent guy he'd gone to school with and who was pulling down good pay in the mortuary game. To others, those he could be pretty sure wouldn't put the bite on him, White had said that SOA paid him twenty-five thousand dollars a year. He admitted to Harry that it was fifteen thousand.

Harry didn't like that at all. "Fifteen grand for all the dirty work you do for them? Jeez, you're a prize chump, Stuie, you're being taken good. Do you have *any* idea who you're tied up with, you dope? This guy Cunningham's Midas and Croesus combined. Didn't you at least ask for fifty, say?"

"Of course I did," lied White. "I'm not some Arkansas hick, ready to jump at the first offer. But they said that was all they could pay, so I thought about it a while and I figured fifteen grand was fifteen grand more than I had. But you figure I was a chump, huh?"

"A prize one."

Goddam them, thought Stuart Curtiss White. Harry Weaver's right. How can a man like me—I'm not out to screw anybody, so how is it that a man like me gets screwed everywhere he turns?

By the time Robin returned to New York from Chicago and was in rehearsals for a second and more heralded appearance on "The Curly Custer Show," Weber had closed the one-picture deal with Sol Aaron of Cambridge Pictures, subject to her signature. She was cool to Weber, and he was cool to her, but she was civil and charming when others were present, and she signed.

Too, he had Vanguard's go-ahead, an agreement with C. Harvey Rhodes's name on it, on "Moore." He had asked for, and received, total production say on the guarantee of a thirteen-week series: a unique Warren Weber package, giving him incontestable control to choose writers, rotating directors, staff, and cast, on condition that a sponsor be sealed and delivered by the Friday agreed upon. Eschewing agencies and all middle-men barnacles, Weber dropped in on jolly, postmaturely young Owen Claffee, a sixty-year-old hepster in an age of twenty-year-old hipsters, who was to Foley Foods what C. Harvey Rhodes was to VBN: After many drinks at Voisin, Claffee admitted that he was indebted to good ol' Warren for having trafficked "Meet Ginger" and "Spy for Sale" to Foley Foods, and added that he was also indebted to good ol' Warren for having furnished him with some swell experiences of, you know, Warren, a—hic, wink—special kind. "It's in the bag, this minute," Weber said, and signed the check, and taxied Claffee to Gloria Barclay's apartment on East 76th, where Gloria and her sometime partner Marilyn, the speedboat with the high boots and modified cat-o'-nine-tails, were waiting.

The following morning, Weber took the signed guarantee to Rhodes. He returned to GWS to learn from Jeanne that Jesse Nash had phoned in. Weber called.

"An idea I have might be beneficial to us both, Mr. Nash," he said. "Will you have lunch with me today, say, at one? Toots Shor's?"

He was not especially surprised by the sullen suspicion in Nash's eyes, but he was monumentally surprised by the size, the immediate star-quality, the distinctive charismatic whammy of the young man who was supposed to be running a revolution over the United States. They shook hands, and, on the way to a table, Weber saw the heads of lunchers turn—not at him, for once, but at Jesse Nash. They weren't looking at a black man in a white man's restaurant, he sensed, and they were only incidentally looking at someone they recognized from paper and magazine pictures and intermittent television appearances. They were looking at Cary Grant and Clark Gable, at a man who causes heads to turn automatically when he walks through a room, because of himself, not because of his name.

Weber had a Scotch and soda, and Nash had tomato juice. "Where did you have that suit made? I like it," said Weber, not really liking the suit, the quality or the cut of it at all, but at a loss for small talk with this man.

"I bought it from off a plain pipe rack," Nash said. "In a black-owned store, up in Harlem." He lighted a cigarette. "You didn't call me to eat lunch so you could admire my clothes. I know you—least I know you once used to be with that man Gundersen who put on some good gut shows when he was alive. And I know you have an ex-wife of mine under real rich lock and key. Other than that, I *don't* know you, Mr. Weber. I don't know why you want to be seen with me in a fancy place like this, 'cept maybe to show off to the other folks that this is Take-a-Nigger-to-Lunch Week."

Weber gritted his teeth and told him about "Moore."

And talked money.

And asked him if he would like to try out for the part.

"Try out?"

"Mr. Nash, don't be a hard-jawed poker player with me, Mr. Nash," Weber said evenly, smiling evenly. "You know show business as well as I do. John Barrymore and Elizabeth Taylor and Minnie Mouse don't try out for parts. Everyone else does, in one way or another, and you know that, and as soon as you remove that chip from your shoulder we'll have a conversation."

To his credit, Nash managed a grin. "Let's have me ask a question or two. The way you lay out this show, it sounds okay. But how's it gonna come out—the way you describe it, with a real punch, or like a nice white man's show, hittin' hard up to the point where it may bug somebody? Nice white men don't go in for buggin' anybody."

"I have full legal control. I call all the shots. If you mean will the integrity of this show get watered down to appease someone, the answer is no. It's going to start strong and stay strong. Why do you think I want you in it?"

"Hmm," Nash said. "All right then, what's my say in it?"

"Your what?"

"You tell me you have two writers, one black, one white. What if I don't like what they write?"

Weber blinked. "This is awfully early in the game to throw curves, isn't it?"

Nodding, Nash said, "That's right. But I got to protect my people, not just me. You could be all for my people, and so could that white scriptwriter, but you two cats don't know what bein' black is, 'cause you're not black. For that matter, your black writer might not know what bein' black is, either. Good intentions aren't near good enough. A show like this has got to be true."

Because the man was right, because the original fanciful thought of Nash as "Moore" was now an active possibility and a fascinating one, Weber said something he had not meant to say. "You'll be in on it," he promised.

"When do you think you'll be set to start shootin'?"

"A month. No more."

"Thirteen weeks in all?"

"Yes, which means about twenty weeks of actual production. About halfway through we'll be able to see how the wind blows, and there's no reason why it shouldn't blow perfectly. That's when we'll plan to shoot beyond the first thirteen scripts and make an entire season of it. You'll have to understand that and consent to it —assuming you do half as well in the director's test as I know you will. If you have other commitments on your time, you'll have to adjust them. We'll need you for the whole tour."

Nash nodded again. "Shouldn't be any sweat, takin' a leave of absence from FREE. If the kind of money you're talkin' about's on the square, I can put what I earn into FREE. Money's somethin' it can always use."

"What you do with your money is your business."

"Yes. I know that, Mr. Weber," Nash said with ice-pick clean-ness, but then he suddenly grinned and as suddenly the air cleared. "What isn't my business is somethin' that sorta interests me. That ex-wife of mine—she must be earnin' a bundle."

"A tidy bundle. But nothing compared to what she'll be earning a few months from now."

"How's she spendin' it, can you tell me?"

"You *are* a nosy mug, aren't you?" Weber declared, and the man grinned. "I'm not, so I wouldn't dream of asking her. We set up a savings and investment plan for her—my partner, Phil Simms, is the money expert, but I've been around for as long as he has, and we've seen our fill of stars and semi-stars who woke up in eternal hock because they didn't put money away—so Robin will be well off even if she retires tomorrow, God forbid. What *she* does with what she keeps is *her* affair."

"Uh-huh. I'm just waitin' for her to marry Coley Dennis—if Coley'd ever lower himself enough to marry black. They're so much alike, they'd make a perfect pair."

Weber knew the opinion many Negroes had of Coley Dennis, very likely justified because Dennis, a great artist, was a Negro who fled from anything Negro. Weber recalled the Florida brawl that had transformed this man Nash from rising star to salaried civil-rightsnik, recalled that Nash had punched Dennis. The details were vague in his mind, and he had no desire to have them refreshed, but he considered the remark lumping Robin and Dennis together a nasty one. "Has it been a few years since you saw Robin?" he asked, and Nash nodded. "Then why would you say a thing like that about her, unless you've personally watched every move she's made since then?" he asked, annoyed that this man had once touched Robin, had slept with her, annoyed that Robin had probably cared for this man.

"I read the papers."

"I see. Those same papers you tell rallies you don't believe for a second? Is that how you get all your current information about Robin?"

Visibly relenting a bit, Nash said, "If she'da spoken one word in public about that cop that killed her brother, that cop flyin' free as a bird, I'da known about it. If she'da given a thin dime outta all the gold she's haulin' in to one rights group or even to her mother, I'da known about it. Oh, well, like you say, it's none of my affair. I'm done with my coffee, how about you?"

"I—yes, I'm done. As far as Robin is concerned—"

"Wait, now. I apologize for raisin' the subject. I don't care all that much, and that's the truth. I'll be headin' on back to 125th Street now. You want to send me a script, I'll be glad to look it over and give you my thoughts."

Weber returned to the office, telling himself that as of this moment no law other than Weber's Law, which dictated that man must be propelled to action by stubbornness as well as reason even if the stubbornness proves idiotic, prevented him from taking steps to replace Jesse Nash at once with a more manageable, less quixotic Negro. "Moore," in the exciting new shapes it was taking daily, wasn't a gimmick project reliant on human tricks. It had merit, and it must not be spoiled.

And yet *Chalmers' Weekly* had come and gone with the low-down on Robin Hamilton as the former Mrs. Jesse Nash, and there had been bursts of concern and ripples of alarm from the sidelines as a consequence, but the sky had not fallen. Nor had there been more than a transitory *qvetch* out of Sol Aaron. Nor had Mitch Brooks, Curly Custer's producer, tried to squeeze out of featuring Robin on Curly's hour. Nor had the demand for Robin's appearance abated in the slightest.

Nor had Nash behaved like anything but a pro. With the press after him, with his antagonism toward Robin and his passion for publicity, he could have played it up big, could have invented and maintained headlines for himself with glorious cock-and-bull stories. Instead, he had consistently, and with dignity, said, "No comment." Nash, who could always be counted on to be chock-full of comment.

No, I'm right, thought Weber. It will all mesh. It will work. I'm sizzling on all burners now, and everything works when I'm on all burners.

For a time he purposely avoided meeting with Robin privately, even though his Chicago anger had dissipated, even though there were long moments when he ached for the touch of her. There were reasons he gave himself: She had to learn that she was his creation as well as his mistress and she had no right to withhold secrets from him; she had to learn, by his avoidance if necessary, that his role was not to pursue her, that her job was to reach out, in love and appreciation, for him.

Love, he thought.

That's what I'm afraid of, that's why I'm keeping away.

Love with a girl there is no future with is one thing. Letting it get out of control is quite another.

At ten o'clock on a Tuesday evening, after the "Curly Custer" taping, Rudi drove Weber and Karen to a party at Curly's duplex near the UN Building. Robin arrived, looking marvelous, and was sweet to Karen who was sweet back, and sang two numbers because Curly asked her to and half the guests pressed her to. Weber observed that she followed one champagne cocktail with a second, and polished both off as if they were doses of medicine. He observed her avoiding him, observed her having another champagne cocktail with a gaunt, long-haired man he did not know and suspected she did not know, and later found her and the gaunt, long-haired man gone. As soon as he could free himself from Karen, he asked the people he could trust who the man was. Those he asked did not know.

When he and Karen left the party, soon after midnight, Robin and the man had not returned. On the way home, Karen said, "Young Miss Hamilton has learned a lot since the Stalwart, but she hasn't yet learned manners."

Weber did not answer. He was thinking of Robin, his Robin, in a stranger's bed. It was hideous if it was true, and he had to contain himself from telling Karen *how* hideous.

Twelve

THERE WERE SEVERAL REASONS why leaving the Curly Custer party with a stranger was a dumb thing to do, Robin knew as she left with the stranger. It was rude to go without saying good night to the Custers. And Warren and probably anyone else who might miss her would almost surely suppose she was disappearing to sleep with the stranger. And the dumbest reason of all was that she went with him simply because he asked her to.

His name was Lamont Winters and he was a skin-and-bones white man, soft-spoken and harmless on a night she needed someone harmless, a part-time playwright-actor-director and semi-invited party-goer, who had evidently followed every detail of her career. They walked in the late Manhattan night and drank endless cups of coffee in a White Tower, and he quietly, gently bawled her out for letting herself be manipulated and exploited by the Warren Webers, by letting herself be forced into becoming a star before she was ready. "You have a grand talent, but it needs nurturing," Mr. Winters said, gracefully stropping his English muffin with a knife full of marmalade. "You think the Webers are giving you the keys to eternal bliss and success. Well, you're mistaken. I hope I'm wrong, but I think they're greedy. They're out to turn a speedy dollar. I'm not against a dollar, speedy or otherwise, but the sin involved here is that you're not being given the time to develop your very real talent. Exploitation, manipulation —that's what's happening to you, my dear. You should wise up, before it's too late, before the bubble bursts. You ought to march yourself up to the Webers and say to them, 'Let me learn my craft, my art. If I'm good now, I'll be great a year from now.' You're young, so very young. You should insist on the right to make all the normal mistakes in private before you allow them to chew you up and dump what's left by the side of the road."

Robin heard him, and thanked him for his interest, and explained that nothing and no one could shake her faith in Warren Weber. They walked all the way to her hotel, still friends. She did not invite him up, because he wasn't acting as though he expected to be invited up. Alone, she thought over what he had said. No, he was all wrong. Warren made her mad—he didn't care for her enough, he didn't try hard enough to trust her and comfort her, and maybe that was the really stupid reason why she had gone off with a stranger, to anger and worry Warren, to pay him back for not being with her twenty-four hours a day to guide and comfort and love her. But Lamont Winters, the part-time this, part-time that, full-time failure, didn't understand anything. Warren, the very good man, wanted only the best for her. For *her*.

And yet she wakened the next morning and the mornings that came after as she had wakened since Chicago: unaccountably burdened. The dreams of fame and heavy Turkish towels and people fussing over her weren't dreams any more, they were one great fact, yet she relished the fact only at fleeting intervals, for the fuss was being made not over her but an invention she could stand at distant sides of rooms and look at. Except for the five-thousand-dollar money order she sent to Mama, all that money would ever buy for her were things. She kept appointments. She took singing lessons when she was told to. She posed for pictures when she was told to. She took acting lessons when she was told to. She was fitted for clothes when she was told to.

She did not sleep well, even with liquor, and she tried to be pleasant and cooperative with the people who were helping her become the star she had once wanted to become. But Lou Patterley complained one afternoon during a vocal lesson that she wasn't giving the hour the concentration it needed, and she tore some sheet music in half and yelled, "Don't you yell at me!"

Mr. Patterley, who hadn't yelled, looked startled, as he should have. "I'm not your trained seal," she railed, banging a fist on the keyboard, "I'm not anybody's trained seal, and not you or anybody has the right to treat me like one! This lesson's over, hear? You don't make enough money to yell at me, ever!"

She apologized, and continued to apologize, long after Mr. Patterley came to and conceded that he probably was working her too hard. "I'm so ashamed," she said, not quite sobbing "I promise I will never talk to you like that, ever again." And she meant it, for she was indeed ashamed, and warned herself that she must never let her nerves get out of control, certainly not in front of this man or anyone who had been brought to help her.

But her nerves would not stay under control at command, despite the liquor, despite the tranquilizers. The next day, as she taxied from a difficult record session to Sardi's on 44th for a newspaper interview, having changed into a gown for later in the evening, she sensed that she should have summoned Ronnie Haley and called off the interview; she felt tense and tired and irritable. The paper was the *San Francisco Afro*-something-or-other, and she would not, absolutely would not, talk on this day with anyone about her ancestors. She entered the still uncrowded restaurant at ten of seven, only twenty minutes late, walking almost successfully with the celebrity carriage one of her instructors of celebrity was teaching her to use for entrances, and she was escorted to Warren's special table in the rear where a young Negro man saw her coming and stood, instantly. "Mr. Hightower, hello, sorry I'm late," she said, and he was going to pull her chair back for her but the captain beat him to it. One of the very first laws she had learned from Warren was that a performer could forget her lines, but she could never afford to forget a newspaperman's name or forget to use it liberally and cordially during an interview.

"I was afraid I was going to be late, myself," he acknowledged, sitting when she sat, a peaceful and rather attractive young man, two shades darker than she, conservatively dressed, clean-shaven, maybe around twenty-six years old, with an accent she could not identify but which was not remotely southern, and his smile was not ingratiating so much as it was calm and assured. "The New York subways are supposed to be a snap to understand, even without a map, but I got on a train in Brooklyn in plenty of time to get here, and I must've made one very wrong change because the one-hour ride took closer to two hours."

He was having a whiskey sour, and Robin asked the captain for one, too. "What were you doing in Brooklyn in the first place?" she asked, remembering Warren's second law: Always begin an interview by getting the interviewer to talk about himself; it shows you're interested in him as a person and he'll tend to go easy with you.

He was in and around New York for a week or so, covering a number of stories for the *San Francisco Afro-American*, he explained. Talking with random citizens of the black community in Brooklyn's Bedford-Stuyvesant was one of them. Meeting with her was another. Show business was not his beat—his specialties were politics and race relations, he said—but the name Robin Hamilton was creating a stir back home, and he was happy to have the chance to have a chat with her, in spite of the taboos.

"What taboos?"

"The ones your press agent Mr. Haley advised my editor about. Your brother. And Jesse Nash. And, I gather, anything dealing with color."

Robin nodded, wishing she were home, wishing she could make him like her at once, sensing he was not someone she could fool or manipulate, yet inexplicably distrustful of him. "That's right," she affirmed. "And you working for a colored paper, that doesn't leave us much to talk about, does it?"

He looked at her. "Readers of black newspapers are interested in lots of subjects, Miss Hamilton."

"You don't have to tell me about black people, Mr. Hightower," she said, more sarcastically than she intended, uncomfortable at being bitchy yet helpless to quit. "I may not beat drums all over the place and say, 'Look at me, I'm colored.' But I'm colored. And believe it or not, there's not a thing you can tell me about being colored." Why am I doing this, she thought, I'm so keyed up and bone tired I could scream but so what, why am I all of a sudden baiting this man I don't know? "Now, do we understand each other before we go on?"

His smile seemed only slightly forced. He nodded. "I'm all for people understanding one another. I admit I'd much rather ask you about you as a person than about your favorite desserts and movie stars, but maybe we can find some middle ground and try to get off to a better start. And be civil in the process."

Who are you, anyway, to give me orders? I just started getting big in show business, and I already have more money than you'll ever see, she thought, and said, carefully not raising her voice and carefully not frowning, "Well, that's something else you don't have to do—tell me to be civil. I didn't go looking for you. You came to me from your little newspaper. If *you* want to be civil, then we can talk for a little while. If you don't, then I'm too busy for you to take up my time."

The whiskey sour came and the waiter went. She waited for young Mr. Hightower (what was his first name? Verne? Yes, Verne Hightower—ridiculous name) to apologize for trying to put her down—he needed a Robin Hamilton interview for his editor, didn't he?—or to jolly her out of her miserable mood.

He did neither. He cocked a controlled eyebrow, and he said, "Look at me. Not past me. At me." She did. His sharp eyes held hers and he said, very quietly, very sternly, "I'm leaving this table in one minute, because I may be from a little newspaper and nobody special, but in spite of all the big ballyhoo I've been hearing about you it appears that you're nobody special, either. All you are, Miss Hamilton—at least all that's getting across to me—is a girl with looks and probably talent and not much else."

Horrified at herself, horrified that he was so exactly right about

her, Robin strove for the words that would beg his pardon, but he
went on, still quietly, still in full control. "It's interesting," he said.
"In this job of mine for this little newspaper I work for, I meet
people with a great deal more to give than overnight wonders like
you have to give. And what always impresses me is that the ones
most useful to themselves and to other people, to the world, are
the ones who never suspect for an instant that the world revolves
around them. I'm sorry I'm wasting your time. You've certainly
wasted mine. I don't have that much to spare here in the East, and
I want to spend it with folks I can respect."

"Please . . ."

"Now I'll pay the check and go—my little newspaper gave me a
little expense account before I came. Everyone says you're going
to be a big star. You're bound to find all the robots you need to
fawn over you."

Softly, throatily, desperately, again unable to meet his gaze,
Robin implored, "Don't go." She paused, then whispered, "Oh,
please."

He could have left, could have continued to twist the knife
deeper. But he frowned at her as though attempting to read her,
and he didn't speak for a moment, and then he said with surprise,
"You're trembling."

"A little. I'm all right."

"Drink your whiskey."

She saw him smile. Holding her breath to stave off the tears that
were churning to appear, she smiled, too obediently, and raised her
glass by its narrow stem and brought it to her lips because he had
ordered her to. "Sure you're all right?" he asked. "I didn't rough
you up too much?"

"Not enough," she said, shaking her head at the cigarette he
offered. "Sometimes—there's no excuse for it—sometimes I have
this terrible habit of trying to make two cents out of the nicest
people I meet. Lately—I wasn't always like this. I'm really a very
crummy person—the last thing I want to be. I see people acting

crummy—crummily—is that a word?—towards other people, and all I want to do is sink right into the floor, I feel so awful. I wish I could be nice."

"When did it begin, this change?"

Robin glanced at his pad and pencil. "Is any of this for publication?"

Gracefully, good-naturedly, he put the pad and pencil out of sight. "No."

He had an eight-thirty dinner appointment, Verne Hightower said after they had talked about themselves, mostly about Robin, for nearly an hour that began awkwardly and then suddenly sped by, but nothing in the way he said it suggested he was impatient with her or eager to duck out. Robin had an eight-thirty appointment, too, she joylessly confessed—she was expected to attend someone's movie premiere at the Criterion—and then she asked him, maybe too brazenly, if he could break his date and go with her. He would like to, he said and maybe he was sincere, but he couldn't. Hastily she studied her calendar. "I have to sing at this benefit at Town Hall tomorrow night," she said. "They promised me I'll only have to sing two numbers and I can be out by ten or so, and I don't have anything special planned for after. Are you doing anything special tomorrow night?"

"I'll know my schedule better in the afternoon." He seemed amused and yet a little less friendly. "Suppose I get in touch with you then, unless that's too late and you want to make other plans?"

"Oh, call, absolutely! I don't know where I'll be when you call, but if you leave a message with Ronnie Haley's office I'll get it. I won't make any plans at all!"

He accepted the check and paid it. Robin wanted to insist that GWS should and would pay it, but decided he might feel she was being superior, and so she was silent. Waiting for change, he said, "I've enjoyed this. We were off on the wrong foot for a minute or two there, but maybe it was just as well—we know each other better."

"I talked my head off."

"I liked it."

"You—*will* call, won't you?"

"Yes."

"Do you like hamburgers? If you like, we can go to my place after Town Hall and I'll cook you up some burgers from the old Hamilton family recipe."

"You?" he asked, grinning. "Somehow I can't picture you as a cook."

"Oh, I am, sort of. You'd be surprised at all the ordinary little things I can do, as long as they don't take brains."

"It's a date—I hope."

Shortly before eight o'clock, Ronnie Haley called for Robin at Sardi's, and on the ride to the theater she asked him if he knew anything about Verne Hightower. "No," he said. "Just that that Frisco paper he writes for is damned influential in the Negro community. I hope you two hit it off."

"Could you find out about him tomorrow, you or someone at your office? He doesn't talk much about himself and I'm—oh, sort of curious."

"Do you mean find out what his marital status is?"

She laughed lightly. "Well, that too, I guess."

The floodlighted sidewalk in front of the Criterion was roped off for the premiere of the new Burt Lancaster picture, and microphones and television cameras and hundreds of people on either side of the theater's entrance greeted the celebrities who arrived. Robin heard herself cheered as she was helped out of the limousine, and she glittered at the microphone as a slick-haired, oily master of ceremonies exclaimed that his spies had informed him that her first, soon to be released album, *Robin on the Wing*, would be a smash, and exclaimed that she was far lovelier in person than her video shots would lead the public to believe, and exclaimed that he *knew* her first motion picture, soon to begin on the Coast, would make her a smash star, and she just had time to thank him and confide how thrilled she was to be here tonight when he subtly edged her away because more celebrities were waiting in line to hear his exclamations. She sat restlessly through the Burt Lancaster movie, Ronnie Haley beside her, and thought about the young man with the ridiculous name of Verne Hightower, and could not remember much of what they had talked about. All she remembered, the important thing she savored, was that he must have liked her or he would have found an excuse to leave earlier. Once he had rightfully pinned her ears back for behaving like a nasty child, he was nice, very, very nice, even though she *had* talked her head off. He was a quiet man, reserved, probably not terribly ambitious, certainly not wildly fascinated by show business, but there was an authority about him, a dignity, a presence that Robin welcomed, responded to. He was strong, not overpowering but confident, and he saw something in her and—

Wait, she thought, could be I'm mistaken. Again. I was sure Jerry Sorin was strong, and he was Kleenex. I was sure Jesse was strong, but no truly strong man lets setbacks drag him down and turn him inside out. Maybe this man I don't really know at all is quiet strength just on the surface, maybe all he can do like a man is shut a girl up when she needs it, and deep down he's just another man like James Lonny Hamilton, who sees something good in me but who's a quitter when you need him most.

Maybe he won't call.

Why does it matter so much? I'll survive, won't I? I keep surviving, I guess.

Why should he bother to call? Of course I remember all that happened. Something got into me the minute I realized he wasn't out to hurt me, and I started to talk and I couldn't stop. I needed to sound entertaining and witty and wise, and I wasn't; I did everything wrong, I didn't let him talk, I didn't wait to learn much about him except that he's not married—or that's what he said—and he's on committees and stuff. I just jabbered about myself, big deal me, about how hard show business is, all the pressures they put on you, silly jabber.

Polite. That's what he was—polite. He's a serious man, concerned about important things, not about a dope kid like me who runs off at the mouth about unimportant things. No, I lost him. Maybe I should've been sexy; I caught him glancing at my body as though he was interested, kind of. He began to fade away long before I said You *will* call, won't you? I was chasing him. Our first meeting together and I was letting him know I need someone to take care of me. What man wants that?

Please call. I need someone strong, someone to take care of me. . . .

Early the next afternoon, Ronnie Haley's secretary Gwen reached Robin by phone, not with a message from Verne Hightower but a rundown on him. "This Mr. H. is evidently quite a guy for twenty-eight years old," Gwen reported. "Born in Minnesota. Worked his way through the University of Minnesota, majored in political science, and he graduated near the tippy-top of his class. He makes his living, not much of one, writing for the *San Francisco Afro-American,* but he wrote a book on Negro history that was published four years ago—it didn't sell well but it got raves from most of the book critics—and if you have all night I'll read off all the civil rights and human rights committees he's active on."

"Is he single?"

"Ah, *that's* why I was put to work on him for you, huh? Wait, let's see. A widower, it says here. He has a daughter, three years old."

Verne Hightower did not phone by eight-fifteen, when Robin had to leave for Town Hall. Nor was there any word from or about him when she returned to her hotel from Town Hall.

Nor was there word the following day, a brutal day of work—but then all days now were brutal. She did receive one telephone call, during a rare breather between being shuttled from one rushed appointment to another. It was her sister Lula, and Robin's immediate thought was of Mama, dead. In these two years, Lula had never tried to reach her by phone.

"No, Mama's doing pretty well," Lula reassured her. "She told me to write you, but I decided to call instead—the name of your hotel was on that money order you sent and that's how I found out where to call. Mama says to tell you she'll always pray for you, honey, but she won't take that money or any money from you."

"Are you calling from home? Is she there?"

"She's out somewhere. These people at FREE keep her on the go. I've begged her not to do so much, she comes home worn out, but it's like talking to a wall. And I've kept telling her you'd probably give anything to see her, be with her, but that's like talking to a wall, too, Robin. I hear her praying for your soul every night, but she's got this stubborn streak, same as always, and she looked at that money order for a long while, and she cried a little, and then she just flushed it down the toilet."

"Please tell me all about her, Lula, all about both of you!" Robin urged. "You couldn't believe how many times a day I've wanted to call up and didn't have the nerve."

"We're getting along, keeping busy. I—well, I'm getting married, for one thing."

"No! How wonderful!" Robin exclaimed, and rose from her chair and set down her glass of rye and ginger ale. "Lula, how wonderful! Who is it? Do I know him?"

"I don't think. Dewey Erskine. I don't think you ever met him— no, of course not, he hasn't been around here but a year. He's a minister, assisting Reverend Fletcher, and he'll be taking over when Reverend Fletcher retires. We started keeping company about six months ago, and, well, last week he popped the question."

"Oh, Lula, that's just marvelous! You must be flying!" said Robin, joyful and, oddly, fleetingly jealous.

"Well, he's a fine man, kind of serious-minded but very considerate. And Mama's just plain tickled, I must admit."

Robin burbled with enthusiasm, firing questions about Dewey Erskine and what the wedding would be like, delighted that her sister was at last going to be happy and that Mama would finally know pleasure, too, but dismayed at being left out. "Why haven't you called me before this, Lula, or written to me except for that letter a long time ago?" she implored, and raised her glass of rye and ginger ale. "I've been so *lonely*, so lonely for my family. You don't hate me, Lula, I know that. You always knew where to find me, or you could've found out. Why can't I be with my family?"

"Because of Mama, honey, stubborn, proud Mama. She pretends like you're gone, like Roland Lee. She calls you a saloon hussy and her baby girl, almost in the same breath, and she knows as much as I do that it's not Christian not to be forgiving but she won't budge an inch."

"What can I *do*? I made one mistake. What can I do so she won't punish me the rest of my life?"

"Nothing, I guess. I don't like that Jesse Nash, but he got his hooks into her to go read those speeches for FREE, and, well, to be honest, he was the one who put that bee in her bonnet about how you shouldn't be forgiven. He took his sweet time about it, he didn't come out and say it right off, but he talked her into believing a lot of nonsense about how you betrayed your family and your people, and she's all mixed up, she doesn't know if she's coming or going, what with all he and that Orville Sanford told her to believe, but that's how it is. You'll just have to accept it."

"You, Lula," said Robin desperately. "You come and see me."

A pause. "Mama wouldn't allow that. And I'd never do anything behind her back."

"She won't *allow*? What are you, a child?"

Another pause. "Yes. Mama's child. Till the day she dies."

Robin drank from her glass, which was shaking. "All right, then, I guess I'd better stop crawling, I guess you'd better tell that to Mama," she said, sounding helplessly hard. "But wait, don't hang up, Lula. I have more money than I know what to do with, and I'm going to have lots more. Can you tell her that not all of it comes from the saloons? I want you both to have money. What's wrong with that? She can buy things with it. You can buy things with it."

"I—could talk with her again. But I know what she'd do with money, even if she'd say all right. It would go to the church, and it would go to FREE. I'd love it if she could have some comforts, if . . . No, it just wouldn't work out, Robin. Mama won't take anything from you."

"Wait, wait, this is silly. *You* take it. I'll send money to you, and you do what's right with it. I'll send it to your bank. Which bank do you have, still Westbrook on Lenox?"

"Yes, but—"

"Please, Lula, don't say no. I want to, I *have* to. Please don't you punish me, too."

". . . All right. I guess it would be all right, even if it would be lying to Mama."

The telephone's red bulb lighted, signaling that a call was waiting for her. "Lula, I have to hang up now. I *am* happy about you and your Minister Erskine."

"I know that."

"We can't see each other, you and I?"

". . . No."

"Lula?"

"Yes, Robin?"

"Tell Mama I'm not a bad girl. Tell her I never have been, and I never will be."

"Good-bye, Robin. God bless you and watch out for you."

The waiting call was from Warren—surprising her, because since Chicago he had relayed information and questions to her by way of Jeanne Prescott and other GWS people and had not once personally phoned her. He didn't sound unfriendly. "I thought you'd like to know," he said, "that I've just finished reading the first complete draft of *Play with Fire*, and I can't see how it can miss."

Play with Fire was the story idea he had sold to Cambridge Pictures for her first movie and had hired some writers to turn into a quick screenplay. "So fast?" she asked, impressed, guardedly friendly. "I've lost all track of time, I've been so busy, but it seems like you put those writers to work just yesterday."

"Not quite, but almost—I chained them to the newel post and fed them nothing but bread and water till they were done. I'd like to get this script to you to read as soon as possible—shooting begins on the fifteenth, which is around the corner. I have a copy of your work schedule here in front of me, and you obviously don't have two consecutive minutes to rest, but when do you think I could send a messenger over with the script?"

Gripping her fingers around her glass, Robin said, "Let me look. I have a voice lesson and an acting lesson this evening, and then Ronnie Haley wants to send some men over to take some pictures. I told him they couldn't stay longer than eleven because I've been running since seven this morning and I have to be up at seven tomorrow morning. But if you're free, maybe *you* could bring it by about eleven."

She imagined she could see him sit up. "That's, ah, possible."

The photographers arrived at nine, minutes before her drama coach left, and time was wasted because, nerves frayed and exhaustion around the bend, she argued with the men, the Negro photographer as well as the white one, that she would hold still for no cheesecake. Exactly at eleven, she said, "That's enough for now. Will you go home now, please?" and left to go to the kitchen, from where she could hear one of the men grumbling about nice, cooperative young kids turning bitcho overnight.

In the kitchen she discovered she had run out of ginger ale. (Warren's been right all along, she reminded herself: having a cleaning woman in here's not enough; I need somebody around, if only to see that I don't run out of milk and eggs and ginger ale and things.) And so she drank tap water with her rye. The taste was repugnant and made her gag briefly, but it warmed her stomach; the second water and rye went down with as much difficulty as the first, but it relaxed her a little.

She had emptied an ice tray into the sink and built a fresh drink of ice and water and rye by the time she heard the photographers close the front door after themselves and their equipment. She carried the glass to the bedroom and stripped for a shower, wanting a warm, sudsy bath but not daring to take the time, for Warren would be here soon and it would not do for him to catch her in the tub and think she was in naked wait for him. Naked, she returned to the living room, sipping from her glass, made sure the front door was shut but unlocked, and went back to the bedroom, where she forced herself to swallow half of the drink. As the shower beat down on her she wondered what had possessed her to invite Warren, who would pick on her again—at this time of night, especially, when her nerves were ready to screech.

Warren was in the living room, fixing himself a drink, when she emerged from the shower and the bedroom, wearing not the expensive, sheer black negligee he had bought her but the expensive, neck-high, floor-length mauve dressing robe she had bought herself. He smiled, and so did she. "Tired?" he asked.

"Mmmm, fall-down tired," she nodded, drying the insides of her ears with a heavy Turkish towel. "Could I have a drink, too?"

"Really? You?"

"Really. Not too much of one."

She sat down on her couch almost formally, having carefully avoided painting her lips or perfuming her body, sat as the Tired Almost-Star, not as Warren's Easy Pickin's. "How did tonight's session go with Lois?" he inquired at the makeshift bar. Lois Farrentino was the drama teacher GWS had hired to try to turn Robin into an actress.

"It could've been better if I hadn't been so pooped."

He chuckled. "I had a talk with her this morning. Lois is like most of the pros I respect—pulling teeth is easier than pulling good news. But fawncy-diction Lois gave you all A's on your report card. She said you have ten or twenty minutes to go before you can play *Medea*, but she said there's no doubt in her mind that you have as much of a future cut out for you as an actress as you do as a singer. That just went and made my whole day. It ought to make yours, too."

"It would," agreed Robin, "if I didn't feel like something being fed through the sausage-grinder. I'm so tired out, at my age. What's going to happen when I'm a gray-haired old lady?"

"Aging," said Warren, bringing her the first drink he had ever brought her, "is, on good days, an imperceptible process. Take that pearl of wisdom from a gray-haired old man who knows all about gray-haired old ladies." He sat with her, and the tenderness was her Warren's tenderness. "I haven't been awfully kind lately, have I, gray-haired old lady?"

Robin melted, though she barely moved. "No wonder," she said. "I've been giving you such a hard time."

They talked, uncomfortable business talk, scrupulously touching no personal bases nor each other, clearing their throats a lot, lovers with reminiscences held in, lovers afraid to look up. He did not ask her about Lamont Winters, the stranger at Curly Custer's party, and so she did not ask him about Jesse. He told her that her part in *Play with Fire* would take three weeks, four at the most, and he told her how much money he would demand and get for her, when the time came to discuss her second picture. Finally Warren kissed her, and the trouble with Warren's kiss was that it was full of sex but not full of love. He brought one of her breasts out from between the folds of the robe, and held it, but she appraised it along with him, and whatever had been spontaneous and meaningful before was forced now, funny-forced, and Warren seemed as relieved as she when she gradually, gracefully moved and got up and said, with a smile, "I hate saying this, but I can hardly keep my eyes open."

Warren smiled, too, the smile artificial and troubled, and assured her he understood, and remarked that he'd had a long day, too, that it might have been smarter to have sent the script over with a messenger, after all. At the door, his eyes were hurt and his kiss was mechanical, but he continued to smile, and he said, "Stay well, dear."

"You too."

Robin bolted the door after him, finished the drink he had made for her, and went to her bedroom to finish the half-filled glass she had left there. They did not help, but she poured milk rather than more liquor, because more liquor would give her a sound sleep, as it had on other recent nights, but she was afraid she was sliding into a dangerous habit, and she was frightened of danger. She took the script to bed, but all she could see on the pages were Warren's cold lips on her cold lips. No, cold wasn't the right word. Hot, then suspicious, then spiritless.

Why? What had happened, what was happening? Why did I move away from him, why didn't he come after me?

Don't leave me, Warren.

Or I have nobody. No Verne Hightowers, no Jesses, nobody.

When the unread script was closed, when sleep would not come, when the tears would neither come nor go, when her overstrung nerves scissored into every joint and muscle, she hurried to the living room, where she drank liquor, and coughed and gagged, and drank more, huddling close to the makeshift bar with her head down so that Mama would not see her.

Thirteen

IN THE HAVILLAND LOBBY, Weber phoned Gloria Barclay because there was no one at home to go to: Karen was in Greenwich with her mother who was ill and old, and their son Skipper was at college in Oregon, and their daughters Nancy and Kay would surely be asleep. Gloria's answering service did not know when Miss Barclay would be in and was there any message? He riffled through his address book for the number of Jeri Paine, the sometime television dancer who couldn't decide whether she wanted to be a fulltime call girl or a Mother Superior, and, under "P," came upon Jeanne Prescott, and telephoned her. "It's late," he said, "but I'd like to come by. I can be there in twenty, thirty minutes."

"Okay," said Jeanne, who lived on West End and whose flat he had never visited. "I'll put some coffee on—and a dress."

Rudi gave him a cigarette because he asked for one. It tasted delicious, and he decided he had been a damned masochistic fool for having given up smoking months ago, at a time when he needed all the small satisfactions he could get. He poured vodka at his back-seat bar and glumly reflected on how withdrawn Robin had been, how rejecting, not because she was tired but maybe because she didn't need him any more; then, uncomfortably, he reflected on how bumbling his own response had been, not insisting or even suggesting that they talk about where they stood with each other.

He wanted Karen. He wished she were not up in Greenwich.

He wanted Robin. He wished love weren't so exorbitantly expensive in so many different ways.

He wished it were earlier, so he could have Rudi take him to Greenwich, where Karen was keeping one of her periodic death-watches. He was fond of Henrietta, his mother-in-law, who had always stuck up for him, defended him to her husband, St. John Vickery, who had been Vickery Chemicals and was now dead, who could not fathom what Karen could see in a non-Christian with a non-future. He liked her and wished she was not going to die soon, as he and Karen knew was inevitable. He was proud of Karen, who could go to pieces when the toast burned but who was Gibralter in crisis, who loved her mother, the last Vickery alive besides herself, and who was taking the old girl's visible deterioration with dignity and responsibility.

Finishing the vodka and pouring another, trying to get just a little high, trying to work through the jumbles in his head that started and stalled with Robin, he made up his mind to take off some time tomorrow and go to Connecticut. To be with Karen, who didn't need him. To cozy Henrietta into thinking she would outlive Methuselah. To find a place for himself.

Strange how things work out, he thought now, going away from Robin Hamilton and toward Jeanne Prescott. Strange, how life changes and stands absolutely still. "*Find* yourself, Warren," Phil said to me all those years ago, when he was waiting for his accountancy degree and I was waiting for the key, any key, that would open the right door and, presto, make me the biggest man in New York. "A smart fella like you, figure out what you want to *do*. You want to be J. P. Morgan and you want to save the world. You can't do both at the same time. Make a choice, but don't *schlepp* your life away making it." All those years ago. Phil could have made the same speech last year, last week, today.

Do I know any more about myself today than I did all those years ago, when I was young, when everybody was young?

Jeanne Prescott was not grumpy as she admitted Weber to her well-ordered yet strangely unpersonalized apartment, but she seemed puzzled as she made him a drink and commented that he looked tired. "Fresh as a daisy," he said, and shook a cigarette from her pack of Commanders on her living room desk and lighted it. He wandered through the room, vacantly examining this end-table chromo and that east-wall Titian reproduction, and then realized that most of the other pictures were Titians.

"What's with this one-man show?" he asked when she brought him the drink.

"Sue me. I dig Titian."

"You dig repi-Titian." She was near him, and he said, "Thanks for taking the curlers out, duchess."

"You'd better thank me." Jeanne grinned and sat at the desk, where her cup of coffee was. "When did you go back on cigarettes? Weren't you the bore who made so much noise about the evils of nicotine when you swore off and made all us addicts at the office feel like criminals for not swearing off with you?"

"I'm quitting after tonight. This is a nice pad you have, Jeannie."

"I know. It has everything, including chairs. Why don't you sit in one, Warren, and tell Aunt Prescott what's bugging you?"

"Nothing's bugging me."

"It's past one in the morning and you didn't drop in from out of the blue to admire my nice pad. What's bugging you?"

Weber sighed, and sat, and nodded. "My wife the analyst calls it decathexis. Or used to, before I revoked her license to practice in the state of New York."

"Deca—who? I'm a country girl from Jersey. I never learned language like that."

"Cathexis means the concentration of psychic energy on particular persons or places or ideas. Decathexis, if my wife the analyst reads me right and she usually does, means I got no adhesion to people, baby, I don't know how to love." He drank. "I sound loaded, don't I? I'm not. I'm the boy who was born with something left out. The capacity to feel and love persons and places and ideas, that's what was left out. I'm trying to figure where I can go for a cathexis transplant." He lifted his glass. "Knock me again, will you?"

As the clearly mystified Jeanne went to freshen his drink, it occurred to Weber that he would regret this inexplicable visit, for Jeanne was his employee first and his friend and one-time bed partner second, but he had nowhere else to go. She knew about "Moore" but not about Jesse Nash, knew about Robin but probably not about the extent of his involvement with Robin, probably knew that he hadn't a good marriage but had only a vague notion of how incomplete he was as a man. He watched her at her bar, half watching him, and suddenly knew, with a swift, involuntary shudder, that he had come to her to talk about Robin because she, patient Jeanne, was black.

"Keep talking, I *guess*," Jeanne said, bringing him the drink; he noticed that it was a tall one, light, with more water than the first one had had. "I'll do my best to follow you."

"How happy are you, Jeannie?"

She sat again, but did a double take. "At past one in the morning, with a great big day ahead of me, and I have to put my hair up all over again? How happy should I be?"

"Why aren't you a married lady with thirty kids jumping into the cookie jar?"

Her frown was quick and precise. "You're a swell fella, Warren, decawhatzis and all, but you just asked me something that's none of your goddam concern."

"Do you have a special guy?"

"That's also none of your goddam concern. How would you like me to give you the third degree about your private life?"

"Be my guest."

"No, you're my guest, and I'll listen to anything you want to tell me, but I don't pry."

"On a number of occasions, Robin and I have slept together."

"Rah-rah for the both of you. So what else is new?"

"Did you know that?"

"I surmised it. What do you want me to do with this scoop, Warren? Scold you, give you my blessings, what? What's your point?"

"You sound testy."

"I'm not testy. I'm confused. You're making me a little uneasy. I don't know why I should be hearing these things."

"I need help, Jeanne."

"From me?"

"Yes."

"Why me?"

"Because you're wise. Because you're black."

"Oh-oh," she said, and lighted a cigarette.

"Because you're wise and black. In that order."

"We blacks always come in second. All right, Warren, tell it like it is to the black Dear Abby."

Weber gulped his second drink and began to talk, with a punctilious, too-soon-nearly-drunk honesty that he suspected could very well plague and haunt him in the morning—or minutes from now. Talking as he rose to pour drinks and take cigarettes, he piled detail upon detail of his prowess as a lover. He got rapidly drunker and talked about Karen, who was not frigid so much as inconsistently responsive. He talked about Robin, about the joy and the complexities of her, about himself and his credentials and credits as a progressive, about his loving her and finding direct and devious ways of retreating so that he wouldn't have to nourish her. He talked about being color blind, and he asked Jeanne if part of him wanted to cut himself off from Robin Hamilton because he had this decathexis thing or because Robin Hamilton was black.

He drank as he waited for her to answer. And tried to remember what he had asked her.

"You're asking the wrong woman, Warren," said Jeanne. "I can't untangle you. Maybe you should ask your wife the analyst."

"Testy again, testy," said Weber, aware that he had eaten one or two more Dexies than usual today yet astonished that he was so sloshed, so irresponsibly, un-Weberly sloshed, even though too many Dexies always made alcohol work fast.

Jeanne got up and there were only traces of kindness in her pretty face. "Is Rudi downstairs?" she asked.

"Rudi? Yeah."

"Then have him take you home, Warren. You don't belong here. I can't help you. You belong home."

"Not the bum's rush. Don't give me the bum's—"

"No, Warren dear, I'm giving you the chance to walk out of here under your own steam, like a man, a man I admire and need to keep admiring. I'll call downstairs. I'll have the night man find Rudi, and Rudi will come up and get you and drive you home."

" 'Come up'? I'm not all that crocked."

"You are, Warren dear. You're good and crocked, and you and I have to face each other tomorrow. I'll call for Rudi and get your coat and—"

Weber grabbed Jeanne and held her buttocks and tried to kiss her. She freed herself, fury and a droplet of compassion in her eyes, and she said, firmly, "No. If you want to lay a colored girl, have Rudi take you up to Harlem. If you want to get laid, period, have Rudi take you to the East Side, West Side, all around the town. I'm sorry, sweetheart, all your white liberal credentials are in order, but some of us colored gals just don't spread on demand."

Mortified, abruptly stone sober, Weber said, "Oh, Christ, Jeanne, I apologize for being such a mess. I honest to Christ apologize. It was—I had to talk to somebody."

"I know, Warren. I'll see you in the office."

He stood with elaborate dignity in the elevator that took him down, because he sensed that the elevator operator sensed he was drunk. Rudi drove him to Sutton Place and had to call and even shake him to bring him awake. He reached the penthouse without help and zigzagged to his and Karen's bedroom, hoping he wouldn't disturb Karen but glad that she was there. She wasn't, and he dimly remembered why, and fell heavily on the bed, planning to rest for just a moment and then get up and take off his clothes.

His valet, Ernest, knocked and came into the room, said, "Good morning," and seemed surprised that Weber was fully dressed.

"Time zit?"

"A few minutes before nine."

"Too early. Go 'way. You know never to get me up unless I leave a call the night before."

"Mrs. Weber's on the phone for you, Mr. Weber, and she says to wake you. She called twice last night."

"Okay, get me some black coffee and put out . . . let's see . . . put out the gray chalk stripe," Weber said, running booze-shaky fingers through his hair, aware of his eight-pound tongue, and reached for the telephone, quickly suspecting that Karen was calling because Henrietta was dead.

He was right. Karen had broken down, or would, but she sounded manifestly contained now, perhaps too much so. Henrietta had passed away at five o'clock in the afternoon. Karen had called him then, couldn't get him, had left word with Louise, Phil's secretary, because Jeanne hadn't been at her desk, nor had Sharon, Jeanne's assistant. She sounded slightly miffed that he hadn't called her or gone to her before this. "I got in late," he said. "The girls and Ernest were asleep, and I went right to bed."

"But you always look at your messages, no matter what time you get home."

It was not a morning for criticism, even mild and understandable criticism, and Weber, sitting up slowly and painfully, unbuttoning his shirt, wondered where the hell Ernest was with the coffee. "Last night I didn't," he said. "I'm sorry, dear. Of course I would've phoned you right away."

"Anyway, the girls are here with me," Karen said. "They were both in the apartment, the first time I called, and they went straight to Grand Central and came here. I didn't even ask them to—they did it on their own. I didn't realize how much they loved their grandmother."

"Did your mother have a bad time?"

"No, I'm sure she didn't. The coma frightened me, and the servants, too, but it helped. She was asleep, and she died."

"How are you, Karen?" he asked, genuinely concerned.

"I'm all right. I'd be better if you could be here with the girls and me."

"Yes. I'll be there as soon as I can."

The coffee came, and Weber told Ernest to put out the new blue suit instead of the chalk stripe. He hadn't the heart to rouse Rudi this early, and so he told Ernest to find a Greenwich train schedule. The coffee didn't settle him but it brought him partially back to life, and ridding himself of the rumpled clothes helped (*My God, I went to sleep with my shoes on!*) and so did the shave and so did the shower. Ernest read him the morning express trains to Greenwich, and by the time he was dressed it was nearly ten o'clock, and he phoned his office and Jeanne was there.

He explained why his appointments would have to be cancelled or postponed, and Jeanne, whose face he wished he could see and read, asked to be remembered to Mrs. Weber. There weren't any appointments that couldn't be put off for a day or two, she said, but she admitted she was curious about one call he'd received and Sharon had taken. Jesse Nash (*"the* Jesse Nash?"*) wanted his call returned—before noon, if possible—and Jeanne gave him Nash's number, which Weber already had. "Why would Jesse Nash be ringing you up?"

"I'll check into it," Weber said evasively, and guessed this was the moment to put on the sackcloth and ashes. "Is there any truth to the rumor in this morning's *National Enquirer* that a man was in your apartment some hours ago and behaved like ten generations of jackasses?"

Jeanne didn't laugh or say oh boy did you have a load on. She said evenly, "It's more than a rumor. And it was more than a disturbing hour or so. I've never thrown the least little weight around, Warren, but I've got to tell you this, and I might as well do it right now. You upset me very much last night. I didn't know how much till hours after you left and I couldn't sleep. You are never to use me again like that. I have the toughest hide in town, and I thought you were the most disgusting man I'd ever met. I don't now, because I've reminded myself of all the good things there are about you. But that doesn't cancel out the bad things I learned about you last night. You do anything like that ever again, and out I scram."

"I hear every word, Jeannie. Believe that."

He phoned Nash, who had read the three "Moore" scripts and liked them. Weber was instantly relieved, and knew why: a Jesse Nash valentine wouldn't automatically have insured that the series was right, but an outright raspberry from Nash would have meant cause for worry that "Moore" was a fixed fight, white liberalism's powder-puff blows at occasionally naughty white exploiters.

"Okay, so far, so good," said Weber, purposely holding in his delight. "I can round up a director and a camera crew, nothing fancy, just enough to make sure your test will be done right for everyone concerned. And the sooner the better. Can you get going immediately if these people are ready?"

"Hold on now, I'm not sayin' I went and fell in love with it, whole hog. I like what I read, sure, but what guarantee'd I have that it's gonna stay punchy like this?"

Weber's temples were killing him. "What guarantee do I have that you can act your way out of a paper bag?" he barked. "What guarantee do I have about *anything*?"

It must have been the way to tuck a tail between Nash's legs, for Nash said, after a moment, "I dig. No real sweat, man."

"Write this name down—Earl Cuff, C-u-f-f," Weber said and gave him Earl's office number. "He handles screen tests. I'm going to call him now. You give him a call in ten minutes or so, and go and do as he tells you."

"You can talk salty, you know?"

"Yes, I know. I'll get over it. We both will. Good-bye."

He phoned Earl, who wasn't in, and told Earl's associate, Cliff Doran, to set up a test as soon as possible, to expect Nash's call, and to get cracking. Then Ernest phoned the lobby for a cab to be waiting, and Weber carried an overnight bag to the elevator and the curb, where he gave Elwood the doorman a dollar for Elwood's half package of cigarettes and the taxi. On the way to Grand Central, the shame of his conduct with Jeanne Prescott seared into him. And on the way, for no reason at all and without announcement, his chest began to hurt him and he had to roll both windows down so that he could breathe more easily.

By the time he was on the express to Greenwich, his chest and his breathing were fine, and he knew the brief taxi fit had been the consequence of too little sleep and too much hangover, that it bore no relation to the long-ago conniption in Gloria Barclay's flat.

He felt all right, despite the hangover. But he tried to ignore Jeanne, and couldn't. What a horse's ass I must have been, he thought, lighting a delicious cigarette. I acted like a man with a crack-up coming.

He felt a hand on his shoulder and looked up to see a scowling conductor pointing, like the Lord banishing Adam and Eve from Eden, to the No Smoking sign. And Warren Weber, who frequently had the muscle to banish the Lord from Eden, immediately dropped the cigarette and crushed it with his heel and said, "I'm awfully sorry. I didn't see the sign."

Caleb Atwood performed many nuisance chores that ate into his day, time-consuming and usually pointless small chores he nonetheless believed necessary because his central responsibility at Vanguard Broadcasting was to run a ship that was tight yet maneuverable. And one means of keeping it fluid was to know what was happening outside the walls of Vanguard Broadcasting. And that was why he read newspapers, and the columnists in newspapers.

A small item in Bart Snyder's column, *I Get Around*, read, in its entirety: "There are Video Row rumblings that Warren Weber's fall season blockbuster for VBN will be an all-Negro dramatic series, with the lead played by—get this—Jesse Nash, the FREEdom fighter."

Furious not because it was a lie but because it was some press agent's lie that the irresponsible Snyder should never have allowed anywhere near a linotyper, Caleb Atwood instantly and personally placed a call to Snyder's apartment, where the colunist's I-don't-know-nothin' maid or somebody reminded him that it was eleven o'clock in the morning and not even World War Three could ever disturb Mr. Snyder's sleep till five in the afternoon. Atwood phoned Snyder's office, where the columnist's right and probably left hand, Iona Fuller, calmly intoned, "You know Bart never gives out information sources, Mr. Atwood. You know that re- porters don't, nor should they. This is the third time in a month you've—" Atwood phoned GWS and was connected with Weber's haughty colored secretary, Jemima Prescott or something, who said that Warren had gone to Connecticut because his mother-in- law had died, and who pretended she knew nothing about the Snyder item. "I saw the item, and it's insane," she said. "Somebody made it up. I'm with Warren day in and day out, and if it held any water, I'd know about it."

"I want your Mr. Weber," said Atwood. "Give me the number in Connecticut."

"Can it wait? His wife's mother died just yesterday and—"

"Yesterday ? Then the funeral's over by now, isn't it?"

"Over?"

"Jews bury—the Jewish people bury their dead right away, within hours. So Mr. Weber should be perfectly free to talk."

"I—well, I wouldn't know anything about that. Here's the num- ber. But he wouldn't be there yet. He phoned me just about an hour ago, and he was just leaving his apartment to go to Green- wich."

Caleb Atwood took the number, hung up, and phoned Green- wich. A man with a foreign accent answered, "Vickery residence," said he didn't know when Mr. Weber was due but would der chentleman care to shpeak mit Missus Veber? Mrs. Weber was summoned and said that Warren was expected presently. Atwood instructed her to have him return the call at once and then asked her what she knew about Jesse Nash and "Moore." She said she knew nothing. "You're Weber's wife and this is a series I'm sure he considers the apex of his career," said Atwood. "How could you conceivably not know anything?"

"Mr. Atwood," said Weber's wife, "I lost my mother yesterday and I would appreciate it if you would not snap at me."

"I am not snapping, madam," said Atwood. "I am attempting to elicit some simple information. Who fed that nauseating, destructive item to Bart Snyder if not your husband? You live with your husband, I presume. Your husband is the most uninterruptible talker of all time. How could you *conceivably* not know anything about—"

It was preposterous, but he heard a click and then dead air. She had hung up on him.

Caleb Atwood again phoned GWS, this time for Philip Simms. Mr. Simms was in a sales meeting, he was told, and could not be disturbed. He directed that Mr. Simms be hauled out of the sales meeting bodily and directed to telephone Mr. Atwood instantly. He replaced the receiver, and tapped each of his two front teeth with his fingernail, and placed several more calls, to Owen Claffee of Foley Foods, the imbecilic millionaire who was sponsoring "Moore" and who said, "Who's Jessie Nash? Name's familiar, but I can't place her," to people who assured Caleb Atwood that the Snyder item was the goofiest and most groundless one they had ever read, to people who didn't know nothin'—nobody knew nothin'—but who told him he'd have to agree, wouldn't he, that if it were true, and it couldn't be, it would make a devil of a provocative show. He felt like hitting someone.

Then Caleb Atwood buzzed Claude Rhodes and said that it was important that he see him. He went to the too-slowly dying old man who, as he expected, had not seen the item and didn't know what to make of it, and said, "This could very well be some grubby press agent's hallucination, Claude. It probably is—I'm still checking it out. But what disturbs me, if I may say so, is that you let Weber talk you into letting him and his tribe have free rein to roller-skate up and down all the offices and corridors of

Vanguard. What am *I* at Vanguard for? Why didn't you at least consult me before you told him to go full speed ahead on this "Moore" idea? What if he does decide to have Nash, or someone of the Nash stripe, sell Owen Claffee's oatmeal?"

"He won't, Caleb. Weber's a sideshow barker, but he's not a dunce. He wouldn't jeopardize himself in the industry, if only because casting that loudmouth Nash in the part is aesthetically as well as commercially untenable."

"The way the agreement is worded, the agreement you signed, it strikes me that Weber can cast anyone he chooses, from Shylock to the Rosenbergs. It strikes me—"

"The Rosenbergs? Those traitors, you mean? Come now, Caleb, you're being extremely dramatic and overwrought on such a lovely morning. Polluted air and all, it's a lovely morning—just look out the window. I do want you to stop being shrill, Caleb. I wasn't born yesterday, as everyone including my Dr. Bronf knows. I hear you. I hear your displeasure with Weber, and I hear your emphasis on the fact that he's Jewish . . ."

"Claude—"

"One moment, Caleb. I'm a sick old man, but there's nothing wrong with my ears. Or my education. I know Shylock was a Jew. I know the Rosenbergs were Jews. I wouldn't dare to ask you where your intelligence and your heart are, Caleb. I'd love to ask you where your urbanity is, though."

It had reached that silly season stage, had it? Christly Claude, the *New Republic* subscriber, the B'nai B'rith speaker, the charter member of the New York Athletic Club that barred Jews, the resident of Darien, the Connecticut welcomer of all the moneyed gentry except the Jewish ones. Inconsistency was an abomination to Caleb Atwood, and equally abominable to him was that he was not in a position, not quite yet, to tell the weary old buffalo to take his brittle bones to a nursing home and let the here-and-now generation take charge of the merchandise.

"Very well, Claude. You deal with Mr. Weber. And Jack the Ripper, or anyone who plays 'Moore.'"

"Thank you, Caleb. I shall. Kindly don't fret so. This can be a very nice, pleasant world, if we give it a ghost of a chance."

Caleb Atwood went back to his office and placed a person-to-person call to Willard Cunningham in Helena, Montana. Willard was an old buffalo, like Claude, though certainly not a weary one. There were some vague pockets of crackpotism in crusty old Willard Cunningham, but Willard Cunningham's philosophic consistency was unswerving and admirable. Caleb Atwood was not an official or unofficial member of Soul of America because he was too busy to join anything and because it would be unbecoming for the public to think of him as a joiner. But if Vanguard was preparing to go to hell in a black Commie handbasket, Willard Cunningham had a right to know.

Fourteen

On THE RIDE to Greenwich, Weber read the *New York Times* and tried to ignore the small, shooting pains in both his upper arms. There was a picture of Robin on page 24, above an item about her having signed to play a featured role in *Play with Fire*. Direction by Leo Osgood. Screenplay by Cyril Ducas and Arnie Abraham, based on a story idea by Warren Weber. Co-starring Mark Fraser, Sunny Storm, and Bruce Corbett. Miss Hamilton would sing, but act as well. The item recounted her swift rise from an unknown to a much-sought-after entertainer, and, thought the *Times* rarely gave him credit for much of anything these days, attributed her success to Warren Weber's personal aegis. It mentioned that she was the sister of the slain Roland Lee Hamilton, and, damn it, added that she was not active in the civil rights movement.

There was, on page 19, a file photograph of Stuart Curtiss White above an article about Soul of America's insistence that, all liberal extremists' lying rumors to the contrary, White was still very much a valuable member of the SOA team, even though he was temporarily unavailable for comment owning to ill health aggravated by the emotional strain placed on him by hectoring enemies. The *Times* recapped the story of the doctored picture of Justice Denny and Nick Stanton, detailed its aftermath—including the belief of certain "informed observers" that the ultraconservative society had used White as a fall guy and had ditched him—and then quoted Harold K. Tucker, SOA's Wasp in charge of Public Relations: "The interesting fact that Denny and Stanton's attorney, or attorneys, have not seen fit to institute a libel suit against us," said Tucker, "is our most sterling vindication. Proof is abundant in our files, available to the proper authorities and at the proper time, that the Supreme Court Judge and the convicted Communist are atheistic Red brothers under the skin. As for Officer White, he has not yet begun to fight, at Soul of America's side, against the foes of freedom and liberty."

SOA, you're an S.O.B., thought Weber, marveling at their sublime *chutzpah*. What do you do when your tail is caught in the gate of a gigantically malicious lie? You calmly turn around and slam that same gate on your enemies' fingers. Picture Horace Denny lowering himself to sue vermin. Picture verminy Nick Stanton, the professional martyr, heightening himself to deny the lie. What was more frightening than annoying was that the SOA S.O.B.'s, groaning under the weight of Willard Cunningham's money, thought they could get away with anything. No, *knew* they could get away with anything, because their only adversaries were logic and reason.

His left upper arm again throbbing but the right upper arm right as rain, Weber took a taxi to the Vickery estate, where he hugged Nancy, the elder of his daughters, who was a few years younger than Robin. She was all right, she said, and so was Mommy, who was with Granny's lawyer, and so, she guessed, was little sister Kay, who was off by herself somewhere.

Karen came to him, the rings deep beneath her eyes, and they embraced. "You look so tired," Karen said.

"You look as if you could use a rest yourself," he said gently. They were at the lip of the drawing room and he could see people there, standing, sitting, milling, people he did not know, Greenwich-looking people, ladies with vegetable-garden hats, a sprinkle of elderly men. Nancy left to go and help Mrs. Turner, the housekeeper, and Weber and Karen went to the music room off the foyer, where they could be alone and where he held her as she wept softly.

"This is the first time I've cried since yesterday," she murmured.

"Crying is good," soothed Weber, who had not cried in years.

Karen poured sherry for them both, and they sat, and she talked about Don Barstow, her mother's attorney. "Don just showed me the will and a list of instructions beyond the will," she said. "Mother never said a word about it to me—and that's odd, because she barely stopped talking these past few nights, almost as though she knew she was about to die and needed to sum up her whole life in a matter of hours—but she left instructions that she was to be cremated, and as soon after her death as possible. I can't think what to make of it. Mother always believed in funerals. She believed it was important to see loved ones lowered into the ground, to accept the reality of death. She thought that cremation was cruel, unreal, to the survivors. And now Don tells me she left this instruction over a year ago. It's . . . unsettling . . . to find out you know so little about someone you were positive you knew everything about."

"What does 'soon as possible' mean?"

"Tomorrow morning—isn't that amazing? There's this mad insistence that she's to be prepared for burial, embalming and coffin and all, even though she's to be cremated—isn't that amazing, too? So it's tomorrow morning, and none of us will be there."

"But we do what Henrietta wanted done."

"Yes," Karen sighed. "Yes, of course, damn it."

"Has anyone called Skipper?" Weber asked, suddenly remembering their son.

"I called him. He offered to fly here, but I told him not to—he's up to his ears in exams, and his coming isn't really necessary. The girls have been a most interesting puzzle, Warren. They've done exactly the opposite of what we would've expected. Nancy's been very mature, very attuned, very supportive, and Kay's become an absolute sphinx. She's terribly moved, I'm sure, but she hasn't spoken three words. She's off walking, all by herself."

"Kay? Sis-boom-bah Kay?" The girls had always been remarkably unalike. Nancy, fifteen, with none of her mother's good looks and presence, was a shy child, reflective, emotional, the one who saw every minor setback or brief disturbance as a major crisis, to be solved, if ever and at all, by others. Kay, thirteen, with all her mother's good looks and teeming with presence, was the mental-health star with a score of friends and scores of genuine, healthy interests, the one who got all the A's and the school trophies and who had it on divine authority that every setback and disturbance would be automatically righted by sundown.

Karen nodded. "This is the first family death she's experienced. She seems mystified, even angry. She was the one who cried when she and Nancy got here, much more than Nancy did, but she hasn't let me hold her or even get near her. Would you talk with her, Warren? I don't know what a father's role or a mother's role is at a time like this, but—"

"Of course."

There was a knock at the door and one of the servants said that a Mrs. Rutledge had to leave and wanted to say good-bye to Mrs. Weber. "I'll be right there, Anna," Karen said, and got up, and, setting her scarcely touched sherry down, told Weber, "Mother and Hazel Rutledge worked on half a dozen committees together—I'd best see her out. Oh, wait, I'm sorry, Warren, I forgot to mention something. Caleb Atwood called you here this morning, trying to reach you. A nasty call, by the way."

"Nasty?"

She told him what Caleb Atwood had said, what she had said, and how brutal and insensitive he had been.

"You go on," Weber directed. "I'll make the call here, and be out soon."

"Your face is all red, Warren. Call him, but don't be brutal and insensitive back."

"Quit joking."

"Talking with him on his level never helps either of you—you've learned that by now. You don't have to be as uncivilized as he is to try to understand him."

"Go on, Karen."

He closed the music room door, lighted a cigarette with unsteady fingers, downed Karen's sherry, and placed the call to New York, shaking with rage. Atwood's secretary explained that Mr.

Atwood was on a *very* important long-distance call and would Mr. Weber hold for just a—

"No, I will not hold," Weber snapped. "You get him on the line immediately. Not a minute from now. Immediately."

It was done. Atwood came on the phone talking. "I want to know about the Snyder item, who—"

"I want you to shut up. I want you to know this. If you *ever* talk to Mrs. Weber again the way you talked to her—*ever*, like she was one of your chattel whores, *ever*—I'm coming to you and beating the living shit out of you. Do you hear me, you sick, rotten, son-of-a-bitch pig?"

"Just one mo—"

Weber slammed the receiver on its cradle, and stood at the music room desk until the furious beats of his heart lessened. Neither arm hurt him, and he was relieved. He drank sherry because it was the only thing in the room to drink, and wondered what the telephone call had accomplished, and realized, with no special pride but with a transient satisfaction, that he had done something unfamiliar to him and yet natural; he had, and always would, with conviction, come to the defense of his wife.

He went to the drawing room and met mourners, and talked with the minister named Howlin and the attorney named Barstow. He listened to some well-meaning, earnest lady who assured him she never missed her two favorite television shows of his, "Family Closet" and "Barnum Was Right," two series he had never had anything to do with. He talked with Nancy, his secondborn, whom he had never understood, and then he excused himself and went looking for his youngest, Kay, whom he had always understood.

He came upon her, a quarter mile or so from the estate, in the woods where he and Karen had walked years and years ago, throwing pebbles into the circular, shining pond. They kissed and hugged, and he scooped up some pebbles, and they had a contest, the winner to receive $850,000 in cash, to see who could throw more pebbles farther.

"What's doing, Katydid?" he asked.

"We're supposed to go to that funeral place tonight to see Gran," Kay said flatly, looking ahead. "I loved Gran, but I don't want to go."

"No one's going to force you, if that's your decision."

"I'll go. I know no one'll make me, but I'll go."

"You can make up your mind later."

"Is Grandma Weber younger than Gran?"

"Yes, five or six years younger."

"Do you think she'll live a long time?"

"We expect so, Katydid. She's strong, and she takes good care of herself." He was touched by her remembering his mother, by her asking the sweet, innocent question. His mother and Henrietta had never met, which had occasionally rankled him even though they would have had next to nothing to talk about because they were thoroughly different kinds of women. Karen had gone with him to Philadelphia several times and had sincerely tried to warm Mom up. And Mom, once she had gradually got over the shock of a Gentile daughter-in-law, had tried to be close, too; had not tried with all her might, for Mom did not know how to negotiate any feeling that was unnatural to her, but she had tried. With the kids, though, the situation was entirely different. Whenever she saw them, Mom soared into paroxysms of grandma-ism, pinching them, coaxing kisses, gorging them with Jewish meals and cake and candy and gum and more Jewish meals, clucking that they looked peaked and weren't eating enough and getting enough sleep, spoiling the hell out of them.

"I hate for people to die," Kay said. "You'll die some day, and Mommy will, too, and if that happens I'll want to die, too."

"Hey, there, Gloomy Gus!" Weber exclaimed, too heartily, draping his arm around her shoulders and bringing her close. "Don't bury us yet. Your mother and I aren't sweet sixteen, but we have a way to go before we turn into doddering old museums."

Kay tried a little smile that didn't work.

"Want to walk back to the house?" he asked.

"No."

How do you talk to a thirteen-year-old girl whose adult wisdom very often scares you and whose first personal knowledge of the reality of death now makes her sound seven years old? He released her and said quietly, "Look, Katydid, dying happens because it's got to happen. Getting sick happens, and getting old, and you and I are the two smartest folks on this planet but we're never going to change things that have to happen. Do you know what we can do, what we smart folks can do? We can work like beavers to be *menshkeit*, your Grandma Weber calls it, real people, solid people, loving life and appreciating it and never squandering a minute of it, work to make ourselves whole and kind and respect ourselves and respect others. We work for that and then, when someone we love dies, we mourn for a while but we don't crack up, we don't crack up over anything, because we're *menshkeit*."

Kay looked up at him, frowning. "Daddy, I love you, and you're the smartest and nicest person there is," she said. "And I'm a kid, I know, and sort of dopey sometimes, but you're talking to me like I'm a baby."

It would have been snotty if Nancy had said it. But Kay said it, said it and was looking at him with love and confusion and a trace of disappointment, and Weber felt the put-down like a slap.

He kissed her forehead. "I'll bone up and try to do better, next time at bat. No fortune cookies, I promise."

She looked alarmed. "Oh, gee, Daddy, did I hurt your feelings? I bet I did, I bet—"

"Not at all, Katydid. You unstuffed me a little, which is what should happen to daddies sometimes. Not as a steady diet, but sometimes." He placed his pebbles into her small hand, displeased with himself but proud of her. "I'll see you back at the ranch, when you're ready to go back. I think I should see how your mother's doing." He kissed her again. "I've been out of touch with you, with all my kids, with my whole doggone family. Wow-ee-wow, but are you going to see a big change! I'm going to slow down mighty soon, and all these hyar Webers are going to be as interwoven as a plate of spaghetti."

He walked slowly back toward the estate and thought, Yes, that's what I do. I slow down. As soon as "Moore" is under control and riding on his own, as soon as I clean up this loose end and that loose end, I quit, the champ retires from the ring undefeated. I have the same weight and all the hair I had when I was twenty, I screw with the same appetite and verve I had when I was twenty.

I'm not twenty, though. I'm forty-four, forty-five in October, and I have a family, and what am I killing myself for?

A sudden image of Robin, naked, popped into his mind, and he walked a little faster toward the house where his wife was waiting.

Liquor had never had much of an important place in the Vickery home since St. John Vickery had gone to his Anglo-Saxon reward, but there was liquor, and Weber furtively drank it as friends arrived with their respects and departed. There was an adequate if half-hearted dinner and then the family went, Weber high but not noticeably high, to the plushy funeral parlor in Greenwich. Kay went along, holding Weber's hand and squeezing it from the time they got out of Henrietta's limousine till after they stood and viewed Henrietta for long minutes. He regarded Karen, who could be so cold, so cool, so rejecting, smiling at her mother's corpse, the smile gracious and calm, saw her reach over and feel the lines and lifeless veins of Henrietta's hand, saw the smile, now wistful but still gracious and calm, remain. He loved Karen, loved her goodness. He was high, and not fully trusting of his impulses, yet he had a sudden, almost irresistible urge to hold her in his arms and tell her he loved her and promise he would be the good husband and father they both wanted him to be.

They rode to the estate, and he stole drinks and talked with his daughters as Karen dealt with yet more friends who arrived with their respects and departed, and then he and Karen were alone on the broad patio facing unending grounds, and Weber was no longer hiding the fact that he was drinking and was well on his way toward getting drunk. Karen knew it, because Karen always knew everything, but, surprisingly, she had a strong drink, too, and then a second.

They sat in a long hammock-sofa, and Weber's hand rested on her thigh as they talked a variety of irrelevant, disconnected subjects. He wanted her, here, now, on this well-made, unwieldly hammock-sofa, knew it was the wrong place as well as the wrong time, recalled her having remarked once upon a time during one of their conversations and during one of her psychoanalytical periods that many healthy couples had intercourse soon after the death of someone close, for intercourse was affirmation and, by its act, professed the will and determination to live. Weber squeezed her thigh, waiting for her to show some sign that she remembered her remark. There was no sign, and soon he removed his hand.

But being with Karen was good, talking with her was good, and he told her that he needed her, and Karen nodded and said she needed him, too, and presently he admitted that he had been an often-thoughtless husband, admitted that he had had women other than Karen during their marriage, vowed that whatever had made him pause with other women had been bottled and would never be let loose again.

"I know about the women, Warren," she said, with neither recrimination nor even special emotion.

He was alarmed. "You do?"

"You're an attractive man, out in the arena where there are attractive women. I haven't been the most receptive mate—I know that. The thought of you making love, or sex, to someone other than me wasn't ever . . . pleasing . . . but, well, why shouldn't you?"

"Never again, Karen. Never. We're going to be a family."

"Warren . . ."

"Yes?"

"The Hamilton girl. Robin Hamilton. Did you ever . . . was there ever anything with her?"

"Oh Lord, no, Karen, never. Believe that."

"I do, Warren. I'm glad you're being so honest and direct. It's healthy, it's promising. Yes, Warren, I'd like for us to be a family, finally. I'd like that very much."

They said good-bye to Henrietta the next morning, and Weber preceded his wife and daughters back to New York, where he phoned Earl Cuff. The Nash test was shot and processed, Cuff said, and looked good. Weber sent a messenger to fetch the film and directed Jeanne, who was reserved and a little formal, to have it set up in the projection room. Waiting, catching up on work that Greenwich had interrupted, he read the *Variety* and *Billboard* reviews of Robin's LP, *Robin on the Wing*. Both notices observed that she had some high and low range problems, and the commanding authority was yet to be established, but that she very definitely knew what she was about, the delivery especially on the soulful numbers could break your heart, and there was every sign that the album would, and should, be a success. Pleased, Weber called her vocal coach, Lou Patterley, who had seen the reviews and who agreed with them. "How's her work coming, generally?" Weber asked.

"Well, there are some good days. Some are lousy," said Lou.

"Lousy?"

"When she's not rested, she's lousy. Anyone would be. Fatigue's bound to affect the vocal cords."

"Fatigue? What does a kid that young know about fatigue?"

"Everything. I spend an hour a day with her—an hour's not enough time and it's too much time. You or someone's slaving her cute black bottom off, Warren. She seems tied up in knots, tense as hell. I was with her yesterday, from four till five, and her voice sounded like a cow being milked with cold fingers."

"That's nerves. She has a lot happening, I agree, but so has every performer who makes it big in a hurry."

"I agree with you agreeing. But there's something I don't understand. I understand the psychology of momentum. But why such nonstop momentum, why such a rush to turn her into Supergirl in five minutes flat? No kid should be as tense as she's been lately. I didn't mind her suddenly jumping down my throat last week when I very, very slightly criticized her for not paying attention. What I didn't like was that it was four o'clock in the afternoon and I smelled liquor on her breath."

Weber tensed. "You're nuts. She's strictly Coca-Cola."

"Okay, I'm nuts. You're the paymaster and you're paying me good, so okay, I'm nuts. But if she cracks, don't say nobody told you about the storm warnings. Robin was a damn nice person not too many weeks ago. She's a handful now, and I can smell the screwed-up prima donna bit right around the corner."

"You're doing an unnecessary amount of smelling. Suppose you coach more and smell less, maestro. I'll handle the mental health."

"You're the paymaster."

Keenly concerned, remembering that she had asked for a drink in her apartment and he had served her one, Weber phoned Robin, who was not in, and left word that she return the call. He summoned Jeanne, told her about Lou Patterley, and asked if she thought they were working Robin too hard. "It's been a rugged schedule, but I wouldn't call it inhuman," said Jeanne. "She's a funny kid—sometimes she acts like she's not the least bit sure of herself, like she's going to collapse. But she's tough, there's no question about that. Liquor? Baloney. I had a couple of highballs in Chicago, and she asked me how I could drink stuff that tasted like medicine."

"Um. All right, Jeannie. Thanks."

"Ah—while I'm here, Warren . . . would you be so kind as to settle something about Jesse Nash? My phone didn't stop, with people asking about the Bart Snyder column."

"Did you remind them what Bart Snyder's initials are?"

"Yes, yes, but that's not what bothers me. You've been brewing something you haven't told me about. There was a time when you always let me in on what you were up to."

He inspected a cigarette, trying to decide whether to light it. "I dimly recall a journey to your home, when I let you in on a great many matters."

"So you did. I'm not talking about your sex life. I'm talking about business. Are you and Jesse Nash baking a cake together?"

"Possibly. I've been coy with you because nothing's definite. When it is, if it is, you'll hear it first."

"Don't mess with that man, Warren. Don't go into something you don't know anything about. He's a dangerous cat. He spells trouble."

"Yes, teacher, I know." Weber supposed his reassuring smile was a patent fake. "Relax, duchess, relax. The wrong kind of trouble is the last kind I want. Now beat it."

When the messenger brought the film test, Weber buzzed Phil and they met in the projection room. Earl Cuff had been more than right: Nash might never cop an Emmy but he was an actor, a distinctly better than adequate actor, with intelligence and bearing and a controlled dynamism. And something else—a hint of savagery beneath the civilized façade. The light went up, and Phil nodded and said, "This should clinch it. Your guy's dandy. We may be walking on soft-boiled eggs, but your guy's dandy."

Weber nodded, too. "I'll get started right away."

"It's a relief in more ways than one—you taking the reins, I mean. I've been dodging everybody—Atwood, the newspapers, Jeanne. I'm surprised you kept Jeanne in the dark, by the way, but all right. I said I didn't know anything about anything, this was your department, and everybody said where there's smoke there's fire, and I said wait till you get back. I hope you're right about this."

"When have I ever been wrong, you plutocrat bookkeeper?"

In his office Weber phoned Jesse Nash's number, was told where Mr. Nash could be reached, reached him and gave him the good news. "Well, that's not bad news at all," Nash drawled.

"Do you have a lawyer?"

"Yeah. Name's Ben Packard."

"Does he know anything about television contracts?"

"I guess. What's there to know? A contract's a contract."

"I'll tell you what. I have a draft of a contract between you and GWS here on my desk. I have a contract lawyer whose office is one floor below mine. I want GWS to be satisfied, but obviously you and your attorney have to be satisfied, too. I want us to wrap this up immediately if possible, but I don't want you coming around later and complaining that you were represented by a lawyer who didn't know how to read a television contract properly. You do as you choose, but I'd like to make a suggestion. Get an attorney who's had experience in this field. Bring him here, or we'll meet wherever you and he say, as long as we don't all waste time planning on a summit conference in Geneva. Don't crowd your own attorney out—have him with you, but have him select the best attorney in this field he can find."

"I like the one I got."

Weber sighed. "Then that's up to you. Will you be in your apartment in, say, an hour from now?"

"I can be."

"All right, a messenger will have this contract in your hands in one hour. It's ten past three now. I suggest you contact your man the minute you hang up. I'd like to get going on this show fast, while the temperature's high. I'm ready to sign this afternoon, this evening, the first thing in the morning. I'll be here for several hours, at least. I'd appreciate it if you'd get back to me as soon as you can."

Nash agreed.

"Okay. I'll be hearing from you," Weber said, and replaced the receiver. He reread the Nash contract provisions that he had recommended and that Phil had altered and modified here and there, and that their lawyer Max Wright had then drawn up. Sure that Jeanne was out of eye- and earshot, he placed the contract in a manila envelope, sealed it, addressed it, and buzzed the bullpen for a messenger to deliver it to Nash uptown. He then phoned his own home to hear, as he had expected to hear, that Karen and the girls had not yet returned. Chasing the day's second Dexie down with a Scotch from his office bar, he wondered what Karen would say if he were to suggest that they board the *Stalwart* again, the two of them in one stateroom and the girls in another. Maybe the affirmation of marriage and family that should have been solidified and strengthened on the Christmas cruise could have another chance at the brass ring, and this time with a real effort on his part. He examined the new raft of Robin offers, damned impressive ones, and studied the glossies Ronnie Haley's photographers had taken of her, okaying some and rejecting others, intrigued anew by the freshness, the loveliness of her, wishing there were some way, some non-Noel Coward way, to take her and Karen and the girls on a cruise together.

Nash called at five on the dot. He had read the contract, had read high points from it to his lawyer on the telephone, and both men were ready and willing to talk, at GWS's convenience. "Hold on," said Weber, and asked Phil on the intercom to come to the apartment that night, and ordered Max Wright on the intercom to come to the apartment that night. Phil and Wright said yes. "Let's meet at my apartment this evening around nine," he told Nash, and gave the address. "That should be more comfortable than some ugly office. Any office looks ugly after sundown."

Robin called, shortly before six, sounding subdued but not especially tired. She had heard about his mother-in-law and was sorry. Beyond that, she was simply returning his call.

"Have you had a chance to read *Play with Fire* yet?" he asked.

"Yes, finally. Scripts aren't easy to read—for me, at least—and I'm not in it very much, but it looks like it'll be a good movie."

"Your part's being fattened up. By the time you get to the Coast, it'll be a different picture and a better one. I didn't realize you had any real acting talent till Lois Farrentino told me—I said all this to you the night I brought you the script, didn't I?—and now that we know it, we're making changes. All right?"

"All right, whatever you say. You know best."

"How are you, Robin? Working too hard?"

"Well, hard, yes, but I'm learning things, so that makes up for it."

"Lou Patterley's been slapping my wrists. He thinks we're killing you."

A pause. "He said that?"

"Are we killing you? Is anyone killing you?"

"Of course not. If I was working too hard, or if I thought I wouldn't be able to keep up the pace, I'd say so, wouldn't I?"

"Have you had any free time for yourself?"

"A little. I even go out on dates."

Slightly stunned, Weber asked, "Dates? Who's the lucky gent?"

"Gents, you mean."

"Is that what I mean? How long do they stay when they take you home?"

Another pause, a longer one. "I don't think that's your business, do you?"

"Isn't it? Why isn't it?"

"I don't think it's been since Chicago—certainly not since you were here the last time."

"That night was a mistake. We were both tired and out of sorts. But I'm not going to believe you and I are done, Robin. We mean too much to each other." He waited. "Do you hear?"

"I hear. I don't want to talk about it, Warren. I just don't."

"Robin—"

"I have to go now. Lois Farrentino's coming for a lesson. I'll . . . see you."

She hung up. Not harshly, but she hung up.

Phil came in and they talked about tonight's meeting. Phil did most of the talking. Weber saw ninety-dollar-a-week black bucks in bed with Robin, Robin who loved Weber, saw their world ending with a whimper and a bang, not even the right bang, and warned himself that he must not allow it to end. Not with so much unsaid, unshared, unloved. Not yet, not yet.

Karen and Nancy were in the penthouse living room when Weber got there—Kay was in her room with a friend, playing records—and he kissed them and apologized for spoiling the evening by inviting some people to talk business. He mentioned that one of the people coming was Jesse Nash, which stopped Nancy in her fifteen-year-old tracks. "Jesse Nash?" Nancy exclaimed. "The civil rights man?"

"The same."

Nancy didn't quite gasp. "Jesse Nash, *here?*"

Amused, he remarked, "Don't bite your toenails. Mr. Nash won't set fire to the drapes. He's arriving with an attorney named Packard. Say now—Nash and Packard. Maybe we ought to've invited General Motors along, in the interests of equal time."

Nancy was visibly upset. "Daddy, you're having a *colored* man here at the house?"

Karen was halfway out of the living room, and kept going. Maybe she hadn't heard Nancy. Maybe she had, and had no urge to get involved.

Weber was outraged. "You'd better come here, young lady," he instructed his daughter, using a sharp tone he had rarely used on either daughter. "Would you repeat that shabby question?"

"Oh, Daddy, you know what I mean—"

"No, I hope I don't. You've had a long, meaningful, constructive life, dedicated to the good of mankind, so you must be an expert in these areas. Would you, in your infinite wisdom, apprise me of what this *"colored* man" jazz is about?"

She seemed shocked and near tears at being spoken to sharply, but Weber read it as an exercise in adolescent dramatics. "You know me better, you know I'm not prejudiced," she said. "It's just, well, we've never had anybody colored here before."

"That's the most ridic—" Weber began, and abruptly realized, with shock of his own, that his daughter was right. Realized that there had never been a conspiracy to invite only whites here, but she was right. Realized that if she did see black as something separate from white, she couldn't be faulted simply as a rich, spoiled brat. When had she, or Kay, ever come across a Negro, except for maids who had come and gone over the years of her young life? Karen had once mentioned that there were two Negro kids in Nancy's private school, both sons of a well-to-do Negro actor—and they, Weber imagined, were the Negroes Nancy knew. He had taken for granted that the children knew where their parents stood on the acceptance and rejection of human beings as human beings, their indifference to the differences of religion or lack of religion, the casts of eyes, the color of skins.

And Nancy was right. This home was full of color-blindness, and no Negro guest had ever entered it.

"I just don't want any more race talk out of you," Weber said, "is that understood?"

She looked baffled, as he knew she should be, and she walked out of the room, head high in a pose of hurt, and he went to find Karen and ask her, "Why haven't there ever been any black faces around here? Are we the worst kind of segregationists—the kind that doesn't know it?"

"We never thought about inviting any."

"That's the point—why haven't we? This is precisely what bugs Negroes the most, I'm sure, and it should, it damn well should. They can grapple with being abused and having their rights shot out from under them. What they must find it holy hell on wheels to deal with is being invisible to us lovely rump-in-the-air whites . . ."

"Should we invite anyone because he's black, or white, or yellow?" Karen said blandly. "It seems to me that patronizing people is as destructive as ignoring them. Shouldn't relationships be natural? You certainly have no reason to be guilty about anything in that direction, Warren. Your offices are integrated. Your shows, even the frothy ones we're not proud of, stopped bowing to the color line long before it was chic."

"That was Charlie's doing."

"Yes, but you could have easily dragged your feet or given in to the networks after Charlie died. You didn't. Are you forgetting your knock-down fights, the shows you slaved on and then shelved and wouldn't let anyone buy because they wouldn't let you have a courtroom judge who was a Negro or a white family's friend who was Negro? I used to think you were mistaken when you refused at those eleventh hours to sell a show after all your work, I thought you were being petulant, too uncompromising, when a character didn't have to be colored. But I was wrong, and I'm a bit ashamed. You had principles, and you believed in them, and you stuck by them, and you proved what you set out to prove."

" 'Had,' 'believed,' 'proved'? How did I get into the past tense?"

Karen smiled, but suddenly she wasn't supportive any longer. "I'm not sure I like the 'Moore' project."

"Oh? Now it comes out, does it? I'm deep in the big muddy with it, and you're not sure you like it."

"Not that I don't like it. I'm not sure I like your motives in doing it."

"Here we go," he sighed. "Okay, Doc, what are my motives?"

"I don't know what they are. What's wrong is that I don't think you know what they are, either. You seem to need to prove something, something about yourself, something separate from seeing a series through that might be socially significant. I could be wrong, Warren, but I have an uncomfortable feeling that you're doing this show not because you believe in what it's saying so much as because you're determined to go on showing authority figures that no one can boss Warren Weber around."

Weber was furious, and did not show it because this was the day that Karen had sent her mother away to be incinerated. "Let's see if dinner's ready," he said.

"Have I made you angry? I don't mean—"

"No, no," he answered quickly, eager to have the jiffy home analyst's crap the hell over with. "I'm hungry. Let's call the girls and eat."

Phil and Max Wright arrived at a few minutes before nine, and at nine twenty-five Jesse Nash arrived with a light-skinned, red-freckled, belligerent-looking Negro who was Ben Packard. Ernest, Weber's valet, served drinks, but Nash and Packard had none; they sat rigid and unsmiling as the talk got under way, and Weber imagined he could hear what Packard had probably lectured Nash on their trip here: "You look out for those white men. Don't fuzzy your brain with drink, don't smile, don't be too friendly with your handshakes, don't let them get the idea for a second that they can put anything over on us because we're black."

The contract was perfectly clear and forthright, free of the mildest loophole or whisper of skulduggery, and Weber knew that Packard knew it, watched him listen to the patient and immaculately concise explanations of Phil the businessman and Max the lawyer, and knew that Packard was going to play it tough for a while because toughness was expected of him. He conceded that the residuals guarantees were fair, and then crisply stated that his client wished twenty percent more money than the contract offered. Phil and Max glanced at Weber though the black men did not, and Weber held up ten fingers. A ten percent across-the-board increase was finally agreed upon, and it appeared that the meeting had reached the dotted-line stage.

But then Nash, who had sat grimly silent throughout the discussions, like a proud chieftain whose dignity was too great to descend to the business of haggling over trivia, spoke up. "Wait," he said. "We don't sign till you put it in the contract that I have the right to approve all scripts."

Weber immediately uncrossed his legs and sat up. "Here's where I come into the picture, gentlemen. Script approval is entirely out of the question."

"Why's that? So you can go antiblack any time it suits your fancy?"

"No, sir, and that's a repulsive statement to make," Weber snapped. "Repulsive and idiotic, because 'Moore' has no purpose at all if an atom of it is used to hurt Negroes. Actors don't get script approval on my shows for the same reason I'm not an actor on my shows—I couldn't be counted on to do a credible job of it. Even if we had thirteen or twenty-six scripts written before we start shooting, which we don't, all kinds of changes are made—technical, dialogue—by the time a segment's in the can. There simply isn't time, once a series is begun, for professionals to take advice from nonprofessionals. No. There is where the foot's put down."

Nash began to rise. "Then we're done discussin'."

His lawyer shot Nash a "Jesus, let's not queer this deal" glance, and Weber said, "Oh, sit down! Too much is involved here for you to get theatrical. Let's talk like reasonable adults. We've ironed out the money end of it, we can work this out, too."

"No, *you* ironed out the money end," asserted Nash, still the proud chieftain. "Ben Packard tried for twenty percent more money because that's his job. You haggled him down to ten. I never said a thing, because money doesn't matter. What I want's what I wanted back at that Shor's restaurant. I'm lookin' to dot every 'i' and cross every 't'. I know a set can be a busy place. I just want to be sure there's *nothin'* in any of those shows that could damage my people. You say, 'talk like reasonable adults.' Well, I don't see anything unreasonable in what I want. I got to have somethin' on paper that says if somethin' in any script is 'way off base about black folks, I get to set you white folks straight. So it's that, or nothin'."

Weber nibbled his lower lip, saw that Nash was deadly serious, and knew he would have to think fast.

"All right," he said. "I'll go along with you."

Everyone looked at him.

"But with this stipulation. You're a little worried about my judgment, which is your right, but there may come a time when I might question your judgment, which is my right. I'll want a referee, a Negro referee. Not an Orville Sanford, but definitely not an Uncle Tom. A moderate, you should excuse the expression. He'll be the best man I can find—I'll guarantee that." He studied his watch, so Nash would see that the discussion had a cutoff point. "On those terms, I'm sure Mr. Wright and Mr. Simms and I are ready to sign, as soon as the clause is added."

Phil and Max Wright and Packard were wise enough to keep still. Nash looked troubled, suspicious, and then he nodded.

The clause was phrased, and Max Wright typed it into the copies of the contract. Weber buzzed Ernest for a fresh round of drinks and smiled at a still-unsmiling Nash. "You'll have a victory drink now, won't you?" he asked.

"No, thanks," Nash replied. "Mr. Packard and I aren't much for wettin' the whistle."

"I'll find Mrs. Weber. I know she'd like to meet you."

Nash wasn't having any. " 'Fraid I'll have to be leavin', soon's we sign. I have this appointment uptown."

Oy, am I going to have my hands full with this guy, Weber sighed to himself, but he shrugged. The signing was done, and there were formal handshakes, and then Nash and Packard were gone.

"This is certainly late in the season for a snowstorm," said Phil.

"That was some pair," said Max, shaking his head. "You would've thought we were going to take out their appendix without an anesthetic."

"What's the difference?" Weber said, hiding his hurt and annoyance. "Everybody got what everybody wanted."

Max and Phil left after one drink and Weber, trying to shake off fresh misgivings about Proud Chieftain Nash, went to the bedroom, where Karen was still awake, to tell her that Nash wasn't Mr. Cordiality but the deal was made and it was a good one. "Nancy wanted to see him," Karen said. "I suppose it's just as well she didn't, if he's so disagreeable. Are you coming to bed, Warren? I think I'm ready to go to sleep. These past days and nights have caught up with me."

"In just a minute. I need to make a couple of notes." He went to his study and drank for ten minutes, to soften the jitters of the last Dexie, which had not quite worn off, and warned the invisible Jesse Nash not to make a fool of him. Karen was not yet asleep when he slid into bed beside her. He held her, without the remotest interest in rousing her or himself.

She gazed at the picture window and asked, "How many women were there, Warren?"

"What?"

"The women you've had . . . relations . . . with since we've been married. Were there lots?"

He remembered having been a drunk blabbermouth on Henrietta's patio and wondered now if it was possible to kick himself while lying down. "No," he lied.

"Are there any now? Last week, last month, I mean?"

"No. You," he lied.

"Don't tell me who any of them were. But were any of them friends of mine?"

"No," he lied. There had been three friends of hers—four if you counted Jane Wilcox, who wasn't her friend so much as Jane's husband, Reed, was Weber's friend. In twenty years there had been three of Karen's friends, hardly a stunning track record. There had been Marge Richmond, she of the foreign language that was Freudese, Marge the professional analysand who held wordily forth on Copulation Anxiety and Coital Relationships and Psychosexual Complexities when she was with Weber and Karen and who croaked, "Gimme," when she and Weber were alone. There had been Mary Ann Frye, the upbeat, never-say-die joy girl whose suicide note had read *Esprit de corps/Was quite a chore.* There had been Iris Spector, the young matron with the jokeable name and the lavish shape, the magazine-article writer whose specialty was marriage and the home and sanctity of both.

"May I ask just one more question?" asked Karen.

"If you have to. This isn't the most enjoyable moment of my life."

"Was there—was there ever Robin Hamilton?"

"I said no when you asked me that in Greenwich. Why's Robin Hamilton a stuck needle with you?"

"I'm not sure. I've seen you look at her, and I've seen her look at you, when you were at one corner of the room and she was at another, and I saw something transmitted. It seemed too personal, too close, too knowing, somehow. I think I'd be deeply hurt if there were anything between you."

"Not a chance," he said, and switched off the light. "Sleep, dear. You've had a long day."

At nine the next morning he phoned Claude Rhodes, perhaps the only man in the broadcasting business who was at the executive desk by a quarter past eight. "Very well, Warren," Rhodes said. "I'll be here."

At 9:41 Weber was in the man's office to announce that the rumors were indeed true, that Jesse Nash would be "Moore" and here was the contract, that Mr. Rhodes more than any man in the industry had the expertise and prescience to recognize that this series couldn't help but raise eyebrows, cause talk, sell merchandise, and give vital meaning to the medium.

"And also to make Vanguard and me legally bound to your wishes," C. Harvey Rhodes said mildly. "I'm sorry I signed an evidently legal agreement with you. Warren, I'm sorry, because I trusted you and you rather betrayed my trust. I'm not certain of what I would have said if you'd told me, your last time here, that you had this young man Nash set for the title role. I do know that you could have been a trifle less underhanded with me. You pulled a fast one, as they say, and I'm too old to be surprised by many things, but I wish you could have been just a bit more candid."

"I didn't have Nash then. His name didn't even enter my mind till after you and I talked."

Rhodes yammered and protested in his soft, courtly way, suggested that there were several devices Vanguard's attorneys could employ to fight the agreement if the project got severely out of hand, and cautioned Weber not to thumb his nose at the public, or at Vanguard. "My thumb isn't on my nose, Mr. Rhodes," said Weber. "It's on the public's pulse."

At GWS he directed Ronnie Haley to start the publicity barrage at once, then spent the afternoon unmooring "Moore," placing and receiving no fewer than twenty-six telephone calls on the project alone. He could not quite meet Jeanne's eyes, but he needed her for dictation, and he nipped her protests in the bud early by ordering, "Let's get some work done around here. You can spank me later, on your own time."

Fifteen

VERNE HIGHTOWER telephoned Robin, four days after he had promised to phone. "Remember me?" he asked.

Hang up on him, she told herself.

"I sure do remember you," she said, not bothering to camouflage her delight. "But I thought maybe you got back on that Brooklyn subway again and got lost forever."

"Actually, I was supposed to've been back home a few days ago, but I went out to Boston and some other stories cropped up and, with one thing and another, I'm still an easterner—at least till the middle of next week. I was wondering if you might be free later this evening for that hamburger you promised me."

"And you didn't show up for."

"I'll explain why when I see you. If I can see you."

Don't be so easy to get, she told herself. Make him squirm a little, make him think there are other pebbles on the beach.

"I'll see that I'm free," she said. "I'm leaving for the Coast, too, in fact, this Sunday, and there's a million things to do, but I'll shift them around, somehow. Ah—what time can you be here?"

"It would have to be some time after eight, depending on the cab situation. I'm on a television show from seven-thirty till eight. The program's called 'Names in the News' if you're near a set and you don't have anything better to do."

"You on television? How exciting! Doing what? You're not nervous, are you? You shouldn't be."

"No, I've been on these panel shows before, and I guess I'm

never nervous when I get to ask the questions. If I ever have to sit there and answer them, I'm sure you'll hear my knees knocking together. Anyway, there'll be two or three other reporters on the program. We're grilling Orville Sanford."

"Gee, is that awful man still around?" asked Robin, thinking at once of Jesse.

"Very much so, I'm afraid. We're firm, then, for tonight?"

Robin gave him her address and he told her what channel he would be on. They said good-bye and she begged him, after he hung up, not to stand her up a second time.

She phoned the market nearest The Havilland and ordered chopped steak and vegetables and desserts. She phoned the liquor shop nearest The Havilland and ordered champagne and whiskey. Then she phoned Gordon Aldrich, the white and sort of handsome trade paper columnist, to say she couldn't meet him tonight in his office, which happened to be in his apartment on Central Park West, because she had this miserable virus, but could she see him the second she returned from California? Ronnie Haley would be mad, because Gordon Aldrich was an influential writer not to be turned down. Gordon Aldrich was mad, although he didn't say so, and she was sure she knew why: there had to be a bed in his office-apartment, and he probably had not planned to sleep in it alone tonight.

She hurried to tidy the apartment and to bathe, although Verne wouldn't arrive for several hours. I suppose I should have said okay to that Gordon Aldrich in his bedroom tonight, she thought, if only to keep Ronnie contented, Ronnie who wants my name in all the papers. Idiotic reason to get in bed with a man. Well, the heck with him. The heck with them all. Verne Hightower called, because he's been thinking about me and he likes me. Maybe he wants sex and that's all. All right, we'll start from there. I lied to Warren, the last time we talked. I said I had dates when I didn't have any. I lied to Warren to hurt Warren because Warren hurt me, but I won't have to lie any more. I'll be the most scintillating woman Verne has ever met, and I'll make him love me, and then

I can tell Warren, and everyone who uses me, I have a man named Verne and he loves me, he cares what happens to me.

Let it happen. Let something go right for me. Let Verne care.

At seven-thirty the apartment gleamed, the hamburgers were ready to be put on the minute he arrived, and she had changed her clothes three times. She glued herself to the television set, wanting a steadying drink but denying herself, for it was vital that she be clear as a bell for him.

Orville Sanford looked as he had looked in the Los Angeles restaurant: urbane and scary, scary even when he smiled—especially when he smiled. There was a white reporter, an old man from some newspaper in Virginia, who was so openly hostile, with sarcastic questions that weren't really questions but bumbling speeches attacking civil rights, and so emotional and badly organized in his anger that the cool and smiling Sanford easily and quickly made mincemeat of him. There was a colored lady reporter who was pure velvet glove, whose allotted minutes of questions about FREE and its aims were so timid and respectful that the cool and smiling Sanford came through as a decent and humane leader.

And then, there on the large screen, was Verne Hightower, all dignity and presence, and he asked, "Are you prepared to confirm or deny, sir, the rather persistent rumor that the real financing that keeps FREE afloat comes from Soul of America, which no one can deny is loaded with money?"

Sanford (still cool, still smiling): "I've heard the rumor. I emphatically deny it, of course. From the very little I know about Soul of America, it's a society made up of white fat cats devoted to preserving and protecting the white establishment. FREE's sole reason for being is to strengthen the hand of all black citizens, most of whom are shackled from cradle to grave by the kind of Soul of America mentality that controls this country. How could we possibly be bedfellows?"

Verne: "To create greater and greater divisions between blacks and whites in the United States. Isn't that FREE's goal?"

Sanford (no longer smiling): "I'm familiar with your newspaper

out in San Francisco, Mr. Hightower, and I know its reputation
for Tomming, so nothing you or it says shocks or surprises me.
Your rag has continually and purposely misrepresented FREE.
Why some black people are so eager to destroy their brothers is
the mystery of the age—but I want this audience to know here and
now that we have nothing but contempt for you and your crowd."

Verne: "My paper and I have no problem defending our credentials, Mr. Sanford, but that's quite beside the point as far as this discussion is concerned. Instead of simply attacking all your critics as
either racists or Toms, mightn't you help clear the air by forth-
rightly answering the most serious charges that keep arising and
aren't really dealt with? I've followed FREE very carefully, sir.
Every rally FREE holds in ghetto neighborhoods has some official
spokesman railing against the Jews, and here"—Verne raised half a
dozen or so papers—"are leaflets distributed regularly in Harlem
and Watts and all black communities, with FREE's imprint, chock
full of vicious anti-Semitism, yet you deny that FREE is anti-
Semitic. At organized street-corner gatherings I've personally attended, FREE's official spokesmen call for violence against everything and anything that isn't black, yet you consistently deny that
FREE supports violence. Now what *is* FREE all about, sir, if it
isn't to reach the most disadvantaged Negroes in America and in-
doctrinate them with a lust for violence?"

Sanford (cool, smiling again, addressing himself to the old white
man from the Virginia newspaper): "I would like to offer you my
apologies, Mr. Stark. Earlier in this program, I thought of you as
an enemy of my people. I'm sure you are. But compared to the
young man who's just finished his catalog of criminal distortions,
and whom I have no intention of dignifying with my attention for
the remainder of the program—compared to him, Mr. Stark, you
are a gentleman of integrity and honor."

The rest of the program tapered off into non sequiturs, and
Robin turned off the moderator's summation in confusion. Verne
Hightower arrived at The Havilland with a bottle of wine at nine
o'clock, by which time Robin had made her fifth change of clothes

—pink cashmere cardigan, pink tweed skirt, moccasins, and pink hair ribbon—and had drunk two glasses of whiskey to fortify her and give her a semblance of equanimity to greet him. She exclaimed that he had been wonderful on the show, and fussed over him, and listened to him through the dinner he complimented. Finally he explained why he had not kept his promise to call.

"I spent that night asking myself where this could lead," he said, "and I decided the fairest thing would be to just steer clear."

"Why?"

"Self-defense, maybe. You were right about what you said before you left Sardi's—you *did* talk your head off. Frankly, most of that show-biz gibberish bored me stiff. And frankly, the only reason I had that day for wanting to see you again was to see if I could sleep with you. There. I'm honest. A blunt, insulting creep maybe, but honest."

Robin regarded him gravely. "There are worse reasons to want to see someone again . . ."

"Not in your case. I didn't learn much about you that day, and I may be all wet, but I got the feeling that the last thing you need from a man is a hello-good-bye hop in the hay. You need a man to take you seriously. I didn't call the next day because the man who takes you seriously should be a man who'll be around, and I'm never in one place for long."

"Then why did you call me today?"

"I kept thinking about you. Gibberish and all, I kept thinking about you. We make an unlikely pair, or we would. You have everything in your career working for you, and if I never make more than eight or nine grand a year I'll be happy as a clam. If you're halfway normal, you go in for parties and dances, and my idea of a swinging evening is collecting clothes for the Southern Box Project. But I'm not a bad guy, Robin Hamilton, and it might be fun to get to know each other."

The evening was ecstasy for Robin, and her watch read midnight only seconds after it read half-past ten. Verne kissed her, and she came apart, and then she did something astonishing and incomprehensible to her. As gracefully as possible, she moved away from him and said, "Let's not—do anything tonight, okay?"

"No?"

"I'm sort of crazy. When you leave here, I bet I'll cut my throat, I want you so much. And I sound like one of those dizzy girls in the confession magazines, but I don't want it to be just sex for you. I want it to be more than that, and if you come back again that means maybe it will be. Do I sound crazy?"

He laughed. "As a loon. And I must be even crazier, because I won't even put up a fight. Any more coffee left, loony?"

Within a week after the publicity began, for Weber a week with little sleep and less food, "Moore" was physically almost ready to roll, the Harlem locations scouted and secured, the staff and cast and crew poised for action. Within a week, too, preparations for the filming of *Play with Fire* were ironed out and completed. The idea of a cocktail party in the penthouse, celebrating Nash's new fortunes and Robin's continuing, growing fortunes, was Weber's, and Karen agreed to it if only, she acknowledged, to wrest him away from the driving work compulsiveness for a few hours. He told Karen to set up the get-together for Friday evening —Robin would leave for the Coast on Sunday, to begin work on Monday—and, after consideration, got in touch with Nash, who stated he just might drop in if nothing important came up. Weber called Robin, without mentioning Nash, and she said she would be glad to come and added that she'd bring Verne Hightower, if he was available.

"Verne Whattower?"

"He writes for a Negro newspaper. He interviewed me, and we became friends. Very good friends."

"By all means," Weber said with deliberate jauntiness, sourly picturing the ninety-dollar-a-week black buck bristling through the door in a fez and goatee.

The Friday cocktail party's fourteen guests were invited to

arrive at six. Weber was home by half past five because he was perspiring on this cool day and his chest felt tight, and because he wanted to oversee the party preparations, and because he wanted Karen. Ernest built him the large martini he requested, and he drank it down, and told one servant to straighten the Rubens and told another servant there weren't nearly enough ash trays or macadamia nuts, and swiftly polished off another martini, and went to the master bedroom, where Karen was in a slip and two cocktail dresses were on the bed. She was obviously deliberating as she kneaded cologne into her skin, and he kissed her eyes and held her warm, bare arm and said,"Hi."

"Eenie meenie," she said. "Which one of these should I wear?"

"Neither. Greet your company like this, and you'll be the party hit of the season. The loveliest. The most desirable, the most delectable—"

"Warren, the guests will be here in—"

"—the most scrumptious, the sexiest, the hotsy-totsiest, the dollbabiest," he said, his voice growing huskier, and his hands were on her thighs and his mouth was close to her ear. "The wildest, the gentlest, the dearest, the greatest, the—"

Her face was red, and she was smiling, but she casually slipped away from him. "No, you don't, Mr. Weber. We have a dress to choose."

"Karen—"

"No, Warren. Stop it. Your guests will be here any minute now."

"Let's . . . now, let me have it now. Later, when they leave, we'll take all the time in the world."

"No."

"Christ, Karen—"

The smile vanished. "This is silly, Warren. We've been all over this a million times. A sexual relationship must have its time and place, or the whole structure of it is meaningless. You may not have 'it' now. What's 'it'? My vagina? If all you married was a vagina, then—"

Weber went, pretending to stroll, back to the living room, where he nodded to Ernest, who served him a martini as grandly ruthless as the first ones had been. He sipped it and drank it, drank it and sipped it, and wandered about the front part of the penthouse, and stoutly embraced Rebecca and Ollie Doyle, the tubby, clean-and-rumpled wife and husband team who were the chief writers of "Meet Ginger" and who believed in coming half gassed to any and all cocktail parties. "The ball and chain here asks me what she should wear to this shindig," Ollie Doyle rasped, "and I says, 'Anything'll that'll look good on the floor,' and she shows up in this Salvation Army special that—"

"My fat lord and master, he should go grab himself a Gehenna rinse," rasped Rebecca Doyle, "he all of a sudden has to know while we're getting ready to come here how you pluralize 'hard on' and—"

"Not all of a sudden," Ollie Doyle rasped. "The problem was eating into me for weeks, day after day, minute after minute, and—"

"The saloon, you barrel of laughs," said Weber, "is over yonder thataway."

" 'Nuff said," rasped Ollie.

"*Soixante-neuf* said," rasped Rebecca.

The cocktail party for fourteen grew to twenty, and thirty, and then infinity, seemingly minutes after a ravishing Robin and her young man Whatzisname arrived. Hightower, it was, Verne Hightower, and there was no fez nor stringy goatee, and he was a good-looking, inexpensively but neatly dressed slim, dark man in his twenties—*thirties? no, late twenties*—and the handshake was firm, the clear eyes were direct, and Weber was an affable host and wanted to smack him for being young and attractive. Karen appeared, wearing the cocktail dress Weber would not have picked yet looking elegant, nonetheless, and Robin shyly complimented the Webers on their lovely home, and gradually guided her escort toward the bar, where the refreshments were.

"Why is she so cold, after all you've done for her?" Karen asked.

"Why are you so cold, after—" Weber began, and stopped.

"What?"

"Here come Ruth and Phil. Let's go say hello."

"What did you start to say, Warren?"

"Nothing. Let's see Ruth and Phil."

"Cold, you said."

"No, Karen, warm as toast. Hot as fire. Cauldrons of adoring heat," Weber said, and left his wife to go to the Simms, who were as rich as he, or nearly as rich, and who would have been more relaxed over a plate of stuffed cabbage at Hebrew National. He kissed Ruth and said, "Helen, thy beauty to me is like those Nicean barks of yore."

"What else could it be?" Ruth said, laughing, and lightly punched his arm. Weber wandered some more, avoiding though never ignoring Robin, who was getting a drink at the bar and then was wandering, too, but with the young man beside her. With Weber, Lois Farrentino watched her, watched the assurance and charm of her as she chatted easily with guests who ate her from a spoon, as she introduced the young man to each of those guests with the grace of a princess, and Weber asked Lois if she had any idea what a bowl of chocolate Jello this Robin Hamilton had been just scant months before.

"Maybe," Lois said. "Maybe you read her wrong. That gal's put together with piano wire. She's talented as all get-out, partly, mainly, because she's tough as nails. I think you read her wrong, Warren. I think she was born tough. And that toughness is what's going to make her the biggest black star in show business."

"You sound like Ronnie Haley talking to Earl Wilson."

"No, I mean it."

He watched her for many minutes and wished she were not drinking with such an interest in drinking, wished her Hightower would order her to switch to soda pop, the drink she had drunk on the *Stalwart*. The party noises were stifling the hi-fi music, and Karen was a queenly and pleasant hostess who greeted and spoke with guests and came by to make peace with Weber, and he apologized for having been an abject slob, and Karen kissed his cheek and lovingly murmured, "Don't get too drunk," and moved to circulate among more guests.

He watched Robin sneaking drinks as he talked with guests, and he drank with conscious compulsiveness and felt himself getting drunk, and her Hightower was talking with Ollie Doyle and whoever else would talk with him because Robin was attaching herself to Dwight Rowland the producer, white-lecher Dwight, and Weber supposed he had spawned a bitch, a black bitch, and could see the shining glow of her bare shoulders from here, yards away, and needed to kiss them.

Then the living room was a firetrap of people and he wished he could stop drinking with such a sense of mission. Over there was Jesse Nash, possibly just arrived (*where did all these other people come from? when did they start coming? when does the overflow leave?*), tall and dead-pan in a not-quite fashionable turtleneck, looking around, looking superior, which was okay, but looking hostile at the same time, which was not okay, looking like an invited guest who shows up to announce that he's just dropped in for a minute because these people are too unimportant for him to waste his time on. Very near to Nash was a slight, light brown, fierce-looking young woman, her frizzy hair short and her flowered toga long, a young woman who didn't look at all African except for the costume but who seemed determined to play African, up-yours African. Weber started to go to them, to welcome them, but they headed for the buffet table, Nash not seeing him, Nash nodding indifferently at friendly people along the way, introducing his young lady to no one.

Robin was at that table, with Rowland and Hightower. Nash didn't appear to notice that she was there until his trick-or-treat date had begun to inspect the food. But he saw her, and she looked up and saw him and her body went rigid as though electric charges were coursing through it. Weber started that way, but the room was noisy, and there were distractions and momentary barriers who wanted to chat with him. When he finally neared the buffet table, close enough to catch some of the words yet far enough away to be relatively unobserved, Nash was speaking to Robin.

"—still the white nigger, gettin' whiter 'n' whiter's the days 'n' the years go by," Nash was taunting, so calmly, so evenly that it seemed as if he were praising rather than attacking. Robin was alarmed and speechless and obviously incapable of turning from him. Dwight Rowland silently excused himself, and winked and shook his head at Weber as he departed. Young Hightower was impassive and still, which rather puzzled Weber. Wasn't he supposed to be her current white knight—whoops—manly protector?

"Say, I got regards for you from Coley Dennis—he says to tell you he's been watchin' your progress and just as soon's you can unload the last o' the dinges, he'll—" Nash was talking like a snotty drunk, but he wasn't drunk, thought Weber, who knew *he* was drunk, too much so to break in. There were eight or ten eavesdroppers at the table, waiting for things to get good and messy, and Weber tried to summon the authority to command, *This is my home and if you're spoiling for a scrap, do it somewhere else.* Robin was taking it all—why, Weber could not imagine—and her manly protector was background furniture.

As Nash kept it up, as the eight or ten eavesdroppers grew in number and gathered, Weber cleared his throat and prepared to interrupt, for the needling was cruel and this was a celebration party, Warren Weber's celebration party in his own home, and this was not an evening for anyone to be cruel to anyone. But then Robin's black escort come to life, advanced a step, and there was something in that single step, something in the way he cocked his head and stood taller than Nash who was almost a head taller than he, that stopped the needling. "Suppose you cool it now," he said softly.

Nash stiffened and glared at Hightower for tense seconds. Then he turned back to Robin, who looked embarrassed and terrified. "This black cat with you, white lady?" he asked, feigning surprise. "When'd you go back to slummin' with us colored fo—"

"I said cool it, man!" Hightower's voice was a fleck louder. "What're you here to prove—that you can push little girls around? That you're blacker than anyone? All you're proving is you've got worse manners than anyone here."

"Oh-oh, 'manners.' Let's all put on the manners so's Massa Honk won't call us savages behind our back, right?" Nash drawled. "Well, nobody's talkin' to you, slick man. I'm talkin' to the ex-colored queen here about black folks forgettin' the one thing that can keep their head above water in White City, and that's pride in bein' black. Might be you could learn a pointer, too, whoever you are, seein's how—"

The young man named Hightower took Robin's arm. "Let's find some better company," he said.

Nash shoved him, and Weber could hear some eavesdroppers gasp. "*You* cool it, slick man!" Nash demanded. "Who do you think you are with that honk jazz about me provin' I'm blacker than anybody? Maybe I *am*, slick man, and what's wrong with that? Huh? It's a crime to be black—that's what Honky's always laid on us. Where does a spade come off, echoin' Honky? You an' your *society* here," he sneered, pointing to the petrified Robin.

"Okay, that does it, the war's over," Weber ordered, the eddies of whiskey in his brain causing the order to come out as mush. He moved unsteadily between the two men, not at all sober but sane enough to try to prevent a brawl that would surely make the morning *News*.

Hightower stepped in front of the weaving Weber to confront Nash. "I'm not a slick man, and I'm not a very tough one, either," he said. "But I'm a man, Nash, and I'll still be a man if you shove me again and I have to shove you back and one of us leaves here without his teeth. My name is Hightower, Nash, for your information, and my skin happens to be black—blacker than yours, incidentally, if one-upmanship grabs you—and White City's handed me some lumps, too, but White City's never been white enough to force me to spend this one life I have hating and whining. Are you reading me, Nash? Or are you too busy proving your black manhood by insulting women and making yourself obnoxious?"

The large room was now entirely filled with eavesdroppers. Even the drunks stopped drinking and stared.

Jesse Nash obviously recognized that he was in the center of the spotlight. He glared at the ring of white faces, and then at Hightower, who hadn't moved an inch. Then he turned to his trick-or-treat young lady, and Weber heard him say, "I've had this ofay party. Let's split."

Their spines were ramrods as they walked out of the living room, up the steps to the foyer, and faced the front door as they waited for Ernest to fetch the simulated African lady's imitation African shawl. They left the penthouse, and the party took all of two or three minutes to resume spontaneity. Weber, lifting a drink from a hired waiter's tray, spotted Karen, who was near the closed terrace doors with Ruth Simms. He could tell, from halfway across the room and with vision and perceptions fogged by far too much liquor, that she was doing her damnedest with Ruth to change the subject to nicer things but that she was unhinged by the graceless spectacle that had taken place in her refined parlor. He looked for Robin, but she was not at the buffet table or anywhere in sight. Young Hightower was still at the table, though, and he went over to him and shook his hand. " 'Lo, champ," he said, and smiled.

Hightower smiled back.

"Get you somep'm drink 'roun' here? Vict'ry drink?" Weber offered, cursing the way he sounded.

"No more, thanks. I have one here, anyway, somewhere. Ah—Robin seems to have disappeared. Have you seen her?"

"Prob'ly in the john. Tha's where lady oughtta be, in genteel temp'ry—tem-po-ra-ry—s'clusion after two gla'iators almos' came to blows over her."

"I'm sorry that things got out of control. And frankly, Mr. Weber, I appreciate having been invited, but I'd do anything to be able to slip out."

To hell with asking him why, with coddling him just because passers-by were giving him the tail of their eyes. "Slip out? Shank o' the evening, wanna slip out? Know who'd go with you? Robin'd go with you, 'cause tha's our Robin, loyal start to finish, always goes with the man what brung her. An' who's the party for? Robin, right?"

"Yes," with a tolerant sigh. "Right."

Weber clapped the young man's back. "Right! Drink up, my frien'. R'lax, r'lax! Hey, Angie!" he cried, calling to the nearby port in a storm that was Angela Ferris, portrait painter and cheery nympho, the seven- or eight-time divorcee who had been crowned Miss America in Atlantic City back in the days of the thirteen original colonies, no spring chicken but a palsy-walsy swinger with terrific legs and a holy crusade in life to ball every man under the sun. Angie Ferris came to Weber and they pecked each other's lips and he goosed her because Karen wasn't around and because he liked Angie and because Angie never objected to anything as long as it was vulgar and in good fun. "Here's Angie Innerspring. Tell it like it is, Ang—you still checking into motels as Angela Ferrish and To Whom It May Conshern?"

Angie laughed and he watched her give Hightower the seductive up and down appraisal that was a reflex with her. "You're soused to the cranberries, you filthy old man," she pretended to criticize. "When are you going to introduce me to this gentleman who I bet doesn't pinch ladies—in public, at least?"

Weber introduced them, and warned Hightower, "See that your chastity belt's s'curely locked, buddy," and made his getaway in search of—what? who? There was a glass on the thick carpet beside a puddle of booze, but people merely stepped over and around it. Maybe Weber would find Robin. Jesse Nash, big-mouth Jesse Nash on whom he was banking damn near everything, was a troublemaker for fair just as everyone had warned, and the reality of this would have to be dealt with. But not tonight, not now. Tomorrow was another day, wasn't it? Wasn't it? He walked through his and Karen's acre of a living room and almost passed Robin without seeing her. She was in a corner, subdued, listening to a man who was breathing on her.

She saw Weber, and lighted up, this lovely and defenseless child. He saw her spill some of the drink on the front of the cocktail dress, and be embarrassed, and laugh in embarrassment for the man, and she excused herself to leave the room and carried what was left of the drink with her.

Weber waited, and followed her.

He found her in the first guest room off the hall. She was at the sink, dabbing a wet washcloth on the stain, and he asked, syllables slurred and eyelids heavy, "Wonder'f you c'n use any help?"

"No, I'm doing fine," she said, and smiled at him.

He held her, and Robin's arms immediately encircled him as he kissed her mouth. His fingers found the clasp of the zipper at the back of her dress and lowered it, and he brought both of her full breasts out of her bra and kissed them with a frenzy that momentarily stupified him. "Dying for you, Warren, dying for you," she breathed, and freed his zipper, and was squeezing him in her hand when Weber heard the door and looked up to see Karen.

Sixteen

Mrs. Weber covered her mouth as though to suppress a gasp, but did not speak. She left the room.

She left the door wide open.

In panic, mortified, quickly righting her clothes, Robin assumed that Warren would quickly take care of the door he had not taken care of before. He did not; he merely stood, shoulders stooped, and blinked, like a man slowly coming awake from a deep sleep. Robin asked him to shut the door, and he nodded, but he moved toward it with such molasses effort that she passed him and shut it and worriedly examined herself in the door's full mirror, as though to judge whether anyone besides Mrs. Weber would be able to tell by her face that she had allowed something very wrong to happen. She hoped he would not touch her, hoped he would not speak.

He did begin to speak, if mumbling was speaking, but she hurried away from him because she was sure that if she stayed another moment he would have apologized, and she could not have endured that. The party seemed louder than ever when she returned to the living room, and she found Verne, whom she had betrayed, and told him she had a headache and needed to go home. Verne said he would get her wrap and take her.

She had left her drink in the room where Warren was, and urgently wanted one, but, waiting for Verne, she stayed far from the bar and from people because otherwise someone would come to her and expect her to speak.

And it did happen, as it had to happen, because to have been caught with her dress undone could not possibly be punishment enough. She looked up from her melancholy shame and saw Mrs. Weber, regal, faultless, white Mrs. Weber, expression blank except for hurt eyes. "How long," the lady asked, "do you think it will take you to get out of my home?"

"I'm going right away, Mrs. Web—"

"That's splendid news," the lady said, and turned on her heel.

Some guests who had been friendly before spotted Robin and came toward her, wanting still to be friendly, but Verne rescued her and guided her to the small vestibule and rang for the elevator. "Are you really feeling bad, or were you having a hard time there?" he asked.

"Both."

In the basement garage, waiting for the chauffeur-driven limousine GWS had hired, she repeated that she wasn't feeling well, and Verne didn't deserve it but she stared straight ahead, tuning him out. "You might want to head right on to your hotel," she said. "The driver can drop me off and then take you."

A little pause. "I don't understand," he said with concern.

Why should you? she thought. She had not known Verne long, but she was certain she knew him well, far better than she had allowed him to know her, and she knew her chilliness wasn't being fair to him at all. "The chauffeur will take you where you want to go, safe and sound," she said. "He's a white man being paid to do as he's told. If I tell him to drive you to China, he'll do as he's told."

"Come *on*, now. What happened upstairs? What did I do wrong?"

Robin didn't answer. She kept seeing Warren's wife, those hurt eyes. How dirty she must have looked through another woman's eyes. . . .

On the ride, she accepted a cigarette and a light, although smoking was a relatively new chore, one she was trying to get the hang of so she would look as sophisticated as Jeanne Prescott and Warren's wife and Lois Farrentino did when they smoked cigarettes.

Verne continued to prod her on what was wrong, whether Jesse Nash had upset her more than she let on, what was making her act so oddly, and she did not answer. He shrugged and said lightly, "I don't mind admitting I was ready to kiss Nash for backing down when he did. He could've dropped me with one punch."

A block from her apartment, Robin looked at him and said, with no animation, clearly but so that the chauffeur wouldn't hear, "I guess you're all ready to jump between the sheets as soon as we get upstairs."

The abruptness startled him, but then he managed a troubled smile. "That's the best offer I've had in, oh, hours," he said.

"So it's settled." Her face was blank. "There's my place up ahead, and if you're really interested I'll send the driver home. If all you want to do is talk, then I'll call up the handyman. It doesn't make that much difference to me. All I want is to get laid, and you're available."

"What the *hell*—" he began, very troubled now, and he reached for her, maybe to cradle and protect her, maybe to tell her how much he was trying to understand. Robin flinched, and slapped his hand, and drew away. "Robin—"

"No, I just changed my mind, I prefer the handyman to goody-goodies like you any day in the week," she exclaimed, and read all the bewilderment and disgust and question marks in his face as the car pulled up to The Havilland. She opened her door herself and instructed the chauffeur, "Take this gentleman to wherever he tells you." To Verne Hightower she said, "Go away and stay away." And she ran.

She rushed into the lobby before he could come after her. Waiting for the elevator, shivering, she recognized with relief and dismay that there was time for him to come after her, and that he did not.

In her bedroom, she poured the rye. It went down better without water because it went down faster, and she coughed, but that was the idea, wasn't it? She stripped, not daring to look at a mirror, and switched on the television set nearest to the bottle of rye. It was only a little past ten o'clock, and she phoned down to the desk for messages. There were many, none important, none from Mama, none from Jesse, none from Warren Weber or Mrs. Weber, none from Verne, and she directed that she was not to be disturbed until she gave the word.

She watched the second half of a Richard Widmark movie, then the Eleven O'Clock News, then thirty minutes of Johnny Carson, then "The Larry Endicott Show," then a movie titled *How's Your Aunt?* with Slim Summerville and Zasu Pitts, whom she had heard of and never seen, and Stepin Fetchit, whom she had heard of, much of, and never seen. Stepin Fetchit wore wrinkled overalls and no shoes, scratched his bald head and bare feet and armpit, and drawled, "Ain' gwine do nuffin' but wuk. Wha' wuk Ah does? Ah saws woods when Ah dream 'bout dem nize cole mellums, bozz, tha's th' wuk Ah does bes'."

She fell asleep, when all her senses were coated and when the bottle was empty.

She wakened at three in the afternoon, awed that she had slept for so many hours, and phoned the desk. The desk read the names of callers, including Mr. Weber who had called three times. Robin attempted to get out of bed, and could not. She swore to Mama that she would never drink alcohol again for as long as she lived. And she swore to Mama that she would go to church—as soon as her head and belly came off the roller coaster, as soon as the pain in her soul lessened, as soon as she would be able to enter a church without shame. Mama said, "Feelin' shame's the best time to go to church." But Robin knew better. She knew God didn't like bad women.

Robin flew to Hollywood and was met at the airport by reporters, and smilingly answered all questions with answers Ronnie Haley had provided her with and which she had memorized on the plane, and by Vic Ennis, who was GWS's publicity man, and by Norman Gaynor, who was Cambridge Pictures' publicity man. A limousine drove her and Ennis at her right and Gaynor at her left—or was it Ennis at her left and Gaynor at her right?—toward town, and one of them lighted her cigarette as the other ogled her crossed legs with flabby subtlety, and she thought, as each of the men interrupted the other with promises of how busy she could expect to be during her seven or eight weeks here: I am here. Here. Not as someone in the background, not as Jesse's girl friend. As Robin Hamilton. Star. Robin Hamilton, Star. Yes, light Robin Hamilton's cigarette. Yes, admire Robin Hamilton's pretty legs. Yes, keep telling Robin Hamilton she's beautiful and you've played her LP so often you've worn it out and this town was built expressly for her. Yes. Yes.

I'm here.

I'm so scared.

I'm here.

They delivered her to the endless suite of a splashy, vast hotel called The Hollywood Haywell, which one of the men, Gaynor or Ennis, claimed was the newest In hotel in town and which the other man, Ennis or Gaynor, claimed made the Beverly Hilton look like a shanty in old shantytown as he slipped a Hollywood Haywell jade ash tray into his plaid jacket pocket. There was a white maid, a middle-aged bowing-and-scraping woman whose name was Sigrid and who would serve her around the clock for the length of her stay in Hollywood. The suite's parlor was crowded with flowers, flowers and candy and big bowls of big fruits and bottles of whisky and telegrams and phone messages and a gold-framed, color photograph of Cambridge Pictures' president, Sol Aaron, a lemony-looking man with pince-nez and sparse hair parted in the middle and an autograph that read, *To Robin Hamilton. Love and luck. Yours and best wishes, Sol Aaron.*

"If you strike out here, honey, you can always hock that frame," said Gaynor or Ennis.

"Stop, Christ sakes, with the jinx talk, will ya!" said Ennis or Gaynor.

Finally Robin was alone except for Sigrid the white maid, and, as Sigrid the white maid mixed a drink of rye and ginger ale, she read her messages. She crumpled the wire that read *Phone at once, Warren,* and set aside others and crumpled still others, and paused to reread the note that read *So many good wishes to you. Hollywood may be busier than Chicago ever was, but may we have dinner while you're here? Kindest, Jack Dickson.* There was a telephone number beneath the name.

The next morning, Monday, a limousine drove her to Cambridge Pictures, where she met too many people and heard too many names and titles to remember, and where she was extravagantly flattered almost to the point of belief. She and Sol Aaron posed for photographs, and *Play with Fire* officially commenced. It was an oddly old-fashioned kind of movie—a pampered, selfish young heiress learns to be human from a poor but kind young man who is working his way through college as an auto mechanic—an old-fashioned movie made modern by the event of the heiress's college roommate, a Negro girl, herself poor, kind, understanding, a consummate philosopher, psychologist, and emotional girder. Robin was the roommate and would share the secondary love interest with the college's young music instructor, a poor, kind, handsome Negro.

The heiress was played by Sunny Storm, an in-vogue blonde semi-actress who shook hands with Robin the first day on the set and said, "Some of the nicest kids I knew when I was a kid were colored." The auto mechanic was played by Mark Fraser, a New York Method actor who asked Robin, the first day on the set, if he could come to her from time to time to discuss motivations between the races, the better for him to fully comprehend his role. The music instructor was played by Bruce Corbett, an off-Broadway actor who had never made a movie before, who drank coffee with Robin the first day on the set and said, "This is really a disgusting script. If I didn't need the bread and the exposure, I wouldn't stay a minute. When you come right down to it, you're still playing Louise Beavers and Butterfly McQueen, and I'm still

playing Mantan Moreland. Times haven't changed for us Hollywood darkies. The theme of this picture's the same as *Gone with
the Wind*—colored folks were put on this earth for the singular
purpose of helping white folks out of jams."

He was wrong, Robin thought; the movie's idea had been Warren's, and Warren's mind just didn't work that way. "There's a
big difference, though," she said. "We play colored people in
college."

"Do we ever!" the actor snorted. "Every one of your lines is
all-wise Confucius. You're so knowledgeable you can't possibly be
human. And I'm so brilliant, so witty, so perfect, that no audience
can be expected to believe a second of my characterization."

"What would be better, then, us playing a janitor and a maid?"

"No, no, but this is plain dishonest. The image of a Negro as
flawless, not a hair out of place, is as dishonest as the image of a
Negro shuffling and kissing Massa's foot. I don't like it. I should've
had more guts when my agent called me up. I was hungry back
East, but I should've held out and waited for the right part to come
along."

You poor dumb soul, thought Robin.

When she was invited to see the rushes, Robin began to believe
she was nearly as good as the Ennises and Gaynors and Aarons
enthusiastically claimed she was. She admitted to herself that she
photographed not merely well but great, and admitted, as the days
went on, that her voice was better than ever and, remarkably, that
she was that very good, very convincing actress up there on that
screen.

Her white maid embarrassed her by waiting on her hand and
foot. The VIP treatment she received from nearly everyone—the
hairdresser, the producer, the chauffeur, interviewers, headwaiters
—buoyed her until she returned to the hotel at night, when she
would drink in private because she was afraid of sleeping pills and
because liquor relaxed her and assured her she could face the following morning with courage she did not have. She was quite

alone on these nights, despite the day's people and excitement, despite the growing indications that *Play with Fire* would make her a star.

When she summoned the nerve, she wrote a letter to Verne, in care of his newspaper in San Francisco, to say what a horrible mess she had been that night in New York, that he had been perfectly right in not getting in touch with her after that night because what real man wanted to bother with a mess, that she read and admired his by-lines in the *Afro-American,* and that she wished him the very best, always.

On the evenings she was not exhausted, she went out with Bruce Corbett, partly because the publicity departments of both GWS and Cambridge thought it would be a smart idea to be seen with him in public and partly because loneliness was something she could see and touch. She almost let him sleep with her, but his two continual monologues—about himself as an actor and himself as a Negro actor who, like all Negroes, should constantly fight for Negro rights—tired her, bored her, oppressed her, and she ordered him out, forever, on the night he accused her of not taking her race and her heritage seriously.

Halfway through the filming of *Play with Fire* she was visited on the set by Jack Dickson, who told her she looked wonderful, told her that the reports of how great she was in the picture were thrilling. They sat in her dressing room and, though it was midday and a tricky scene with Sunny Storm was ahead of her, she instructed Sigrid to serve her and her guest some drinks. They toasted each other and talked about his brother Marty, who sent regards and who wanted her for a Marty Dickson TV special.

"That's not up to me," she said. "Warren handles everything."

He peered at his cigarette. "May I put a bee in your bonnet that Warren won't thank me for, Robin? Warren's shortchanging you."

"Short—Cheating me, you mean? That's the sil—"

"Oh, no, I don't mean that at all. Warren's worst enemies've never charged him with pocketing a nickel that wasn't his. I mean he's shortchanging your career. News travels fast in this business, and what I hear everywhere I go is that this is when Warren should be giving you all his attention, because the deals important people want to offer you are coming in thick and fast, and he's putting all his time into that Jesse Nash thing in New York. The gossip goes that he's not doing right by you."

"He has so far. I owe him everything."

"Everything? Your talent? Your talent that improves every minute of every day? You have a contract with him, don't you? He makes a profit from your talents, doesn't he? Or is it all altruism on his part?"

Robin didn't snap at him. "I appreciate your interest," she said, "but I really don't want to talk about it. I'm not all that ambitious. If Warren isn't working for me day and night he has some reason, and I can live with it."

"But—"

"If you promise never to bring up that subject again, I'll let you buy me some dinner sometime."

They had dinner together, a quiet, back-booth Italian dinner two nights later, and he was attentive and easy to be with and he did not once mention Warren. On a glorious late Sunday morning he called for her in an ostentatious but good-humored foreign roadster and drove her to his compact, masculine, and cheerful house in Malibu, which was only yards from the ocean. His valet, an old, spavined, frowning Negro he introduced as Coolidge, built and served bullshots, which were bouillon cubes and whiskey and other medicinal ingredients, and which Jack Dickson called booze broth and proclaimed to be civilization's dynamic cure for man's most diabolical temporary disease, the morning-after shakes. Robin loved it, though she was guilty about drinking before lunch, and he showed her around, and she was restless because she had not decided why she had come here, why she was asking to get involved with another white man when it was pointless, and she asked if they would swim. He guided her to a small house on the beach, carrying her drink and his own, and pointed to a galaxy of ladies' swimsuits, all styles and all sizes. Handing her her drink, smiling at her with a compact, masculine, cheerful smile, he said, "It's a little indecent to be athletic this early in the day, but all right, take your pick. I'll be changing in the next room, and I promise not to peek at your pick through the holes in the wall."

"You wouldn't peek."

"That's what I've just finished saying. I wouldn't peek," he said, and she believed him. He was a sexy man—not as immediately, flying-sparks sexy as Warren, but sexy—but she had the feeling, as she'd had since she'd first met him, at Jesse's opening night at Phideau's, that he was not a huffer and puffer. She appreciated that—and she did not.

Because it fit, and because it would save time between them that would otherwise be frittered in feinting and circling, in holding off, in postponing what she wished and did not wish to be postponed, Robin chose a blood-red bikini. It hid almost nothing, it accentuated the curves, planes, and angles of a body too mature to fill two strips of cloth, it made her look so laughably, spilling-over sexy that it almost became sexless. She finished the bullshot for courage, stepped into sandals, and sauntered out of the small house and onto the beach, where he was in swim trunks, looking young except for the grey hair on his chest and the start of a potbelly.

"Lordamercy," he said.

"Is it okay?" she asked. "If you think I'll shame anybody, I'll scoot right on back and change."

"I'm scandalized."

"You are? I'll change."

"Can I watch?"

"No, I'll put on something else. It was just a joke, I—"

"Don't you dare. I like. I'll be rubbing these old eyes all day, but I like."

Robin laughed lightly and moved as lightly toward the ocean, aware with the eyes in back of her head that he was watching every muscle, every ripple, every line, that she had almost nothing on and that he was feasting on the absurd sight of her. She walked into the surf, which was cold only for moments, and then gracefully dove under the first mild wave and swam, though she did not swim well, in the showy way Esther Williams swam in the movies on television. He came to her and swam with her. She was in Malibu, not Guadeloupe, with a reserved man she merely trusted, not with Warren.

Maybe this was better. Maybe.

They did not bother to dress when they came out of the water, because a pitcher of drinks awaited them on the patio and because the hot sun began at once to dry them. They drank in the sun and Robin realized how skillfully liquor, if it was paced right, could send bothersome inhibitions off and away. The bikini had started as a joke, or a kind of joke. It wasn't a joke now; her host's furtive glances said it wasn't a joke. Without liquor, she would not have been able to sit in this beach chair and calmly, or seemingly calmly, exhibit herself. With liquor shyness dissolved. As he talked about the headaches that kept cropping up daily as Marty's manager, about Marty who was becoming riddled with arthritis and who had more than enough money to quit the grind of show business but who never would, she did more than sit. She crossed and uncrossed her legs. She leaned forward for him to light her cigarette and hunched her shoulders so that her breasts pressed together, and her eyes met his eyes with a look that was deep and provocative as she caught the flame from his lighter. Coolidge served a lunch of cold salmon and Caesar salad, giving her the "You Hussy" glare. They ate it, and drank some more as they waited for the lunch to be digested, and then swam again. Coolidge had left for the day by the time they returned to the patio, and Jack Dickson said, "There's a shower next to the bathhouse, but there's a better one in here. Plenty of towels, and the water's guaranteed hot."

"My clothes are in the bathhouse."

"I'll get them."

Her clothes were on the laundry hamper when she emerged from a long shower, and the bathroom door was ajar. "Are you there?" she called. "What about your shower?"

"I had mine, at the bathhouse."

"What are you doing?"

"Getting dressed."

"I can't find any towels," she said, stuffing towels into the hamper.

"Look at the rack beside the john."

"Nope. Not a one."

Silence. Then: "That's funny, I was sure there were. Wait a second and I'll hand you one." She waited eight seconds and he tapped at the bathroom door. "Here it is. I'll—"

She opened the door so that he could see her and she gasped and quickly covered herself here and there and here and there with her hands and said, "Oh, my, the door went and flung open, didn't it?"

He was wearing white undershorts, and he looked startled. Robin did not smile or show a hint of invitation. But Jack Dickson knew he was invited.

The lovely thing about Jack Dickson was that everything he did as a lover was right. He was gentle, and his patience was generous.

The awful thing about Jack Dickson was that she had barely recovered from the final tingles of ecstasy when he said they must be together always, which was right, and that she should get out of her contract with Weber and let him represent her, which was not at all right. Cavanaugh, *the* Cavanaugh, could be talked into signing her—this minute—for a three-picture deal, at double the price for each that Sol Aaron was paying her for this one picture. Weber was asleep at the switch. He, Jack Dickson, could get her a percentage, could . . .

"What's wrong?" he asked. "Why are you looking like that?"

"You son of a bitch," she said, carefully enunciating each word.

"Whaat?"

She hastened to the bathroom, where she dressed. She could not find her left shoe, but she hastened out of the house, past him, clutching her purse, and walked and walked until she came to a store that was open. It was a pharmacy, and she asked the man behind a counter where she could get a taxi. And she wept before she could finish the question, and the man put her in a chair and waved a white plastic stick under her nose, and he left her to make a telephone call. After a while, a taxi came and drove her to the hotel.

At ten o'clock California time, Warren called, and she accepted, urgently accepted, the call. "How are you, Robin?" he asked.

"All right, I guess."

Every studio was after her, on the basis of *Play with Fire* reports, he said. He was signing her up with Onyx. She was guaranteed $250,000, plus ten percent of the net gross. It was a sweet money script, and she would begin thirty days after the completion of *Play with Fire*.

"Onyx?" she said. "Did you try Cavanaugh?"

"Who? Anthony Cavanaugh?"

"Yes."

"What are you, selling five-and-dime ribbons? Tony Cavanaugh offered forty-one five, top price, flat, and suggested a musical version of *Uncle Tom's Cabin*, with you in the title role. You'd play either Uncle Tom or the cabin, or maybe he was figuring on a dual role for the same price. I never did get it straight, because I hung up on him. What's this with Cavanaugh?"

"Nothing. I just heard his name. I heard he was big."

"Will you let me advise you who's big?"

"Yes."

"What's this barbed wire, Robin? Why haven't you accepted any of my calls?"

"Why haven't you been out here?"

"I've been busy."

"So have I," she said.

"I'll be there the instant I can."

"All right, Warren," she said, and told Sigrid the maid she wanted a drink.

Waiting for sleep that was necessary, for she would have to look rested and fresh for tomorrow's close-up shots, she read Verne Hightower's newspaper columns from the past three days. The second one, Friday's, was a call to all members of FREE to either resign from it and give their allegiance and contributions to civil rights movements far worthier and more truly dedicated to their welfare, or to work to reorganize FREE and to begin by ousting Orville Sanford and replacing him with a leader who understood black citizens' real aspirations and needs. He called, in an open letter, on Jesse Nash to help bring changes about, suggesting that for all his bombastic speeches, all his public support for revolution, Jesse was the only spokesman for FREE who had never uttered a word in public that could be construed as anti-Semitic, or a word that endorsed indiscriminate violence. "If you're not sold on the idea, Jesse Nash, that the most expedient and lastingly effective way for the black man to attain his rights is to set fire to everything and everyone not black," Verne wrote, "what in the world are you still doing in FREE? The white man has a lot to answer to us for. But so has Orville Sanford, the man you call your leader but who obviously is not leading *you* by the nose. It is men like you, men many of us still respect, who can make FREE free."

Everything, thought Robin, was going to change for me, going to be different when I became enough of a star to have a chauffeur drive me around. Nothing's changed. Nothing's different.

She called to Sigrid, and Sigrid helped her to get to sleep by serving her all the rye in Hollywood, California.

Seventeen

KAREN DID NOT move out of the penthouse at once, because of the children. "The girls are in bed. I can't very well pack them and take them to Greenwich, or wherever, tonight," she said when the last party guests left. "But I won't spend another night under the same roof with you, and certainly not tonight. You're reeking of liquor, you can hardly stand, but I won't have you sleeping in the study or anywhere in this apartment. I need you out of here, Warren. If Rudi isn't available, then have one of the men in the lobby get you a cab. You are not to stay here tonight, and let's please not have a scene."

"Karen . . ."

"No," she said abruptly. "Not a word. I want to divorce you. You're a liar, and dishonorable, and cold—you've always been cold, and I pretended for twenty years that you were something else, and you're not, you never will be because you never can be. I've loved you for possibly five years out of twenty, which isn't good enough. Get out of here, Warren. Now. Get out of this family I tried with all my might to keep together."

A taxi took him to his club at The Yarnall, where one of the night men escorted him to a room and where he slept. He wakened at seven in the morning, feeling unutterably healthy, and it wasn't until he had shaved and showered and started for his office that he realized he hadn't a trace of hangover. Recollection made him feel wretched, but physically he had not felt this sound in years.

His daughters' school terms were over, and Karen took them to

Greenwich. His valet, Ernest, called him when they had gone, with two bags of clothing, and added that the Webers' housekeeper, Mrs. Neilsen, had been instructed to pack more clothing and belongings to be collected in a day or two.

He phoned Karen. She was indeed serious. She was consulting Henrietta's attorney, Don Barstow, who would represent her in the divorce. "This is lunacy," Weber said. "You can't break up a marriage and a home just like that!"

"Yes, I can."

"The girls—you can't turn my children against me because of one incident while I was drunk."

"Yes, I can do that, too. Will that hurt you possibly a tenth as much as you've hurt me? The girls were bewildered and asked questions, naturally. But they made it clear that they want to be with their mother, not their father. I didn't have to handcuff them to get them out of the apartment."

"Not Kay. Kay's crazy about me. You're either poisoning her mind, or you're lying . . ."

"No, I'm not a liar, Warren. Lying is your gift, not mine. You're right about one thing—your one drunken incident, as you call it, isn't why I'm divorcing you. But I didn't realize till last night that I've been in the process of divorcing you for the past ten years. Your trashy colored sweetheart merely served to break the camel's back."

"I'm coming up to Greenwich right—"

"You won't be let in. I've seen to that. Good-bye, Warren."

She'll get over it, he thought after the initial helpless rage lessened. This is hell-hath-no-fury stuff, as temporary as all snits. I'll let her cool off, and then she and the girls will come back, as if nothing had happened. He phoned Robin, who would not talk with him. That needed cooling off, too.

He absorbed himself in "Moore," working closely with Ronnie Haley to make certain that the trades and the public knew there was not only a big new series coming in the fall, but the biggest, the freshest, the most provocative and trailblazing and dramatic and uncompromising series to ever hit the tube. He spent money, thousands upon thousands of dollars of it, to prime the public for it months in advance, to force the public to talk about it and wait for it. He worked his writers hard to come up with one punchy script after another, and they must have been excellent because he was enthusiastic over what he read, and Emmett Lovell, the Negro "referee" he retained suggested only minor changes. And, wonder of wonders, Jesse Nash grumbled occasionally but did not really growl.

The project was going perfectly, almost frighteningly so. As expected, unreachable stars learned that the signing of Brad Hammond and the Beaumonts was not a publicity fiction but a fact and scrambled to join the parade of guest stars. Rhodes and Owen Claffee left Weber alone. And, additional and miraculous wonder of wonders, he stopped into "21" several nights before "Moore" was to go into physical production, and Caleb Atwood smiled and waved at him from a corner table. He waved back but stayed at the bar with two ABC men who were pumping him, trying to learn if "Moore" was going to be as socko and commercially viable as the reports predicted, trying to learn if he had dealt with Caleb directly or gone over Caleb's head. "Just look at Caleb's smiling face," he said. "That should answer all questions." It was not an answer at all, of course. Clearly, Atwood had two exquisite reasons to be gunning for him—he *had* gone over his head, and he had done it with a show that had to be a large chicken bone in Atwood's throat. But the fact remained that Caleb was leaving him alone, too, and that proved further that everything about "Moore" was cream and silk, that nothing could go wrong. He didn't bother to touch wood. He bought a new round of drinks for the ABC men and himself instead.

The day before the first *Moore* segment was to begin shooting, he heard from Max Wright, his attorney, who had heard from Don Barstow, Karen's attorney. Karen and the girls had flown to

London on a holiday, Max reported, and she was indeed seeking a divorce; Barstow's charge would be mental cruelty. "Ignore it," Weber angrily ordered.

"What's that?"

"You heard me. It's noise, and it doesn't mean anything. It's a B-movie waiting game and it'll blow over. Just ignore it."

On that same day a worried Phil came into Weber's office, having heard about Karen. "It'll blow over," Weber repeated. "You know Karen—she could no more be divorced than she could scrub floors. She'll be back."

On that same day he received a long-distance call from his son Skipper, who had a letter from Mom in London, something about separating from Dad, and what was going on? "Nothing, Skip," said Weber. "Your mother and I had a disagreement about something, and you know how women can be, even great women like your mother. They get overly emotional and they need time to calm down at their own pace. Don't be upset, it'll blow over. Listen, old man, when are you coming to New York? It's about time you and I did up the town, isn't it?"

And on that same day Mel Hebranck's nurse phoned to remind him that his appointment for a checkup was long overdue, and that Dr. Hebranck wanted her to emphasize the necessity of periodic examinations. "I've been busy," said Weber. "But I promise to get back to you in a day or two."

Then it was time to go back to "Moore."

Kevin Beaumont and Margalo Wells, the movies' highest-priced husband-and-wife acting team, kept their word and flew to New York to appear in the first segment of "Moore." Weber set them up at The Drake and sent them flowers and champagne and pretty Margalo's most abiding passion after sex, kosher salami. Neither had ever been closer to Harlem than El Morocco, and Weber was secretly concerned about how they would receive Harlem or how Harlem would receive them. They breathed aristocracy, they were used to being catered to, and there was the strong possibility that they and the ghetto might not hit it off. He and Rudi escorted them to the series' basic set, a building on 125th Street, and he discovered there was no cause for concern; colored kids mobbed them for autographs, and the couple, who normally fled from crowds, radiated patience and good humor. They hit it off immediately and splendidly with the technical crew, most of whom, on Weber's request and Nash's insistence, were Negro, and Weber's jaw fell when they were introduced to Jesse, who temporarily mislaid his antagonism to white faces and told them he'd admired them in their last two movies. "That's surely praise from Caesar," Weber confided to them when Jesse was called away. "Nash admires nobody."

"He admired me more than he admired you," Margalo teased Kevin.

"That's because you have keen insights, an ability to communicate the depth of your character, and large boobs, my dear," Kevin said.

The Beaumonts were kidders, but they were workhorses, too, and they knew exactly what they were doing. The script's story line involved them almost as much as it involved the Jim Moore character: Caseworker Moore is called to the tenement home of one of his clients, a Negro mother whose teen-aged son has gotten mixed up with a bunch of bad kids, including a renegade white girl who fancies herself in love with him. Moore finds the boy—a decent, hard-working kid now high on marijuana and indolence—and becomes intrigued with the neurotic white girl, who has moved to Harlem from nowhere and who has turned against the white world. He tracks down her wealthy parents (the Beaumonts), who are relieved that their daughter is alive, who concede that she's always been headstrong and difficult in spite of all the advantages they've given her, and who are baffled to know why she chose a grubby life in grubby Harlem as a means of hurting them and herself. Moore effects a reconciliation between them and their daughter and they take her away from the ghetto, after they tell Moore that they had never trained her to be a racist and after Moore hears the mother's unexpected and emotional confession that she and her husband had indeed always answered the girl's inquisitive, intelligent questions about the advantaged and disadvantaged with platitudes and outright distortions. Then Moore goes to his most pertinent task, which is to try to reclaim the boy, who has been wrecked—though maybe not forever—by poverty, and the conditions of poverty, and platitudes and outright distortions. By the platitudes and distortions of a system in which he was formed.

The Beaumonts packed a week's worth of work into three days, and Weber and Rudi took them to the airport for their flight to London, where they would begin a new picture. Weber asked them to look up Karen and the girls, who were most likely at Claridge's, and told them, because they were his friends, that Karen had left him. Kevin was upset, but Margalo was shocked. "That can't be!" she exclaimed. "Karen, steady, peaceful Karen? *Why?*"

Because they were his friends, and because he needed their reactions, he said, "It seems my esteemed wife found me with my hand caught in the dishwasher. The dishwasher had large boobs like you, and she was thirty-seven years old if she was an inch."

"She walked out for *that?* For cheating?" Margalo cried.

Kevin groaned. "Saintly Mary and Joseph," he sighed. "How quaint. If Puss here and I had a *sou* for every time we played house with—"

"Will you see her?" Weber asked. "I'm sure she's just stewing and letting me stew. But will you see her and tell her Daddykins loves her and wants her back home?"

"You dreary ape!" Margalo snapped. "*You* go to her! Take your club out of the cave and drag her home by the hair—that's what she's waiting for!"

"I can't get away, not with 'Moore' clicking."

"How long does it take to fly there?" said Kevin. "You can go and be back in two days."

"See her, will you?" Weber repeated. "Tell her I need her."

Troubles with Jesse, which Weber had anticipated and hoped could be put off at least until the series was rolling evenly, were not put off. Brad Hammond, the show's second guest star, reigned in the spotlight during his five days of work, and Nash stayed out of his path, though he visibly had the sulks. The director, Jay Eaton, went to Weber. "I can dig long-time stars bitching about this and that. I can even dig losers bitching about this and that," Jay objected. "But I can't dig a cat like Prince Jesse bitching about anything. He's not a loser, but he's sure no long-time star."

"What's the bitching?"

"*I'm* the one who should raise sand, because he's wasting everybody's time, mainly mine. He jumps on Dottie for not throwing him lines fast enough. He butted into a run-through with Zelda to tell her there's black folks and there's niggers and she was reading her lines like a nigger. And he's on my back, not that it's a federal case—yet—but he chases me around. He says a black man wouldn't emphasize a word the way I want him to emphasize it. He's telling me a black man wouldn't do this or wouldn't do that. He's telling *me* how a black man talks and acts and doesn't talk and act! *Me!* Who does he figure *I* am, Leif Erikson?"

"Can he act?"

"Hell, yes, but I've directed a hundred colored cats smarter than he is, better actors than he is, and they do their job and they let me do mine. So he can act, so what? When he's John Gielgud, *then* I'll let him educate me on how to put a show together."

"I'll have a talk with him, Jay. Settle down."

During a break, Weber went to Nash and reported the beefs. "What's biting you, Jesse? The night we signed your contract you agreed that a set can be a busy place, and you said you had no intention of dotting every 'i' and crossing every 't.' I'm getting the idea that that's exactly what you're trying to do."

"We agreed on something else, that night. You talked about a referee. You were gonna get in a black man to size up the scripts and say whether they read right."

"And I kept my end of the bargain. I wanted Emmett Lovell, and you okayed him." Emmett Lovell was a Negro satirist, poet, and novelist who had the high respect of most thinking blacks and whites, although Weber was beginning to wonder if there was a thinking black who could agree with a thinking white on any issue completely except that the official end of official slavery had occurred in the year 1865. Weber had introduced Jesse and Emmett to each other. Jesse had seemed satisfied.

"Well, who you hired was the wrong black man. The piddly changes and suggestions Lovell's been makin' coulda been made by Jim Eastland."

"Goddam you, cut it out!" Weber stormed. "You can pull your paranoid crap on the gullible nose-pickers, but don't try it on me any more. You're not black, you're sick! When you were in diapers, Emmett Lovell was risking his ass leading Deep South blacks past the shotguns up to the desk on voter registration day. That's when you were in *diapers*, young prince, when getting shot for telling off the redneck law was a hell of a lot more likely than it is today. Who the hell do you dream you are, you burrhead-come-lately, to put down a man like Lovell? Your tongue never stops with one noble speech after another, but what in hell have you *done*, for all your publicity, for all your chances to be a leader, except to whine 'White power structure, white power structure'? If you're such a marvel of an expert on the minds of men, then why don't you climb off your can and do something constructive instead of knocking a giant like Emmett Lovell, who's been in the battles you've sat home and read about?"

He didn't wait for an answer, if there was to be one. He stalked away. He was inviting increased tension, the last thing a filmed series needed, he suspected. But he had come close to socking the man, who, he also suspected, could probably beat him to a pulp.

Curiously, the proud Nash came to him some minutes later and, curiously, he didn't seem nearly as belligerent as Weber would have expected. "I signed on to this show 'cause I wanted it to be good, just like you," he said. "Not just good, but true. I didn't say much when I read those first scripts. I told you they were okay, because at least they didn't hurt my people or poke fun at them. I mostly said okay 'cause I figured we'd do a couple of them that don't say much of anything, and then we'd get movin' and do some shows that really hit home. Well, I been readin' more scripts, and looks to me like all you're plannin' is more of the same."

" 'Don't say much of anything'?" Weber argued, though quietly; this was not a time to match short fuses again. "These scripts are strong meat. Look, Jesse, I'm sorry I piled into you before. I realize that if you had control of the show, you'd have one theme, and that theme would be the conviction of the entire white world for murder. I'm not being sarcastic—in fact, as much as I'm able, I guess I can understand that. But you're being unrealistic, and you're definitely being unfair when you claim we're not saying much of anything. If attacking forced ghetto living, and the whole concept of second-class citizenship, isn't saying much of anything, if stressing the dignity and courage of the Negro people isn't—"

"You don't follow me," said Nash as quietly, as though he recognized the need, too, of talking without exclamation points. "There's a pattern. The scripts are startin' to come out of the same cookie-cutter. If we keep doin' these same stories, we won't be damagin' black folks but we won't be helpin' them, either, or helpin' whites to learn somethin'. And wasn't that what you were all about, to help, not just say tenements got rats? Old Eastland knows tenements got rats."

"Okay, I'll try to follow you."

Jesse Nash lit a cigarette. "You didn't mean to, and the writers probably didn't mean to, but every one of these stories ends up on pretty much the same note—that the black man's got hard times, but the best way to stand up straight is to get a little help from outside and mainly to help himself. You bet I'm lookin' for this to be a pro-black show, but I never said anything about it bein' anti-white. I want it true, to tell it like it is. There's honks with their heel on our neck—that's how come we can't stand up straight, that's how come a *little* help from outside isn't gonna help us—*or* them—near enough. If you really and truly wanna make somethin' outta this show, what you oughtta do, you oughtta tear up some of these once-over-lightly scripts and tackle somethin' that'll make everybody sit up and take notice."

"Such as what?"

"True stories, not made-up stories. Base 'Moore' on somethin' that really took place—in Harlem, not in some rich scriptwriter's head."

"Such as?"

Nash paused. "The Roland Lee Hamilton case."

Weber squinted at him.

"What could be more natural?" Nash went on, a whit more quickly. "It'd take guts—the law men in this town wouldn't like you nohow—but I met you at that Shor's restaurant that day 'cause I'd heard you were a white man with guts, 'least once upon a time you had guts. Now, what tells it like it is, better and stronger—frettin' over a poor little rich white kid who thinks she wants to be black 'cause her parents didn't bring her up right, or showin' what's real, an innocent fourteen-year-old colored boy gunned down by a white cop that goes scot-free? You're not only the man that says he wants to do what's right, you're Weber the showman. You tell me which story carries more of a wallop."

"I know the Hamilton case has meant a lot to you—"

"That's right, and it still means a lot 'cause what it says about my people and your people, simple as pie, is what folks've been writin' in books for hundreds and hundreds of years. You're a smart fella. You got to know that."

"The Hamilton case, eh? It's not exactly a chapter out of 'Beverly Hillbillies,' is it?"

"Not exactly, no."

"Give me a while, will you, Jesse? Maybe we'll talk about it some more."

"Sure," Nash said, and walked away. Weber watched him go, the half-assed Messiah he disliked, the young man he cautiously admired. Jesse Nash was so passionate, so half-cocked in his full passion that he didn't know which end was up and that was why his inflexible judgments had to be watched like a hawk. Going anywhere near the Hamilton case was out of the question, of course—yet admiration was in order. Because of passion in the midst of platitudes, and because he was a pro. Like Robin, he was a gamble that might pay off. He was unhappy and surely part of the reason he was unhappy was that he hungered to be a bigger man than he was capable of being, yet there was no denying that people looked at him as he walked, as people had looked at him in Toots Shor's and would always look at him, anywhere. People didn't look at minor or even major celebrities for long. They never tired of looking at someone who had whatzis, however—presence, charisma, glow, force, whatever you call it. Nash had it. The sad hell of it, thought Weber, wasn't that he was a rebel without a cause. He was loaded with cause. The sad hell of it was that he didn't know where, or how, to carry it.

Weber had overseen the first "Moore" show from inception to completion. At GWS, he had Ozzie run it again, and studied it, and told Ozzie to run the second show's rough cut. Nash's performances were sturdy, often more incisive than the dialogue warranted. The work, the diligence, the strive for perfectionism showed. Jay Eaton could be credited for much. But Eaton wasn't on that screen playing Moore; Jesse Nash was, and you believed there was a good man named Moore, because of Jesse's interpretation.

And Weber came to see, gradually and almost firmly, why Nash had been bitching, why he was unhappy. The scripts were bullets, but rubber bullets. The gloss of show biz, years of show-biz know-how, intruded at each of the screen's four corners and in the center where the gut was supposed to be. Nothing being said about black pain was phony, yet nothing about black pain was being said in words and ways that were new, unsafe, disturbing. I've been a hot-air liberal, thought Weber. I've played it safe. How did Heywood Broun put it? "A liberal is a man who leaves the room when the fight starts." Nash, that unpleasant, hostile, inflexible, half-cocked toothache, is absolutely right. I've constructed a series that informs white America that tenements have rats. That's all it says.

The Hamilton case remained out of the question, but he inter-commed Edith, the lady martinet in charge of GWS's research department, and ordered the complete file to date on the Roland Lee Hamilton case. Edith said it would take a while. "Round it all up," Weber directed, "and have one of the boys deliver it to my apartment."

He went to his apartment, which had servants and no family, well after midnight, and the file was on his desk. He read every clipping, every column, trying to ignore the references to Robin because she had no significant relevance to the boy's story, and he could not ignore them because of course she had a great deal of relevance, to the story and to Weber. Did she suffer very much? he wondered. The clips didn't say. The clips dated within the first weeks after the murder mentioned her only as Sister Robin. No clip quoted Sister Robin, no clip differentiated her particularly from Sister Lula or Mother Willie Mae. Yet she must have grieved, Weber thought. My beautiful, sad, young, dumb, brilliant, closed-off Robin must have, surely must have, must surely still.

He wrote pages upon pages of notes, and then he slept. He wakened at nine o'clock, on his own, and knew that Jesse was as right as an unpleasant Messiah could be. The Hamilton story would play. It would relate painful and undiluted truths. If Weber were to die a minute after it was wrapped up and in the can, the *Times* and the world would remember that Warren Weber had told *this* story on television.

"Moore" 's writers, white Gene Trowbridge and black Carl Montgomery, heard him out and respectfully advised him that his belfry had bats, that treading on the toes such an hour show would step on would be unprofitable toes to step on, that one libel suit had a pesky habit of encouraging others, that "Moore" belonged on the air, not in litigation. "Write it," said Weber, and shoved the Hamilton file and his own pages of notes across the desk. "Tell it, as Carl's brethren like to chant, like it is. Fiction is Jim Moore as the family's caseworker. Fact is the Hamilton case—everything that's in the record. Don't pull a single punch. And don't teach law to me. You're not legally responsible for 'Moore'—I am."

Phil, who was perfectly content to leave all creative decisions up to Weber, and who had supported every decision on the series from the outset, scratched his temple when Weber brought him the news that Ronnie Haley had been instructed to tell the public, by way of column plants and news items, that a semifictionalized recreation of the Hamilton death and its aftermath could be looked forward to as the high point of television's fall season, and that it would be recreated on "Moore." "I think you should call Haley and tell him to hold off for the time being," Phil advised. "Get your script first, and then get your clearance."

"What clearance? City Hall's permission for me to tell the truth?"

"Is 'Moore' a news story or a pretend story?"

"It's both. As of this morning, it's both."

"Stubborn *schlemiel* Warren," Phil sighed. "I never poke my head out of a ledger, but I know better than that. A news story, you can invite principals to speak for themselves and let them hang themselves. A pretend story, you can't name names and not expect to have the slightest mistake, the tiniest error, fall on you like a building."

"Who was the bookkeeper bellyaching to stop already with the 'Our Favorite Husband' *chozzerai*?"

"I was. And I still am. All I'm saying is, ironclad contract or no ironclad contract, Vanguard has a legal department that'll give us all *unglück* we can do without at our age."

"Don't sass me, Mr. Shimolovich, suh. If something is right, it's right. If something is truthful, it's truthful. I've handled a hotter cage of tigers than this before, and I will again."

Phil shrugged.

On the day the column plants began to appear, Weber took a call from Caleb Atwood, who was unexpectedly disarming. "Well,

I've got to admit you pulled it off, Warren," Atwood said. "I saw one of the segments, the one with the Beaumonts, and it's a gem."

Oh-oh, thought Weber. "Thank you, Caleb, but I wouldn't've imagined that would be your stick of tea."

"Here we go again—'Caleb, you fascist pig,'" Atwood said lightly. "I was against the project because I was afraid it wouldn't work, that's all, not because of its liberal orientation. I'm a practical man, I hope—I realize there are political views other than mine. What I'm calling about is, if the rest of the series keeps the quality I saw last night, you'll've proved me wrong, and I'm man enough to admit it."

"Thanks again, Caleb. I'm man enough to come out and ask one question. Considering that I went to the old man to sell the package, and considering that our last phone conversation was a little less than loving, why are you being so chummy now?"

"You're a truly suspicious cuss, aren't you?"

"Yep. Card-carrying."

"That's regrettable, because what's past is past—the show is a reality now, and I'd be a fool if I didn't face up to that. I do have a few constructive suggestions to make, because I want to see a series with integrity succeed and, frankly, because a Vanguard show that cooks on all burners helps not only Vanguard's image but Vanguard's solvency as well."

"What suggestions do you have in mind?"

"Oh, not on the phone, Warren. Let's meet for lunch tomorrow and kick it around. Can you make it tomorrow?"

Weber read his calendar. "I can make it."

"Fine. Twelve-thirty, at Fonda?"

They met at La Fonda del Sol, and Weber ordered a bloody mary. Atwood ordered the same, without vodka. "We really have been behaving like a pair of temperamental adolescents, Warren," Atwood acknowledged, "and it hasn't benefited either of us. I was sore as a boil that you went to Claude, and, to be honest, I still believe you were unthinking and highhanded. Your attitude would be the same if our roles were reversed. But I wasn't very graceful, either, especially when I made that unpardonable call to your wife in her hour of grief."

"Okay, we're even. Now we can be sweethearts again."

Atwood, who didn't like to smile, smiled. "Speaking of sweethearts, I'd personally love to know if you're finding Mr. Nash a sweetheart. Aside from other objections I've heard about him, I've heard he doesn't have the sunniest personality."

"He has an objectionable personality. He also has a bundle of talent, and he works harder than any comparatively new pro I've met, to see that things are done right. There are problems, sure, but because he's a perfectionist, like most pros, not because of his personality. He hasn't given us a second of trouble as far as the concept or the conduct of the show is concerned, if that's what you've heard."

"That's refreshing to hear—a black militant who's content to act, to follow directions. Which brings me to what I've been reading about your plans to devote a segment to the Hamilton thing, what was his name, Ronald Lou or—"

"Roland Lee," corrected Weber, who knew that Atwood knew.

"Yes. Whose idea was it?"

"Mine."

"Can you get away with it?"

"Why not?"

"It's still extremely controversial, for one thing."

"That's why I'm doing it."

"For another thing, you'll be naming names, won't you, unless you do it as straight fiction? Do you intend to give the real names of the Chief of Police, and the Mayor, and the District Attorney, and this Orville Sanford, and all the people who were involved? For that matter, Jesse Nash, too?"

"How we're going to attack it is still on the drawing board. I haven't decided anything definite yet. But if I decide to run it that way, all down the line, then I'll bone up on all the libel and slander laws and do it right, even if it kicks some VIP tails—*particularly* if it kicks some VIP tails." Weber glanced at Caleb.

"Why? Are you about to sermon me on why boats shouldn't be rocked?"

Atwood, who didn't like to laugh, chuckled. "That's precisely why I suggested this lunch," he asserted, buttering a hard roll and, Weber continued to suspect, possibly buttering Weber. "May I be frank?"

Weber nodded, and wondered if he would ever learn to trust the frankness of people who asked if they may be frank.

"I don't deny that normally I'd rather not see any boats in this business rocked. But at the same time I'm convinced that where a high viewer rating is indicated—here's Caleb the sordid capitalist again—boats certainly can be rocked. My feeling is, Warren—and maybe you're way ahead of me, maybe you've already worked all this out more than you say you have—is that telling this colored lad's story exactly as it happened is the *only* way to tell it, not only because bending a fact here and there would diminish its integrity but because the truth can get us a stratospheric rating."

"You surprise me, Caleb," Weber said, and nodded to the waiter for another bloody mary. "I was waiting for you to con me out of doing the segment at all. Failing that, I was waiting for you to recommend that we have the Hamilton boy gun down a few white women and children before he bites the dust."

The smile again. "What am I going to do with you? I've already admitted that I didn't want 'Moore' on Vanguard in the first place. Now that it will be on, now that you've shown that it has viewer identification as well as quality, let's see if we can't pull out all the stops and give it the kind of muscle that will guarantee steady viewership after you've run out of the Hammond and Wells and Beaumont big-gun names—and guarantee that Foley Foods will renew for more money. Don't skirt a single fact. But, by the same token, don't stack all the cards on the side of the Negroes."

"Oh? Where should I stack the cards?"

"That's my point—nowhere. On neither side. Obviously, if you're doing a show involving the Negroes, you can't offend Negro consumers—nor, morally, should you. But if truth is what we're seeking to show, it strikes me that you're obligated to show both sides of the story, the white side as well as the black. Otherwise, it's another tract, and that can't serve justice, let alone truth."

"I'm not so sure the case was ever that tidy, Caleb—a legitimate white side and a legitimate black side. There are plenty of whites who thought, and still think, that the entire case was a disgrace, that too many whites connected with it were thoroughly despicable sons of bitches."

"Probably so. But why leave yourself and the series open, vulnerable to unnecessary criticism? Why let anyone accuse you of presenting the story in anything but a balanced way? Balance always strengthens truth."

"Well, let's see. We could turn the second half of the hour over to Soul of America. They could come out with the white pillow cases over their heads and explain, in a balanced way, why the Hamilton kid should've been lynched instead of shot."

"Oh, stop that nonsense—that's not worthy of you. What I suggest—strongly suggest—is that you let the chips fall where they may, in the interests of arriving at the truth, and at the same time buy yourself a little legal protection. I can think of one way. Find the one man who knows the truth, the only man who knows exactly what happened."

"Who would that be?"

"Put on your thinking cap, Warren. The policeman. I think his name is White."

The waiter brought the second bloody mary, and Weber stared at his glass. "Caleb," he said slowly, "I wouldn't believe that vicious *schlang* if he told me water was wet."

Atwood raised his menu and studied it. "All right. I almost expected that reaction," he said.

"What reaction, that that cop is a vicious *schlang?*"

"No, whatever a *schlang* is. That a liberal—you call yourself a liberal—listens to all viewpoints, every single viewpoint except the ones he doesn't happen to agree with. That's unfortunate. And, if I may be perfectly frank, that's why liberals are morally bankrupt.

They cry for truth, but only their own truth. I admit I'm disappointed. Believe it or not, there are aspects of the liberalist philosophy that I've always respected, and there's a part of me that's wanted for years to be a liberal. But you liberals won't let me be one—you're all high-sounding and yet you all invariably insult my intelligence."

It was Weber's turn to smile. "Lefty Caleb—well, my stars and garters. Tell me, is the rumor true that your hero Willard Chase Cunningham is really a Communist posing as a reactionary in order to ruin the reactionary cause?"

Atwood's eyes left the menu. "My *hero* Willard Cunningham? Now what's that supposed to mean?"

"Well, sidekick if not hero. Don't you both drink out of the same cup?"

"Ah, there we have it—guilt by association is evil, except when the liberals go in for it. I deal with Cunningham because he sponsors some Vanguard properties. I also deal with *your* hero from Foley Foods, Owen Claffee, who's a member of SANE and some other peculiar organizations—I've dealt with him because he's a Vanguard sponsor. It happens that there are some things about Cunningham I agree with and some I don't. What's your inference, that I beat the drums for Soul of America?"

"No, no," said Weber, slightly amused. "I'm merely curious about your selling me the cop who, coincidentally or not, is Willard Cunningham's manservant."

Yet another Atwood smile. "Let's not go back to being our old temperamental adolescent selves with each other, Warren. I'm not *selling* you that policeman, or anyone. I've never laid eyes on Stuart White except for newspaper pictures and once, I think, when I caught him on television. I don't know him, nor do I have any interest in knowing him. But consider it from a practical standpoint. With all sides heard, you'd run no risk of being accused of pandering to the far left. And by paying White a little money and making him a technical adviser, you—"

"*Technical* adviser? Are you out of—"

"Let me finish. I assume the man needs money and an ego boost. By giving him a fancy title like that, and a few dollars, you're home clear as far as the threat of a lawsuit is concerned. And don't think there won't be libel lawyers honing their blades for you otherwise."

Weber shook his head in mock wonder. "You're a thinker and planner, aren't you, Caleb?"

"That's all I'm paid for. Warren, if you feel you can honorably approach that segment without consulting the one eyewitness to the colored boy's death, then more power to you. As you've evidently informed Rhodes more than once, 'Moore' is your baby from beginning to end. I don't care about your taking satisfaction in rubbing my nose in the fact. What I care about, what I live for, is Vanguard. And realistic thinking and realistic planning. In many ways, you and I are very much alike."

Weber grinned. "Caleb, your purity and innocence make me want to marry you."

"What?"

"Nothing. I'll give the cop some thought. Now let's find that waiter."

Even Jeanne, who had been against "Moore" in the beginning and then dead set against it because of Nash, admitted after she saw the first two segments in the GWS projection room that the show had all the elements of a hit—not only as a money-maker but as a crowd-pleaser with bite. She went further and admitted, grudgingly, that Nash, who did not appeal to her personally or as a black spokesman or any kind of spokesman, was surprisingly effective. "But don't think I'm mellowing," she cautioned. "I'd say Lucifer was an effective television actor if he was. That doesn't mean I buy his hostility toward air-conditioning."

The incessant publicity barrage paid off, or promised to. Unethically, perhaps, Weber screened the segments for Gar Kelly of Norfolk Tobacco and Sherman Howe of Monarch Airlines, at different times, not telling either man about the other, certainly not telling Owen Claffee. Each man enthusiastically offered to top Foley Foods' budget for the second thirteen weeks. "Top it? You'll have to do better than top it," Weber half-jokingly declared. "If I decide to take this gold mine out of Foley's hands after the first thirteen weeks, I'll expect you to turn the keys to your store over to me." There had been times when he had broken his neck trying to stop money men like Kelly and Howe from yawning. Now they were watching him yawn. If he sensed, by the time the fourth or fifth segment was safely in the can, that Foley Foods just might have half a hesitation at renewing at a hell of a lot sweeter budget, here was insurance, cushy, nose-thumbing insurance.

All his energy went into the Hamilton story.

Jesse was pleased, which pleased Weber inordinately, and became cooperative and pliable on the set, which pleased Jay Eaton. Weber did not discuss the small, possible likelihood of conferring, or having someone with an iron stomach confer, with Stuart White. It seemed unlikely that such an assignation couldn't be brought off to "Moore"'s advantage. But Weber could not dismiss Caleb Atwood's notion, harebrained and more than conceivably self-serving and gradually sensible as it was, because gradually it *was* sensible. Because a signed release by the cop, if he knows how to write his name, *will* take the worry of a nuisance suit off my shoulders, Weber thought. And because I must be consistent, or I'm nothing. I wear these bright signs reading *Kiss Me, I'm a Liberal*. And what's a liberal? A conservative, we are taught in the Gospel According to Saint Smug, is a gracious thunderbolt with 3.2 children; has a wife who guiltily brands herself a nymphomaniac if she desires sexual intercourse 1.3 times over any single calendar and/or fiscal year and whose charitable works include the strenuous protesting of UNICEF sending milk to any baby born under the hammer-and-sickle emblem; is urged by Jehovah, the Great Capitalist in the Sky, to abhor sin, sloth, and the remains of Eleanor Roosevelt; is satisfied in his heart of superior hearts that indolence is the sole cause of poverty; is a compassionate fighter in God's Holy Crusade to save mankind by comforting the comfortable and afflicting the afflicted.

Neat. Swell. But what's a liberal? A liberal is supposed to be Saint Smug's natural enemy. A liberal's mission is to be curious, intelligently and selectively, and committed to truth, without prior, set postures of arrogance.

Of course Atwood's notion can't be sloughed off simply because I don't like or trust him. If I sincerely want truth, then I can't arrive at it without finding Stuart White.

Finding him may involve searching through several reams of used toilet paper. But would Charlie Gundersen have been content to give the final television word on Jan Masaryk's suicide without first checking out anyone who had been, could have been, in the room when Masaryk had supposedly jumped?

He phoned Atwood. "I'm willing to see Stuart White," he said. "What's your pipeline to him?"

"Pipeline? I've never laid eyes on him."

"I know, you told me that at lunch last week. You know my style, Caleb—when my mind's made up about something, I get awfully impatient twiddling my thumbs waiting for the action to begin. Can you lay your eyes on him—like, today? Or can you lay eyes on someone who can lay eyes on him?

"That's—possible. I can have a discreet phone call or two placed."

"There's my bully courier."

"Moore" 's fourth show's guest star was Donna McLerie, a popular lowbrow comedienne who had never played a straight role before and, until Weber's offbeat casting brainstorm, had never been thought by anyone to be anything but a highly competent pie-in-the-face thrower and receiver. Jesse disliked her from the outset. "Get her off me, or get somebody else for the part," he demanded of Weber. "I got no love for white women. I 'specially got no love for white women that wanna cozy up to me 'cause I'm a black stud."

"Don't pat yourself on the back," Weber said, chuckling. "Donna enjoys being studded. Pigmentation is quite irrelevant, believe me."

"I don't dig this story, either, while we're at it. I didn't go for it when I read it, and I go for it even less now. What're we doin' with a *funny* story on a show that's supposed to be anything but funny?"

"Change of pace; we can't have gloom and doom week in and week out. And the script's not meant to be funny. There are jokes, because jokes fit part of the characterization, but it's not ha-ha funny. Which intrigues me, by the way, now that you bring it up. Didn't you start out as a comic?"

"That was a long while a—"

"Yes, but what was wrong with it? Your *shtick* was that you said important things with jokes. It was a damned good *shtick*."

"That was when I didn't know any better. There's no room or time for jokes with black people these days. We been laughin' and singin' and dancin' for you all long enough."

"Oh, Jesse, you really can be a pompous jerk when you set your mind to it. What is it you *want?* I'm working on the Hamilton show. I'd start the shooting today if we had a script, but we don't have one yet, not one that's thought out and ready to go. We do have this one, the McLerie one, and so we work while we're waiting for the big one to be right. When are you and I going to stop circling each other? This series is working fine, and I'm being as cooperative as I know how to be. I've given in on just about everything to keep you happy. What more can I do?"

"You can keep me posted on the Hamilton story. If this *is* the big one, I have a right to have a hand in it."

Weber sighed. "Again with the ultimata. Which hand are you offering? I won't fire Eaton and let you direct it. I won't fire Wes Kirby and let you shoot it. I won't fire Montgomery and Trowbridge and let you write it. I could fire myself, if that would reassure you."

"I wanna be let in on what's happenin'—after all, I did more'n follow the case in the papers. Who you castin' for the boy's sister, for instance?"

"Robin? Nobody. She has no place in the story."

"She doesn't, huh? A sister who bugs off when her family needs her most, who cops out when there's trouble? No place for that in the story?"

"What's your interest? Would you just happen to have an actress lady friend who's breaking into show business and who'd be perfect in the part?"

"No, but I'm interested. I'd be interested in what'd happen if you told your white nigger Robin to come out of hiding and play the part herself."

"Are you serious?"

"Day and night. I'm serious about everything, day and night."

It was a masterpiece of an idea; it was so unthinkable it was a masterpiece; the ratings would be so high that Atwood would wet himself. "What makes you think Robin would consent to do it, assuming it wasn't in the worst possible taste, which it is?"

Nash frowned. "Consent? Now I wonder why she wouldn't consent to stand on her head from now till Armageddon if you told her to. Aren't you the cat she owes everything to, body and soul? And why would she object to playing a part with truth in it? Is she afraid people will get the idea she's a nigger?"

"It wouldn't work," said Weber, tasting the publicity coup of Robin in "Moore." "For one reason, forget the gross of other reasons, bringing you and her together on the same show would be like assigning a bridal suite to Ben-Gurion and Nasser."

"Oh, it'd never happen—by the time you'd pry her away for two minutes from haulin' in all that gold she'd never of seen if she hadn't been a murdered kid's big sister, by that time we'd all be well into the ninety-ninth show. It was just an idea. Like you say, it'd be in bad taste. Bad taste—that means you'd maybe be afraid to tell her what to do, what with all the gold she's coinin' for the two of you."

"Christ, Nash, one of these days—"

"Uh-huh, I'm an uppity nigger. But I'm a *black* nigger, and that's better'n bein' a white one. Though your hot-shot new picture star might disagree."

Atwood phoned. White was out of town, he was informed, but was expected back in several days.

"Inform your informant that I'll be out of town for several days, too," said Weber, "and that I'll request a holy audience with Mr. White when *I* get back."

"Done and done, Warren. You're using your head," Atwood said, sounding happy. "The simple release won't be any problem— it can be drawn up right away and signed before the two of you meet. Any suggestion on what to pay him, to bind the deal?"

"I'll pay him what his time is worth, if the dickering stays within the realm of practicability. I may even go as high as two cents. Oh, hell, I don't know. You work that out."

On impulse—*will I ever live long enough to do anything big except by impulse?*—he directed Jeanne to make a jet reservation to L.A. He then wrote a letter to Karen, in care of Claridge's, London, told her he loved her and the children, and vowed he would revere and nourish her if she and the children would take the next flight home.

Then, because he was afraid to be alone, he called Gloria Barclay to say he would be right over. A telephone operator, not the answering service, reported that the number was disconnected till further notice. He called Jeri Paine, who was in and who wanted to be taken to a discotheque. "I want to come to your place," he said, "and have you serve me a drink and scramble two eggs."

"What am I, a cook?"

"Yes, a cook, and a faithful lover. For two hundred dollars, I want you to be both."

"That's always the way you come on, like I'm a prostitute."

"But that's what you are, my darling, that's where you shine. You're surely not a dancer. What will it take to make you admit you're a prostitute, two dollars tacked on to the two hundred?"

She hung up.

Weber, weary to the soul, was about to phone The Bringer to bring him a companion, preferably one who knew how to scramble eggs. He raised the receiver, but replaced it. He didn't want eggs. He didn't want cold thighs. "Relate" was Karen's showy word. Screw relating. If relating to another human being was a matter of climbing over brambles when he was this weary, then screw all relating. Rudi drove him home, where he told Ernest to stir a strenuous martini and told Mrs. Nielsen to scramble some eggs, and undressed in his and Karen's bedroom. He drank Ernest's martini, but he was sound asleep when the eggs were ready.

Eighteen

ON A FREE SATURDAY, two weeks before the completion of *Play with Fire*, Robin donned smoked glasses and rode a taxi to an address on Hawthorne Street in Watts, where she asked the aproned Negro lady who opened the door if this was where Sarah Glenda Hicks lived. Two weeks or more before, she had read a badly spelled letter, written to her in pencil and on lined paper, from a Mrs. Randolph Hicks. Mrs. Hicks had never asked a famous person for any favor, she wrote, but she was begging Miss Hamilton for a favor now. Her boy, Randolph, Jr., had died in the service. Her husband, Randolph, Sr., was dead, too. Her girl, Sarah Glenda, fourteen come October, was at home in bed with the kidney disease Miss Hamilton had been on the TV talking about, and the doctor said that Sarah Glenda had half a year to live at most, and Sarah Glenda had all of Miss Hamilton's photos and magazine stories and played her record album all the time and didn't know she was going to die and wanted to be a big colored star just like Miss Hamilton. Could Miss Hamilton find it in her heart to come and visit the child if only for a minute or two, not bring anything, it had to be understood that Mrs. Hicks wasn't asking for anything but a minute or two of her time?

"Law, law, you just come right in!" the lady cried, wiping her hands on her apron and then touching her black-gray hair with her fingers, as though trying to recall if it was combed. "You did come, Miz Hamilton, bless God you did come, now didn'cha? Ain't that just the grandest!"

"I'm sorry I took so long," Robin said shyly in the parlor that was tiny yet spotless, and remembered with shame that she had put off coming because she couldn't have been sure if the request was legitimate and, more, because she had dreaded the prospect of going to Watts which, she had heard, looked better than Harlem from a passing car but was Harlem, nonetheless. She had, she knew, heard correctly. Poverty was everywhere around and in this house. The house was clean, as Mama kept her own home clean ("You keeps your home clean jus' like you got to keep your soul clean," Mama would say, "and, 'sides, you never know who's maybe gonna pay you a call"), but the poverty, the sin and the degradation of poverty, was filthy, and Robin wished she had had less showoff-expensive clothes to wear here.

Mrs. Hicks offered her some homemade fudge, and chattered her appreciation, interrupting herself after each dozenth word to apologize for the looks of the house, and soon Robin knew she was a good woman, not seeking a handout. Someone—who?—had warned her long before her second television show that she would be barraged by people seeking handouts, and Someone had been right; at least half of her mail was loaded with hard-luck stories and pleas for as much money as she could afford by tomorrow at the latest. But Mrs. Hicks, younger than Mama, almost as stout, not as bright as Mama but every bit as real and recognizably decent, was not a leech. The lady repeated everything she had written in the letter, in fuller detail, and then excused herself to go and prepare Sarah Glenda for the most grandest news that had ever come to Hawthorne Street.

Robin waited uneasily, walking from corner to corner in the little parlor with the stained flowered wallpaper, touching the glass candy dish with the inscription *Ezekiel Baptist Church, Moline* printed on its face, examining the two large framed charcoal drawings of an old colored man and an old colored lady, hearing, "No, Mama! Really! Here? Mama, don't you make up no jokes like that, now!" from the other side of the thin wall. Then Mrs. Hicks came back, her too-old eyes bright with happy tears, and took

Robin into a bedroom, where a homely girl, thirteen years old and looking both ten and eighty, almost lost in the great brass bed, gawked in awe and disbelief. Robin, shoulders straightened, nearly as ill at ease as the girl, went to her with an artificial smile she hoped wasn't transparent, and said, "Hello, Sarah Glenda. I'm Robin."

"Oh my, oh my," the girl breathed. "Oh my."

"Can I sit with you for a little while?"

"Oh my, Miss Hamilton, I can't stand it, you come here to see *me?*"

"That's what I did," Robin said, and sat in the straight-backed chair near the bed. "I hear you're planning to be a big star, is that right?"

It took five minutes to reassure the girl that Robin was real and that she was interested in any young lady who wanted to be a star. She stayed for an hour, a thoroughly uncomfortable hour, for she lied throughout, about how hard work and clean living had made her a star and how hard work and clean living could let Sarah Glenda be anything she wished to be, about how pretty and fresh and intelligent the homely, almost slow-witted, dying girl was, about how being colored no longer stood in the way of a young person's realizing a dream, about the furs and beautiful clothes and fine restaurants and attention that were the benefits of stardom, about how she would help Sarah Glenda become a famous star. Finally she said, "I have to go now, but I don't know when I had a nicer time. Now you just remember one thing, if you don't re- member anything else. If you want something, anything, hard enough, you can get it, you can do anything you want to do. The first thing you want to do is get up out of that old bed just as soon as you can. You have a whole lot of friends, and I'm one of them. Mind your mama, like I've always tried to mind mine, and don't ever think anything but happy thoughts, and remember I'm going to help you earn lots of fine clothes and a big house. You hear me now?"

The girl nodded, still awed.

Robin kissed her, sickened by the death she smelled, and murmured, "Be a good girl and strong, darling. I'll be back to see you, and we'll go to the beach and lie in the sun and we'll drink so much cold lemonade we'll get sick to our stomach."

In the parlor and then on the stoop in front of the house, she was impatient as Mrs. Hicks kept blessing her. She asked if the child had been seen by more than one doctor. "Well, there wasn't but one," the woman admitted. "Dr. Carley, the welfare doctor they give us. He's just the nicest man—"

"Is he a specialist in this sickness she has?"

"No, but they tells me this Dr. Carley, he's a good doctor, and he do come ever by 'n' by to look in on us. And our church, they been so *nice*, they're the ones give us the li'l television set Sarah Glenda sets so much store by, and the li'l Victrola. And Miz Smiff from the parish, she's the fine lady went out an' bought Sarah Glenda your nice phonograph record. Oh, we got such nice people helpin' us, bless God, an' then you come, a real tonic, tha's what you been, a real tonic—"

"Has she been in a hospital?"

"Oncet. Uh-huh, oncet. They treat her purty good an' they study her, but tha's when Dr. Carley says ain't nothin' more to help, she be jus' as good off in her own bed. So I bring her back, an' I prays day an' night, night an' day the Good Lord look down on us, so's—"

"Mrs. Hicks, I met a doctor, a Dr. Mosher, when I was on that telethon for this kidney disease. He's a specialist, and if anybody could help Sarah Glenda, he could. What I want you to do, I want you to let her go into a hospital where this Dr. Mosher is and have him take some tests, or whatever. Will you let me call him and make some arrangements?"

"Oh, Miz Hamilton, that'd cost *money!* I couldn't have you nor nobody else takin' on a burden—"

"It wouldn't cost anything. Dr. Mosher would do it as a favor to me," Robin lied. "All right?"

"Ah, bless God, bless you, Miz Hamilton, bless God. I been

prayin' and prayin' for help for my li'l girl, but I couldn't never ask nobody big to go out their way. You a joy, a Christian joy, I gonna ask the Lord to bless you all you' days."

A taxi was not available for blocks after blocks of walking through Watts, so Robin took a bus until she spotted a taxi stand. In the cab, riding away, she cried freely. She cried with rage at Mrs. Randolph Hicks, Sr., for having allowed segregation to grind her down to the point where she had not sought all avenues of help that might save or prolong her child's life, for having believed that dumb darkies were supposed to be thankful for crumbs. And she cried with rage at her own dishonesty, at having filled a dying child with an hour of white fairy tales.

Returning to The Haywell, she phoned Dr. Mosher's nurse and directed that Sarah Hicks was to be admitted to Cedars of Lebanon Hospital as Dr. Mosher's patient at once, that she be given all treatment and care necessary, and that she, Robin, be billed for everything. Then, although it was Saturday, she phoned Matt Keyes, one of GWS's West Coast accountants, and directed that a thousand dollars in cash be charged against her account and dispatched immediately to Mrs. Hicks, and gave him the Watts address, and told him to tell Mrs. Hicks that the money was to be spent on necessities, including anything that might make Sarah happy. She then accepted a call from Vic Ennis, GWS's West Coast publicity man, who pleaded with her to reconsider and go to the Standish party in Pacific Palisades, where everybody who *mattered* would be, and where her appearance could do herself and her career and GWS a world of good. She agreed, because she had not gone to the raft of other parties since she had come to glamorous, anchorless Hollywood, and because she was weary of getting tight alone. The party was for nine o'clock, and Vic Ennis, brash and young and finger-snapping, called for her early, long before she was ready. She gave Sigrid the night off and summoned him into the bedroom, where she sat in the negligee Warren had given her on the night of the first Larry Endicott show, before a mirror, and brushed her hair. Her back was to him, though she saw every clothed twitch of him in the mirror, and she said, looking at him and at the drink on the dresser in front of her, "I'll bet you work at your job every minute. What does your wife say about you being out, working, on a Saturday night?"

"We're separated. Ah—maybe you know who she is. Sandra Doherty? She was in the last Presley picture?"

He was too heavy, gross, too jowly for his age, and he was not attractive, and for a moment she could not remember if he was Ennis or Gaynor, and so he was exactly the right man to be cheap with, to be cheap for. She was about to part the folds of the negligee and let it fall from her shoulders and down her back. She was about to ask him if he loved her and if the party would wait.

And, because he would not be able to understand, because he might think she really wanted him, she caught herself in time.

As she tried to remember his question, he asked, "So, ah, what do you say? We better head on out to good old P.P., right? Fashionably late is one thing, but showing up when the band's playing 'Three O'Clock in the Morning,' that I call bad form."

"You're right," she said, and brushed her hair more quickly. "I'll be ready soon, Norman."

"Vic."

"I'm sorry. Vic. I won't be long at all."

"Yeah. Well, let's snap it up, doll. Everybody who *matters* is waiting for you out in good old P.P."

In good old P.P. the celebrities swarmed around her and around themselves, and she was asked who would be Number One in her Hall of Fame, Joe Louis or Jackie Robinson, and she drank and answered, "Stepin Fetchit, because if there hadn't been a Stepin Fetchit there wouldn't have been a Sidney Poitier." A lady celebrity said, "You're putting us on," and a man celebrity looked thoughtful and said, "No, wait, Kim, there's something in what Miss Jefferson says. That's a *fascinating* point, *fascinating*." A nonmale noncelebrity kept serving her drinks, and she drank. A non-female noncelebrity asked her what her next picture was going to be. *"Snow White,"* she answered. "I play the title role."

"You poor thing."

"What?"

"How you must have been hurt—wounded, *crucified*—to say a thing like that. How I pray I could do anything, *anything*, to right the wrongs you and your people have suffered under we fucking white storm troopers all these years. Listen, have you tried Madge's fondue yet? It'll send you smack out of your *skull*."

A lady celebrity—Madge, the hostess, wearing toreador pants, a too-tight sweater, a too-tight smile, and hoop earrings, waddled to her after half an hour and declared, "We're all delirious that you came, darling. Vic Ennis says you'd be delirious to sing a couple of chunes. Yessee? Let's see, where did Barney the bowlegged piano-player disappear to? You wait right here, darling, and—"

"You hold your breath, darling."

"Hmmm?"

"How many songs are you interested in?"

"Oh, I can't project. Till you've had enough, till the kiddies here start to get loopy and disruptive, I don't know, whatever you say."

"Fine. I charge a thousand dollars a song."

"Hmmm?"

"A thousand dollars. I've committed eight songs to memory. That's eight thousand dollars. Do you have a check for eight thousand dollars, hmmm?"

"What are you saying?"

"Madge, Midge, Smadge-Smidge, whatever your name is, you quit looking around and look at me."

"I'm *looking!*"

"I don't want to sing."

"Well, Jesus God, darling, if you don't *want* to, who's around here to *force* you? I just thought you might *want* to."

"I just thought, after an hour here, my hostess would've come up to say hello before this, and would've said something besides, 'Get ready to sing.' Madge, Midge, I'm talking to you now and you're not even listening to me, you're looking all around, every-where but at me."

"Oh, God, there come the Barretts, and look at the May's base-ment Mainbocher she has on! Oh, God. What were you saying, darling, hmmm?"

Robin went to Vic Ennis. "Would you mind taking me home?" she asked.

"Home? This early, home? All these big people here, are you nuts?"

"Yes, home. Or I telephone Mr. Weber and tell him you gave me an argument."

"Home," he said.

The next morning was Sunday and Robin went to the first Protestant church nearest to The Haywell. She was not moved nor touched, but she could imagine Mama sitting beside her, and she enjoyed the enjoyment of the congregation. She went back to The Haywell, where the desk clerk handed her a message from Verne Hightower with a San Francisco telephone number. Her vision blurred, and excitement made her legs wobbly as she rushed up-stairs, and she tried to breathe.

Verne was reserved, though not really formal. "I plan to be in L.A. this afternoon," he said. "I'm calling at the last minute, but would you be free for a late lunch?"

"O God, Verne . . . Oh, you called . . . I'm so happy you—I treated you like dirt and you've forgiven me, I'm so happy you called!"

They met at the hotel's coffee shop at three o'clock, and he looked at her as if he liked her, and Robin warned herself: he came all this way to see you but not to listen to you moan and groan and gush and carry on like a baby. Don't ruin this. And she talked, and knew she was doing everything wrong, everything, and could not stop. She had missed him terribly, she declared, not once but surely too many times. She explained the night in New York without explaining anything, for she could tell him about all the men since Jerry Sorin but not about that drunk, unbelievable minute in Warren's guest room as he had waited in Warren's parlor, and she babbled apologies for that disastrous ride in the chauffeur-driven car, and said, "I'm so grateful you forgive me."

"It's not a matter of forgiving or not forgiving," Verne said. "Or of apologizing. I'm just interested to know why we were getting along so well on the way to that party and why you behaved like some half-dollar tramp when we left it."

"Why didn't you get out of the car with me and find out?"

"Because I decided you were too screwed up to bother with."

"What changed your mind?" Robin asked him, and asked herself, Why am I all of a sudden sounding snippy?

"Your letter, partly. My waking up, mainly. You were calling for help and it took me a while to hear."

"Yes. It took you weeks and weeks to hear. It took you till today to come to me."

"Easy, Robin," he cautioned softly. "I don't like to be nagged."

Sensing his annoyance, scared of it, she lowered her eyes and nodded.

"I could say I flew here expressly to see you, but that wouldn't be true. There's some work I'm in town for. Not everything revolves around you, young lady, although I can appreciate that it must be a job to resist believing all your publici—"

"Why are we fighting?"

He laughed. "We do seem to be clawing, don't we?"

The studio kept a convertible at Robin's disposal in the hotel garage. Driving to a quiet beach, Verne explained that he was in Los Angeles to cover a Roger Beckley for Senator fund-raising dinner tonight at the Roosevelt; he would be staying there overnight and flying back home tomorrow. They walked in the mid-afternoon sun in bare feet and they talked, now freely, now guardedly, now freely again—Robin about Mama and Roland Lee and Jesse and most of the men, most but not Warren, about needing to find out who she was; Verne about his wife Joetta whom he'd loved and his little girl Diane whom he worshiped, about the work that had sustained him and kept him from going under after Joetta died, about the world he wanted, made up of the best and most productive that was in the Jesse Nashes.

Then they found themselves at a part of the beach where there was no life but theirs, and he was kissing her, Verne was kissing her.

It was meant to be a peaceful kiss, a kiss of affection, simple, innocent of ardor. It started that way. And it might have ended simply, without flares. But Robin held him and would not let him stop kissing her, and they sank to the sand in embrace and then it was Verne who would not stop until his hands pressed and fondled her and those hands released her breasts from her bra and held them and he kissed them, Verne breathing hard, all of him hard. She was ashamed that there had been any man before him, and she was alarmed that she felt love though not passion, but her fingers searched the muscled ridges of his back, and she breathed hard, too, and whimpered, so he would think he had set her on fire.

He stopped. He kissed her once more, and then sat up so that he could not touch her.

"We were talking about—what—something," he said.

Robin sat up, too, troubled. "What happened?"

"I almost loused us up once and for all, that's what happened. Here in the sand, with this watch saying, 'Get it over with fast because you have to hurry back to the Roosevelt for that dinner at seven-fifteen on the dot.' My mistake, Robin. Bad mistake."

He'll leave me, she thought in horror. He'll take me home, and all he'll remember is that I moan and groan about myself and all he'll think of me as is a drag, and he'll just leave me. "Fast is all right," she said quietly, desperately. "Anything you do is all right, don't you know that?"

"No, it can't be just for me. Lord, I do sound pompous and Boy Scouty. Let's wait and—"

"You want me, Verne."

"Of course I—"

"And I want you. I need you, I love you, I want to love you—here, now, fast, slow, any way, any way is right." Swiftly she brought her blouse off and brushed the unclasped bra away and thrust herself at him, into his arms, and he seemed stupified, but for only a moment. He said her name. He touched her hair, and cupped her cheeks in the damp palms of his hands. And then those hands were stroking heat into her flesh, and clothes disappeared by those hands, and his weight was on her and presently in her, and she could hear the half-spoken words of endearment. Meeting his every rise and fall, matching him stroke for stroke, holding him, loving him, she whispered, "Darling, love, darling," baffled, oppressed that this was Verne, Verne who would lead her out of the tunnel, far from the halls of mirrors, and that she could only make dishonest sounds and only pretend to be stirred and shaken by the urgent force of him that would soon shoot a lava of love into her. Impossible, impossible, men I didn't like, men I didn't know, I was close to orgasm the second after they started, and there's no passion now, only love, but you will never know that, dearest Verne. Here. Feel how I squeeze you. See how I move so I can get you deeper, deeper. Ah, I need you, need you, Verne dearest, here they go high in the air and wrapping tight around your spine so every stroke will be easier for you.

"Oh, Robin, baby . . ."

"Yes, darling, yes."

"Trying hold back . . ."

"Don't, don't, don't, I'm ready, darling, you're driving me crazy, say 'love', don't say you love me, you don't have to say that, just say love." Say you love me. Say something to help me, what kind of fantastic perversity is this, you're scalding me and I can't feel you, I can't feel anything except that I'm a freak, a phony, not a woman. Love, you're saying. Oh, yes, keep saying it, oh how good that you're saying it and saying it. You're hurting my breast. You're hurting me. Enjoy me, darling Verne. Oh, you are, you are, you are, he's loving me, he loves me, does he know, will he know I'm lying, that I'm hugging him and I don't feel anything?

They held each other when it was done. Will I ever know him well enough to tell him that good men are the only men I can love and strangers are the only men I can come with?

They were silent for many minutes on the drive back to the city, and Robin felt him still inside her and no longer near her, certain she did not have him, certain she did and would, certain of everything, certain of nothing. The car radio was on, and soon they heard Robin Hamilton singing "If I Were a Bell."

"Now this is what I call a small world," Verne declared, visibly brightening.

"Looks like you can't escape me," she said, certain she should be light, certain she should be serious.

Say "I wouldn't want to," she prayed. He didn't. He listened with her till the end of the record, and listened to the disk jockey ramble on about Robin Hamilton the overnight sensation, and asked, "How does that make you feel—to turn a knob and hear yourself? Bowled over?"

"You bowl me over more. I shouldn't admit things like that, should I? A girl is supposed to keep a man guessing."

He just smiled, and Robin hated him for not telling her he was wild about her. "I wish I could've invited you to go with me to this dinner tonight," he remarked. "I couldn't, anyway, because we working stiffs aren't allowed to bring guests. And, anyway, I couldn't see you going ray-ray-ray during a bunch of political speeches."

"I could, too! Who—what did you say this man's name is that wants to be a senator? Roger Buckley?"

Verne's quick glance of surprise conveyed that she could as well have asked "Who's George Washington?" "Beckley," he corrected. "Roger Beckley's the Negro congressman who thinks he has a chance for the Senate. And he just may have, with luck and with enough support."

"I wish I could go. I'd keep out of everybody's way, and I wouldn't ask dumb questions."

"You'd show up and they'd all ignore Beckley and elect you senator on the spot."

"Oh, yeah, fat chance."

"You'd be the best-built senator in history."

"Then you admit it. You like my build."

"What's not to like?"

"Did you like it, Verne? Was I good? Did I disappoint you?"

"Dammit, Robin, will you stop acting like some starved waif?"

"I'm sorry . . ."

He smiled again, but this time he freed his right hand from the wheel just long enough to playfully muss her hair. Everything was right again. The gesture meant that everything would always be right.

At The Haywell she asked, "Will you come back, when you've finished work over there?"

"What time do you have to get up in the morning?"

"Early, but that doesn't matter. I can get by on five minutes sleep a night. What does your room at the Roosevelt care if it isn't slept in tonight?"

"I'll see what time we break up. If it's going to be too late—sometimes these dinners never break up—I'll call you."

"Don't call, Verne. Just come." It was the worst thing possible to say, she knew, but she said, "I need you. I don't want to be alone."

". . . Okay."

Robin wanted him to use the convertible to get to the hotel, but he said he would just as soon leave it in the Haywell garage and take a cab, because L.A. evening traffic was never a pleasure to negotiate. She went to her suite, a girl again, a nearly fulfilled girl who must get ready for a heavy date at home with a swell young man. Sigrid asked if Miss Hamilton would care for a drink. "No, I'll have a chop, and salad, and some tea," said Robin, for the only people who drank alone were lonely people. She had Verne. Not yet, not completely, not so he knew it. But she had him, and she would never have to drink whiskey, or sleep with strangers, or be frightened, ever again.

Sigrid served her in bed. She ate as she read tomorrow's scenes, and thought about the flight she would make to San Francisco, Verne's stomping ground, the minute the movie was done. She would tell Warren she wasn't going to start work in a new movie in thirty days. She would tell Warren about Verne and how important Verne was, and if Warren didn't like it he could lump it—Warren, who was so sure he knew what was best for her, from a contract she should sign to the kind of shoes she should wear. She would prove to Verne that she was a good girl, really, a good person, and his little daughter Diane would love her and she would love Diane, and Verne would marry her and she would give him lots more children, and she would never again be lonely and scared. Working at memorizing one of tomorrow's scenes with Sunny Storm, she again felt Verne inside her, and she pressed her legs together to hold him tighter, to relive today on the beach and to share it with him. The heat that had not gathered then gathered now.

Please hurry, Verne, she thought.

He called at eleven to say it looked as if it would be well past midnight before he could get away, that it probably would be wiser to see her next when they could have, say, a long weekend together, when they wouldn't have to be so conscious of calendars and clocks.

"I see," she said coldly, watching the ship sail. "You could've been more honest before, you know. If you didn't have any intention of coming, you could've told me so before."

"Quit that, Robin," he said, and she could hear voices in the background. "I did plan to come, but I have to leave first thing in the morning for a big work day, and you have to go to work early, too. We'll see each other before you go back to New York. That's a promise."

He means it. He's got to mean it. "You—you promise now?"

"Yes. I liked being with you today, Robin. I sincerely mean that. Look, I've got to get back. Sleep well, hear?"

When she heard Sigrid's light switch off, she went to the parlor and drank a little ginger ale and a lot of whiskey. The movie on television was *Love Finds Andy Hardy*, with Mickey Rooney, Judy Garland, and Lana Turner. They all looked so very young.

The end of *Play with Fire* was to be delayed a week because the director, Leo Osgood, decided that Robin should sing an additional number and be written into two additional scenes, and that involved shifting and reshooting some scenes already shot. Robin liked the decision, for, though there were members of the company who snubbed her and whom she therefore had to snub in return, there also were people like Sunny Storm who accepted her and warmed her, people who made her believe with their compliments that she had skill and worth. And she liked the decision, too, for it meant she would be on the same coast with Verne, who was bound to write or call her soon, that much longer.

But Warren, reached by phone, would have none of it. "I smell Sol Aaron's fine old Italian hand in all of this," Warren objected, "and I'm going to phone him and say no, with some choice four-letter words. He sees you're money in the bank, and he's losing you after this picture, and he wants to squeeze all the goodies he can out of you for the same flat sum he's paying you."

"What if you get him to pay more?"

"How much more? Twenty million more? Not worth it—you have fatter fish to fry away from Aaron's studio. Don't you say anything to Osgood or Aaron or anyone—I'll handle everything."

"Warren, I met this young man who—"

"You've heard me now, haven't you? If anyone says 'boo' to you, you refer them to me. I have to get off the phone now, Robin, to call Aaron. I'll be out there, first chance I get."

Warren called her the very next day. He said he would catch a plane the following morning, not to see Aaron, whom he had set straight, but to see Robin. There was something exciting he had to discuss with her.

Again Robin started to talk about Verne. She didn't. It could wait a day, and it was a subject too big, too important, to talk about on a long-distance telephone.

That was the day Sol Aaron, the lemony-looking little man with the old-fashioned pince-nez, asked her to leave the set for a few minutes to come to his office. She went because Mr. Aaron had been kind to her in many small ways, had gone out of his way to make her as comfortable as possible at Cambridge Pictures. He showed her his desk photographs of Mrs. Aaron and his late, sainted mother and his grandchildren, he showed her the framed commendation given him by the NAACP, he told her rather wistfully that he regretted "usually nice" Warren Weber's lack of cooperation, told her he hoped she would never forget that she'd got her start in motion pictures at Cambridge, and then patted her breast and told her he was a very lonely man and asked her to be kind and considerate, maybe tonight. Robin thanked him and said she was going to be married immediately after the movie was finished.

That was the day she received a snide, insulting letter from a civil rights organization, "congratulating" her for being the only prominent black entertainer in or around Los Angeles to refuse to appear at its benefit next Tuesday night. Robin had planned to appear, but Ronnie Haley's Hollywood office had checked her calendar and discovered that she had been booked weeks before to appear at another benefit on that evening. She had sent the organization money and a personal letter of explanation and apology, and the sarcastic tone of the reply hurt.

And that was the day the letter from Verne arrived. She had written to him, four night before, because she had not been able to reach him by telephone. Nervous, neglected, not entirely sober, she had alternately called him the only man she would ever love and criticized him for always being off somewhere when—didn't he know?—she loved him, needed him, needed his strength and goodness. Waking the next morning she was sure the letter had been wrong, but she remembered having dropped the letter in the hotel's mail chute.

> *Robin*, his letter read,
> *I have of course not been honest with you.*
> *There are some couples who are simply not right for each other, and never can be, no matter how hard either or both tries. I am fond of you, as you are of me, but we are two such people, for a number of reasons that can't be changed or altered, and I am writing you this letter, after a too-long stretch of vacillation, to tell you we won't be seeing each other again.*
> *You call me strong. Had I been a stronger, more sensible man, I would have known very soon after we met that there is no possibility of a future for us. I only wish I could have faced up to this early, certainly before that afternoon on the beach.*
> *It is not my right to blame you for being as needful as you are. There is, or there ought to be, some sensitive and patient man who can recognize your many admirable impulses and go about filling your needs, which to me seem bottomless. I can't help you. Nor could you help me. I want to marry again some day, because my little girl needs a mother and, I increasingly find, I don't like being unmarried. You and I never even re-motely approached the subject of marriage and, for all I know, the subject may hold no interest for you. But I am at a point in life, Robin, where the woman I get serious about must be the one I want to marry. I am being cruel, but I feel the man you want is one who will come running at a snap of your fingers.*

There was more. He wrote that he was sorry they couldn't have done better together, wished there weren't so many strikes against them. He wished her success, in her career and in life. Then there was no more letter, no more Verne.

After she had read the letter through for the eighth or eightieth time, searching for the line she had missed, the line that read April

Fool and I'll be there at once, someone knocked at her studio trailer door and called that she was wanted on the set. She stopped crying, not remembering that she had started, or when, and called back, "Have them wait. Find Miss Storm and ask her to come here."

"Mr. Osgood, he says—"

"Tell Miss Storm to come here!"

She cried again, and kept crying after Sunny Storm entered the trailer. Sunny, blonde and taffee-pull pretty, almost always good-naturedly profane, full of hang-ups, mostly over men, but a friend with lots of common sense, was instantly concerned. Robin pushed the letter across the dressing table to her and struggled to compose herself as Sunny read it. She had told Sunny everything about Verne, everything.

"The superior son of a bitch," Sunny declared.

"No . . ."

"Sticks around till he can climb in your box and then says, 'Ta ta, deary, I'm too good for you.' The stinkin' spade!"

"No, no. It's my fault. You were right all along. You kept warning me not to act so possessive."

"But he came back for more, didn't he, your dignified, holy, square professor? Your oh-so-honorable superdinge sends you packing, but he sure made sure he got laid first." Sunny knew where the whiskey was, took the bottle by its neck from the bottom drawer, and poured two stiff shots. "Here. Get a little juiced and write on the blackboard one hundred times—'No guy's worth sagging over.'" Robin took the glass, although a complex take lay ahead on the set. "You know what you do tonight, baby? You come with me. You ever been to a bang?"

"A what?"

"A bango. There's one tonight, just off the Strip. Community singing, community balling, plenty of pot but the good stuff, maybe some horse in the back room but I don't dig horse and you shouldn't, either. All the rest'll be good for what ails you."

"No, thanks."

"Oh, don't go square-hair on me. You'd be doing me a favor, besides yourself a favor, you'd be helping me and all the colored folks. I've been trying to integrate gang bangs for years. The closest I ever came was when I brought a high-yaller bull dike, but she spent the whole night cussing everybody out because she belonged to two minority groups. Whaddaya say? It's all for laughs. You could use some."

A knock at the door. "Hey, ladies, what's holdin' up the works? Mr. Osgood's yellin'!"

"You go and enjoy yourself, Sunny," said Robin. "I'll get into bed with a book."

"A book? Now that's a hell of a thing to get in bed with." Sunny Storm kissed her cheek and patted the same breast Sol Aaron had patted, and Robin sadly supposed she knew why so much of this sexpot girl's talk was peppered with ridiculing references to dikes and lezzos and butches. "Let me know if you change your mind, baby. This is a short life. If we don't get as many laughs and kicks out of it as we can, what good is it?"

"Ladies!" the man outside called. "You comin'?"

"Yeah, baby, on the double!" Sunny called back. They finished their drinks quickly. Robin, repairing her face almost as quickly, felt Sunny's hand on her hip, and saw her in the mirror, but was careful not to react. "I could skip the party tonight and you and I could have one of our own," Sunny said in a near whisper, all the breeziness gone. "You ever have a white chick? I've had a squad of spades, but never a spade chick. Might be a real kick, dig?"

"Let's go on the set," Robin said, frowning, suddenly remembering Chicago and sick Porter Blair, poor Porter Blair who had made her ill but who had not uttered a word about color. "Leo's going to have a fit."

Mercifully, Verne Hightower did not intrude on the long and difficult take. Sunny Storm was the one who was uncharacteristically out of pace and blew her lines, whereas Robin astonished herself and probably the other pros by flubbing nothing, by missing not a single cue, by taking the scene that was Sunny's and turning it into her own. Sunny, as the love-struck co-ed, wept that Danny had ditched her and was running around with other girls. Robin, as the wise friend, assured her that Danny would come back, and held her to comfort her. Sunny's monologue was long. Robin's function in the scene was to listen and say there-there. She listened with her soul exposed. After the take, when Sunny was out of earshot, Leo Osgood beamed and said, "My God, but you were gorgeous! Those *eyes*—the compassion, the empathy, the understanding, the young proud *madonna* quality that came through . . . I wanted to leave everything and go to church to beg forgiveness for getting an erection! Excuse the language, Rob. You know me."

"Yes," she said coolly. "Don't worry about me. I don't shock easily any more."

"I can't wait to see the rushes. Sunny's manager may throw up a howl, but if Wes's camera caught half of what I caught, nine-tenths of this scene'll be a series of close-ups of you."

"Do what you like. Are we done for the day? It's almost six o'clock, and my feet are sore."

Gary Hebert, a young, white, friendly-when-she-was-friendly writer who was doing a magazine article on her and who had followed her around for the past week, walked up to her as she left the set. He offered to drive her home and, on the way, eke out a bit more copy. Robin agreed, because she suspected she had been unnecessarily short and rude and not cooperative enough during the week with this not very forceful young man who was trying to earn a living, and because the chauffeur who drove her to and from the studio got on her nerves when she was alone in the back seat by gabbing on and on about how he had once been Cecil B. DeMille's favorite stunt man.

In his mauve bug of a sports car, she did not like Gary Hebert's musky cologne, or his pipe, or his tweedy clothes that seemed studied and out of keeping with his mauve car and Southern California, or the questions he clearly wanted to ask about growing up pretty in Harlem and hadn't the courage or sense to ask directly. But it was time to be pleasant with him, to stop playing smoked-glasses movie star. Verne's letter had been solemnly then defiantly torn into shreds and flushed down the studio trailer's john. Verne had not gone down with it, and maybe never would, but he was in the past now, without the help of Sunny Storm's orgies, with Robin's own determination, and she would keep him there.

"I haven't been awfully nice to you," she acknowledged to Gary Hebert, crossing her legs.

He didn't smile. He shrugged. "I've interviewed stars before. It took me a while, but I understand how many emotional pulls and pressures there can be that have nothing to do with me. Now I wear a bullet-proof vest."

"How old are you?"

"Me? Thirty. The day before yesterday, in fact."

"Happy birthday. Happily married?"

"Well, married." A glimmer of a smile. "Say, who's the interviewer here?"

"I am. I daydream sometimes that I'm a writer. I've always admired writers, if you think that can go into your story. Did you always want to be a writer?"

Robin tuned him out as he talked. She recrossed her legs and wondered if Sunny had been kidding or if there really was an orgy going on somewhere tonight. She wondered what would have happened if she'd told Sunny, "I'll go, if I can just watch." Would I go to one? If the people were just sick and not mean, if I drank enough, if no one made me smoke any marijuana or take any narcotics, would I ever try something like that? How spontaneous is it, how much of it is planned, how many people do it at one time? If you can get uninhibited enough, can you do it and not have to commit suicide the next day?

Why am I thinking about it? Why am I curious?

Because if the people aren't mean and too sick, it makes a kind of sense. The more the merrier. The more people there are, the fewer names, the fewer faces. The more people doing it, the less dirty you have to feel. It must be something to do it and not feel dirty.

"—and that's about all there is to tell, that's how I got into this writing game," said Gary Hebert. "There's The Haywell."

"Would you like to come up for a quick drink? If you give me your word you won't write anything about my drinking anything but Seven-Up?"

"Sure."

Sigrid served cocktails and Robin pantomimed for her to scat. When they were alone, Robin freshened her own drink, walked about the room, and asked, "How many movie stars have you been to bed with?"

She thought she could hear him gulp. "A fair share," he said. "No spectacular number."

She grinned and pretended to be casual as she unbuttoned her white blouse. "It's stuffy in here, isn't it? I've complained about the air-conditioning in this room, but they say they'll fix it and they never do. Or they do, and it goes right back on the blink," she said. "How are they in bed? Movie stars."

Was he as calm as he appeared after the gulp? "Some good, some not so good. It all depends on the person and on the circumstance."

"It always does." Robin nodded and brought the white blouse off her brown shoulders, the scooped-out bra tight against her breasts. "I hope you don't mind me walking around like this, but I can't stand a stuffy room. Can you? I haven't been in the movies long enough to compare notes with stars. I read somewhere that they're usually frigid because—what's that fourteen-dollar word?— because they're so narcissistic." She went to him with her drink and smiled. "If you promise to keep your pencil in your pocket— your writing pencil, I mean—I'll bet you could find one movie star who isn't frigid."

Why am I doing this?

I don't like this man. I don't even hate him.

He could write all this in his magazine. He doesn't owe me anything.

Why am I doing this, a day before Warren gets here?

Why, Verne or no Verne? Why am I doing this?

Vic Ennis—no, Hebert, Gary Hebert, the man who was not happily married but, well, married—sat forward, and his face clouded. Robin stood close to him and showed him the zipper at the side of her skirt. "If you're doing research," she said, "this zipper starts here and goes all the way down to here."

He got up, but not toward her. "That would create a problem," he said in a furry voice. "It would—uh—color the objectivity of the, uh, whole article."

"When do you get to know your movie stars on an intimate basis? After you've written your articles?"

"I was—just, uh, talking. I never mix business with, I never, uh, fool around on any assignment. That's a strict rule with me."

"Why? Because I'm ugly?" she asked, and unhooked the bra and let it fall. "Because I'm so ugly?"

"I'd better, uh, go right on, Miss Hamil—"

"*Why?* Because I'm *ugly?*"

The stridency surely shocked him nearly as much as it shocked her.

"Miss Hamilton," he said, "you're—I've got to say this so you won't be offended—you know you're anything but ugly, Jesus, you're the most beautiful Negress in show business today, I—well, I've been around but the, uh, plain truth is there's nobody who's ever been more in favor of civil rights, uh, watchacallit human rights, I wrote a two-parter for *McCall's* on civil rights and the mail that came in—"

Robin picked up her brassiere and her blouse. "I understand," she said. "You go home now, or wherever it is you go. I have some things to do."

"What I want to say—"

"Yes, yes," said Robin, suddenly exhausted. "See yourself out, will you? Oh, and put a handkerchief over your hand when you turn the doorknob. That would be an awful way to catch our syphilis."

She went into the bedroom and locked the door. If he knocked or called to her she did not hear, for she hastened into the bathroom and turned the tub faucets as hard and full as they would turn. She stripped off all her clothes and, within moments, the tub was filled with water.

She was deep in the tub when the wall phone rang. The operator asked her if she was in for a Miss Storm. "All right," she said.

"The community sing tonight, baby?" Sunny asked. "I can pick you up in, say, an hour."

"Not tonight, Sunny. Maybe another time."

"Bushed?"

"A little. I'm in the tub now, trying to revive."

"Yeah? You wanna dig a coincidence? I'm here in the September Morn, too, all ready to catch a shower. I bet you look fantastic."

"Not very."

Sunny's voice got confidential, conspiratorial. "Let's forget the community sing. I'm not all that far from your pad. I can be there in forty-five minutes, maybe less. I'll bring a couple of dried leaves and flowers and we'll have a soft little community sing of our own."

"Oh, you should've called five minutes sooner, Sunny. A really big date's coming over in a little while. I'm over Verne already. This cat's bringing heavy artillery. Full of laughs, too."

"The greatest. Take care, baby."

"You, too, Sunny," Robin said, and replaced the receiver.

Why did you leave me, Verne? she asked. Why does everybody who means something leave me?

"Why won't you do it?" Weber asked.

"Because it's wrong," Robin answered. "That's all. Because it would be wrong."

They were in Stefanino's and people were covertly staring at her, at the star. In New York, so few months ago, she had been an almost star, with rough edges. Now, every edge was artfully smoothed, Weber observed, and she turned her head like a star, raised her coffee cup like a star, breathed like a star, and the package was real, unforced; years from today she might take in washing, God forbid, but she would remain a star.

She would not do the television show, she quietly, stubbornly insisted, even though Weber, treading lightly, assured her that Jesse had agreed the idea was a brilliant one and promised to be thoroughly cooperative. Even though the series would benefit by the luster of her name. Even though her appearance would be an ideal way to effect a reconciliation with her mother. Even though, he added without scolding, she owed him something—and her brother, too. "Whatever I owe Roland Lee, I can't pay him, not so he'll know it," she said. "I owe you everything, or nearly everything. And I'd do anything else you wanted, but not this. I got where I am, wherever I am, by not making it look like I was trying to use Roland Lee to help me, and I'm not going to change now. Don't keep at me, Warren. I want to see my mother again. But I won't do this. I can't do it."

Autograph hounds were off limits at Stefanino's, but a woman stopped at the table for one, and Robin graciously gave it.

"You sign your name on a menu as if you've been doing it all your life," Weber commented as the woman gushed away.

"I feel like I've been out here all my life. Oh, I hate sounding so hard, especially with you. I guess I'm still scared, and that's why I act so high and mighty sometimes. Some people at the studio don't like me; they think I put on airs, or I'm mean. I don't mean to be mean to anybody. I'm just scared."

"Scared of what?"

Robin shrugged. "It sounds so corny. Scared of success, scared of all the fuss over me. It's corny, and maybe it sounds insane, too. What I'd love more than anything in the world would be to live in a little house with a nice husband who earns enough to buy groceries."

Weber pretended to be amused. "You wouldn't have mountains of trouble, at this stage of the game, finding a man who fits that qualification."

"I found one. Or I thought I did."

He did not pretend to be amused. "You did, did you?"

"You met him on—that night. Verne Hightower, remember? Anyway, he was the man I'd love to live in a little house with, but he turned me down."

"*He* turned *you* down? That newspaperman? Could he even afford groceries?"

"Gee, I hope I misunderstand you, Warren."

"I hope you don't. Whatever else you forget about what we've been to each other, I hope you'll never forget that I want the best for you. Is that as high as you can raise your sights, a sweet-talker who makes a couple of dollars an hour?"

"What a man earns doesn't matter."

"But what you earn, and will earn, matters. You're on the road to a million a year, Robin, and more! You be realistic, the next time one of these sweet-talkers rings your bell when you're vulnerable. How long would the vine-covered cottage suit you, now that you've slept on the silk sheets? How long would a fellow like that, any fellow on a salary, stay put with a bride who can blow her nose and command fifty grand? It's romantic, and it works in a script, but that's the only place it works."

"Then what are you telling me to do?"

"I'm telling you to recognize, first and foremost, that you've priced yourself out of vine-covered cottages."

"Then I don't have a right to a life of my own, is that what you're—"

"Obviously I didn't say anything like that. I'm saying—"

"Are you saying I should just be a money machine until I find a black man who makes the kind of money I make?"

She had a point. "There are other colors than black," he said lamely.

"There are? Like what?"

A public restaurant was a hell of an unseemly place for soul-baring. "I've missed you, Robin."

"What does that have to do with what we were talking about?"

"Karen left me. She took my children."

Robin appeared jolted. "Because of that night?"

"Yes."

"That's . . . terrible."

"Don't you turn me out, dearest. That's really what I came to California to say."

It was a cheap ploy, he knew, crude and morally repulsive, but it connected. She was visibly moved.

"I have to do what I have to do," she said. But her voice was unsteady.

"I know you do, Robin."

She served Weber a highball when they got to her hotel, and played a record, and did not speak, and behaved as though she did not want to be touched. She seemed agitated—by him, maybe, maybe by demons that had nothing to do with him—and then she asked, from twenty feet away, "What happened to us that time?"

"What time?"

"The last time we were together. When you brought me that

script in New York, and we were like strangers. We acted like we should've been saying 'Mr. Weber' and 'Miss Hamilton.' "

"You were so tired that ni—"

"No, no, that doesn't explain anything," she said, still far away. "Even today, before, in the restaurant—it was like we were strangers, like we never loved each other. Did we? Were we in love?"

"Not 'were.' 'Are.' Always. Nothing can change that," he said firmly, because she needed to hear it, and, he realized, because he needed to hear it, too.

"Then why am I over here, why aren't we comfortable with each other even if we're fighting? I told you everything good I have I owe to you, but it's more than just owing something. I'm always going to love you, Warren. You don't want to marry me and I don't want to marry you; I love Verne, I think, and you love your wife, but that's different, that's something else. I'm . . . even if Verne came back right this minute, I still think I'd have to die if it turned out everything you and I were together got lost . . ."

Her eyes misted, and she lighted a cigarette. "God, no wonder nobody stays with me for long. I never stop talking, and whatever I say always comes out all nutty. I never give a man room to breathe."

Weber went to her, touched at recognizing that of course Robin was right: no matter how many serious lovers there had been before or to come, they were Warren and Robin, very special lovers.

She turned away slightly. "No, don't come near me."

"Why not?"

"I don't want us to have sex. That never solves anything."

"Holding you can solve something. Telling you I love you, and meaning it, can solve everything. For both of us." He kissed her, trying to convey warmth rather than instant lust. Robin responded, but with a careful control; and she looked at him sadly, as if to gauge his sincerity, as if she wished there were some way they could make love without sex.

She slipped slowly, lithely, out of his arms and turned to face the living room window. "Please don't touch me, Warren," she said in a dragging voice. "You don't understand. I can't go to bed with you. When you're this close to me that's all I can think about, and I don't want to, I want to think about something else . . ."

Weber stood behind her and his arms circled her waist. "Quick, see the falling star?" he asked quietly.

"Where?"

"Anywhere you look. Remember what I said on the boat—that I see a falling star and I can't think of a thing to wish for?"

"Yes . . ."

"Living without you is an awfully aimless way to live, Robin darling."

She tensed. Weber pressed himself against her, held her more tightly, kissed her neck. She brought his hand to her breast, and she gasped and her voice broke as she muttered, "God, God, God . . ." and he pressed harder and his Robin was berserk with the need to kiss him, wildly and repeatedly, to be kissed, to have him.

And suddenly she stopped and moved away, gazing gravely at her sweater on the rug, the sweater she had helped him take off, gazed gravely at him and at what she had released with a febrile tug of his zipper. Her eyes announced her disgust and sorrow at the wildness that was and was not hers, and she shook her head and walked slowly into her bedroom and softly closed the door.

Righting his clothes, feeling foolish, his head pounding, Weber gulped his drink and paced. He found an Erroll Garner LP and replaced the record on the turntable with it. Pouring another drink, he studied the glass until the incomparable piano began. She wants love, he thought. I want love. I forgot I love her—how in hell could I forget that? And here's the extent of the love I'm able to give. It measures precisely six and one-eighth inches when encouraged—what was the name of that lunatic girl who got curious that night in Lausanne and phoned down to room service for a tape measure?—and it's a shockingly limited love offering. And so am I.

Presently he tapped at her door. No answer. "Robin?"

"Yes."

"May I come in?"

A pause. "Yes."

The ceiling light was on and the bedcovers had not been turned down. She wore her floor-length housecoat, and she stood at the bedroom window. She did not resist him as he guided her to the bed, but neither did she welcome him until long after they lay under the covers. Then her body was warm and hot, hot and warm and hot, and clearly she did not want him to stop.

Later, though not much later, he gently resumed the arguments for her doing "Moore." He gently mentioned her mother again. He gently alluded again to the gratefulness she owed him. He gently reminded her that she could not seal herself off entirely and forever from the fact of who her brother had been, and was.

She gazed at something, nothing, past him.

"What is it?" he asked when she was silent too long.

"There was a man a couple of weeks ago, more than a couple, who wanted to sell me something," she said. "I didn't know how much he wanted to sell it. I thought he wanted to make love to me, and I guess I wanted him to—I forget why, now—and I let him. Then he went back to his sales talk, maybe thirty seconds after he was done making love. I called him a bad name and I ran out of his house."

"O God, darling, don't think for a moment—"

"I don't. But I've got to think something about something sometime. Please don't ever do that again, Warren. I don't know what I am—a harem girl, or some big star who can tell everybody to go take a flying leap, or colored, or white, or not either one—but I'm a person, I'm trying to be a person. I don't blame you for this altogether, I guess I could've told you no. But don't make love to me ever again to get something out of me."

Weber was mortified. Through most of the night he talked to her, listened to her, comforted her.

And he flew back to New York in the morning with her promise that she would do the show.

Montgomery and Trowbridge brought him a script draft so skill-fully devised and so punchily written that Weber exulted, "We could cast Lee Marvin in the kid's part and have Guy Kibbee play the cop, and we'd still win a gross of Emmys!"

But he reread it, and he wasn't so sure.

Something jarred, something was out of kilter.

The cop, he had to admit. Every other character leaped off the pages with meat and muscle, but the cop was pallid, a one-dimensional stereotype; his motive in shooting, his dialogue, his characterization were as lifeless as the rest of the script was crackle and force. On the flight back from the Coast, Weber had changed his mind about meeting with White. But that had been before he'd read and reread this script, the script that would be Warren Weber's re-entry into Charlie Gundersen's league.

Without comment, he let Nash see the draft. Nash claimed it still didn't hit hard enough, but at least he didn't grumble or indicate he planned to be a pest. Testing the water, Weber mentioned that the sister's part would be beefed up and that Robin would play herself.

Jesse stared at him. "Well, now, appears like we got us an all-star cast," he drawled. "How'd you swing that?"

"I saw your argument—that the way to get to the truth is to go to the actual sources. Robin agreed."

"But what'd she say when you explained she'd have to mix with colored folks. Or haven't you broken it to her yet?"

"Lay off, Jesse," Weber said sharply. "And hear me. Robin doesn't intend to bicker. If you do, stay a pro and save your needling or whatever you have in mind for any time except working hours. Do you hear?"

Nash shrugged.

Testing the water further, Weber said casually, "The only character that still bothers me is the cop. He's unconvincing—nothing about him comes through. I wish the writers could've had some way to know how he really talks, how he moves . . ."

"Uh. I could sure find out how he moves. Just get that scum

bastard within five miles of me, and we'd see how he moves. I'd kill him, with these bare hands. If anybody around here asked that trash bastard for the time of day, I'd kill him and then I'd walk off the show and keep walkin'."

Weber, lightly, very lightly, the smile full: "Off the contract, too?"

"What contract?"

"Yours. The contract on a show that represents a lot of people's sweat and a lot of people's money."

"Why, sure I could. There's a white cat name of Marty Dickson. Ask him whether I could or couldn't."

Weber laughed. "I never met a man who could get worked up so fast over nothing. Let's drop it, Jesse, whatever it was. Of course no one's going to mess with that cop."

On the phone, Caleb Atwood confided that Stuart White had signed the release and was ready for a meeting. Weber ordered it for Saturday afternoon, when "Moore" wouldn't be filming, in his own office. The meeting was to be a private one, between Weber and White, without seconds or lieutenants. "I'm emphasizing secrecy, for White's own good," he said. "I haven't discussed this with Nash, naturally, but he'd have the cop's hide if he ever found out."

"I understand perfectly," said Atwood. "Why does Nash have to know anything? This is something between you and the series, isn't it?"

Replacing the receiver, Weber rubbed his upper arms, which hadn't hurt for a while and which hurt now. Scotch, and a cigarette, helped. He remembered that his appointment with Mel Hebranck was overdue and dialed Mel's number himself, so that Jeanne or Jeanne's assistant wouldn't wonder why he wanted his doctor. Mel's line was busy. Weber went back to work. He didn't think of placing the call again until late in the evening, when Mel was probably at home in bed with his wife. I wish I could be home in bed with Karen, Weber thought. I wish I could wrap Robin in these arms and hold her for the rest of my life. I wish I could take

Margalo Beaumont's advice and drag Karen away from London by the hair. I wish I could be a *mensh*. I wish. I wish. I wish. If wishes were horses, right? I wish.

Caleb Atwood placed a call to Stuart Curtiss White.

Then he placed a call to Jesse Nash.

Then, although his was a busy day, he laced his fingers across his chest and smiled at his office's picture window.

Play with Fire was finished on a Friday afternoon, but Robin did not go to the cast and crew party, nor did she even pause to say good-bye to Leo Osgood or Sunny. She had considered flying immediately to Warren, who was, in spite of the very little he was able to give, the man who would always look out for her, who would hurt her but who was the one man who would never mean to.

Instead she flew to San Francisco, determined to call Verne. He was not expecting her, and he might want to hang up on her, but she would beg him to stay on the telephone, beg him to see her. She would make him see that they *were* right for each other, that she would do everything in her power to prove it—give up her career, give her life to him, plead with him for one more chance to show she was the woman he wanted, needed, could love. Verne wouldn't send her out. She had been thoughtless, impossible, given him nothing and expected so much, and that was why he had written that letter, had had to write it. But she would be better, she would grow up and be his woman.

At the airport, she called the *Afro-American*. The lady who answered kept her waiting, and then came back to the phone to say that Mr. Hightower had taken a leave of absence to head up the Roger Beckley for Senator campaign in San Francisco. "Where can I reach him?" she demanded. "It's very important." The lady wasn't at liberty to furnish her with his home number but recommended she contact the Beckley headquarters and, after another minute of keeping her waiting, came back with the number.

A lady at that number said that yes, Mr. Hightower was in, and asked who was calling. "Robin Hamilton," said Robin. "Just one minute," the lady said, and Robin waited, the receiver tight against her ear, for a minute and then for too many minutes. There were background sounds, calls and typewriter pecks and busy noises and only a word here and there that she could catch and hold. A man's voice came on the line and said, "Who's this calling, please?"

"Robin Hamilton," she repeated.

"That's for who? Verne Hightower?"

"Yes. Robin Hamilton for Mr. Hightower."

"He's not here."

"He's . . . but the lady who answered the phone said—"

Curtly: "He's not here. He's moving around from place to place and we don't know when we'll hear from him. He should be back in a week or so, you want to try him then?"

Click.

Robin blinked at the black telephone box in front of her. She sat upright, holding the receiver, until she heard on-and-off buzzing sounds, impersonal yet insistent, that said, The call's over, the call's over, the call's over, another coin please, he wants you out of his hair, hang up and put another dime in please to be told he wants you out of his hair, another dime please . . .

The next nonstop flight to New York would leave in an hour and a quarter. "Where does the very next flight out of here go?" she asked the man at the ticket window, dazed, wounded, cloudy, full of on-and-off buzzing sounds. The question seemed to puzzle him, but he checked and reported there was a plane loading now for Cleveland. She bought a ticket.

The jet landed late at night in Cleveland, where she had never been and where she knew no one. There were taxis, but they passed her, or accepted white passengers who came behind her, or explained that they weren't going in her direction before she explained which direction she was going. Finally a Negro driver let her into his cab and began the meter. She remembered the name of the Hotel Kingsley in Cleveland; Warren had once mentioned that it had the city's one smart club and he would have her booked there when he got to it and if her price could be met.

"The Kingsley," she said. Minutes later, she asked, "Are there liquor stores still open?"

"No. Late for that."

The Kingsley had no rooms available, the desk clerk claimed grandly, only a suite, at eighty dollars a night. "I'll take it," Robin said, behind dark glasses, and registered as R. Nash, New York, N.Y. A colored bellhop followed her with her one bag—the studio had sent her luggage on to The Havilland in New York—and impassively preceded her into a clean, serviceable suite that, she was certain, no white guest would have been asked to pay eighty dollars for. The bellhop was husky and mildly attractive, older looking than Verne, maybe Jesse's age or a year older. He didn't speak as he opened closet doors and raised window shades and made sure the television set worked, but there was something about his manner that didn't spell lifetime bellhop.

Robin didn't tip him. She kept her coat on and asked, "Can you bring me two or three bottles of whiskey? Rye, preferably, but I'll settle for what you can get as long as it's not Scotch."

He stayed impassive, as though he were used to the request this late at night. "I'll do my best."

"How long will it take?"

"Not long. Ten minutes. Five."

"Thank you."

Alone, she switched the set on so there would be sounds. Still wearing her coat and dark glasses, she emptied the refrigerator's ice tray and then sat huddled, cold in this warm apartment, determined not to cry, in front of the television set, watching Larry Endicott, "The Midnight Son." He was interviewing a pretty Negro girl unfamiliar to Robin. The girl wasn't as pretty as Robin or as well put together, but she did have a sweetness and a sort of charm, and Larry Endicott and the other performers around the table were congratulating her on her first album, which they guaranteed was a cinch to be a hit.

The rye arrived, three quarts of it, and Robin removed her

glasses but not her coat and asked the bellhop if he would have some with her.

"I don't go off for an hour or so," he said.

"I'll be here," she said and gave him two twenty-dollar bills for the liquor. "Will you come back then?"

"May be a problem. I can come up in the service elevator, but anybody sees me walking the corridor in street clothes might get a little touchy."

"Will you try?"

"Sure."

"What's your name?"

"Bill."

"Good, Bill. My name's Sunny. I'll leave the latch off."

"No, I wouldn't advise that. I'd get canned if they found out downstairs I said this, but this is one hotel you shouldn't leave your door unlocked, even if you're in the room. Burglars hold a convention around here just about every night."

"All right."

She let him out and would, of course, not let him back in. Who was he? What did she know about him? Where was the sign on his chest promising not to rob her, beat her up, kill her? Cleveland was raining. She lowered all the shades and turned up the television sound, but she could still hear the rain. She got drunk quickly. By the time she heard the door's tranquil chime, she had showered and brushed her hair and perfumed her body and changed into the short filmy nightgown that showed her thighs, yet she had managed to drink so much that her walk was unsteady. Bob (*Bob? Bill?*) had on a heavy suit and a small bow tie, and his face was nearly as frozen as before, in spite of what she was wearing, what she was promising. "All quiet on the western front?" she asked, and smiled.

"No sweat. Nobody saw me. Leaving may not be so easy, though."

"You're a real worry wart. I'll make it worth the risk," she said brightly, locking the door. "I'll try."

He poured his own drink, and one for her. They sat in the living room, in the deep cushions of the sofa, Robin's hem recklessly high and so what? and he told her, because she asked, that he was from Chillicothe, that he'd done four years in the Navy, that he was off to a late start but he was going to school along with the kids, learning to be a machinist. Then he said, "I've heard you on the radio a few times, coming to work, and I saw you, just once, on 'The Curly Custer Show,' I think it was. I think I read in the *Plain Dealer* you're supposed to be out in Hollywood, making a movie."

"Who? Who're you talking to?"

"You. I don't know much about actors and singers and that, but I know who you are. Maybe it's none of my business . . ."

"Maybe it isn't. My name's Sunny."

He saluted. "Okay, Sunny. Whatever you say."

Robin leaned back, facing him, holding her glass tightly, and crossed her ankles over his legs. "I say, why say anything? Who wantsa talk?"

His hand traveled over her leg, over her thigh, and Robin shut her eyes and gasped pleasure and misery. The hand stopped, as if waiting to be invited further. She took it and whispered, "Bedroom."

There, she shook her head when he began to switch off lights, for darkness might have lent dignity to the night. They undressed like a married couple dully used to each other—and that was fitting, too, perfectly fitting—but then Robin saw him. He made Verne, and Jesse, and Warren, look like boys. "God," she breathed. "You'll *slaughter* a girl!"

"Claim to fame."

Minutes later—*how many? the liquor stopped time and rushed it* —there were two urgencies, for him and for him never to have brought her here, wherever here was. Chicago? Cleveland. Cleveland, Ohio. Why was she in Cleveland, Ohio? "You'll murder me with that . . ."

"Let's see." Ah, how nice was the touch of a stranger.

"No."

"Let's see," he said, and lay beside her—gently, gently, gently. "Let's see."

"You'll hurt me. I can't stand to be hurt."

"Here."

"Be careful."

"Here," he repeated.

"Slow. Slow."

"Uh-huh. Little by little."

"Say you love me," she whispered.

"Yeah. I love you."

"Like you mean it. Say you love me like you mean it."

Silence. Deeper. Silence.

"Don't leave me. Will you?"

"No." Deeper.

"I love you."

Silence. Then she was moving with him, so he would think she loved him, and he moaned as it happened for him, and she let him hold her for the respectable minute (*minutes? seconds?*) afterward and left him to get the bottle and glasses and bring them back. He drank with her but he did not keep up with her, and Robin didn't care. She fell asleep for a little while or a long while and was brought fuzzily awake by him, by its happening again. The sleep had not sobered her, but she suddenly, clearly recalled that she had put her purse with lots of cash on the bedroom bureau. She saw it now and wondered why he had not taken it and gone away.

Then it was daylight, though Cleveland, Ohio, was still raining, and she was ill. He was gone, but the purse was on the bureau, and she inspected it after she vomited. Nothing had been touched. Her watch read five before two. She phoned for coffee, and began to drink again, to steady herself, to get organized enough to have someone call an airline and find out when a plane could take her somewhere. A bath did not help, but the liquor surprised her by not making her gag, and she continued to drink, even when she donned her coat to admit the white waiter with the coffee. His studious stare transparently asked, *What's a colored girl doing in a ritzy suite, boozing it up early in the day?* The coffee did not help.

Four drinks (*three? five?*) put her back to sleep. The phone woke her and for a time she did not know who the man was who called himself Bill. He could, he said, trade tricks with another guy and be off at nine o'clock. Was she staying another night?

"Sure. All year."

"There's this jazz joint across town. Want to go, meet some of my buddies?"

"No."

"I'll try to come there to you, then."

She slept again.

She slept, incredibly, till after eight. She phoned for a club sandwich and coffee, but did not touch the tray. When Bill arrived, she was still in her nightgown, trying to make the liquor work the magic it had worked before. The rain had not let up. She greeted him only by taking off her gown and walking solemnly, glass in hand, to the bedroom.

"That isn't the only reason I'm here," he declared, following her.

"It's my only reason," she said and turned the bedroom radio up to full volume. "Well, let's go. Let's get started."

Music blasted. He moved to lower it, but she cried, "Don't you go near that!"

He pressed the button that silenced it. Robin started to rail at him, and then they heard the living room door chime.

"Oh-oh," he said.

"Forget it. We won't answer it."

"I saw Dunphy when I was coming up the hall, but I was sure he didn't see me. Oh, hell, now they got me . . ."

"Nobody's got you. Who's *they?* Nobody's got anybody!" The chime sounded again as she charged to the door, glass still in hand, certain of madness, and called, "Nobody home!"

"This is Dunphy. Security."

"Whadda I care? What do you want?"

"Open this door, please."

" 'Open this door, open this door,' I'm a paying guest, damn it!"

she roared, and unlocked the door and stormed, "All right, you came to see something? Take a good look!"

There were two men, and they saw her nakedness, and her glass, and her frightened defiance, and her madness. They were inside before she could block them, and one of the men said, "Bill Jessup back there?" to no one. He went to the bedroom as the other man tried not to stare. Robin ran to the bathroom and locked herself in it, trembling as she heard angry voices, one of the voices saying nigger whorehouse, trembling as the front door closed, trembling for many minutes after she was alone in the suite.

She trembled as she answered the phone.

"This is Mr. Sheppard, the night manager, Miss—ah—Nash. You will kindly be out of your suite, and prepared to settle your account, in the next quarter of an hour."

"No," she said softly, frightened to leave in the rain. "You can't make me leave."

"Indeed we can. Please don't force us to call the police."

In the lobby thirty minutes later, she was conscious of weaving, conscious of humiliation, conscious of anger around her, conscious of people—"Isn't that Robin Hamilton, the singer?" she heard and did not turn—and the cashier informed her he could accept a credit card but not a personal check, which was white talk, she supposed, but decided it was just as well; *Robin Hamilton* was printed on her checks. She paid in cash and did not wait for a receipt. She said, "The airport," to the taxi driver, who started his motor and who advised, "I'll get you there, lady, but keep your fingers crossed. We haven't had a steady rain like this in ten, twelve years. Last they said on the radio an hour or so ago, ain't any planes leaving Cleveland."

"Let's go and see." Humiliation returned. Would they have called the police? If I was white, would they have acted the same way?

Maybe no, maybe yes. But I know how I acted. I'm still drunk, but I know all I did, and being drunk doesn't excuse any of it. Being black doesn't excuse any of it.

At the airport, she was told there would be no flights until the weather began to clear, probably not till morning. In the restaurant, she ate a ham sandwich and drank three cups of black coffee. The waiting room was cold and crowded, yet not impersonal enough; people gawked at her, or she imagined they did, and that was the same thing. She checked into the motel nearest the airport and left word that she be called as soon as there was a definite flight to New York. Sleep would not come, but she was glad she had not brought any of the liquor with her from the Kingsley. She was not sure why the prospect of going back to New York scared her. Yet it did.

The morning sky was hazy. In the jet to New York, turning the Cleveland newspaper pages to the entertainment section, she saw a photograph of Mrs. Randolph Hicks, Sr. Sarah Glenda Hicks was dead, the victim of uremic poisoning. Dr. Francis M. Mosher was quoted as saying that the plucky, valiant child had been at death's door for months, that early, proper attention might have prolonged her life, possibly for years. Robin saw why the *Herald-Examiner* had printed the small story. Mrs. Hicks detailed everything that Robin Hamilton had done. The child had been closer to death than anyone had thought, but Robin Hamilton was to be blessed for her care and concern and money and prayers.

In her Havilland apartment, Robin was met with a barrage of messages. The one that mattered was the request to call her sister Lula.

"Mama's been in Sydenham for the past three days, Robin," said Lula. "I wanted to take her down to Mount Sinai or Lenox Hill or one of those hospitals downtown, but she said Sydenham, up here, or nothing. She's sick, Robin. She's very sick. I've spent every penny you've sent me for the best there is, and this new doctor, Doctor Barry, says she won't live long. Why couldn't I get hold of you till now, Robin? I've been trying everywhere."

Mama was asleep when Robin got to Sydenham at five minutes past four in the afternoon. The first sight of her, after an age away, was shocking. Willie Mae Hamilton's soft, always smooth skin hung in creases and folds; the cheeks, once padded with fat, were hollow. Her hair had been jet black with only a few strands of gray, always pulled back and curled into a bun on top of her head; now it was all frosty white, changing and distorting her appearance even more than the loose skin did, and it too was loose, long, uncharacteristically unkempt. She had always been neat as a pin, had always insisted that as long as you were allowed to walk the earth you owed it to others and yourself to look presentable. If Mama was really alive, Robin thought, eager to touch the cheek, the hand, afraid to, if Mama sensed she was going to go on living, she'd never let anyone see her hair like this. . . .

Mama continued to sleep. Lula left the hospital for short periods during the next two days, but Robin stayed in the waiting room, dozing, waking with a start, walking, suspended. She looked into her mother's room at least once every half hour, although each of the three nurses assured her she would be told the second her mother came awake. And then she was called, in the middle of a morning while Lula was downstairs for coffee, and the nurse cautioned her to keep the visit brief and took her to Willie Mae Hamilton.

Heavy folds burdened Mama's eyes, but amazingly, gloriously, the eyes were bright and alert. There were moments of no movement, no expression, and then Mama raised her arms and extended them, and Robin hurried into them and kissed her mother's cheeks and chin and eyes and head, held her mother who was holding her, begged herself not to cry, and cried.

And Mama cried, too, for a little while.

"Don't you go on, angel, don't you go on," she said, and Robin knew she wasn't going to die. Dying people had dying voices, and Mama's deep voice was as strong as ever. "I'm doin' just grand. You remember to call up Miz Jeffrey on the telephone that I can't come to her today?"

Robin froze. Mama had stopped cleaning Mrs. Jeffrey's apartment on Riverside Drive when the old woman had died ten years ago. Mama had missed only one day of working for Mrs. Jeffrey, because of a cold, and she had felt bad about it.

"Yes, Mama. I called."

"She put out that I couldn't come? You tell her 'bout this pesky cold?"

"She said for you to take your time and get well."

"Hate leavin' her in the lurch, fine lady like Miz Jeffrey." She released Robin and soon Robin saw a flicker of a question in her eyes. "Now don't that beat all, me recallin' poor ole Miz Jeffrey after all these years?" She shook her head and blinked hard. "What you doin' here, Robin Beverly? You s'posed to be some place . . . Funny. Funniest thing. I can't seem to hold onto a thought in the head for longer'n a wink. Gittin' old, mebbe." She chuckled, and sighed. "I figger I'm a mite tired, angel. You leave me rest a bit."

"Of course, Mama," Robin said. "I won't be far away."

She leaned to kiss her, but Mama's head turned. "Mind you don't catch this cold. You an' Lula make sure Roland Lee's got fresh clothes for church in the mornin', hear? And see the three of you gets there on time, not like last Sunday. You pay a call on the Lord's House, it's only fittin' you git there prompt." She squeezed Robin's hand. "Oh, I can see it just so clear!"

"See what, Mama?"

"You wearin' that purty blue taffeta I'm fixin' for Easter Sunday. You'll make us all strut like a peacock, how nice you'll look. Jus' keep holdin' my hand, li'l precious," she said, and Robin did not leave until she was asleep and the morning nurse whispered that it would be best to go.

In the corridor, shaken yet unable to free more tears, Robin understood with stinging shame the selfish reason she was praying for Mama to live. If she dies like this, she thought, I won't hear her say she forgives me. I won't even hear her say she'll never forgive me. All it will be is . . . this. Mama remembering only the little girl in the Easter Sunday dress, the little girl before the sins.

That night, Robin and Lula stood as they saw Dr. Barry come into the waiting room, and Robin was relieved because his face was not as somber as usual. "Why don't you ladies go home and get a comfortable night's sleep for a change?" he said. "Nothing's going to happen between now and morning. I've just been in and she's holding her own, which is a darned good sign."

"We'll stay," said Lula.

"That's up to you." The doctor shrugged and left them.

The sisters slept. The wall clock read a quarter of four in the morning when a white man in a white gown, with *Dr. Ramirez* printed on an inch of wood pinned to the gown, walked to them and said, "You moathah jos' die."

The service was held in Reverend Fletcher's church. Robin, who no longer cried and wondered why, would not allow Orville Sanford to attend, nor would she allow his flowers from FREE to be brought into the church, but she was pleased that Warren came. She was surprised, and pleased, that Jesse came with Warren, and sat beside him.

Warren and Jesse rode with her and Lula to the cemetery in Westchester. Neither then, nor during the burial, nor on the ride back to the city, did she cry. The car took them to the Harlem apartment house. Warren, who had been so thoughtful and supportive from the moment he had heard about Mama, stirred restlessly in the car as though he felt out of place, and Robin tried to make it easy for him by touching his hand and saying, "Don't bother to come up, Warren. Thank you for everything."

"You'll be all right?"

"Fine. Thanks again."

She and Lula got out. And so did Jesse, who surprised Robin, and probably Lula as well, by going with her and Lula to the apartment.

Two neighbor ladies—Mrs. Bantry and old Miss Shaw—and Reverend Fletcher's wife were in the warmly sunlit apartment, straightening slipcovers and preparing mounds and mounds of food. Others arrived in time, including Lula's beau, Reverend Dewey

Erskine, a shy young man Robin liked at once. Mrs. Bantry began to cry, and then so did nice Mrs. Brown, and they were joined by the older ladies, and soon by a softly weeping Lula, but Robin still could not cry. She left Jesse talking with Lula's beau, and she walked through the apartment that had been hers, and she felt foreign to it, as out of place as Warren would have. The neighbors had been polite, had told her how pretty she looked, had asked her questions about being on television and in the movies. Yet they were Mama's friends, not hers, and that meant they disapproved of her.

She was changing her clothes in the bedroom she had shared with Lula when Lula came in to change, too. "So many people are coming and nobody's leaving. I can't imagine where we'll put them all," Lula said.

"Mama had a lot of friends."

"I wish I had a little more nerve. I'd tell Mr. Nash he's not welcome here."

"Why, Lula?"

"He's a hypocrite. It's not proper to speak bad of anyone, but that's what he is. He pushed Mama, even when he knew how worn out she was. Different things wore her out and killed her, but Mr. Nash can take some of the blame."

"Maybe that's why he's here, because he's sorry."

"Maybe. Maybe it doesn't matter."

In the parlor Robin went to Jesse, who seemed subdued and even friendly. This was my husband, she thought. I was this man's wife and good things happened, a long time ago but not that long, before bitterness got him, before everything that Cleveland was all about got me. He doesn't hate me, he can't. He did at Warren's party—he hated me, or someone, something, himself, but these aren't the eyes of a man who hates. This is Jesse, my husband, my lover.

"You up to goin' back to work, Robin?" he asked.

"I'll have to be," she answered, and smiled. "Warren's not pressing, of course, but I expect he'll need to get started soon on the TV show. I'd have no right to hold him up."

"You sure do figure you owe that man a whole mess o' dues, don't you?"

"Yes. Why shouldn't I?"

"Oh, you should, you should. One thing about darlin' Warren, he gives his word on somethin', he sticks to it." There was an uncomfortable pause. "Well, now. The last time we saw each other, that wasn't a very pleasant occasion, either, was it? That night I chewed you out in front of all those folks. I didn't know when to quit talkin'. I shouldn't'a started."

"It's over."

"That guy with you that night—name didn't mean beans to me till the next day. That's when I found out who he is. You still seein' him?"

"No. . . . Are you still seeing that girl you were with?"

Jesse frowned. "Which one was that? Oh, her. Shoot, that wasn't anything." He grinned. "Say, you are lookin' mighty classy, Robin. And to think, you might still just be driftin' along, hadn't been for darlin' Warren. Yep, touchin' how darlin' Warren turns us all into gold."

"Jesse, what are you up to? Are you and Warren having an argument about something? I know when you're being sarcastic. If you two are having troubles, I don't want to hear about it."

"That's my Robin, always with her head under the covers where it's safe. Trust is one thing. Knowin' your enemy's somethin' else."

"Enemy? Warren Weber, do you mean? Jesse, I won't stand here and—"

"Won't what? Believe darlin' Warren's your enemy till you get it proved? Tomorrow's Saturday. What you doin' at two o'clock?"

"Why?"

"I'll take you to darlin' Warren's office tomorrow at two, if you don't tell him between now and then we're comin'. You might learn somethin' about who's on your side and who isn't. I'll come for you at half-past one. If the information I got about darlin' Warren's wrong, I hereby promise an' guarantee I'll empty his trash cans till I drop and I'll turn all my salary over to the KKK. Fair enough, Robin? Half-past one."

Old Miss Shaw limped up to Robin, to say that Reverend Fletcher was about to make his departure and wished everyone to gather for a final prayer. Jesse, appearing to catch the chill in Lula's glances, stole out of the apartment during the prayer. Robin bowed her head and asked Mama to forgive her, as she had at the church and the cemetery, for being a sinner. When Reverend Fletcher left, she decided she hadn't Lula's strength for talking with the guests, so many kinds of them, so she went to Mama's bedroom, where she tried to cry and could not, where all she could feel was shame, here in Mama's room with Mama everywhere in it, the shame of having been kicked out of a fancy hotel as though she were what she was, a common slut. Someone had returned the Bible and reading glasses Mama had insisted on taking to the hospital, and Robin picked them up and held them. She looked in Mama's top dresser drawer and found a blue imitation sapphire ring she had never seen Mama wear, and dozens of religious pamphlets. She found photographs of herself and Lula when they had been very young, and she found a picture of Roland Lee, who couldn't have been more than four years old, wearing a cowboy hat and sitting on a wooden pony. She found old wrinkled letters tied together with an elastic band. And she found her father's postcard, the one from Detroit that read *Am fine be good. Jas Lonny H.*

There were no clothes in the bureau or closet. Mama had instructed that, on her death, all her clothes be immediately given to poor people who could make use of them.

The imitation sapphire ring had cost a dollar, if that. Robin put it in her pocket, and would never part with it.

Promptly at two o'clock on Saturday afternoon, Weber admitted Stuart White to his office. He ignored the outstretched hand. "Sit there," he directed, and pointed.

"Real nice layout you have here," the cop said, the wide collar of his floral sports shirt out over the collar of his plaid sports jacket. "The rent alone I bet adds up to plenty."

"It's expensive," Weber agreed, walking to his desk. "How expensive were you, by the way? I never did get around to asking Atwood what you were paid."

"Do you mean for being the technical adviser on this television show? Well, it was all right. Not much. I sort of had the idea you'd sweeten the pot a little extra, on your own."

"By all means. Be fair to yourself. I realize your time is valuable."

"Well, let's be fair to each other," said White, sitting, obviously eager to be friendly. "I know you're not the type man to try and jew a fella down. How's—ah—a hundred dollars? Seventy-five?"

"Let's split the difference. I'll write you a check for eighty-seven-fifty. When we're done."

"Right now wouldn't be a bad time, like they say."

"When we're done."

"Sure, whatever, that's fine with me. Wait—what're you doing with that machine?"

"I'm getting ready to tape our conversation."

"Uh—why? I'm not sure I go along with that."

"Are you hiding something?"

"Now you know better than that. It's just . . . well, why would you want to tape what we say? Don't you trust me or something?"

"Not very much, Mr. White, but that isn't my reason for using the machine. I want the 'Moore' writers to learn your cadence, your speech patterns. That's worth the extra eighty-seven-fifty, isn't it?"

"Well, yeah, but—listen, what's that stuff about not trusting me very much? That's no way to start a talk."

Weber nodded. "You're right. You're a man of honor or Caleb Atwood wouldn't have brought us together. I apologize."

"Okay. But that tape recorder, that's out. I wouldn't talk natural with it on."

Sitting at his desk, Weber leaned to switch the machine off, then sat back and pushed the button under the arm of his chair that set the other recorder White couldn't see into operation. "Very well, you win. Begin at the beginning, Mr. White. Don't omit a thing."

White began not a reminiscence but a speech, surely the canned performance of the lecture circuit, and Weber interrupted him. "I didn't make myself clear. I don't want to hear the talk you memorized for church and patriotic groups. I know you're a red-blooded, loyal American, and I applaud you for it, but by 'begin at the beginning' I mean what happened from the instant you saw Roland Lee Hamilton in the Harlem alley."

White began again, and talked for ten minutes or more, punctuating every other sentence with a whiny, self-pitying stab at Them, and the office door opened and Weber looked up and saw Jesse Nash.

So did White. What shocked Weber most was that White did not appear to be shocked at all, not even surprised.

"Hello, boys. Who's cuttin' the cards?" Nash said, and Weber's heart lurched because Nash stepped to one side and Robin, looking stunned, came into the office with him.

Weber stood. Stuart White blinked and asked, "What's going on here, Mr. Weber? Nash, I know. That girl, that's Robin Hamilton, isn't it? You kept saying you were worried they'd ever find out the two of us were having these meetings. I never much cared, one way or the other, but you were working so hard to keep them off the trail. Who slipped up?"

A frame, thought Weber. You goddam contemptible scum, you and Atwood really went to town, didn't you?

"I dig the way you keep your word, darlin' Warren," Nash said. "I dig how you steer clear of garbage like this."

"Lis-sen . . ." said White.

Turning to Robin, Nash said, but for all to hear, "Here's how it hangs, doll. Here's the white man that murdered your brother, and here's the white man that's treatin' him to all the ice cream sundaes."

"Shut up, Jesse," Weber demanded, and demanded of White, "What do you know about this?"

"Now's the last time you tell me to shut up, massa," Nash said. "I'm done. I clear out." He asked Robin, "You comin' or you stayin'? I'm sure Mr. Whitey'd be glad to show you the blood on his hands."

"You cruddy, big-mouth ape!" White spluttered, and he shot up and advanced toward Nash. They were both tall, but the cop was obviously a man of immense physical strength. "Where the hell do you get off talkin' that shit to me?"

"Touch me," said Nash. "Lay one bloody finger on me, and you ride out of here in a canvas bag."

"That's enough, both of you!" Weber exclaimed, moving toward them, fully aware that he had been caught in the middle, fully aware that "Moore" was done.

But then Robin walked forward from the doorway with slow steps, her face as blank as a sleepwalker's. The cop seemed to freeze.

She stood no more than inches from him, and tears formed in her eyes, and soon small whimpers were choking in her throat. She raised her hand above her head, poising it there for a moment, and then she slapped White's cheek with such precise and extra- ordinary force that he surely was stupefied as much by her power as by the act. "Killer," she whispered. She pushed him so that he fell backward into his chair and she slapped and punched his head, and swooped up the nearest object on Weber's desk, which was a heavy marble ash tray, and brought it down with a sickening crack on his head.

"Killer!" she screamed. "Killer, killer, killer!"

White lunged to his feet and started for her, his huge fist set to smash, and Weber knew he couldn't get there fast enough even as he started moving. But then, incredibly, White crumpled to his knees, and Weber saw the blood pouring down the man's head. White pawed the air weakly, and terrible noises chugged from him.

Nash moved toward him, but Weber called, "Stop!" Nash hesi- tated. "If you kill him, you won't get off free the way he did," Weber said. He sat on his knees next to White, looking at the cuts and the blood, and asked, "Can you hear me?"

White nodded.

"Walk out of this office and out of this building."

"I can't."

"Walk out of this building," Weber said evenly. "Go to At-wood, and Soul of America, and whatever other filth you earn your living from, and tell them Warren Weber said it takes more than a pitiful little turd like you to beat him." He rose and, almost gently, placed White's straw hat, with the gaudy red-green hat-band, on White's bloody head. "Now," he said. "Get up now, little man, and take your stench out of here."

The cop lumbered to his feet and swayed toward the door. He leaned on the frame for a moment, then turned to them again. "Nobody understands," he said sadly. "I didn't shoot that nigger kid on purpose. I didn't even know him."

He went out.

And Weber looked for Robin and did not see her, or her purse. "Where did Robin go?"

They both hurried to the corridor, past the slowly moving Stuart White. They saw the elevator indicator lowering to the lobby, and they returned to the office. Fatigue engulfed Weber as he lit a cigarette. "There's one thing you have to believe, Jesse," he said. "I didn't entirely play straight with you, but I swear to you I never met that cop till today. Nor did I ever intend—"

"Save it," Nash said flatly. "What I know, what I always knew and pretended for a time it wasn't so, is somethin' you don't face up to 'cause you're white. Not as white as the cop, maybe, but white. White people lie, even when they don't mean to, and the plain fact is those lies aren't ever gonna stop, long as black folks are stalled some place between bein' slaves and bein' free."

"This crap today was Caleb Atwood's doing. He engineered the—"

Nash nodded. "That's just a name to me. All white folks're just names to me. Ol' Robin's just free enough that she can listen to you tell her what to do and then decide what she wants to do. Not too much doubt she'll decide to go along with the plantation owner. But I'm all decided. I'm goin' home."

"Where's home?"

"Orville Sanford. FREE."

"God Almighty, what a pigheaded fool you can be, Jesse. What does that mean? Making street-corner speeches and collecting dues for Sanford from Negroes who can't afford the rent? Why, when you can earn a fortune for your Mr. Sanford by doing 'Moore,' and not so incidentally using 'Moore' to teach us white devils about human rights? Since when is a soapbox a more effective means of communicating ideas than a major network?"

"When I'm on a soapbox, nobody tells me to compromise anything."

" 'Compromise,' " Weber sighed, wishing his body didn't ache so. "Lord, don't you have the feeling I have, that you and I've been over this ground a hundred times?"

"I sure do. And that's how come we'll never cut it together, you and I, or any white man and black man—there's just never an interpreter handy to translate two different languages. So, you might call this a declaration of war. It'll be a funny sorta war. I hate everything you are, but I don't hate you. Kinda hard for a white man to dig, isn't it?"

At last Weber was alone, and he called Mel Hebranck's office. The answering service told him that Dr. Hebranck was away for the weekend and referred him to the doctor's associate, Dr. Whitney, whom Weber did not know at all. He placed a transatlantic call to Claridge's in London, and was advised that Mrs. Weber and children had checked out. "Where can they be reached?" he asked, and was told Villa Medici in Florence. He tried there, and Karen was not in her suite, and he left word that it was urgent that Mrs. Weber return his call. Then he telephoned Caleb Atwood's home number on this Saturday afternoon and was told that Mr. Atwood could be reached at the New York Athletic Club. The New York Athletic Club kept him waiting for five minutes, and he felt terribly tired as he waited, and he finally was told that Mr. Atwood was having a rubdown and would ring him back, if Mr. Weber would leave his number.

"Mr. Atwood knows where I am."

Then he drank, because liquor would remove the aches in his body.

He called Nora Gundersen in Evanston, and she was in and profoundly happy to hear from him. She had written to him to thank him for the wire and flowers, as had her daughter Pat when Pat's baby was born, and she flooded him with questions. He was fit, he said, and so were Karen and the kids. Nora had been reading about "Moore" and thought it was awfully exciting. "I'm going to sound like an old nag, which I am," she said, "but this is the kind of show you should've been doing all along."

"Agreed, agreed. But I'm young yet. I'm just starting to revolutionize the world. Karen's proud as punch. You will be, too, when you see the result."

"I've always been proud of you, Warren. I'm so glad you've sunk your teeth into something I'll want to watch. I love you, Warren, and I'm proud of you, but I must confess I gave 'Meet Ginger' and—what's that other gem, 'Spy for Sale'?—exactly two trial examinations each, and they didn't grab me, as we teen-agers say. I'm *so* glad for you, Warren."

"Just wait till the boy wonder really takes off, Nora. You'll burn incense in adoration. Charlie's alive and breathing his usual masterful flame somewhere. He'll be proudest of all—and that's why *I'm* alive and breathing."

When Weber was into his fourth double Scotch and water, Atwood phoned. "Hi there, Warren," he said. "What's up?"

"Your lunch, Caleb. I'm afraid things didn't pan out. Stuart Curtiss Scum did his patriotic darnedest, but Jesse Nash is staying with 'Moore,' bigger and stronger than ever. By the way, Mr. White was struck about the head and body while he was here. Your lawyer, or Willard Cunningham's lawyers, or White's own lawyer from the Yellow Pages, will instruct him that he's been injured and that the publicity for Soul of America will be manifold if Nash or I, or both of us, are sued in the tabloid headlines for eighty zillion bucks. I would counsel you to counsel White, Caleb,

that he cease and desist from any such foolishness. Or I will go to
the tabloid headlines myself and, for starters, unearth those hideous
but provable stories about your extended personal association with
gorgeous Gilbert Booth." Gilbert Booth was a famous playwright
and a drunk who kept ketting into transient trouble in bars that
catered to homosexuals.

Pause. "I can't talk here . . ."

"You don't have to talk," said Weber. "Listen. Me and Admiral
Farragut, we've not yet begun to fight. 'Moore' is my culmination, my epitaph, and *dreck* like you can't touch me. I'm *Weber*,
buddy, I'm the true mover and shaker. You may get half a foot-
note in the books, baby, but those books are gonna be crammed
full of Warren Weber. Remember that. You've just begun to do
battle with Warren Weber."

He hung up, and drank, and phoned Robin. Robin didn't answer,
and he left word that it was urgent that she return his call. He
drank some more, until his body was not weightless but relatively
free of aches and of pain, and he removed his shoes and lay on the
office couch to await Karen's call, or Robin's call, or someone's
loving call.

If anyone called, Warren Weber did not hear, for he fell into
a drugged sleep.

C. Harvey Rhodes called Caleb Atwood to his office on the morning Caleb Atwood returned from a Miami sales conference.

" 'Moore' hasn't been quite laid to rest," he said. "Weber paid
everyone involved and took the segments that were finished and
sold them to Payson."

"That doesn't surprise me, Claude," said Caleb, looking dapper
and tanned and very healthy. "Payson is the ash-can channel.
They've bought discards before and they'll buy them again. What
did they pay Weber, do you know? More than five dollars?"

"Not much more. The segments will be shown as individual
dramas, none related to the other. I gather they'll be aired on
evenings when there aren't hockey games."

"That's interesting. I saw Nelson Lane in Palm Beach, Claude, and I think we have the Thursday-night-at-nine slot sewn up." He spread his fingers to simulate a marquee. " 'Donna McLerie Time.' So far, McLerie's done only specials and guest shots. NBC and the others've been after her for a long while to head her own weekly show, and they've all struck out. I think, I *think* I have her. I reminded Lane of how well we've done for him in the past, and one thing led to another—I incidentally supplied him with a willowy lady friend of mine, an English chum from the Old Vic, and that may well have tipped the scales—"

"Caleb, what are you magpieing about?"

"What am I what?"

"Today I clean out my desk, paper clips, plaques and all, and check out. This evening I get into an airplane and go to Munich and check into a sanitorium where a Dr. Bronf will try to keep me alive for another month."

"I'm sure I'm not following you, Claude."

"Indeed you are. I'm as sorry as I'm—ah—certain you are. I'm sorry, too, that the last hurrah, as it were, is 'Donna McLerie Time.' I'm not sure I like Warren Weber. I'm not sure I ever approved of this 'Moore' project. I loathed Weber's underhanded tactics. But I wish 'Moore' could have had a chance. I wish you hadn't destroyed it before it caught its second wind."

"*I?* Claude, you're the magpie, you're chattering like an old, ah—"

"Like an old cardiac who's ready for the box. I made several simple telephone calls before I called for you, Caleb. I find you own a goodly number of shares of Vanguard, which guarantees you solvency in Vanguard till you sell or till death do you part. But you don't own an automatic right to this chair I'm sitting in. Nor do you have a lease on your own chair. You are to pack your paper clips and plaques and whatnot, Caleb, and leave Vanguard Broadcasting within the hour. Otherwise, you will be escorted out. I have advised my attorney that I wish my successor to be Adam Pritchard. My attorney advises me that only a board of directors' meeting can choose or not choose Pritchard. I advised my attorney that if you steamroll your name over Pritchard's, every newspaper, every trade paper, every agency and sponsor and potential sponsor, every soul who has ever invested a penny or a moment in Vanguard is to learn that I detest you and all I've permitted you to do to Vanguard, and that if you take over, you will be assuming a chair that morally is not yours."

Typical of Caleb, thought Rhodes, he heard and retained only what he wanted to hear and retain. "Pritchard? That *embryo?* What's that foul-mouthed camp follower ever done for the industry?"

"Pritchard lies somewhere between what you are and what I used to be and what Warren Weber could have become. He's processed normal commercial television trivia. He also was instrumental in setting up educational and public affairs television when all the conventional roadblocks were in force. He's a maverick. He may kill or cure, but mavericks have begun to please me."

"Would you be so pleased, so luxurious in your pleasure, if you weren't on your way to . . . uh . . ."

"The boneyard? Probably not," Rhodes conceded. "Collect those paper clips, Caleb. If there is such a thing as a soul, I really do dislike yours. Mine is nothing to brag about, but yours is absolutely unspeakable."

"Claude, now honestly, we've got to—"

"Get out of here, Caleb. At once."

Twenty

JESSE NASH RETURNED to FREE, for there was no place else to go. Orville Sanford privately admitted, when pressed, that FREE *was* being bankrolled in part by Soul of America, but what was the difference as long as there was money to help unite blacks? He assured Nash that SOA gave the money with no strings attached. Nash believed him because there was no one else to believe, and told audiences that would listen that white America's evil had begun in earnest after 1865.

Lula Hamilton was made pregnant nine weeks after she and Dewey Erskine were married in Reverend Fletcher's church. If the baby was to be a boy, his name would be Roland Lee Erskine.

Several days before C. Harvey Rhodes's death, Vanguard Broadcasting's board of directors elected Adam Pritchard as its president and accepted Caleb Atwood's resignation. Atwood retained his Vanguard stock and went to work for Willard Chase Cunningham in two capacities: as Cunningham's advertising chief, and, as the press release stated, "to streamline and modernize Soul of America, in order that the patriotic society can bring its urgent message to the American people as effectively as possible."

Stuart Curtiss White sustained no serious physical injuries and he was advised against suing Weber and Nash. His contract with Soul of America was not to be renewed, he learned, and the few people at SOA who were in when he called were friendly but had no suggestions of where he could get a job. He spent a frantic month, as his bank balance dwindled, in seeking some well-paid position that could make use of his celebrity. One of his pals at McLeod's Tavern, Gus Pernell, had a cousin named Andy who was a part-time free-lance writer and who, Gus believed, just might be the guy to write Stuie's autobiography and make Stuie rich. Andy charged him $100 to ghostwrite an outline to show to book publishers, and they agreed they would share equally in the profits. There were not profits, because no publisher showed interest in the book. A pulp magazine called *Bombshell* wanted White's name on its cover and offered him fifty dollars for an article on International Communism. Andy wrote the article and collected half the money. Stuart Curtiss White then took a job as a clerk in his brother-in-law Al's liquor store in the Bronx. The job lasted five days. At least fifty percent of Al's regular customers were colored, and when some of them learned who Al's brother-in-law was, they spread the word around the neighborhood and began to do business at the liquor store in the next block. White told his wife Lucille that something big would turn up soon.

Robin Hamilton ran from Warren Weber's office because she was appalled by her own violence as much as by the world's, and because she was convinced that she would lose her mind if she stayed a second longer. She saw Warren again, but the bounce, the zest she had so often associated him with had somehow evaporated. He looked drawn and weary. His talk was filled with plans, as always, yet his voice was oddly spiritless, as though he didn't truly believe what he was saying, as though he didn't really care. On the day she was to fly back to California, he kissed her cheek and said, "Don't love me, Robin, but don't hate me. Promise me you'll never hate me."

In Hollywood she started *Cherish the Night* for Onyx Pictures; it was a big-budget movie written expressly for her, a movie that made far greater demands on her talents than *Play with Fire* had, and she watched her drinking because there were mornings when it showed in her face, and she began to go to parties. At one she met Hal Saunders, a white, attentive man who was not at all direct when she asked him what his work was. She learned, on their second meaningless date, that he didn't work at very much; Dad had left him no money worries, and, at thirty, he was considering a number of lines to go into, nothing definite.

At another party she met George Nichols, a black electronics engineer she had two carefully nursed drinks with, and he seemed stable, mature, a man with a responsible career, a man who would never have to depend on a wife's money or be threatened that she might outshine him. She decided she could like him very much, and then a smiling colored lady came to them and he introduced Miss Hamilton to his wife Joyce.

At another party she met Dickie Wendell, a jovial black musician who was intelligent and amusing. She agreed to let him see her home, but she mentioned his name when she and another black guest, Ginny Oakes, repaired lipstick together in a dressing room. Ginny warned her, "Don't get mixed up with that character, Rob. He's strictly bad news. Dickie can be fun, but he's always in some kind of hot water, or looking for it. He's done time twice for kiting checks, I know for a fact, and he goes for women with bread."

"What do I do, Ginny?" Robin asked flatly.

"About what?"

"What do you do when you're paid like you're white, and everybody treats you like you're white, but not really because you're not white? Black people don't want me because I have so much, or that's what they think, and they think I want to be white and so they don't want me. White people want me only to here and no further. Where do I go? Where do I belong?"

"Heck, you're still a baby," said nice Ginny, a dancer whom some Negroes rightly considered rich because she earned more than $10,000 a year, and whom Negroes approved of because she had married black. "Have a ball for a few more years. Belong where *you* want to belong, and quit worrying so much. You're ruling the roost."

Robin escaped Dickie Wendell and went home by herself.

The third time Sunny Storm phoned her with an invitation that gradually became a plea that they get together, either alone or at a bang, she finally, firmly, replied, "No, not either way, Sunny. I'm working as hard as I know how to get to know myself, and you're not good for me. Please don't call me again."

"Well, well. The Queen of Sheba, huh?"

"No, not at all," she said, and quietly hung up on the friend she liked and would forever have to avoid. She went to dinner with Vincent Reardon, a pleasant enough young Negro bachelor who worked in the Onyx art department, but the evening was ruined because the modest restaurant he took her to was the best he could afford, and she did not mind but he did. When Hal Saunders called her the next day for dinner, she accepted rather than eat alone. They dined well, and Hal scarcely glanced at the expensive check before he signed it, and he again seemed to her to be a weak man, but that was the night she let him kiss her in his car, the night she told him that, if he would be patient, some time soon she would invite him up.

She saw her work on the picture steadily improve, and it was good to know that she was good. By the end of the third week of shooting Archer Ryan, the movie's director and producer, a shaggy man who could be a tyrant on the set, hugged her and exclaimed, "We're in, bonbon! These next eight weeks are going to zip by like a minute. I ought to say you're so good that I'm frightened, but there's nothing to be frightened about. This is my thirty-sixth picture, and I know when everything meshes right and when it doesn't, and everything around here's meshing like crazy—your performance, the tempo, the feel, the whole bit. You're guaranteed to grab an Oscar nomination, and unless somebody screws up somewhere, you're going to grab the Oscar. How about that? How about being the first female black star to win it in a starring role?"

"How about if I faint?" she asked, trying to be flip and not succeeding, for she was touched by this thoroughly professional, no-nonsense man's expressions of faith.

"No time. Come on, back to the mines. Damn, *damn*, but I'm a happy old kid when I have real pros to work with!"

That night she let Hal sleep with her. She told him what Archer Ryan had said, and he was elated and declared, "You did it all yourself. A lot of people helped you, I'm sure, but no one gave you your talent. You deserve every great thing that happens to you." Robin decided that she liked Hal Saunders, decided that maybe he was the man, or the type of man, best for her. The silver spoon was still in his mouth, he was good schools and impeccable manners and grooming, a traveler and observer, sweet and supportive and without a trace of personality, a thirty-year-old teen-ager, bland and directionless, someone equipped to do for her because he had the time and because he lacked the equipment to do for himself. He did not stimulate her, but he did not scare her. He was a fair lover. She was sure that, had she raised her hand seconds before his release, he would have stopped and obediently gone home if she ordered him to, there to stay until summoned.

It was, she supposed, a terrible reason to feel comfortable with a man.

On a Thursday evening, when *Cherish the Night* was five weeks old and moving no less smoothly, Hal drove Robin toward the spacious apartment Onyx had rented for her, and she asked him if he would marry her.

He looked at her and drove through a red light.

"It would work," she said. "The color thing wouldn't get in our way—we wouldn't let it. So much is happening to me, so much, so fast, more and more every day, I can't keep my head above water. You'd be such a help to me, Hal, details and everything, you'd see that I don't meet myself coming and going. And I'd do everything to be a wonderful wife."

Hal, crewcut and boyish, didn't speak for two blocks. Then: "It's certainly something to think over."

"What's there to think over? Would your mother and your brothers leave the country if you brought home a colored girl?"

"Oh, that's got nothing to do with anything. My first wife was a stripper—not that I'm making any comparisons—and my mother's pretty conservative and straitlaced Back Bay, but she lived through Vicki. She'll live through anything." He clenched his jaw and his knuckles whitened on the steering wheel. "Listen, you know what? It's a great idea, a *great* idea! Why not? I love you. Sure, why not?"

When they reached the front of her building, he was furious with enthusiasm. "Elope, that's what we'll do!" he declared. "We'll get the blood tests right away and—how long does it take in California to finalize these things? Vicki and I eloped in New Hampshire—and the second it's okay we'll do it!"

Robin told him not to come up now but at ten or so, because a reporter from a Los Angeles paper was coming to interview her. They kissed, in the doorman's full and shocked view, and Hal burbled his joy. "Ten," Robin said.

She let herself into the apartment and heard Sigrid say, "Ah, one moment, please, I will see, I think she is here." Sigrid bustled out of the kitchen and asked, "You will talk with Mr. Weber from New York, on the telephone now?"

Robin hurried to the bedroom. Warren's voice sounded as weary as it had when she had last seen him, but there was a fleck more spirit in it. "Can you drop everything this Saturday afternoon at half-past four your time and watch 'Moore' on Channel Ten?"

"Of course, Warren. Is it being shown all over the country?"

"Ah—yes, but not at the same time. L.A. has one of the segments booked for Saturday; we'll get it here a week or a couple of weeks later. I'm glad we're getting *some* mileage out of it. And, hey, what's this I hear about you knockin' 'em all dead out there in that picture? The reports say you're stupendous."

"Well, half stupendous, maybe. I think I may even start to be happy, one of these days."

"Really? Then that's what matters, dear. That's what's stupendous. Are you keeping company with anyone, serious-like?"

"Yes. I'll tell you all about it when I see you. I wish you were happy, Warren. You haven't been for a long time. I wish you could be the happiest man in the world."

"I'll give you a scoop, Deirdre of the Happies. I'm on my way. Karen and the kids are coming home to Pappy tomorrow."

"Oh, how wonderf—"

"Yep, and Pappy has other happy-Pappy irons in the happy fire. A young Turk named Pritchard's running the store at Vanguard now, and he's young and progressive and serious about feeding some backbone to television. You were too young to remember a series I had something to do with years ago, called 'The Gundersen Journal.' It was a news show, and it was a real kick in the guts. Well, I've been huddling hard with Adam Pritchard, and I'm finally, finally, finally going to do 'The Journal,' with a twenty-six-week guarantee, and look out below, sweetheart, Pappy and television are going to form a gigantic mutual admiration society yet!"

"How wonderful, Warren, how wonderful!"

"You take care, Robin darling. Watch your hat and coat in the beanery, and watch your health, and watch out for wolves and dragons. And watch Weber go, darling. Just watch."

Robin changed into slacks and a sweater, and Sigrid brought her a small drink and a large salad. Shortly before eight a plump red-head named Maxine Revere arrived for the kind of innocuous interview Robin had become used to and had learned to handle with ease. They hit it off almost at once because Miss Revere, slip showing, lip rouge caked, stockings twisted, complaining about sinuses, was an instantaneously warm woman, and sure she'd like a drink, and she acknowledged, "I'm embarrassed to come to you after you've probably put in a strenuous day and ask if you enjoy being a star in the movies."

They laughed. The hour of trite questions and trite answers sped, and sped all the faster because Sigrid kept bringing drinks and because Miss Hamilton became Robin and Miss Revere became Maxine so quickly and so naturally. At nine, the harmless, dumb interview ran out of steam, but Maxine seemed in no rush to go, and Robin ordered Sigrid to leave the bottle and the ice bucket. "Are you married, Maxine?" she asked.

"Me? No, I was missed, as my Great Aunt Eloise used to say about herself. Some day, maybe. I'm thirty-nine, next stop Dooms-ville, and not getting a pound thinner. So that day better come soon."

"Can everything be off the record now?"

"Sure. That's why I never got any farther along in this game than I have—when someone says something's off the record, I close my book. If I ever opened it, I'd be the richest overweight dame in Hollywood. But that's my professional failing—I never print the goodies unless I'm given full speed ahead."

"I'm getting married. But I can't let you print it till I see the ring—which could be in a matter of days. If I see it, I'll let you have the story first. All right?"

"You bet. My pencil's tucked away—I guarantee that—but if you want a gal to dish the dirt with, here I am, all big fat ears. Who's the lucky cuss?"

They drank, and Robin talked about Harold Beacham Courtney Saunders III, the rich man's son she supposed she should marry because he wouldn't do anything to hurt her, and what did Maxine think? "I personally think you're a damn fool to marry a man to answer your fan mail and scrape the carrots, but who am I to hand out advice?" Maxine commented and nodded for a fresh drink.

Pouring Maxine, pouring herself, Robin went on talking; she went back to Jerry Sorin and on to Jesse and Warren and Verne and Cleveland. They were girls alone in confidence, and Robin, relieved, said, "I had to talk to somebody," when it was nearly ten o'clock and Maxine was ready to leave.

"You sound apologetic," Maxine comforted. "Why? And why are you crying?"

"I miss my mother. There are so many things I want to say to her."

Maxine Revere hugged her. "I know. I lost mine six years ago. You be a good girl and let me know when to run the story about your Mr. Saunders, okay? And I'll be around any time you want a pudgy shoulder to bawl on."

"Thanks, Maxine. You're a real friend."

Precisely at ten, Hal arrived. He burbled love and plans, and he stayed the night.

On Friday Robin asked Archer to shoot around her for a few

hours. She and Hal took out a marriage license, and a doctor gave them blood tests.

On Saturday Hal flew to Massachusetts to break the news to his mother, who would be far less upset if he told her of his plans in person; it was a matter of some delicacy, he explained. Naturally his mother couldn't stop him from marrying anyone he pleased, but if she were to decide he was being spiteful, there was the small likelihood that he would be omitted from her will, and the inheritance he had received from his father wouldn't last forever. Robin worked at the studio till one, and went to her apartment to change and swim in the building's outdoor pool, aware in both sorrow and mischievous I'll-show-them glee that the building's white residents were civil to her because she was Robin Hamilton but quietly grumbled to one another when she entered their swimming pool. Her telephone was ringing when she returned to the apartment, but it stopped instants before she picked up the receiver. She left the receiver off the cradle, for Warren's show was about to go on, and she owed it to him to let nothing disturb her during it.

The Saturday afternoon papers had come, and she leafed through the *Afro-American* as she waited for four-thirty. Verne's column was still missing from it because he was still working on Roger Beckley's campaign—even the white papers were now predicting that Roger Beckley had an excellent chance of winning the election—but she had got into the habit of reading the *Afro-American*, and liked much of it, and identified herself with all of it when she was able, with its dignity, with its pride. On her own she had subscribed to other black newspapers, too, the *Chicago Defender* and the *Amsterdam News*, and she read them when there was time and her need for a family was at its greatest. Black newspapers were family, Robin was discovering, distant relatives, perhaps, gently scolding but welcome letters from home reminding her that her family loved her even if she didn't write home more often. Chain-smoking now, realizing she would suffer with Warren and for him if his show was less than perfect, she read the editorial page, the page where Verne's column had appeared. She could not understand the editorial on reapportionment, nor could she understand it when she read it again, but she tried, and she wished there was someone to explain it to her so that she would be a better person and people wouldn't just look at her but listen to her.

Hal would explain it all to her when he got back. Hal was good at these things; he didn't have many thoughts of his own, but he read a lot and he knew a lot. He would explain it, if she remembered to ask him. Hal was very patient.

At 4:29 she switched on Channel 10, surely a bitter pill for Warren; you watched Channel 10 in Los Angeles only when there was nothing else on television to watch. And she wondered again, as she had wondered all these weeks, why Verne had fled from her.

"Moore" came on, and Robin watched it, engrossed. It was a splendid, perfect show, over too soon, and in its last quarter hour she felt she knew what Warren had been trying to do, how sincere he had been, and was—not as a lover, for as that he was a fraud and a self-deceiver—but as a good man who wished for the world to be good. She saw Jesse on the screen and was surprised that she had no feeling about him, nearly none. She did not see Warren on the screen but knew that his stamp was all over it.

Then it was 5:28 and the final commercials played, and Robin was impressed and proud and thought, Someone should tell this man, and right away, what a fine show he's done, what a fine man he is. I've never really told him he's a fine man; I'm always letting him tell me how wonderful *I* am. . . .

She phoned Warren's office in New York, not really expecting him to be there on this weekend afternoon, and she was right; there was no answer. She dialed his home and thought, I must be very careful not to make him think I'm calling to cheer up a loser. He sounded like a loser when he called me the other night, with all that phony cheer, all those big plans that somehow didn't ring true. It's temporary. I'll praise him to the skies because he deserves it. I won't mention Hal, not until I know for sure that his wife and children are really back home with him.

Warren's valet answered, and she identified herself. He asked her to wait a moment and then she heard Jeanne Prescott's voice. "Hi, Jeanne," she said. "What're you doing there? Where's the great man?"

"My God, haven't you heard?"

Robin squeezed the receiver and could not remember a single one of the dozens of prayers Mama had taught her. "Jeanne . . ."

"Warren had a heart attack this morning at about ten-thirty. He was chasing his younger daughter, that's Kay, around the apartment; they were playing, and he dropped dead."

Then Jeanne was talking a lot, in a flat, strangely cold voice, and then her voice suddenly broke and she wept, and Robin could only shake with cold for there was no way possible for Warren to die; Mama yes, but not Warren who was here in this room, bursting with life. And then it was true because Jeanne kept saying it was true, the body was still in the apartment because it couldn't be moved—not Warren, but *it*—until a coroner arrived, and the telephones hadn't stopped ringing, it was amazing that the news could spread so fast but people were calling from places thousands of miles from New York and are you still there, Robin, can you hear me, will you come to the funeral?

"Yes. Good-bye, Jeanne," Robin whispered, and softly brought down the receiver, and was awed that she was numb yet her body was shivering.

Her telephone rang and she let it ring until it would not go away. She answered it, and Hy Stearns, who was a press agent for Onyx was bleating at her ear. She heard some of it, that he had been calling and calling all afternoon, and where was she for Christ's sakes, and had she read that fat bitch Revere's article in the afternoon paper, and what the hell was it with that pack of lies, and what the hell's goin' on here?

"What?"

"What 'what'?" Hy Stearns blazed. "You sloshed or somep'm, you can't make out what I'm sayin'? That fat pig Maxine *Revere*, I'm talkin' about! Do you have the paper there or don'cha? I'll *mutilate* Revere for this, all the scoops I've handed her! Somebody oughtta fix you, too, so you could keep your trap shut. The way I figure it, the only thing you didn't confess to her is that you screw dogs and cats. Where the hell was your *brain*, if you got one, I wanna know? Don't you know this kinda shit's what gives a slob like Revere her two-bit bonuses? If you had this terrific urge to tell all, why didn't you come to me, and I coulda worked it out so these humpin' the milkman confessions could be printed so they'd help the picture. This way—"

"I—I can't talk now."

"You can't. Why didn't you say that to Revere the other—"

Robin hung up and decided, when the shivering lessened and after many minutes of sitting very still and not answering the telephone, which rang and rang and rang, that she could not stay here because Warren was in every inch of this room and would be in every inch of the other rooms. There was no one to call. She wanted to walk, but there was nowhere in Los Angeles to walk. Onyx had presented her with a convertible, and it was in the garage of the building, but she did not know how to drive it. Sigrid did, but she had given Sigrid the weekend off.

She phoned the garage, and Mr. Persons checked and said yes, Sparks, one of the building's handymen, was available and would take her when she was ready. She left the apartment, carrying only cigarettes and a lighter and the afternoon newspaper. Mr. Sparks was a Negro with three prominent, terrible gold teeth, old but not elderly, and he remarked that she ought to have a coat because the day was turning chill. In the back seat, riding to the beach, she had no trouble finding the article. It was on page 3, and there was a recent picture of her, a fairly recent picture of Warren—maybe the same picture the paper would use to illustrate his obituary tomorrow—and a picture of Hal that must have been taken years ago, for he looked barely out of his teens. Little of what she had confided to Maxine Revere was missing. The long story gave the impression throughout that it was an exclusive interview freely granted. The deadly quotes seemed accurate, and Robin wondered how the woman could have remembered so much without having taken a single note.

The story even contained information Robin had not known. It told, briefly but in effective detail, the saga of the wealthy, aristocratic Saunders family. It called Harold Saunders I an empire builder, Harold Saunders II a tycoon, and Harold Saunders III a playboy. It suggested that when and if the marriage came off, the society world might never stop rocking.

Twilight was beginning to shade the sky as the car reached the beach. Mr. Sparks stayed in the car and Robin walked along the water's edge. She had never been on a beach at quite this time of day before, and she was intrigued by its peacefulness and its activity. Dozens of gulls and scores of smaller birds were feverishly busy, chattering, screeching—except for one gull, which stood on a wood post and looked at her. Robin looked back, to stare it down, but it wouldn't be stared down, it looked and it looked, and Robin raised her arm and waved to it, would have called to it if it could have heard her over the din. It kept looking, and she did call. She called, "Hey, hello, old Mr. Seagull," and it continued to look for a few more moments and then it jumped from the post and soared about as though it was showing off for her, and then it flew down to where the other gulls were.

The early evening *was* turning chill, as Mr. Sparks had warned, but she walked. She had said yes when Jeanne had asked her if she would go to the funeral. She couldn't, of course; Mrs. Weber wouldn't permit it.

Hal would be back from Massachusetts by then and, until Warren was put into the ground, Hal would hold her.

Hal or someone would.

If he came back, if he said they could get married, the marriage would last a while, maybe a long, long while. If he didn't come back, she would survive. She always survived.

Robin stopped. No, she thought. Surviving isn't good enough, surviving isn't something to settle for. Surviving is what the Sunny Storms do.

In another couple of years, less, I can be Sunny Storm.

No. That's not nearly anything to settle for.

If I'm going to have to answer to somebody about the Maxine Revere article, and I will, I've got to do more than just survive.

If there's someone who'll love me, not for a while or even a long, long while but forever, I've got to give him more than a body and a barrel of tears.

If I'm going to grow up, I've got to do more than pay someone to do it for me.

How do you grow up? How do you stop waiting to be rescued, waiting for one good Warren or another to charge up at the right minute and put you back together for a day with Scotch tape?

You start, by yourself. You do what Mama did, what even Warren, strong, weak, restless, troubled, kind Warren did when he was able: you find what there is that's good in you, and you build on that. You try, anyway.

Robin walked until it was dark, until she was satisfied she could return to the apartment and not be uncomfortable with Warren's certain presence. For a few minutes she was anxious and just a little frightened, because she had walked too far and she could not be sure how near Mr. Sparks was in his car. She was relieved when she saw the headlights.

Mr. Sparks jumped out of the car the moment he saw her and draped his jacket over her shoulders. "Careful you don't take you death, chile," he scolded.

"Oh, I never get cold," Robin said, but she liked having the jacket around her.

On the drive back to the city, Mr. Sparks remarked that he never seemed to exercise enough, and asked if she took these long walks often. "Not often enough," she answered. "Today was special. I wanted to get some thinking done."

"An' did you do it?"

"Kind of. I'm trying to work on a puzzle. I'm trying to figure myself out."

He chuckled. "That there's some tall order for ever'body."

"Yes. There are people who do it, though."

At the apartment house she gave him three ten-dollar bills, all the cash in her purse. Mr. Sparks protested, but she made him take the money, and thanked him for his time, and stopped in the lobby for messages, feeling rather well, almost at peace. There were telephone messages and telegrams. One telegram she read in the elevator was signed *Verne*.

It was addressed to her in care of the studio. One of the Onyx boys had brought it here, along with some of the other messages.

Robin. Just learned about Warren Weber. Deeply sorry for you. Certain it hurts. If anything I can do am at L.A. Roosevelt, Beckley Headquarters. Warm regards. Verne.

For many minutes after she was in the apartment, moved and hopeful and worried, Robin could not be sure if she dared to call, what she could say and how she would sound if she did. The telegram couldn't have come from the same man who had told her in a letter that she wasn't worth him. Yet it was; Verne was sending concern, not coldness, not pity but sympathy. Verne, who had walked away from her because he'd decided there was nothing to stay for, was telling her that something had touched her and that he understood.

She phoned the Roosevelt at a minute before eight. A man said he would give her name to Mr. Hightower, who was somewhere in the hotel but would have to be tracked down. She left her number.

When Verne called, twenty minutes later, Robin had changed into a blouse and slacks and was drinking the strong coffee she had brewed, and testing her voice to judge if it sounded controlled, contained. "How've you been, Robin?" he asked.

"Nice and healthy, Verne. Busy. What about you?"

"Busy. Extremely busy. I was hopping all over the state, but for the past few weeks I've been limiting it pretty much to shuttling between upstate and here. Are you flying to the funeral?"

". . . I don't know yet. We'll see. I want to thank you for your telegram, Verne. I appreciate it."

"I was debating about sending it. After that letter I wrote, you'd've had every right to tell me to get lost."

Be smart, she thought. "What letter?"

Dead air. "You didn't get a letter from me?"

"No. When? I was wondering what happened to you."

"I . . . well, as I said, keeping on the go. And reading about you, every chance I've had. You're really going great guns, and I couldn't be happier for you. Proud, even, if a man can be proud of something he hasn't accomplished."

Then he hadn't read Maxine Revere.

He asked if he could see her sometime. Robin said, "Yes. Tonight, if you're free. I'm not doing much of anything."

"Have you had dinner yet?"

"No. Have you?"

"Let me remember. Two limp hot dogs, on the run, about three o'clock this afternoon. How far are you from the Roosevelt, do you know? I can leave here in a couple of minutes and pick you up."

She told him her address. Then Robin Hamilton, the child of Willie Mae and James Lonnie Hamilton, the child of Jesse Nash, the child of Warren Weber, the maybe-woman, brushed her hair and drank more coffee and chose the evening coat she would wear. Between now and the time he called for her, there was the possibility that Verne would hear about Maxine Revere. Or eventually he would. Eventually he should, must.

Preparing herself, Robin Hamilton, Willie Mae's daughter, lit a cigarette and stabbed it into an ash tray because it gave her no pleasure, and found a placid, pleasurable instrumental on the radio, and tied a ribbon in her hair, and waited.

Presently, the call came. Verne was in the lobby and asked if she was ready.

"I'll be right down," Robin said. "Two minutes. One."

About the Author

MORTON COOPER was born in Greensburg, Pennsylvania. After stints as a disc jockey and writer-actor on local radio stations, he moved to New York and attended Martha Foley's Short Story Workshop at Columbia University. He has written several paperback originals, both fiction and nonfiction; has composed lyrics for a number of songs; was eastern correspondent for the *Chicago Defender*, a leading Negro newspaper; and has written hundreds of magazine articles dealing with scores of subjects from civil rights to sports, politics to entertainment. In 1966 he co-authored Lita Grey Chaplin's story, MY LIFE WITH CHAPLIN, and in 1967 he combined his long-time fascination with show business and politics in the hugely successful novel, THE KING, which explored the collision point of these two worlds. In BLACK STAR he has again returned to familiar ground and to the meeting of two worlds in the story of a beautiful Negro girl's rise to stardom in a time of violent turmoil and cynical exploitation.